Praise for The El Cholo Feeling Passes:

"Demands the immediate attention of readers." — *The Times-Picayune*

"*The El Cholo Feeling Passes* is a moveable feast."
— *The Atlanta Journal-Constitution*

"*The El Cholo Feeling* is at once happiness and anguish, the sense of wonderful times as perishable as margaritas or love or friendship itself. The finest moment in the world (which for Richard Janus, irrevocably, is defined not as accomplishment, or promotion, or developing one's reputation or even wildly making love, but something better: eating potato chips and watching old movies on the tube with best friends, or making up fake German phrases, or shooting pool) is melting even as we touch it. That's life, Fredrick Barton tells us, and if we don't know that, we don't know beans." — *Los Angeles Times*

"I found myself laughing out loud." — *Creative Loafing*

"It's a kind of *Fear of Flying* for men, and it's terrific — a funny, poignant, always powerful story of one man's search for identity in the 1970s when the women's movement first began to turn male-female relationships upside-down. I had the El Cholo Feeling many times while reading this wonderful novel." — *Waldenbooks Newsweekly*

"A dark comedy, bizarrely amusing and deeply disturbing."
— *The Eccentric Newspapers*

"Resplendent. All who read *The El Cholo Feeling Passes* can laugh and laugh again." — *The Georgia Librarian*

"Hilariously funny." — *The Pilot Newspapers*

"Los Angeles is the setting for the last third of this book, and never has the sad side, the poor side, the unachieving sweet side of a city been so lovingly delineated." — *Los Angeles Times*

D1367148

"*The El Cholo Feeling Passes* recalls the work of the young Philip Roth. Faith Cleaver is one of the most finely crafted and utterly believable women in contemporary fiction. Richard Janus is as interesting and rich a figure as has appeared in American fiction since John Updike's *Rabbit Run*." — *Gambit*

"Exploring its dynamic characters Richard Janus and Faith Cleaver, *The El Cholo Feeling Passes* is funny, tender and thoughtful."
    — *Greenville Daily Reflector*

"*The El Cholo Feeling Passes* is a powerful, poignant book."
    — *Chronicle Newspapers*

"Seeming to masquerade like Mardi Gras as a novel about a young reasonable American male who needs to make a career choice, the novel is, in truth, a gut-wrenching, justifiably emotional tale about religion, sex, family and place." — *The Times-Picayune*

"*The El Cholo Feeling Passes* is both funny and sad as its characters search for their identities in a topsy-turvy world. It's an excellent novel."
    — *Baton Rouge Morning Advocate*

"*The El Cholo Feeling Passes* is a remarkable novel displaying a keen insight into the mental struggles between man and wife. Richard Janus and Faith Cleaver are highly complex and original characters, and Fredrick Barton has apparently peered into their very souls to create two completely believable and sympathetic characters."
    — *The Sun-Herald*

"Utterly honest, utterly forgiving." — *Los Angeles Times*

"Fredrick Barton has an incredible ear for dialogue, especially the angry give and take of marital arguments, during which two people who love each other seem to always find ways to wound. This is an important book, one of the best, most accurate looks at what has been called the baby boom generation." — *The Eccentric Newspapers*

"A funny vision of the absurd world we take for granted."
    — *The Times-Picayune*

THE
EL CHOLO
FEELING
PASSES

Also by Fredrick Barton

Black And White On The Rocks (originally published as *With Extreme Prejudice*)
Courting Pandemonium
A House Divided
Ash Wednesday (a play in verse)

THE EL CHOLO FEELING PASSES

A Novel By

Fredrick Barton

UNIVERSITY OF
NEW ORLEANS
PRESS CLASSICS

First published in the United States of America by Peachtree Publishers, Ltd., 1985

Library of Congress Cataloguing-in-Publication data
Barton, Fredrick
The El Cholo Feeling Passes
p. cm.
ISBN 0-9728143-2-9 (2003 edition)
previously published by Peachtree Publishing, ISBN 0-931948-78-9;
ISBN 0-440-20077-6 (paperback edition)

Book design by David Alcorn
Jacket design by Mark R. Bacon and Gregory A. Melancon
Jacket photo courtesy of El Cholo Restaurants, not to be reprinted
without permission of Ron Salisbury of R.B.I., Newport Beach, CA.
Printed in the United States of America

University of New Orleans Press
2045 Lakeshore Drive
New Orleans, LA 70122

For
Joyce Markrid Dombourian, of course

Preface to the 2003 Edition

Reading *The El Cholo Feeling Passes* as I prepared the 2003 edition, I was struck by how much has changed since its primary setting in the early 1970s and even since its original publication in 1985. The glass ceiling still exists, as any statistical study of top-level leadership across almost any profession attests. And equal pay for equal work has yet to be achieved. But salary gaps are smaller than they were. And all the professions, from medicine to law to engineering to architecture to higher education are open to and peopled by women who didn't enjoy anything approaching comparable access and acceptance thirty years ago.

Women who came of age in the 1990s and since have been extensively, if, obviously, not entirely, spared the kind of gender prejudice experienced by women only a generation earlier. The vastly greater opportunities, psychic as well as economic, available to women in their twenties and early thirties today are the direct result of the determination of those brave women in the late 1960s and 1970s who founded and soldiered the Women's Movement.

Like my main character, Richard Janus, I taught high school in the early 1970s, and I am astonished to remember that my school had no interscholastic sports program for its female students. The only athletic opportunities for young women at my school were intramural, and the male coaches griped openly about having to surrender gym and field facilities for those activities, even though the women got to use them only about three hours per week. One of the Women's Movement's first and most enduring triumphs was the passage of the Title IX legislation that requires gender equity in interscholastic sports. In short, today's female volleyball, basketball and soccer players have access to facilities, coaching and competition completely unavailable to the women of the generation of Faith Cleaver, *El Cholo's* main female character.

Faith and her fellow baby-boom females were raised in the 1950s to be housewives and mothers. They were encouraged to express their athletic gifts by becoming cheerleaders and cavorting in flouncy skirts before a crowd gathered to watch the games of their male classmates. Their own potential athletic skills were seldom nurtured in any meaningful way at all. Middle-class families often expected their daughters to earn college degrees, but only to enter such professions as nursing or primary or secondary education. Even those valuable careers were not expected to be defining, however. A woman's status was tied to that of her husband and someday, perhaps, enhanced by the achievements of her male offspring.

And then, for those women in college during the decade from 1965 to

1975, very much changed, very quickly. Those who had been raised to be one thing were suddenly asked by their peers, but frequently not supported by their own families, to be something quite different. Most women of Faith's generation have their stories. When my sister Dana, now a mental health therapist who supervises field work for the University of Michigan's prestigious School of Social Work, was in high school, she was told by our father, a good, but in this case critically misguided man, that she should take typing, shorthand and other secretarial courses so she'd "have something to fall back on" if she didn't get married right out of college.

Such advice inflicted untold damage to the confidence of those who endured it. It made the women of Faith's generation sometimes uncertain and often understandably angry. And then they found themselves falling in love with men like Richard Janus and me, who had been raised by men like their own fathers, falling in love with men like Richard Janus whose instincts were fundamentally benign but whose experience and presumptions rendered them functionally blind.

Gender prejudice endures, no doubt, but it is neither as pervasive and certainly not as acceptable as it was not long ago. In sum, it seems to me now, that when *The El Cholo Feeling Passes* was first published, its context was sociological whereas it is now more extensively historical. I hope this new edition finds young readers, and I hope that those women in their twenties and thirties who may discover the book for the first time recognize the fire through which women like Faith walked to tear down barriers and open the way for those to come.

In one way, though, the story of Faith Cleaver and Richard Janus is not confined to a particular turbulent era. Marriages still founder and fail. Divorces still occur. And sometimes, surprisingly often in fact, couples who find more heartache than contentment in living with each other, separate sadly, call a surrender to their efforts to remain united, all the while still loving each other and suffering all the more because they do. That's a story that hasn't changed, and as long as individual human personality survives, it probably won't.

Fredrick Barton
New Orleans
March, 2003

It takes a secure man to love a liberated woman.
—T-shirt on Bourbon Street, New Orleans

Security is a kind of death.
—Tennessee Williams

1

The Acknowledgments

*T*he *El Cholo Feeling Passes: A Digression,* which is not a doctoral dissertation in United States history, is the product of the author's mind alone. But the contributions of many have made the final preparation of this volume possible. With fear that I might inadvertently omit someone of crucial importance, I am deeply indebted to:

Mrs. Almak Acen, who first made history challenging and set me on the road to never writing a doctoral dissertation;

Dr. Ernest Chiron, who became my undergraduate mentor, ignored my irresponsibilities, befriended me, cajoled and supported me, and kept me straight on the path to never writing a doctoral dissertation;

Dr. Hanson Bennet, who would not become my undergraduate mentor, befriend me, cajole or support me, and thus insured that my doctoral dissertation would never be written in history rather than English;

Dr. Warren Burden, my graduate chairman, whom I have been reputed to resemble and who set examples for me that were difficult to follow;

The Comstock Putney Fortran Foundation, which provided me with four years of crucial financial support during my graduate study and made it possible for me not to write a doctoral dissertation without going into debt;

The Alumni Library at Lancaster College (my alma mater), whose research materials were so meager that I could not early learn how torpifying I might find historical scholarship;

The University of California at Los Angeles, for awarding me a teaching fellowship so that I could learn that teaching college students is rewarding enough to make me feel truly miserable that I hate historical research;

The James Pearson Library, the National Endowment for the Humanities, and the Shell Oil Company, all of whom awarded me research grants so that I could transfer lines from dusty documents onto shiny, ruled notecards which themselves have become dusty;

The many friends of my life whom I've tried with mixed success to keep from also becoming dusty;

Cally Martin, my special friend, who helped me see that not writing a doctoral dissertation might have some advantages;

And Faith Cleaver, who provided the final challenge in my struggle not to write my doctoral dissertation—Faith my friend, my critic, my antagonist, my wife.

R.A.J.
Santa Monica
July, 1976

The El Cholo Feeling Passes: A Digression
by
Richard Albert Janus

Submitted *in lieu* of fulfillment
Of the requirements
For the degree of Doctor of Philosophy in History
At the University of California, Los Angeles
July 4, 1976

To the Doctoral Committee:
Dr. Warren J. Burden,
chairperson
Dr. Jonathan B. Stein
Dr. Thomas W. Greene

Memo: To the members of the doctoral committee—
Burden, Stein and Greene
Re: The dissertation of Richard A. Janus
From: Richard A. Janus

You are perhaps intrigued by my title. I realize that when each of you opened this manuscript you expected to find herein a doctoral thesis on King Philip's War. Had you read the acknowledgments which precede this note, you'd have had some clue that what followed was not what you anticipated. But I'm sure you didn't. Acknowledgments are quite personal stuff and of interest really only to the author and the acknowledged.

To remind those of you whose minds it might have slipped, King Philip's War was not an obscure engagement fought on behalf of a sixteenth-century Spanish monarch. Rather it was an obscure engagement fought in 1675 and 1676 between the Puritans of New England and their Algonkian Indian neighbors. King Philip was an Algonkian Indian chief. Philip wasn't his real name, of course. His real name was Metacom. But the English settlers called him Philip (his older brother, Wamsutta, they called Alexander). It was just their way of having a little fun—giving a grand classical name to the leader of a people they considered inferior to (though greatly more troublesome than) their draft animals. Southern plantation owners later took similar joy in naming their slaves Augustus, Cicero, Cassius, and the like.

In the war which has come to bear his derisive English name, Metacom very nearly got even. At one point he controlled the Massachusetts countryside to within fifteen miles of Boston, and his successes drove the Bay colony leaders to the verge of panic. Three hundred years later Metacom's successes drove me to the verge of a dissertation. But this is largely irrelevant because King Philip's War is the topic of a dissertation that I have decided not to write.

When my wife found me composing this note instead of the introduction to my thesis, she queried, "Don't you like Indians anymore?"

"Sure, I still like Indians," I replied. And it was true—though I know hardly any that are still alive. "Some of my best friends are Indians. It's just that I don't want my daughter's father to spend the rest of his life writing about one."

Faith looked at me without smiling. "You haven't got a daughter," she said. "And if you don't do your dissertation, you're not *gonna* have a daughter. Or any other kind of child. If you don't get your Ph.D., you won't get a job. If you don't get a job, we're too poor to have a kid."

"I know we don't have a daughter," I protested. Faith was always literal when it suited her purposes. "I was just trying to make a joke," I said and started to explain.

"A joke?" she interrupted. "You're making a joke out of your life, is what you're doing."

Doing my best Groucho Marx impersonation, I replied, "I'd rather be making my life out of a joke." But she was genuinely upset with me and not to be humored out of it.

She drummed her fingers on my desk and brushed them across the yellow legal pad I had been writing on. Shaking her head, she said in a voice redolent with both defeat and contempt, "What a waste, Janus, what a waste."

But my period of studying Indians has not been a waste. I have learned that Indians were not hopeless, helpless savages who were the passive recipients of the historical course plotted for them by white people. Rather I have learned that Indians were active agents in their own history.

Hence my suspicions that I am not an Indian were confirmed. I am not an Indian because I *am* a hopeless, helpless recipient of the historical course plotted for me by white people. I have *not* been an active agent in my own history. But then it comes as no real surprise to me that I am not an Indian. I never had the talents to be a good Indian. Only those, I was always told, to be a chief.

I am already twenty-eight years old and have recently been overwhelmed by the realization that in only twelve more years I will be forty years old. My waistline has begun to spread. I am fearful that any day now I will feel the urge to take up jogging. I occasionally find a gray hair or two, especially in my beard. My ankles, which were always weak, now sprain themselves the moment I set foot on a basketball court. Sometimes they sprain themselves when I walk down the street. I've had to buy a pair of glasses. Soon, I guess, I will have to begin wearing them.

I have never had any particular ambitions to be an actor, but I find it disturbing that men younger than myself have already become stars. I can't name a specific actor right off hand, but that's because I seldom go to the movies anymore. I never have the time. Not writing my dissertation has proved to be very demanding, filling my leisure as thoroughly as it has my work hours.

Was Robert Redford already in the movies when he was younger than twenty-eight? I'm pretty sure that neither Jack Nicholson nor Dustin Hoffman was. Not in any good movies anyway. But there's no solace in that fact. Because without a doubt, long before either turned twenty-eight he was preparing to be in the movies.

I, on the other hand, am preparing to be an historian. Something I'd just as soon not be.

Exactly the same sort of trauma sweeps over me whenever I watch an athletic contest on television. I watch a lot of sports on TV. I have the time since I seldom go to the movies. All the young men shooting jump shots, stealing bases and making diving one-handed pass receptions are under twenty-eight. Except for those who are older, of course, who are mostly baseball players and quarterbacks. But again, there is hardly any solace for me in those who are older because they all reached the major leagues before they turned twenty-eight. I'm already twenty-eight and haven't even reached the minors.

And what about writers? Fitzgerald was only twenty-four when he published *This Side of Paradise*. *The Sun Also Rises* appeared when Hemingway was twenty-seven. Faulkner, of course, didn't publish a book until he was twenty-nine, but what are the chances I'll write *Soldier's Pay* in the next year?

But lest I give a misimpression, it isn't just the accomplishments of the young and famous that depress me. A college pal of mine always wanted to be a lawyer. Three years ago he graduated from law school, and now it drives me crazy when he cancels our tennis dates because he has to be in court. I want to have to be in court, too, and I don't even want to be a lawyer. My grandfather is nearly eighty years old. He still gets up every day and goes to his little jewelry store where he repairs watches. He doesn't have to—he's made plenty enough money to retire on. But he likes repairing watches and so he keeps on doing it. He started doing it when he was seventeen.

So how do I measure up with these examples great and small? I seem only to know that I don't want to be an historian. And I am little consoled by the fact that as days go by I am increasingly successful at not being one.

Which is precisely why I am overwhelmed at the thought of being forty in only twelve years. Twelve years is nothing. Twelve years is yesterday when I was sixteen, playing basketball, dating girls, being embarrassed over wearing braces, getting pimples and preparing to be in college. And twelve years is tomorrow when I'll commence being old, preparing to die without ever getting to be—no, without ever *trying* to be—a ballplayer or even a movie star. I would never have attempted such exotic and difficult careers, for always I was too mature. Easily, unquestionably, I was too mature.

Maturity. That, I think, is the nub of my problem. Always my strongest trait, maturity has exerted a powerful influence on my life. Even in elementary school I was mature. My teachers always said I was among their most mature pupils. Usually they said I *was* their most mature pupil. I loved being mature. I strove for it. I competed with others at having more of it. On my report cards I always got checks in Maturity. Of course, I always got checks in Finishes What He Starts, too, but that's another story. If they had given grades, instead of just checks in Maturity, I'm sure I would have gotten A's. I got A's in everything else.

"Your son is exceptionally mature for his age," my teachers regularly told my mother when they met her at Parents' Night.

"We're very fortunate, his father and I," my mother just as regularly intoned proudly. "We deserve none of the credit. His father and I have always felt that we should just throw our children into the sea of life and let them sink or swim on their own. We are very gratified that Richie has always swum at the head of his class."

I was so mature as a child that I never said I wanted to be a baseball player when I grew up. That was strange, since the only thing I wanted to be as a child was a baseball player. But if you told people that you wanted to be a baseball player when you grew up, they never said, "Oh, what a mature young man you are." Instead they said, "Oh, that's nice," which meant, "Boy, that's dumb." So I told everyone I wanted to be a doctor when I grew up, and they all responded wonderfully: "Oh, what a mature young man you are." I craved hearing it.

Of course, most everyone I told that I wanted to be a doctor was an adult. Every time I told a kid I wanted to be a doctor, the kid said, "Boy, are you dumb." That's because every kid in my neighborhood wanted to be a baseball player when he grew up.

As the years passed, my expressed intention to pursue a career in science mutated somewhat, and I decide to indoctrinate myself with a Ph.D. instead of an M.D. But my fundamental goal remained unchanged. I found that I could be considered just as mature for wanting to be a college professor as I could for wanting to be a doctor.

My single-minded pursuit of maturity had other manifestations, one being that early on I cultivated lust. In the fifth grade I secretly confided to my friend B. F. Johnson, "Lipstick tastes better than bubble gum." I'd heard Wally Cleaver tell Eddie Haskell that on "Leave It To Beaver." I figured Wally ought to know.

And as my father often pointed out, "One thing leads to another." In this case, the desire to taste lipstick quickly led to the desire to taste a far more forbidden fruit. I wanted to screw girls. I was uncertain how. Ignorant of female genitalia, I was even uncertain exactly where. But I was not at all uncertain that I wanted to screw them. As long as they didn't get pregnant. Being mature, I had to go to college and couldn't encumber myself with financial responsibilities at the age of only ten. So before I knew what it was, I believed deeply in contraception.

In the sixth grade, fertilized by my commitment to contraception, I cultivated lust intensely. I grew up in New Orleans, you see, and we pre-teens took very seriously the fact that we lived in Sin City. We felt obliged to sin as young as possible. I always suspected this was easier for my mostly Catholic peers to accomplish than it was for me. As a Baptist, I didn't have a weekly confession to make; I didn't have a moment when my sins could be admitted and instantly forgiven. Instead, I was just required to be perfect. But being perfect, I learned, was far easier prior to sixth grade than it was afterwards.

With a fifth-grade hankering for the taste of lipstick tuning my antenna, I began to hear the sixth-grade boys talking about parties they attended where they danced with girls and kissed them while playing spin the bottle and post office. *Kincaid* parties they were called.

Kincaid parties! What *were* Kincaid parties? I wanted to be in the sixth grade immediately. *I* wanted to dance with girls and kiss them while playing spin the bottle and post office. Oh, those Kincaid parties. Just saying the word *Kincaid* alone in my darkened room at night gave me a moist and tingling and deliciously sinful feeling. It also made me feel so excruciatingly guilty that I sought out my parents for some indirect confession.

"The sixth graders are having Kincaid parties," I told them.

"What are Kincaid parties?" my father and mother asked.

"They're parties where you dance with girls and play spin the bottle and post office," I said.

"Sixth graders?" my mother asked.

"Uh huh."

"Why are you telling us this?" my father asked.

"I dunno," I shrugged.

"Well what do *you* think about these Kincaid parties?" he pursued. I hated that tactic. Instead of just telling me that Kincaid parties were symptomatic of our creeping national decay, were insidious vestiges of Sodom, were cancerous growths on the morals of America's young or were the diabolical workshops of Satan incarnate, he made *me* analyze the situation.

"I dunno," I said.

"Don't you think that's dangerous," my mother said to my father, "for sixth graders to be kissing and that sort of thing?"

"One thing does lead to another," my father opined. They both looked at me.

I opted for a cliché. "People who play with fire, I guess, are liable to get burned."

"People who go swimming in fast-running streams," my mother said solemnly, "are liable to get swept away."

"Perhaps by the time you get to sixth grade," my father said, "they won't have these Kincaid parties."

And my father was right, of course. When I got to sixth grade there *were* no Kincaid parties. There never had been any Kincaid parties. *Kincaid parties,* a term which for a whole year of my life was as erotically evocative as *cunnilingus, mènage á trois* and *orgy* would later become, was a term, it seems, I'd made up. Or creatively misheard, I guess. For there *were* parties when I got to sixth grade. And if the reality of those parties didn't quite match the fantasy of Kincaid parties, there nonetheless were parties where I danced with girls and kissed them while playing spin the bottle and post office.

In conjunction with New Orleans's long Mardi Gras season, there were *King Cake* parties. It was an old New Orleans tradition, I learned. King Cake parties began shortly after Christmas. Near the end of the first party, the hostess would serve slices from an oval sweet roll—the King Cake. Inside one of the slices was a tiny pink baby doll (or sometimes a penny, but usually a tiny pink baby doll). Whichever guest got the baby doll became responsible for giving the next party. If a girl got the doll, she became Queen and chose a boy to serve as King and host of her party. If a boy got the doll, he likewise chose a Queen. At the end of each party a new King Cake was served and a new Royal Couple was selected. The round of parties continued until the advent of Lent forced everyone to stop having fun.

Actually my fun stopped on Mardi Gras eve. (Lent, for those of you who don't follow the church calendar, begins the day after Fat Tuesday.) It was the year's last King Cake party. I had become a seasoned veteran of the King Cake scene. Before the parties began, I had never danced with a girl. Now I was a regular Gene Kelly. For every record on some classmate's cubical, 45 r.p.m. record player, I chose a partner, squeezed her as much as she'd allow and moved my feet about in something approximating a regular pattern. Occasionally that pattern and the record's rhythm were even in sync.

Late in the evening on Mardi Gras eve, while dancing with Adrienne Bandeau, I became aroused, or, as we New Orlenian males would later tend to say, I got on the bone. It was hardly the first time I had done so. Muffled incantations of *Kincaid parties* had rendered me regularly in that condition during the preceding year. But this night was the first time I had gotten on the bone in the presence of someone else. I wasn't at all embarrassed. Being a mature sixth grader, I knew that my condition was natural, if dangerous. I also had on baggy pants.

But I didn't get on the bone from dancing with Adrienne Bandeau. She would barely let me close enough to her for that. I got on the bone because B.F. Johnson had taken Pamela deVane outside in the bushes where I knew they were making out. Before the party that night, B.F. Johnson had asked me if I'd ever made out. He said that playing spin the bottle and post office was okay, but really just kid stuff, and that he was planning to put the make on somebody at the party.

In addition to being my friend, B.F. Johnson was my chief rival for being the most mature student in the sixth grade. Even if he never bothered to claim he wanted to be a doctor when he grew up. Lately it had seemed to me that he was winning the maturity race.

When I'd asked him whom he was planning to put the make on at the last King Cake party, he'd said, "Adrienne Bandeau. I think she's the best-looking girl in the sixth grade."

"What about Janice Martin," I suggested. "She's got really big titties."

But B.F. responded, "If I wanted to feel foam rubber, I'd go to Sears." I didn't immediately understand what B.F.'s snub meant, but my admiration for his maturity soared.

"I think I'll put the make on Pamela deVane," I said.

Things, of course, hadn't gone quite according to plan: B.F. was in the bushes making out with Pamela, and I was on the bone while dancing with Adrienne Bandeau. It was time, I decided, to make my move.

Using superior muscle more than charm, I managed to pull Adrienne close enough to whisper through her sprayed black hair, "Let's go outside in the bushes."

She pulled back from me and said with a funny smile tugging at the corners of her mouth, "What for?"

"You know," I said with a bold grin.

"No, I don't," Adrienne Bandeau said, tilting her head a bit but still showing that hesitant almost-smile.

I raised my eyebrows and then touched the back of my wrist to the top of my forehead. "B.F. and Pam are out there," I explained.

"So?" Adrienne Bandeau said.

I stepped close to her again and said quietly, "Don't you want to make out?"

"No," she said as if I'd asked her if she'd like another Coke.

With the palm of my hand, I mopped the dampness out of the brush of my flattop. "Why not?" I asked.

"Because we're barely twelve years old," Adrienne Bandeau said.

"Well," I responded with a display of forensic wizardry, "it's either now or never." The expression was a favorite of my father's. It did not prove particularly popular with Adrienne Bandeau, however. She didn't say so, but when she turned and walked away from me, it was clear that she'd chosen the second option. She probably didn't realize how firmly I already believed in contraception.

But I am nothing if not a hard trier. (I have even tried hard to be an historian, haven't I?) When B.F. Johnson and Pamela deVane returned to the party, I asked Pamela to dance. And at what I considered the appropriate moment, as Frankie Avalon crooned, "When a girl changes from bobby socks, to stockings…," I whispered to Pamela in a voice volatilely mixed with honeysuckle and desperation, "Let's go outside in the bushes."

"What for?" Pamela deVane said.

"You know," I said, wet with yearning.

"No, I don't," Pamela deVane said, wrinkling her forehead to emphasize her perplexity.

She was playing hard to get, I figured. I tightened my embrace on her and moved her through my awkward repertoire of slow-dancing flourishes. When the song ended, I boldly continued to hold her and whispered again. "Let's go outside in the bushes. Like you and B.F. did."

"Uh uh," Pamela deVane whispered back. She didn't try to wiggle away from me, though, and I was sure she was still playing hard to get.

"Come on," I urged, perhaps adding a seductive wink.

"No," Pamela deVane said.

"Why not?"

"Because you're barely twelve years old," Pamela deVane answered with a giggle. It was the giggle, I think, that finally succeeded in deflating me.

I wanted to point out that she and B.F. Johnson, neither of whom probably knew a damn thing about contraception, were barely twelve years old, too. But somehow I sensed that this early skirmish, like the whole of the battle of the sexes, was not to be determined on the basis of debate.

Though battered by the events at the party, my maturity nonetheless rescued me from double humiliation on Mardi Gras eve. When my parents picked me up, they sensed that I was unhappy about something.

"Didn't you have fun?" my mother asked.

"It was okay," I said from the back seat of our family Dodge.

"That doesn't sound very enthusiastic," my mother said.

"I thought you always enjoyed these Kincaid parties," my father added, making a loud wet sucking noise on his pipe.

"King Cake," I said.

"What?" my father said. He was distracted because he was trying to drive and use a cigarette lighter to relight his pipe at the same time.

"King Cake," I repeated. "They're King Cake parties. Not Kincaid."

"Whatever," my father said. "I thought you always enjoyed them."

"They're okay," I shrugged as my father tried to eye me in the dimness though the rearview mirror.

"Honey," my mother said. "Aren't you going to tell us what happened that upset you?"

"It's either now or never," my father said.

So I told him. Omitting the hard particulars, of course. I told them that Adrienne Bandeau and Pamela deVane liked B.F. Johnson better than me.

My mother clucked in consolation. "It's obvious," she said, "that you're just too mature for those silly girls. You're clearly more mature than B.F. Johnson. I wouldn't give this another thought."

My father exhaled a gray cloud of smoke and recommended, "Just remember, son, there are always other fish in the sea."

My parents liked marine analogies. My father often said of his position at the small local Baptist College that he liked being "a big fish in a small pond."

Applying my father's current counsel, I began to think of Janice Martin. I wished I had asked her to go with me into the bushes. That night I dreamed of taking her swimming and that she let me slip my hand inside her bathing suit to feel her large, soft breasts. When I awoke on Mardi Gras morning with a recovered hard-on, I knew, even though the experience had been only a dream, that I much preferred actually feeling breasts to feeling foam rubber at Sears.

Useful as it was for recovering from certain setbacks, sometimes my maturity got me into trouble. In the days of my *Kincaid* fantasies, when I was still in fifth grade, my class had square-dancing twice a week on the school's asphalt playground. The blacktop was covered with basketball courts. Steel backboards and rims without nets towered over irregular yellow lines that were painted in the days when the foul circle and narrow three-second lane really looked like a keyhole. The courts were never used because no one in grade school knew how to play basketball and older kids in the neighborhood would not play on rims without nets.

Also unused were the shuffleboard courts. A shuffleboard disk will not slide accurately on a cracked asphalt surface whose best function seemed to be inflicting torn blue jeans on all the boys and skinned knees on all the girls. But we never worried about this bit of misplanning because our school owned no shuffleboard equipment for us to be unable to use.

The cracked blacktop, however, did prove useful for square-dancing. Every Tuesday and Thursday afternoon the boys from the fifth grade classes lined up on one side of the asphalt, the girls on the other. Using one of those brown and tan institutional record players that was plugged into an outlet via a hundred-foot extension cord run through a classroom window, some teacher switched on "Pomp and Circumstance." And the grand march began. We walked to the pavement's end, made crisp ninety-degree turns, marched toward each other and found our partners at the center. From week to week no one knew whose partner he or she would be. There were good partners like Pamela deVane, Janice Martin and Adrienne Bandeau who had already begun to wear bras. We like to feel the thin straps across their backs as we danced.

But all the boys lived in terror of the day they would have to dance with Booga.

Booga's real name was Karen Mert. She was ugly and fat and no one liked her. Booga picked her nose. But that alone did not terrify us. Peter Cross, who was a holy roller, picked his nose and no one called him Booga. Everyone called him Peter Cross. But Karen Mert we all called Booga. B.F. Johnson had named her that because, as he pointed out, "Karen Mert *eats* boogers." No one except B.F. Johnson ever exactly saw Karen Mert eat boogers, but everyone took B.F.'s word for it. Why would he make it up? Soon everyone said, "Karen Mert eats boogers."

Along with the rest, I too said, "Karen Mert eats boogers."

Then B.F. Johnson named her Booga and no one ever called her Karen again. Everyone said, "Booga eats boogers." And it must have been true because everyone said she did.

Booga's presence in the girls' line across from us transformed the grand march into Russian roulette. But whichever boy had to dance with her suffered a fate worse than death. He was teased by his classmates; he was called Booga's boyfriend; he was reported to have been seen kissing her; it was suggested he had become converted by her and had turned to booger eating himself.

For weeks I escaped the fate of becoming Booga's square-dancing partner. But then one dismal day "Pomp and Circumstance" brought us together. I was terrified but smart, and I quickly fashioned a method to keep the booganess from rubbing off on me. I pulled my hands up inside my long-sleeved shirt, a feat accomplished by flexing my elbows and tucking my thumbs inside loosely made fists. This contortion made my shoulders hunch up around my neck so that I must have looked as if I was doing an imitation of Frankenstein. But my skin never touched Booga's, and I was saved. I was saved, that is, until a teacher who was not even my own spied my contortion. She was waiting for me outside my classroom after school that day. "Richie Janus," she said sternly.

"Yes ma'am," I said.

"Why did you have your hands in your sleeves during square-dancing today?"

"I dunno," I squirmed.

"It was because you were dancing with Karen Mert, wasn't it?"

No, it was because I was dancing with Booga. "Yes ma'am," I answered quietly, with my eyes on the pavement made cool by the shadows of late afternoon.

"Do you call her names like the others?"

"No ma'am," I said, still refusing to meet her gaze. She took my chin in her hands and pulled my face around until I was forced to look at her. "Not where she can hear," I added.

The teacher's eyes mingled anger and sorrow. "You know better than that," she said. "You shouldn't call her names at all. All of you taunt her. She hasn't a single friend in this school. Richie, have you ever thought how that poor child feels?"

I hadn't. One side of me resented being scolded, argued that it was Booga who ate boogers, not me. But another side of me suddenly understood something easily more frightening than having to square-dance with the school outcast. In recognizing Karen Mert's hopeless loneliness, I was forced to see for the first time my own powerful capacity for evil. I stared around me at the walkways and courtyard of my school. I knew them like the rooms of my own house. But at the moment they seemed like some new place, foreign and hostile.

"I'm disappointed in you, Richie," concluded the teacher who was not even my own. "You're a nice boy, a leader. You're more mature than the other boys in your grade. You should set an example for them. Will you do that from now on?"

"Yes ma'am," I said honestly and with determination.

After that day, all the boys in the fifth grade wore long-sleeved shirts on square-dancing days.

While I'm indulging in mature confession, Dr. Burden, let me confess this: I am a cheater. I've just never been caught. My maturity has always been there to save me.

For instance, in the eighth grade, I cheated on a Latin test. I was forced to do it, because I was afraid that without cheating I might not get a very high grade. This was sound reasoning in the best tradition of Leo Durocher and Richard Nixon. I was so afraid that I didn't go to school the day the test was given. I got diarrhea instead.

Sickness served me well in the eighth grade, and it has served me well since. Elective diarrhea has continued to plague me. And I have also contracted every strain of flu, an ulcer it turned out I didn't have, sprained ankles and a brief but acute case of the heartbreak of psoriasis.

At other times I have been well served by manslaughter. To provide funerals for me to attend coincident with the due dates of papers I couldn't write, or tests I wasn't prepared for, I have killed off all my aunts and uncles, some cousins who were very, very dear to me (usually by suicide—I drove them to it) and my grandparents several times each. I have generally refrained from patricide and matricide. But in desperate moments I have afflicted the members of my immediate family with automobile accidents, broken limbs, appendicitis, breast lumps and operable hemorrhoids.

That time in the eighth grade, however, I used diarrhea to stay home and thus avoid not getting a very high grade on my Latin test. On the Wednesday I returned to school, my teacher, Mrs. Brisket, sent me to the lunchroom, as I knew she would, so that I could make up the exam undisturbed by the proceedings of the class. In the lunchroom I proceeded to copy all the answers, except those I couldn't find and which probably did not exist, out of the Latin textbook I had augustly brought with me.

It was a Caesarean performance. By answering Mrs. Brisket's ten-point bonus question correctly, I made 103. This would have been terrific had not my friend Ronald Demart also made 103. He, too, had been sick for the test the day before. I don't know what was wrong with him, but whatever he had, it was terminal. It finally killed him when the Claymore mine he stepped on in the Mekong Delta blew him to bits.

Mrs. Brisket had sent him with me to the cafeteria to take his exam, but Ronald Demart hadn't been smart enough to bring his textbook along. When I saw that he was struggling, I offered him my test paper, and he copied all the answers off my sheet. Including those I had made up to the questions whose answers I couldn't find. Since these answers probably didn't exist, the ones I made up were wrong. Conspicuously so. And when Mrs. Brisket discovered that my conspicuously wrong answers were identical to those of Ronald Demart, she became suspicious.

"Richie and Ronald," Mrs. Brisket said, "may I see the two of you after class?"

"Yes ma'am," we answered.

"You boys made 103 on your tests," Mrs. Brisket said as the other members of the class filed from the room. Ronald and I exchanged quick, furtive smiles. "But I am concerned that you cheated." We stopped smiling.

Ronald looked away, ran a hand across the top of his crewcut head and adjusted his thick, dark-rimmed glasses. I thrust my hands into the front pockets of my jeans and shifted my weight nervously from one leg to the other. I knew I had to force myself to look Mrs. Brisket straight in the eye. When I did, I had to hold my eyes abnormally wide in order to control a spasm of blinking. "I…I don't know what happened," I stammered, searching in panic for some lie to acquit us, sure that my behavior was hopelessly guilty. What was she going to do? Could I be expelled for cheating on one test? Would they read my name over the school's intercom? Would my parents be notified?

But rather than the iron-edged, gelid tones of the prosecutor, Mrs. Brisket spoke to us in a sad voice that was barely louder than a whisper. "Never mind," she said. "I'm going to ignore what has happened this time. You are both nice boys. But this must never happen again. Do you understand?"

"Yes ma'am," we replied in unison.

"Ronald, you may go. I want to speak to you further, Richie." When Ronald had gone, she said to me, "I know what happened on that test. You let Ronald copy your test paper, didn't you?"

I felt like a quarterback when one of his linemen holds a defender to prevent him from being thrown for a loss. I knew that my escape was unjust, but I ran for daylight nonetheless. "Yes ma'am," I replied after an instant's hesitation. I tried to infuse my voice with contrition and reluctance.

"You are one of the brightest, most mature young men in our school. You must act to set an example for the other boys. Do you understand?" I nodded and she continued. "I know you were just trying to help him, Richie. But it's no favor to help someone cheat. Cheaters never gain."

And she was right, of course, because Ronald Demart has since died.

2

1969

"This salt shaker likes you," Faith Cleaver said. Her green eyes glinted as she shook the dark red hair off her freckled face. In her hand a salt shaker danced its way across the formica table top and leaped onto Richard Janus's arm. "This salt shaker likes you. And so does this fork," Faith said, giggling in her mock-babyish voice. The fork pirouetted its way around the ashtray and coffee cups to join the gyrating salt shaker.

"They like your medallion, too," Faith continued, and the salt shaker and fork began a tap dance on the peace medal he wore inside his denim jacket over a black, turtleneck sweater.

When Faith put the fork and salt shaker down to take a drag from her cigarette, Janus lifted a cup to his lips. He smiled pensively a moment at her over the rim. "I'm glad you like it," he responded. "My father gave it to me. He made it from a piece of shrapnel that was cut out of his back after his plane went down over Antwegen during World War II."

Faith truncated her habitual activity of rolling the ash off the end of her cigarette and said, "Wow," so quickly that the smoke from her most recent puff burst forth in one large, thick gray cloud. She lifted the medallion away from Janus's chest with her finger tips and bent over the table to examine it more closely. "That's an amazing story," she said. "I guess this is a very special symbol for you then, isn't it?"

"Yes," Janus said. "I was very moved when my father gave it to me."

"Was he a pilot?"

"Who?" Janus said, springing his trap.

"Your father." Faith picked her cigarette up, tapped the ash off its end and cocked her head just a bit, as if wondering what she had somehow missed.

"No, he was a chaplain," Janus said.

"Why was he flying over Antwegen?"

"He wasn't."

"He wasn't?" Faith said, looking out of the corners of her eyes. She took a deep drag on her cigarette. Coolly she asked, "Did I mispronounce the name of the town?"

"How do you know it was a town?" Janus stared at Faith. Had she returned his gaze, as he wanted, she might have noticed that although he did not smile, the skin had gone tight over his cheekbones and the lower lids of his eyes had gone puffy.

"Well, I just assumed. It wasn't a town? What was it?" Faith said.

"I don't know."

"Well, it's your father's story. Why don't you know?"

"I made it up."

Faith laughed. Two ha ha's exactly. "You made up this Antwegen, or whatever, where your father was shot down?"

"That too."

The smile slowly edged out of Faith's face. She crushed out her cigarette and fished a new one from her pack of Winstons. She wet her lips before mouthing the new cigarette and said, "Are you trying to put me on?"

"No."

"Well, what all did you make up?" Faith asked.

"The whole thing."

"About your father getting shot down?" Janus nodded. "The injured back? The shrapnel? Everything?" Janus nodded. "Why?" Faith asked.

"It makes a good story, don't you think? A much better story than that my mother gave it to me for Christmas. It's such a good story, in fact, that it should be true even though it isn't."

Faith shook her head rapidly, as if she were trying to shake away some insect. It seemed she didn't know whether to laugh or feel offended, as if she wasn't sure whether she was being flirted with or ridiculed. She decided to change the subject. Working her face into what Janus considered a sarcastic smile, she said, "I heard you were nominated for a Rhodes Scholarship. Congratulations."

"Thank you."

"What do you think your chances are?" Janus held up his hand and curled his thumb and index finger into a zero. "Why so optimistic?" Faith said.

"Because I'm too good an athlete and not good enough a student."

"Wait a minute," Faith said. "I'm not as dumb as I look, you know. Bill Bradley was an All-American, and he won a Rhodes Scholarship."

"True. But Gail Goodrich was All America the same year and *didn't* win a Rhodes Scholarship."

"Maybe he wasn't a very good student," Faith argued.

"My point precisely," Janus said and lightly rapped his knuckles on the table top.

"What?" Faith said, laughing genuinely this time. "You're crazy. Besides, you're no All-American anyway…I mean," she added hurriedly, "I know you're good. I've been to the games. Everyone says what a good passer you are and all. But…."

"You're absolutely right," Janus interjected. "I think you've put your finger right on it. I won't win a Rhodes Scholarship because I'm too good a student and not good enough an athlete. Now that I think of it, there have been many poor athletes, likely hundreds even, who have failed to win Rhodes Scholarships."

"Maybe you won't win because you're crazy," Faith suggested.

"A factor it saddens me to consider," Janus acknowledged.

He picked Faith's cigarette from the ashtray and took a deep drag.

"Hey," she said, snatching it back from him, "you shouldn't do that. You're in training."

"All the more reason why I should do it. Actually, only athletes in training *should* smoke. A new medical study has demonstrated that nicotine stimulation, when supplemented by regular hard exercise, promotes long-term heart resiliency." Janus tried to take the cigarette again, but she held it away from him.

"You're making that up, too," Faith said.

"Yes," Janus admitted, "I am."

An awkward silence followed. Both Faith and Janus searched for something new to say, but neither discovered anything quickly enough. Faith nervously lifted her empty coffee cup, and Janus, observing her, jumped up without comment, to get refills. On the way back from the coffee urn, he paused to squint out the night-blackened window which looked out over the snow-covered grounds of Lancaster College. He didn't know exactly what he was looking for, but it didn't matter anyway. With his hands full, he couldn't block out the bright light that surrounded him, so all he could see at the window was a reflection of himself.

When Janus returned to the table, Faith was holding a smoldering cigarette in her left hand and was drumming the fingers of her right. Janus put the fresh cups of coffee on the table and made a quick silly face. "Blind dates are fun, huh?" he said.

Faith exhaled a long stream of smoke upward and repositioned her left elbow on the formica so that her arm was held upright with the wrist cocked back and the cigarette wedged in the V of her first two fingers. With the tip of her tongue, she licked the left corner of her mouth. "You're not in a fraternity, are you," she said in a voice that seemed studiedly indifferent. Janus shook his head. "Why not?" Faith continued. "Why didn't you pledge Delta Chi? All jocks pledge Delta Chi. Especially the basketball players."

"I guess I don't want to be like all jocks," Janus said.

"Feeling a little superior, are you?" Faith said, talking through her teeth.

Janus felt a bit like he'd been slapped. "No," he responded slowly. "I guess I'm just adept at giving misimpressions about myself."

Faith reached across the table and laid her left hand on Janus's arm. "Oh, Richard," she said, squeezing his arm a little and in the process dropping ash on him, "are you feeling disliked?"

"I don't know. Am I being disliked?" Janus asked with a dry laugh.

"Well, you *are* making an ash of yourself," Faith giggled. She rubbed the ash into Janus's forearm and added, "Or perhaps I'm making an ash out of you. But I don't think you're being disliked. Because," she said, picking up one of her props again, "this fork likes you." And the fork began to dance again as Faith hummed "Light My Fire" through her giggles.

Faith and Janus left the student union and walked outside into the frigid January air. After a few steps Janus grabbed her shoulders to stop her. He wondered if she thought he was going to kiss her. Instead, he reached across her body with his right arm and circled it behind her knees.

"What are you doing?" she squealed. Pulling forward on her legs and steadying her body with his left hand on her stomach, he flipped her backwards 270 degrees onto his shoulder.

"Carrying you home," he said. "What do you think *you're* doing?"

"It looks like I'm riding home on your shoulder. I don't suppose you could be convinced to put me down."

"Nope. Shall we sing?"

"No!"

"Good," Janus said and burst into his gravelly baritone.

> "High above an Alpha's garter,
> High above her knee,
> Lies the secret of my ardor,
> Her virginity.
>
> Lay her gently,
> Oh so gently,
> Lay her in the grass,
> Oh what I would surely die for:
> A piece of Alpha ...."

"Put me down," Faith demanded.

"Sure little Alpha. I've carried you home, and now I'll put you down." Janus loosened his grip on her and let her slide to the ground.

"I don't think that's very funny," Faith said, smoothing her wool skirt.

"Okay. Sure *big* Alpha."

"I don't think your song is funny."

"Good. Because it isn't my song. It's an old Delta Chi song. I just wanted to show you that I could have been a Delta Chi if I'd wanted to." Janus locked his arms behind his back. "Will you go out with me again?"

"When?" Faith asked.

"How about two weeks? For Winter Festival. Simon and Garfunkel will be here."

"I've already got plans. Sorry."

"How about next weekend then?"

"I really am sorry," Faith laughed, "but I've got plans then, too."

"I see," Janus said with a short dry laugh. "Maybe we can try some time later on, then." He didn't mean it as a question but as a prelude to retreat.

Faith surprised him by saying, "I'm not busy the weekend *after* Winter Festival."

"Hey, great. No, that's not great. What I mean is that we have games both Friday and Saturday night that week."

"We could do something afterwards," Faith suggested. "Don't you guys always party after you play at home?"

Janus smiled. "I'd like to say I have a date."

"Why?" she asked.

"So you'd think I have a tight social calendar, too."

"You don't have to take me out," Faith said.

"Maybe I should just go out with a fork. It seems I'm rather popular with tableware. Are there any cute spoons in your sorority that I might like?"

"Should I say none for a gay blade like yourself?" Faith said, laughing.

"I really wish you wouldn't."

"Then perhaps I should say I'd better go in before I freeze my little Alpha ass off." Janus laughed, and Faith stuck out her gloved hand to him. When he took it, she gently pulled him to her and kissed him lightly on the cheek. "Thank you, Rich," she said. "For the coffee and the conversation. I enjoyed myself tonight." She turned then and hurried into her sorority house, her brown Villager skirt dancing after her in the January wind.

By the Wednesday after Winter Festival, Lancaster was in the frigid grips of the season's ugliest weather. The temperature had not climbed above zero in three days. When Janus started home from basketball practice, he determined it was too cold to make the ten-block walk without stopping to warm up. When he reached the student union, he went inside and made his way to the bookstore. He had planned to browse a while in the fiction section, but he spotted Faith in the gift department.

Coming up behind her, Janus drew back his arm to swat her on the rump, like a coach sending a player into the game. But halfway through the motion he decided that the slap might cause Faith to drop the crested sorority tankard she was holding. So instead, he announced himself by saying, "I was just wondering whether a friendly swat on your fanny would cause you to drop that beer mug you're holding."

"It might cause me to drop it on your head," Faith said without turning around.

"Do you even know *who* it is you are threatening with dire bodily harm?" Janus asked.

Faith turned around to face him and discovered that he had not yet undone the hood of his down parka. Typically, Janus had not taken the time to cool down properly after practice before showering, nor had he allowed time after the shower for his hair to dry. On his way from the gym, the strands of his dark brown hair that had strayed outside the hood of his jacket had frozen into hard black icicles. Thawing now, they dropped beads of water like tears down his flushed face.

"From the looks of you, I might guess the Abominable Snowman," Faith said.

Janus brushed at the water trickling down his cheeks and said, "Well, now certain cliché-mongering sportswriters *have* been known to say I have ice water in my veins, but...."

"I had more in mind your deep-frozen heart," Faith interrupted. She tilted her head the way she did when she wanted to signal her listener that she wasn't serious. But her eyes were glassy and lacked their usual teasing flash.

Janus looked genuinely perplexed. He searched for a riposte. Finding nothing, he said, "How did you enjoy the Festival this year? I saw you at the concert." Janus licked his lips and raised his eyebrows. "You seemed to be having a good time. Fraternity boy, Delta Chi, I believe."

Faith cocked her head. "Oh, were you at the concert? I'm surprised. I mean, I heard that your social calendar filled out nicely, but I would have guessed you'd just have skipped the preliminaries and gotten right to the main event."

"What are you talking about?" he said, laughing. He pulled the string under his chin and finally pushed the hood back off his head.

Faith turned and set the mug back on its plexiglass shelf and began to pull on her dark leather gloves. "Let's just say I heard you had a pretty good time yourself," she said in a tone of finality.

Thinking he had been dismissed, Janus said as much to himself as to Faith, "Word does get around."

Faith looked up sharply. "Well, you can't really have expected that I wouldn't hear when you asked out one of my sorority sisters."

Janus pulled his own gloves back on now. He showed his teeth in a little smile. "You don't think I did that to nettle you, do you?"

"Nettle?" Faith wrinkled her face as if she had smelled a bad odor. "What's this *nettle*? Who uses a word like *nettle*?"

"You don't think I did it to *bug* you?" Janus amended.

"Oh, that occurred to me at first," Faith said. "But when Grace called in for an overnight, I figured that I was pretty far from your mind."

She began to walk down the aisle toward the exit. Janus stepped quickly around her into her path to face her. "Not true," he declared. "You're never far from my mind."

"Right, Janus. All the time you were with Grace, you were thinking of me. Wo ho." Faith rolled her eyes.

"Hey, it wasn't what you're insinuating," he said.

"All I know is that cute little Gracie Lamm came dragging into the house at 11 A.M. Sunday morning looking as if she had slept in her clothes."

"That's because she did sleep in her clothes," Janus pointed out.

Faith smiled and said, "Right. People often sleep in their clothes. I even shower in mine. Saves an awful lot of time that way. Does require a drip-dry wardrobe, however."

Janus laughed. "Look Faith. Grace did sleep at my apartment. She did sleep in my bed even. We got home from a party late. It was either both of us in my bed or one of us on the sofa. I couldn't ask the lady to sleep on the sofa. I may be a Midwesterner now, but at heart I'm still a Southern gentleman. On the other hand, it was unthinkable for *me* to sleep on the sofa. It's only about half as long as I am. But sleeping is all we did in the bed. I swear it. Don't you believe me?"

Faith looked at him for a long time before answering with a shake of her head. "No. Who *would* believe a story like that?"

"You could ask Grace," Janus suggested.

"Who would believe any story told by a slut?"

Janus chewed at the stub of his thumb nail. "What could I do to convince you?"

"Nothing," she said.

Janus raised his hands palm up to his shoulders. "What can I say? Do you still want to go to the party after the game on Saturday?"

"Oh, absolutely," Faith said.

Faith was waiting in the corridor when Janus emerged from the locker room still trying to rub his hair dry with a white towel. She dropped her cigarette on the tile floor, crushed it out under one of her Weejun loafers and blew a stream of smoke away from him out of the corner of her mouth.

"How about a victory kiss," she said, approaching him. Janus pulled the towel away from his head and lowered his cheek toward her. "Now, we can do better than that," she said, taking his face in both hands and turning it so that she could kiss him fully on the mouth. "Ah just *love* athletic heroes," she said with a giggle, raising her eyebrows and fluttering her lashes. She put her arm through his, letting her breast graze his elbow as they started to walk down the hall toward the exit, past the glass cases of tarnishing trophies. "You were super tonight, Rich," she said.

"I was?" Janus said. "How was I super?"

"Let's see. Four for seven from the field. Five for five from the line. And three rebounds," Faith said. "But the important thing was your floor game. Only *one* turnover and *eight* assists."

"I didn't know you were such a fan," Janus said.

"Oh, but ah ayam," Faith said, squeezing his arm and laughing at her exaggerated accent. "Ah just *love* athletic heroes."

"Where did you get the stats?" Janus said.

"Why, ah kept 'em myself in my little old notebook," Faith said.

Before going into the cold, Janus wrapped the towel around his head and pulled up the hood of his jacket. Faith made him wait so that she could tie the hood's drawstring under his chin.

"Now, doesn't mah athletic hero look just like an Indian papoose," Faith said.

"I thought I was supposed to look like the Abominable Snowman."

"Nope, you're the Abominable Snowman when you take out Gracie Lamm. When you take me out, you're a cute little Indian papoose." Faith stood on her tiptoes and kissed him on the nose. She took his gloved hand in hers as they walked to the car.

After Janus had let her into his white Volkswagen bus and settled himself behind the wheel, he asked what she thought of the defense he had played.

"Just soopuh, honey chile. Everything you did tonight was just soopah."

"My man led them in scoring, you know," Janus said.

"He did? Then he must be really good, huh?"

"Or maybe I'm not very good at defense," Janus said.

Faith patted him in the middle of his thigh as he started the engine. "Oh, come on, Mr. Athletic Hero. I'll bet there's not anything you're not good at." Faith licked her lips and laughed. "Where are we going?" she asked.

"To a party. That's what you requested, isn't it?" Janus pulled the bus out of the parking lot and onto the street.

"Oh, yes suh. Ah do love pahties. And ah do so hope we can have owasevs a good time. Just a gay old time. Don't you hope so, too?"

"Why, Miz Faith," Janus said. "Ah had you pegged for a Midwestun gal, but hearin' you talk so, I believe in yo haht yore as Southan as a magnolia blossom."

"Oh, ah ayam, suh, ah ayam. Ah'm as Southan as hominy grits and black-eyed Susans."

"That's black-eyed peas," Janus said.

"Oh, and black-eyed peas, too. Ah just *love* black-eyed peas. Almost as much as tall, Southan, athletic heroes." Faith laid her hand on Janus's thigh again and pressed her fingers around his knee as he maneuvered the car into a parking space in front of the Delta Chi house. "Well bless mah Kentucky fried hawt," Faith said, pressing a hand to her sweatered bosom. "Are you, suh, takin' me to one of those wild fraternity pahties? Ah do so hope you plan to protect my honah. Ah heah these Delta Chi boys are such animals."

Inside, Janus led Faith downstairs to a large den where a stereo blared and two dozen couples were dancing. As they forged through the crowd to get cups of beer from a keg in the corner, he was greeted with a chorus of "Nice game tonight, Tricks."

Janus's nickname had a dual etymology. It originally developed after an overzealous sports publicist described his ball handling as "magic." His teammates decided that only a "trickster" was magic. So for a time in his freshman year, he was "Trickster." Ultimately, though, the name was shortened to Tricks. More recently Janus's friends claimed that his nickname derived from the name he shared with Richard Nixon.

When they each had a full cup of beer, Janus showed Faith to a small room with a large naugahyde sofa where the music was not quite so loud. By the time they sat down, Faith had emptied half her beer cup.

"They call you Tricks, huh?" Faith said, lighting a cigarette.

"Yep." Janus nodded and took a sip from his cup.

"What kind of tricks do *you* do? *I* like to make things disappear." She tilted the cup to her lips and drained it, wiping her grinning mouth afterwards with the back of her hand. "More, Tricks," she said, holding the empty cup out to him. Janus laughed, handed his cup to Faith and went back to the keg to refill hers. When he returned, she had finished his beer, too, and was dancing by herself in the middle of the room to the Doors's "Whiskey Bar." Janus took a large swallow from the fresh cup and sat down on the couch to watch her. She mugged and occasionally exaggerated her motions. Near the song's end she stuck her tongue in her cheek and jabbed at it with her index finger. The undercutting gestures notwithstanding, she was performing for him. And she was good.

When the song ended, she sat down next to him so that their legs and shoulders were touching. "Gimme that beer, big boy," she said, doing Mae West.

"Uh uh," Janus said, holding the cup away from her. "This one's mine."

Faith picked up the empty cup which Janus had left with her and said, "*This* one's yours. The one you're holding is *mine*."

"Nope," Janus said and turned his face away from her to take a sip from the cup. "Possession, as they say, is nine-tenths of the law. Whatever that means."

"No!" Faith said, leaning over him and taking the cup. "This is *my* beer." She stuck out her lower lip like a spoiled child. "And it's *my* trick to make things disappear. You haven't told me what your tricks are yet, Tricks." Faith giggled and drank from the cup. "Wo," she said and ran a hand over her face. She smiled at him showing all her teeth.

"Maybe I like to make things disappear too sometimes," Janus said, taking the cup back and drinking from it.

"What things, Tricks?" Faith asked, pursing her lips and opening her eyes wide. "Little sorority girls' clothes, maybe?" She laughed and then kissed him quickly on the lips.

Janus laughed, too, and put his arm around her shoulders. "Is that a *question* or a suggestion?" he asked. There was a buzzing in the crowd of partiers outside the room. The volume of the stereo was turned up and Mick Jagger began to rasp, "I cain't get no sa-tis-fac-tion."

Faith turned to face Janus, pulling her knees up on the couch between them. "Why suh," she said. "It's a question, of co-us. Ah'm just an innocent little Southan gal who's still as virgin as the day she was bawun. Whatevah would ah know about a man makin' a woman's clothes disappear?" She took the beer away from him and finished it.

"Then you mean they're playing my song?" Janus asked.

"Why, Tricks, honey," she drawled, snuggling back into the crook of his arm. "Ah'd hope you'd be satisfied just bein' heah with me right now."

Janus laughed and squeezed her shoulder a little. "I like you, Faith," he said.

"That's good, Tricks. It means you've got good taste."

When Janus took Faith back to the sorority house that night, he asked her at the door if he could see her again.

"Sure," she said, "if you don't mind a girl who drinks too much and can dance too well for you."

"Well, not as long as she remains as virgin as the day she was born."

"Then you better take me out again soon," Faith said, putting her hands on his shoulders.

He put his arms around her waist, pulled her close and just before kissing her said, "How's next Friday?"

She let her lips part slightly, but when his tongue darted into her mouth, she drew back her head and giggled, "Now suh. We musn't get too familiar so soon." Then she laid her cheek next to his and patted him on the back of his neck.

Faith and Janus had driven the forty-five miles north from Lancaster into Chicago's loop to see a movie. On the way home they drove in silence by the starkness of the Robert Taylor homes which towered over the Dan Ryan Expressway. Through the choking air of Calumet, WLS blared out the top forty over the whine of the Volkswagen engine.

When "A Bridge Over Troubled Waters" ended, Janus switched off the radio. He pulled on the heating lever to increase the flow of warm air. Without looking at Faith, he said, "Do you always fall asleep in movies?" These were the first words spoken since claiming the faded white bus from the parking garage. And Janus uttered them with misgiving. He was puzzled by Faith's brief responses to his remarks, by the absence of her usual banter. He was genuinely annoyed with her for falling asleep in the film. But he feared that addressing the matter directly would unalterably sour an evening that was salvageable. So he had decided to dismiss his annoyance and hope to resurrect the feeling of camaraderie that had united them through dinner and drinks before the show. But when the silence of the ride lengthened to fifteen minutes, he blurted out his question without ever abandoning his determination not to.

"Not always," Faith answered slowly. "But it's happened before. It wasn't a comment on my company."

Janus was partially relieved that she hadn't responded hostilely. He patted her leg where the wool skirt gave way to rough nylon stretched taut over her knee. "It's not late," he said.

"I know," she said with a sigh. "I think maybe I'm anemic or something. I get plenty of sleep, but I'm always tired." When Janus didn't comment, she continued. "But it doesn't take going to the movies with Richard Janus to give me a case of the nods. I've fallen asleep in class. Last week I fell asleep in church."

Seizing a chance to interject levity, Janus said, "I *always* fall asleep in church."

"I'm sure you don't even go to church, Janus," Faith replied.

"True. But only because I find it so difficult to get comfortable stretched out in a pew." He expected her to laugh, but she only yawned and laid her head against the window. She was asleep by the time they arrived back on campus.

Janus nudged her awake. She awoke grinning and said, "Hi." She wiped a trickle of saliva off her chin with the back of a closed fist. "Oops, I think I drooled. I'd make somebody a good puppy, huh, Richie?" she said.

"Shall I take you on home," Janus offered, "or would you like to stop by my apartment for a nightcap?"

"A nightcap? A *nightcap?*" Faith howled. "Where did you pick up that line?" She began to poke him in the side with an index finger until, laughing, he told her to stop. "A nightcap?" she said.

"Would you care to have a drink with me before you go home?"

"No," Faith said. "No, I don't think I'd like a drink."

"All right," Janus said, not surprised, but trying to mask his disappointment.

"Because," Faith added, "*I* want a *nightcap.*"

In his cramped apartment, Janus stood at the sink in the front room that served as living room, study and kitchen. He quickly washed two glasses and filled them with gin and tonic, dropping in ice from the lone tray that would fit in his tiny, yellowing refrigerator. He brought one of the drinks to Faith and sat down with the other beside her on the ragged sofa that he had tried to spruce up by covering with an extra bedspread. Faith drank as thirstily as she had the week before at the Delta Chi party, and before Janus had finished half his drink, he had to make her another.

Faith surveyed his cramped bookshelves. She asked him if he had read all the books they contained. He lied and told her yes.

"Which ones do you like best?" she asked. When Janus laughed, she added quickly, "Why is that a funny question? Is that a stupid thing to say?" She began to busy herself finding a cigarette to light.

"Of course it isn't stupid," Janus said, returning to the couch with Faith's fresh drink.

"Why did you laugh then?"

"I laughed, because, well, I have books on so many different topics, from so many different fields. I never thought about liking some of them best." Janus took a sip from his gin and added, "But it isn't an unreasonable question, I guess. It certainly isn't stupid."

"Pick three," Faith said.

"Just three?"

"Three," Faith said.

He took her cigarette and puffed at it. Then he said he'd pick *The Mind of the South*, because it explained to him where he'd come from; *The Plague*, because it outlined for him how to live; and *Catch-22*, because it showed him where he wanted to go: anywhere but to war.

"And of those three," she said, "which is your favorite?"

"That's hard," Janus replied. "*Catch-22*, I guess. The world is so absurd, and Heller gets it just right. And, God, it's funny. That's why it's my favorite, I guess. Because life is so ridiculous, our best hope is to laugh. Laugh raucously, laugh cynically, laugh hopelessly, but laugh." Janus was embarrassed when he stopped talking; he realized that he hadn't been answering Faith's question at all but had been talking to himself. So he added, "That's why I like you, Faith. You make me laugh. You're not afraid to be silly."

He felt it was time for a joke, but Faith crushed out her cigarette and said, "You know, you're not like most of the guys I've gone out with. Are you sure you want to go out with a dingbat like me?"

He protested that he hardly thought her a dingbat and pointed out that it was he, not she, who had suggested they have a *nightcap*. She laughed a little and her seriousness seemed to lift away like a shroud being pulled from a statue.

"Maybe you just like me because I'm cute. I *am* cute, you know," she said in her silly voice. She drained her drink, and when she set the glass on the floor, Janus kissed her softly and for a long time on her mouth. She let his tongue play over her lips and teeth. And after the kiss he lay back on the couch and pulled her down beside him, her head on his chest. He stroked her thick, frizzy hair and ran his hand over her shoulders and down to the small of her back.

"Are you going to take me to bed, Richie?" she asked quietly.

"If you'd like me to."

"I won't know what to do," she said.

"I think you'll find it comes naturally," Janus said and laughed silently at his joke. He got up and led her by the hand to his bedroom.

She sat on the foot of the bed, slid backwards until her feet were off the ground and then jiggled her legs. "Somehow," Faith said, "I feel like I did when I was a little girl, and my father would take me into his bedroom, first to scold me and then to spank me." She laughed and looked at him. "I guess we get undressed now, huh?" she said.

"That would make a good beginning," Janus said.

Faith tugged at her sweater. When she got it turned inside out over her head, her arms stretched out straight, she squealed, "Help me, help me. I'm stuck," and jiggled her legs up and down again.

Janus had undressed. He sat beside her and pulled her sweater off. Carefully, he turned it right side out and laid it on the night table. He kissed her cheek and neck, unbuttoned her blouse, slipped it off and laid it on the sweater. Faith reached behind herself, unsnapped her bra and shrugged it off.

"Not so good in the tits department, huh?" she said.

Janus pulled a pillow from under the spread and laid Faith's head on it. Her half-naked body seemed especially vulnerable to him, and he was oddly moved to discover her body as freckled as her face. Gently he kissed her in the hollow at the bottom of her neck and on each breast. "Just fine in the tits department, I'd say," he assured her.

"I thought most men like big ones," Faith said.

"I'm not most men, and I like Faith's ones." He pulled back the covers and let them drop to the floor at the end of the bed. They kissed again, long and hard, tongues probing deep into one another's mouths. Janus squeezed her breasts and rubbed each nipple erect. He ran a flat hand down over her stomach and under the top of her skirt, his fingers teasing at the beginnings of her pubic hair. He found the zipper on the side of her skirt and pulled it down. She arched her back so that he could slip it off. He kneeled on the bed at her waist and cupped a hand over the slight bulge of flesh inside her thigh between her panties and the top of her stockings. As he freed the nylons from her garter belt, he bent and kissed her there.

When she was finally naked, Janus moved between her legs. He could feel them tense as he rolled on top of her, so he made no effort to penetrate her.

"You won't hurt me, will you, Rich?" Faith whispered.

"No," he said softly. "I won't hurt you, Faith. I won't ever hurt you." He kissed her ear and her cheek. He kissed under her chin and her neck and her breasts again and between them and under them. He scooted backwards on his knees and kissed her navel and then nestled his face in the sparse flame of her dark red pubic hair. He breathed deeply the rich, musky perfume of her and kissed her there and down inside each thigh. When his tongue found her clitoris, she gasped and twined her fingers in his hair.

When she came, Faith cried out as if she were in pain. She began to moan, "Stop. Stop it." But Janus wouldn't quit until she began to laugh and twist her legs, which were clamped around his head. He crawled alongside her then, put his arms around her and squeezed her tightly against him. He brushed the hair off her face and kissed her lightly on each closed eyelid and on her nose.

Faith opened her eyes and looked at him evenly. "Do you do that to all your girlfriends?" she asked.

"No."

"Don't lie," Faith said sharply and then tried to turn away from him.

But he held her and turned her face to him again. "What do you want me to say?"

"I want you to tell me the truth," Faith said. "I always want you to tell me the truth?"

"Oh," Janus said smiling. "But what if I just tell you the truth instead. How about that?"

"Are you *going* to tell me the truth?" Faith said.

"Yes."

"Well?"

"Well what?" Janus said.

Faith made a low rumble of exasperation in her throat. "Do you do that to all your girlfriends?"

"No."

"You're impossible." Faith put the heels of both her hands against his chest and pushed him away from her.

"No," Janus corrected her, "I'm very possible."

Faith sat up and grabbed the sheet from the foot of the bed. She drew it up under her arms. "Does that mean you expect me to reciprocate?" she said.

"I expect very little from a girl who falls asleep in the middle of *Lion in Winter*," Janus responded too quickly, wishing instantly that he hadn't.

She gave him that even, expressionless look again. "Hey, that really made you mad, huh?"

"No, not really. I mean it wasn't my usual experience. Most of my dates manage to stay awake. But I wouldn't say I'm mad. I'm not acting mad, am I?"

Faith lay down again, scrunching the sheet around her with her elbows. Finally, she said, "You're gonna have to take me the way I am, you know."

"That's the way I'd like to take you, sweetheart," Janus replied, doing Bogey, even though he knew she couldn't see the twitch.

Faith ignored him. Staring at the ceiling, she said, "You'll have to be patient with me. There are lots of things I don't know. I'm very innocent."

Janus didn't know how to respond. Faith turned on her side to face him when he didn't answer. She pulled the wound sheet out from under her and spread it over him, leaving her arm across his chest. "Do you think you love me, Rich?" she said.

Janus didn't want to say that he loved her. He felt that the question was unfair. He liked her. He was charmed by her. But *love* her? He hadn't known her nearly long enough for that, he thought.

Faith's hand began to move down over his body, stirring him quickly to heightened arousal.

On the other hand, Janus recognized that Faith expected him to say that he loved her, would feel abused if he didn't. He slipped his arm underneath her head, pulled her close to him and said softly into her hair, "I do think I'm falling in love with you, Faith." And as he said it, he reflected that perhaps it was even true.

3

I dreamed about New Orleans last night. It must have been caused by all the stories about my childhood I was telling. I moved away from my native city between my junior and senior years in high school. I've been back only once since then. I have lived in the Midwest. Now I live in L.A. But I have never stopped thinking of myself as a New Orleanian. You didn't know that, did you, Dr. Burden?

The time of my dream was the present, but in it I was younger-looking, trimmer, harder and tanner. My graying front tooth, which was broken by an elbow in a high school game against Elgin, was whole again. I was wearing dark sandals with tire-tread soles. My jeans fit snugly, but my wide, Indian-tooled belt didn't bite me because the bulge around my waist had disappeared. For reasons known only in the world of dreams, I was wearing my green basketball jersey, my white number 34 displayed prominently on both the front and back.

It seems I had flown to New Orleans because I found myself standing outside the airport where I found a bus to take me across town. As I rode across the city, I noted how different it looked. There were new buildings which sometimes blocked out old landmarks. The trees were all taller and grown more closely together. Distances were shorter, and there generally seemed to be less space.

When the bus arrived in the Gentilly section of the city, my old neighborhood, I disembarked at a terminal next to the Zesto Ice Cream stand, which stood across Chef Menteur Highway from the subdivision where I had grown up. As I waited on the curb to cross the street, I suddenly realized that I didn't know what I was doing. I didn't know why I had come again to New Orleans. I tried to think of something to do. I tried to think of someone to contact. But I realized there was no longer anyone in New Orleans I knew.

I wondered in my dream, as I have so often wondered awake, what had happened to my childhood friends? What had they become? What did they value? Which, if any, had become hippies? Which had demonstrated against the war in Vietnam? Which had worked for Gene McCarthy or Robert Kennedy? Which had voted for George McGovern?

Then, as dreams are wont, Carter Percy drove into the Zesto Ice Cream parking lot. I recognized him at once. He looked exactly like his father. But his eyes passed over me without recognition. At first I figured that my long hair camouflaged me. He had never seen me without a flattop. But, of course, he failed to recognize me because dreamers are often hard to see.

Carter Percy had been my best friend. I had not seen him since 1965. Other than his name, I knew nothing about this man I had been so close to as a boy. I was afraid to speak to him, afraid that the man he had become would destroy my memory of the boy I loved.

The outlines of Carter's powerful upper body were still visible underneath his long-sleeved blue shirt, but his belly now swelled over his belt, just as his father's had. His hairline had receded. Soon he would be bald. His feet dragged the ground as he slouched to the window of the ice cream stand to order cones for himself and the two children waiting in the car.

As Carter returned to his car, I stopped him, on impulse, without deciding to do it. "Carter Percy," I said, sticking out my hand. He looked confused as he tried to juggle the three cones into one hand in order to clasp mine with the other. One of the cones slid from his grasp, smeared his left hand and hit the blacktopped pavement with a sickening splat.

"Jeez, I'm sorry," I said. I was sorry to have bothered him. I had no idea what it was I wanted to say to him. But he did not look annoyed. Only resigned. "Do you remember a guy named Richard Janus?" I said.

His face contorted, and he squinted as if he were trying to make out something very dim. "Richie?" he said. "Richie Janus?" Carter smiled and extended his large right hand toward me. It was dry and cool; his grip was surprisingly limp for such a large man.

Holding that thick, flaccid hand, I recalled an entirely different Carter from the one I now confronted. He had been a burly kid in grammar school. But by the time we started junior high, all his weight had turned to muscle. He was never particularly tall, but he had the strength of a giant.

On our seventh grade football team, Carter played center and I played quarterback. He took immense pride in knocking down people who tried to tackle me when I passed or ran. He was so strong that not even the ninth-grade boys dared to challenge him. And because of his fierce loyalty to me,

I too was spared the hazing that seventh graders often experience at the hands of their older schoolmates. No one stole my gym clothing, no one rubbed liniment into my jockstrap, no one smashed insects between the pages of my textbooks. I was Carter's best friend, and no one was willing to mess with him as the price for messing with me.

Carter's habit of protecting me was so ingrained that it functioned even when he disagreed with me. Like brothers, we sometimes had our disputes, but to the world we presented a united front.

It was during our seventh-grade year that the public school system in New Orleans was finally racially integrated. Of course, it was only token integration: a half dozen black little girls were placed in two grade-school classrooms. Our junior high was unaffected. We had spent our short lifetimes surrounded by invisible black people, and that was not really going to change. Nonetheless, many in the city were upset. Angry talk and violent proclamations began to fill the halls of our junior high school. A demonstration was planned. On the day the black children were to be brought to their new school, weeks after the fall term had begun, all the students at our junior high were to stage a walkout after lunch. Carter planned to walk with the others. I knew that I couldn't.

I don't want to give the impression that I was brave. On the contrary, I was terrified. Even at twelve, I was aware enough of the explosive nature of racial hatred to know that taking a pro-integration stand could physically endanger me. And I certainly had no genuine concern for black people. Although my city was more than forty percent black, I didn't know a single black person. My parents, however, were among that small group of Southern whites who supported civil rights. They had taught me to say *Negro* instead of *nigger*. I never said either, of course, because until my seventh-grade year, the opportunity to refer to black people never arose.

Though I usually discussed important things with my parents, I didn't inform them of the planned walkout. I knew they would order me to stay in school. At first I planned to join the walkout and explain to them, when they found out, that I was afraid to resist. But as the day approached, I abandoned that plan because I knew how disappointed they would be in me. I knew that their disappointment would be so great they wouldn't even bother to punish me, but would look at me with dejected eyes that said they wished I didn't belong to them. Horrible as rejection by my classmates would be, rejection by my family loomed as decidedly worse. Undoubtedly, I was a coward. And it was for cowardly reasons that I resolved to resist the walkout.

The same was hardly true of Carter. He was not a particularly racist kid—I never remember hearing him use the word *nigger* either, for like me, he found no occasion to refer to black people at all—but insofar as he thought about integration, he was against it. And so, like most of the kids in our school, he planned to join the protest.

On the day of the walkout, Carter and I ate our lunch together as usual. When the lunch period ended and students began to march outside instead of back to class, Carter rose to join them. He motioned for me to come, but I didn't move. "Come on," he said.

"I'm not going," I answered. "It isn't right. My parents say it isn't right."

Carter looked at me strangely. "You're not gonna walk out?" he asked. I stared at the smeared cafeteria table top and shook my head. I neither answered nor moved. We were the last two kids in the lunchroom. A ninth grader, one of the protest ringleaders, came back inside. He called for us to come out. Neither of us answered. Carter said to me, "Richie, we gotta go outside. Your parents won't even find out."

"They'll find out," I said without looking at him.

"The ninth grader, who was as big as Carter, came over to us. "You two guys gonna join the walkout or what?" Neither of us looked at him. "Hey, you two a couple of nigger lovers?" he said.

Carter turned to him. In a menacing voice that rumbled from the bottom of his throat, he said, "If you want your ass kicked up around your shoulders, you'll say that to me again."

The ninth grader took a half-step backwards. Perhaps he hadn't really expected resistance, had tossed the epithet at us not as a challenge but as a goad to hurry us outside. Shocked by Carter's threat, he turned to me. "What about you, Janus?" he said. "You want to marry one of those little pickaninnies? I bet you are a *nigger* lover. A pussy-faced, ass-kissing…." He didn't finish his abuse because Carter moved deliberately forward and struck him a terrific blow in the stomach. The kid bent double and gagged, both hands clutching at his waist. I thought he was going to throw up. Still bent over, he stumbled toward the door. When he reached it, he called back, "I'll get you guys." For some reason, he singled me out. "I'll get you, Janus," he said.

But Carter corrected him. "Wrong, asshole. You got me this time, and anytime you mess with Richie, you still got me." The kid didn't linger to argue. "What do we do now?" Carter asked me.

"We go to class, I guess," I said. "We're already late."

"Yeah, I guess we are," Carter said. He smiled at me and motioned with his head for me to get up. "I guess we *are* nigger lovers now, huh?" As we walked toward the stairwell, he added, "I don't feel any different."

And it turned out that we weren't any different. The principal let the protesters stay outside for a while, then told them he acknowledged their protest and asked them to return inside. And they did so. And the ninth-grade kid who had caught us was evidently less concerned with the fact that we were nigger lovers than with the fact that he had been beaten by a seventh grader. Carter and I saw him around school, but he never tried to make trouble.

Do you think I really remembered all that in the middle of my dream when I shook Carter's hand? Probably I didn't. But I usually recall it when I think of him. That's why the dream made me so sad, because in it Carter was no longer invincible. Rather he was flabby and growing old, seemingly defeated in a way I had never known him.

In the dream, still holding my hand, Carter turned and handed the two surviving cones through the car window to his children. Wiping his left hand on the seat of his trousers, he turned back to me and clasped his other hand around mine. "Jeez, you look good," he said. "You still living up in Chicago?"

"No," I said. "I live out in L.A. now. I'm working on a degree in history at UCLA."

"Wow," Carter said. "Still in school. Must be nice."

"Yeah. It is," I agreed. My mind raced for something else to say, not another biographical fact or question but something that could bridge the gulf between us and make us instantly buddies again. "Well...," I began, not knowing as I did so whether I would finish the sentence with some fabricated excuse for why it was necessary for me to leave abruptly or instead ask some question about his family.

"How're your folks?" Carter asked before I could say anything. He had always been fond of my family.

"Great. Just great," I said. I didn't want to tell him that my parents had divorced my first year in college. "And yours?" I asked.

"Mom's just fine," Carter said. "Still living at the same place. Dad passed away two years ago."

"Oh, I'm sorry," I said, realizing as I did so that it would place an unfair onus on Carter to acknowledge this late and useless, if not perfunctory, condolence. "I didn't know," I added. It didn't help.

Carter shook his head briefly. But then he smiled and clapped me on the shoulder with a curled hand. "Man, it's good to see you," he said. "How long you going to be in town?"

"Just this evening," I said quickly.

"Gee. Damn," Carter said. "I'd like you to meet my wife. And Mom would love to see you." Not true, I thought. Carter's mom and wife would be no less uncomfortable with me than he was.

"I may be back soon," I said. "I'll give you a call next time."

"You've got to do that. Man, it's been so long." About ten years, not counting dreams.

"It was great running into you like this, Carter," I said.

"Let me give you my card before you go," he said. He reached into the hip pocket of his baggy pants and pulled out his wallet. Handing me a two-by-three inch business card that read "Percy Realty" across the top, he said, "This has both my home phone and business phone on it." (I could hear Woody Allen dead pan, "Right there on that tiny little card?")

Forgive me, Carter. As I examined your card, I wondered if you had become one of those realtors guilty of racial steering. Oh me of little faith.

"And hey," Carter said, "don't go without letting me introduce you to my kids." He took my elbow and pulled me to the car window. "Kids," he said, "this is your daddy's old friend, Mr. Janus." And to me he said, "This is Cathy and little Sammy." He rubbed each child's head as he introduced them. Reluctantly then, Carter climbed into his car, started the engine, and began slowly to back out of the lot. "You be sure to call," he said as he pulled away.

"I will," I promised. Then I was alone again in the funny amber light of my dream, standing on the street curb in front of the Zesto Ice Cream stand. It was then that I noticed I was clutching my old plaid gym bag, into which I had stuffed all the clothes for my trip. In dreams, one travels light.

My trips to New Orleans were not always made in dreams. When I was a senior in high school, I actually did go back. It was a time my persistent maturity worked against me.

I was living near Chicago with my parents. I never escaped being the new kid in school that year, but my prowess on the basketball court helped me to make new friends. And my unconscious skill at imitation caused my Southern accent to erode somewhat toward the flat speech patterns of the Midwest. By the time my first snowy winter had given way to a dreary, rainy spring, I was no longer being called a hillbilly and thought of myself as accepted.

It was common at that time for high school seniors living near Chicago to give themselves a tan for Easter. They did this, normally, by crowding four or more into some parent's car and driving around the clock to somewhere in Florida (Fort Lauderdale, for some reason, was regarded as the prestige spot) where they would meet or quickly make friends with whom to share the cost of a motel room. Shelter was the key concern in these arrangements. Comfort did not even make the priority list.

In other words, the more the merrier. The more people sharing a room, the less it cost per individual; eight people in a room with two double beds was considered just about right, for no one would really occupy the room save to change clothes or use the bathroom, except between the hours of two and six

A.M., when all would be so exhausted that a floor to sleep on seemed a privilege rather than an inconvenience. All other hours of the day they would spend either lying in the sun baking their bodies or searching frantically for some older or older-looking person to buy them six-packs of beer, which they would consume retchingly past the point of inebriation. After a week of this, they would crowd their tender bodies back into the car and drive around the clock so as to arrive home just in time to be absent for the resumption of classes. If they were lucky, they managed to supply their return with enough beer to make the trip truly terrifying.

The value of such a journey was unquestioned. Fried bodies were badges of merit envied by all underclassmen and stay-at-home peers. Beer got consumed in staggering quantities, and if not for the first time, then for the first time on weekdays, before noon and without fear of parental discovery. But of most long-lasting significance, the trip provided the continuing opportunity to boast of sexual conquests over beautiful blond girls from Southern towns, which, of course, were never made.

Even the underclassmen were well aware that these conquests were never made. How could anyone make it with beautiful blond Southern girls in the still pristine middle sixties in motel rooms crowded with eight other guys, or on beaches crowded with several million red bodies, almost none of whom were yet liberated enough to wear bikinis?

So, of course, everyone believed passionately in the veracity of these sexual triumphs nonetheless.

I ached to go to Florida to give myself a tan for Easter, and I was deathly afraid that my parents might let me go. Being a mature kid, I had never indulged in the adolescent rite of surreptitious beer drinking. As an athlete in training, I had never much wanted to. I was paranoid for days after tasting a glass of wine on New Year's Eve that my coach would find out and bench me. Even more, I was seriously worried that one of the girls I was firmly confident I would never screw might get pregnant.

I did own a condom, however. A pharmacist gave it to me when I worked as a clerk at Walgreen's the summer after my sophomore year. He gave it to me because he thought I didn't know what one was and might find it useful. Neither of which was true. I had no need for a rubber, but I certainly knew what one was. I just didn't know they had names.

A customer came into the drugstore my first day on the job and said to me rather quietly, "I'd like a box of Trojans, please."

"Yes, sir," I said. I began to fumble through drawers trying to avoid appearing bewildered. The only Trojans I knew anything about played football for Southern Cal. When I finally determined that I wouldn't be lucky enough to discover them accidentally, I called across the store to my boss,

"Mr. Pierce, this gentleman wants a box of Trojans."

I did my job well. "If ever you can't find something, ask," Mr. Pierce had instructed earlier when I reported for work. "Never keep the customer waiting."

"I'll take care of this, son," Mr. Pierce said after hurrying to my side. "You go straighten shelves." He had already detected that I hated to straighten shelves. "I'm sorry about the boy," Mr. Pierce said to the customer. "It's his first day on the job. How many would you like, sir?"

"Three dozen will do," the customer said.

My adult experience has been that three dozen will do for about a year.

"Come here, son," Mr. Pierce called to me after the customer left. When I got behind the counter, he opened the drawer in which condoms were kept and pointed at the neatly stacked boxes. "Learn the names of these," he ordered. "If a customer wants any of these, just sell it to him without conversation." Mr. Pierce fixed me with a penetrating stare. Then his face softened into a smile and he said, "Do you know what these are for?"

"Uh, no sir," I lied. I did know, but I figured it was better to feign ignorance than be forced to find the delicate words to prove I knew if he challenged me.

Mr. Pierce chuckled and shook his head at me. "Well, soon you will," he said. He started to turn away, made one of those half motions to leave. Then he stopped and slowly pulled the drawer with the condoms open again. He picked up one of the small boxes of Trojans, took one of the foil-wrapped rubbers from it and slipped the rest of the box into his front pocket. "Here, take this," he said. "And when you find out what it's for, you'll know you got something from old Nick Pierce besides a job."

And he was right, of course. From old Nick Pierce I got in trouble when my mother found the Trojan in my wallet, where I kept it in case I needed it quickly, which, of course, I never did.

I still had that Trojan my senior year in high school, having retrieved it from the trash can after my mother threw it away in disgust with the aquatic admonition, "People without life jackets seldom venture into deep water." But I was little comforted by my possession. For one thing, it was old. How long did such items remain potent (anti-potent?)? But more important, what if the girl whom I surely would not screw wanted to twice? I would be lost because I lacked the courage actually to purchase another in a drugstore. And I was naively unaware that they were available in exotic varieties in most gas stations between Chicago and Florida.

So I was relieved, if disappointed, when none of my new friends suggested going to Florida to give ourselves a tan for Easter.

Some of my friends, however, did suggest that we make a trip to New Orleans over Easter break. Actually, it was originally my idea, but I only suggested it confident that everyone would rather go to Florida. "I lived in New Orleans all my life," I pointed out. "I can show y'all the city. We can get together with some of my old friends and play some basketball. Man, I'd love to take you guys down Bourbon Street."

"New Orleans, huh?" Wayne Franklin said, wiping at a beard he didn't have. Wayne was headed for Princeton the next year. He was the guy in our class who always wore a buttoned-down, oxford-cloth shirt. He was considered the most sophisticated of my new friends. I wonder why he later joined the Marines.

"Yeah," I said, surprised but pleased to have my suggestion considered seriously.

"New Orleans is a pretty cool town," offered Bubba Pals, who has since become a psychologist and calls himself Dr. Thomas Pals.

"New Orleans," Wayne repeated. "You know, that's not a half-bad idea, Janus. I mean, most people go to Florida. But *anybody* can go to Florida. But now New Orleans, that's something not just anybody can do."

"Is there any place we could get a tan?" Bubba Pals asked.

"Sure, at Pontchartrain Beach. And I could also show you guys the Battle of New Orleans battleground. And Jackson Square, St. Louis Cathedral, the Cabildo. We could eat hot doughnuts at Morning Call and walk around the French Quarter."

"I'm interested in Bourbon Street," Wayne said.

"Bourbon Street is part of the Quarter," I replied.

"Did you ever go down Bourbon Street when you lived there?" Wayne inquired.

"Of course," I said quickly, half-truthfully. "I went down Bourbon Street all the time. The drinking age limit in Louisiana is eighteen."

"So?" Wayne said.

"So a mature-looking guy can get served at sixteen or seventeen, maybe even fifteen," I responded.

"Really?" Bubba Pals asked.

"Sure. Look, New Orleans is a real open town. It's a seaport, the second largest in the country as a matter of fact. To New York. The place is crawling with sailors. All the bar owners serve the sailors, and they don't bug them about I.D.'s. Lots of them are only seventeen. Folks in New Orleans figure that if a guy is old enough to serve his country, he's old enough to get a drink."

I had made all of this up. I thought it had the ring of truth, but Wayne was not convinced. "Did you ever do any drinking then? You never drink now."

"Yeah, I used to tip a few. A couple of times. You know, in the summer after baseball was over. Once, a friend and I took some dates down Bourbon

Street. We caught a couple of shows, then went to a place called Pat O'Brien's and had a drink they call a hurricane. We didn't have any trouble getting served." Why was I doing this?

"What's a hurricane like?" Bubba asked.

Fortunately, I had a vague idea. "I don't know what kind of booze is in it. I didn't ask or anything. It's a big pink drink that comes in a special glass. Pat O'Brien hurricanes are renowned in New Orleans. People often keep the glasses for souvenirs."

"What did you drink at the other place?" Wayne asked.

"What other place?" I said.

"You said you went to some shows or something."

"Oh. Martinis," I said, hoping that no one would ask me what went into a martini. "On the rocks."

"I stick to beer," Bubba announced.

"The shows you went to," Wayne continued his interrogation, "these were strip shows?"

"Yeah," I said. "I only went in that one time. Pat O'Brien's isn't a strip club. I forget the names of the places we went in."

"You took girls to a strip joint?" Bubba said, agape.

"Sure. New Orleans girls are like that. They don't care."

"Man," Bubba said. "I gotta go now. I want you to introduce me to some New Orleans women."

And so we all agreed to ask our parents if we could go to New Orleans over Easter vacation. I was worried that such an agreement might result in belying my boasts, but basically I remained confident that my parents would not let me go. They had never let me go anywhere before. And if all else failed, I could always come down with a case of diarrhea.

On the other hand, I thought that perhaps I could actually handle the trip, should my parents decide to let me go. I *had* been down Bourbon Street before, even if I hadn't really been inside a strip joint or tasted any more alcohol than was contained in that one glass of wine on New Year's Eve.

I had been down Bourbon Street many times. It was a must trip every time my parents had out-of-town guests. They all would sit around drinking coffee and visiting until ten o'clock or so. Then the husband guest would begin to hint around that he'd like to see why New Orleans was known as Sin City. So was there anything really wrong with a drive down Bourbon Street? He'd heard so much about it. My father would eye my mother and say that it really wasn't all that exciting, just your usual collage of honky-tonks: crowded, loud and dirty. And then the wife guest would ask it if was true that they really let those women dance "buck nekkid" like that. And my mother would nod and say that she couldn't imagine why in the world anyone would want to see a sad old herd of sea cows shake their flabby behinds anyway. And then my father would remark that Bourbon Street was what New Orleanians mistook for culture, and everyone would laugh.

Then someone would call to the kids in the other room, and we would all pile into our Dodge station wagon, the kids in the back, peering out over the tailgate. When we got into the stop-and-go traffic on Bourbon Street and could hear the barkers' songs, the wife guest would say how disgraceful it was and that at *least* the kids should be told not to look. And one of the kids would ask why that lady didn't have any clothes on. The adults would shake their heads and someone would wonder just what the world was coming to.

And a good time was had by all.

I think my parents greatly enjoyed these trips down Bourbon Street. I think it helped reinforce their conviction about themselves—that they weren't prudish like the other members of the Baptist college faculty and their wives.

And I suspect that they enjoyed the sexual stimulation. There weren't any pornographic magazines on the racks of the local drugstore in those days, no *Penthouse* or *Hustler* or *Club* with their pictures of lovely girls whose faces you never notice because they're sitting around naked with their legs spread. There was only *Playboy* in those days, and it was considered so risque that it was either wrapped in cellophane to prohibit casual voyeurism or sold over-the-counter only. And this despite the fact that in those days *Playboy* was reluctant to photograph nipples, much less pubic hair and the freshly barbered specifics of the female genitalia.

So unlike myself in these more liberated times, my father couldn't stop off to tease his imagination whenever he went to the Drug King. Drug Kings didn't exist. And drugstores had soda fountains instead of pornographic magazines.

To prod their imagination, my parents had to drive down Bourbon Street with out-of-town guests. They still couldn't see nipples or pubic hair, of course, since the dancers were required to wear pasties and keep themselves neatly trimmed to the edges of their ample G-strings. But what they *could* see was a rawer kind of sex than was available anywhere else. They seemed to enjoy it. And I hope that afterwards they went home and read one another salient portions of the Frank Yerby novels they owned.

Anyway, with my growing confidence that I could handle the situation, I asked my parents if I could go to New Orleans over Easter break. A part of me still hoped that they would say no, but I argued strongly for their permission. I would have to work during the coming summer, I reminded them. And after that there was college. It might be a long time before I would get to go home again.

My father sucked his pipe and made no response. Perhaps it was either now or never, I pointed out. To which my father said, "All right, son. I think your mother and I can trust you to be responsible and have a good time with your friends. I think we can count on you not to disappoint us. Your mother and I have always regarded you as a mature young man."

"Oh, New Orleans," my mother said. "I get homesick just listening to you talk about it." She put her arm around my shoulder and said to my father, "Remember those days when we would go crabbing on Pontchartrain before dawn?" My father and I both nodded, and my mother gave my shoulder a squeeze. "I'm jealous already that you're getting to go. You can show the other boys all the sights. The battleground in Chalmette, Jackson Square, St. Louis Cathedral, the French Market, the Audubon Park aquarium."

And so it was set, and when I didn't get diarrhea, I was forced to go to New Orleans. Bubba Pals, Wayne Franklin and I crowded into Bubba's parents' car and drove around the clock to my native city, where we crowded into a motel room with only two beds. We flipped for the beds. I won the floor.

We spent the next morning baking ourselves at Pontchartrain Beach. We challenged one another to start a conversation with any girl that came near us, but not even Wayne had the courage. Finally a red and yellow beach ball rolled near our towels. It was soon followed by two blond girls who had been batting it around. We flirted with them and learned that they were from Iowa and were in town with their parents. Even though they weren't Southern girls, I had my trusty Trojan ready. But nothing happened. At noon they left. By five o'clock we were sunburned and bored. Bubba and I decided to call some of my friends and arrange a basketball game. But Wayne said, "Screw basketball, man. We can play basketball in Chicago." And he was right, of course; we could have played basketball in Chicago. But it turned out that we couldn't play in New Orleans. B.F. Johnson, his parents said, was away at military school. And Carter Percy's mother informed me that Carter and several others had gone to Fort Lauderdale for their Easter break.

So we returned to the motel, showered and dressed. After supper we headed down Bourbon Street. We went into the first bar we came across offering striptease entertainment, a place called The Treasure Chest. Some old fish nets, a rusty anchor and a decidedly putrid odor, ineffectively masked with the smell of disinfectant, provided the atmosphere. A blinking neon sign outside, alternately lighting the words GIRLS GIRLS GIRLS, provided the incentive. The Treasure Chest was a small rectangular room with but one row of tables against the wall across from the bar. Behind and above the bartender's walk was the stripper's stage, a bare, dirty piece of reinforced plywood. No show was in progress when we entered.

We beat back the shroud of cigarette smoke and situated ourselves at a table across from the center of the stage. A waitress materialized out of the gloom. "What can I bring you boys?" she asked. I looked sidelong at Bubba and Wayne.

"What are you having, Rich?" Bubba asked.

"I'll have a martini," I said to the waitress. "On the rocks."

"The same for me," Wayne said.

"Me too," Bubba said, preferring a beer.

The first "girl" on the stage was a plump, homely woman introduced by the bartender-announcer as Cindy. She looked at least forty. Her belly was swollen and loose below her navel. A jagged appendectomy scar ran up out of her G-string toward her hip bone.

Cindy's face was blank as she came on stage. It had never been a pretty face, though perhaps it was once not unattractive. But now it was lined and empty, beyond sad, devoid of expression. Her sunken eyes looked through the two men and three horny boys in the room, not to places or even times far away, but to nothing.

Cindy appeared on stage in what in other settings would be called a bra and panties. Music we could barely hear began to play on a phonograph, and Cindy proceeded to engage in what might be termed skipping. It certainly wasn't dancing. Slowly, from one end of the plywood to the other, she skipped and occasionally shook her shoulders so that her large, drooping breasts swung from side to side. After a while she reached behind herself and, without a change of her blank expression, unhooked the bra, shrugged it into her hand and twirled it around on her index finger. Covering her nipples were silver, sequined pasties.

"This is really livin', guys," Wayne said, drumming his fingers on the damp table top.

"Sure is," Bubba Pals said.

"No kidding," I agreed and forced a grin.

But, of course, this was not really living. Neither for Cindy nor her audience. She was not the erotic sensation we had come down Bourbon Street to find. And in the end, we paid her little mind. We paid her little mind because in the middle of her act, the waitress showed up with our drinks and billed us $2.75 per martini. On the rocks. This was before Mr. Nixon introduced stagflation, remember—a time when a good summer job for a high school student was likely to earn him only $1.75 for an hour of labor. And no sooner had we paid for our martinis than were we obliged to begin drinking them. It was an awful experience. Martinis, I discovered, tasted worse than bad medicine, worse than the paregoric my mother forced me to swallow when I had a stomachache, a remedy which inevitably caused me to throw up.

Far too long we sat in The Treasure Chest, unable to escape, chained by martinis we hated but were determined to finish. We sat, wishing to imbibe by osmosis, taking our drinks only in tiny sips, nursing our olives to counteract the alcohol. Wayne bought a pack of Newport cigarettes, and we all sucked at the menthol to kill the taste of the gin. Through Cindy and Cathy and Cleopatra we sat, much to the annoyance of our waitress who kept checking our glasses, astounded to find out how slowly we could drink. When Cindy returned with her bra back on, we forced down the last of our drinks and left. GIRLS GIRLS GIRLS, it seems, was a euphemism for girl, girl, girl.

Back out on Bourbon Street, we walked for a while. Wayne continued to puff on Newports. I stopped at a storefront concession and bought a pack of Lifesavers. We watched two young black boys tap-dance on the sidewalk outside a Dixieland jazz club. When the song ended, the smaller of the two boys walked among the tourists with a straw boater soliciting money. Bubba gave him a quarter. We walked the length of Bourbon Street and then back again to Canal. Wayne said it was time we had ourselves another drink. Bubba and I looked at one another.

"I kinda got a headache," Bubba said.

"Yeah, and I'm sorta tired," I added. "Maybe we ought to call it a night."

Wayne acted amazed. "What a couple of pussies I end up with," he said. "Here we are in New Orleans, and you guys want to call it a night after one fucking drink." But despite his protesting, he fell in step with us as we began to move in the direction of the motel.

"It won't hurt us to get a little sleep," I argued.

"All that sun really wiped me out," Bubba said.

"Grandmothers," Wayne chided. "You guys are a couple of grandmothers. I get out of crummy Chicago only to spend my vacation in New Orleans with *grandmothers*. Why don't you two guys have silver-blue hair like the other members of your age group?" Neither Bubba nor I responded. We were in league against him, but I think both of us felt that his charge against us was essentially fair.

"At least we could get a six-pack," Wayne urged after a few more steps. "Or would you guys prefer I make you hot toddies."

"I *could* drink a beer or two," Bubba admitted. He looked at me to see if he had violated our unspoken pact.

"Fine with me," I said.

Our agreeing to get the beer seemed to brighten Wayne's mood. I doubted that he was thoroughly miffed about cutting short our first experience on Bourbon Street. It hadn't been much fun. Despite his ridiculing, he had made no genuinely concerted effort to prolong our stay. I suspected he only *thought* that we should have been more adventuresome and was satisfied to shrug the burden of our early retirement onto other shoulders.

Unfortunately, Wayne's lighter mood was not to last. To busy ourselves while we drank, we began a poker game. We played only penny ante, but Wayne's wild and aggressive betting soon put him in a hole. When Bubba took a large pot in a crazy game rife with wild cards called baseball, Wayne couldn't bear it anymore. He smashed his hand down on the bed we had been using as a card table, sending coins jingling to the floor. Bubba and I started to laugh, but a look in Wayne's desperate eyes made us stop. "Fuck you guys!" he screamed.

"Fuck you guys," he repeated more quietly, walking to the closet where he took out his sports jacket. Putting it on, shaking his head at us, he said, "I can't believe you guys. We're in New Orleans, and all you guys want to do is sip piss water and play piss poker. I'm going back to Bourbon Street." Wayne smoothed his hair in the mirror by the door and left. When he had gone, Bubba and I looked at each other and broke into laughter that I think we both realized had a tinny, nervous edge.

Later, in the dark, waiting for sleep, Bubba and I talked. He told me that Wayne was jealous of me, that he had counted on being the basketball star his senior year, but that my arrival had rendered him just another player. I protested, argued how good Wayne was, how important he had been to the team. "But *you* were the star," Bubba pointed out, "not Wayne. *You* were the leading scorer. *You* made All-Conference. *You* got what Wayne wanted. And then you turned around and became his friend, too. That was maybe the worst part. It squeezed him out of his right to resent you."

"I never knew," I said.

"No," Bubba responded. "I didn't think you did."

The next morning I led the way to Morning Call, a café in the French Quarter whose tiny menu offered only milk, café au lait and hot, rectangular, French pastries which were eaten sprinkled with powdered sugar. The menu designated these last items "beignets," but New Orleanians called them simply "doughnuts." With our elbows resting in the sticky-grit, sugar residue which coated the marble counter top, we stared at ourselves in the bright mirrors tinged with naked light bulbs. It was as if we were actors making up for a performance.

We sipped our strong, sweet coffee as Wayne bragged expansively, but gently, about his adventures of the night before. He had found a place, he told us, far more exciting than The Treasure Chest, and had conversed with a friendly waitress named Terry who sometimes doubled as a stripper. She had sat occasionally at Wayne's table and smoked a cigarette. She liked college boys, she told him, was working, in fact, to save up enough money so that she could go to college herself. She'd like to major in art, she thought. She spent lots of her days in Jackson Square, sketching. She hadn't tried to sell anything yet, but she might soon, and she would really like to show Wayne some of her work. Wayne thought she was about twenty, not much older. He had told her that he was a sophomore at Princeton. Later in the evening, as she sat with him and watched one of the strippers work, she asked if he would like to see her dance. He said yes, of course, and she kissed him on the side of his nose. Then she brought him a Tom Collins and refused to let him pay for it. He really hadn't known what to do after that. He really liked her and was convinced she was genuine, not just some hooker with an especially subtle approach. Still, he had the distinct feeling that he could sleep with her if he played his cards just right.

"What *I* want to know," Bubba said when Wayne had finished his tale and was trying to brush the flecks of powdered sugar off his blue, buttoned-down shirt, "is, does she have any friends?" I laughed out loud, and first Bubba, then Wayne, joined in.

"I did tell her about you guys," Wayne said. "I told her that we were buddies from high school and that both of you went to school in the Midwest. She said she'd like to meet you, and I promised we would stop in tonight."

"At least you could have gotten us into Harvard," I said.

"I think I'd prefer pre-med at Oxford myself," Bubba said, affecting a British accent.

"I'm sorry about the geographical restrictions," Wayne said. "Within the Midwest, however, you're free to attend any school you choose. You could go to Chicago or Michigan or Northwestern."

"How about Lancaster College," Bubba said, looking at me but holding a straight face.

"Isn't that a girls' school?" Wayne said. Both of them laughed.

"I think I'll tell her I go to Amherst," I said. "Do you think she'll be impressed?"

"Amherst is in Massachusetts, asshole," Wayne said.

"Ah, but I'll just explain to her that to a snotty Princeton man, anything which isn't Ivy League is only Midwest."

"How about we can the academic small talk and discuss the important issue before us," Bubba interjected. "The who, what, where, when and how big the bra size of these slightly soiled Southern women Wayne is going to lead us to tonight."

"Did I say Terry was going to fix you two juveniles up?" Wayne asked.

"Didn't you?" I asked.

"I was sure he said that," Bubba said to me.

"At least tell us it's possible," I urged.

"Anything's possible," Wayne shrugged. "Even finding women for you two."

"Then we're all set," Bubba said. "Is it nearly night yet?"

Wayne looked at his watch. "It's nearly eleven," he said. We stood, brushed powder from our trousers and began to make our way among the cluttered tables of the café into the pungent air of a New Orleans spring day. As we walked along Decatur Street back toward Jackson Square, Wayne threw his arms around our shoulders and informed us with the air of a benevolent older brother that we were getting drunk on Tom Collinses that night and that the first round was on him.

In a state of relaxed anticipation, we spent the day as tourists, visited the Cabildo and the Cathedral and walked on the edges of a guided tour around the Square. So much of the history of New Orleans is contained in the old buildings which stand there in the Quarter's core. I recall being fascinated at all I learned that day. I recall wishing once or twice that I had a pad on which to take notes. But I don't *remember* any of it. What I *remember* was the tingling in my loins over what lay in store that night: a night of real drinking, a night of carousing with wicked women, whom, I was confident, we would not find waiting for us.

After sandwiches for supper, showers and donning shirts with ties, Wayne took us to a bar called The Dairy. When we entered the large room, Wayne stopped us near the door, waiting for his eyes to adjust from the red and gray-blue light of the street to the interior dimness. He was looking for Terry. When he failed to spot her after a few moments, he motioned us to follow him, remarking that he'd just take the same seat he'd had last night. A trim young woman greeted us at the tiny round table we took on a raised tier against the far wall from the stage. Like the other waitresses moving about the room, she wore a milkmaid costume. Her short blond hair was mostly concealed under a soft cloth cap shaped like a pie crust turned upside down.

"We'd really like to sit in Terry's station," Wayne said to her.

"What?" she said. "Who?"

"Terry," Wayne said. "Where is Terry working tonight?" He was very patient.

The waitress looked at us without speaking. Finally, she seemed to remember something and moved away without answering Wayne's query. In a moment she returned. "Terry isn't working tonight," she said. "This is her night off. Sorry. Would you like to order something from me? My name is Sharon."

Both Bubba and I looked quickly at Wayne to see what he wanted to do, but his face was as rigid as a mask. "I think we'd like three Tom Collinses,"

Bubba said, and when the waitress brought the drinks, he paid for them.

Wayne finished two cigarettes from his pack and went to a machine near the door to get more. When he sat back down, he drained his drink and summoned the waitress and ordered another round for which he paid. We didn't mention the disappointment he obviously felt. I bought a third round, and gradually we began to exchange crude remarks about the strippers who were plying their trade across from us. They were fairly young and fairly attractive. Unlike the women at The Treasure Chest, they actually did dance. They came out fully dressed and, between shimmies and struts, slowly disrobed. A post ran from floor to ceiling at center stage, and at the climax of each girl's number, when she was down to a G-string and pasties, when all the prancing and tit swinging and ass swishing was done, she squatted with the pole between her legs and humped it to a simulated orgasm. Measured against what one can see today in porno houses, the act was relatively tame. But for three boys unused to the alcohol coursing through their veins, it was very erotic stuff. We hooted and leered, smirked and lusted. And forever we ordered new rounds. Round after round of Tom Collinses were purchased and consumed, and stripper after stripper was ogled until we had seen all the girls at least twice and pole and thigh had begun to blur into one and we had gotten too drunk to care any longer. We began to talk among ourselves and reminisce like long-lost friends about events which were barely months old.

Finally, we tried to stumble our way back to the motel. Bubba didn't make it three blocks before he threw up. The sound of his retching made me gag, and in trying to outrun it, I managed to separate myself from my companions. Alone in the motel, I undressed, careening from wall to closet to bed to my pallet. There in my sleeping bag, I discovered the terror of closing one's eyes. The room began to turn when I lay down. With my eyes closed, it raced out of control. Somewhere, growing up in a teetotaling household I can't imagine where, I remembered that it was supposed to help if you could get one foot planted securely flat on the floor. I swung my leg and learned immediately how impossible that advice is to follow when you're *sleeping* on the floor. For the first time in my life, I got sick from too much booze. Unfortunately, it would not be the last.

Before stirring from my sleeping bag the next morning, I resolved never again to go down Bourbon Street. I further resolved never again to touch a drop of alcohol. It took me only hours to break both resolutions.

When the three of us were up and vaguely certain that we were still alive, we discovered that the previous night's debauch had so severely drained our meager funds that we could afford only more night in New Orleans. A debate ensued about how to spend our last day. Bubba and Wayne opted for a jaunt to the Mississippi Gulf Coast, a drive of some seventy-five miles. I decided to try to visit with Janice Martin.

Janice Martin, you all may remember, was the object of my earliest sexual fantasies, the large-breasted sixth grader whom B.F. Johnson suspected of bra padding. What you could not know was that Janice Martin later became my steady high-school girlfriend, the wearer of my letter sweater and ring. During the summer after my departure from New Orleans to Chicago, we wrote each other daily pledges of our undying love. But after school began in the fall, we mutually agreed that it would be a shame to waste our senior years pining for each other from a distance of a thousand miles. We were, after all, mature kids. For a time, our flagging correspondence continued to proclaim the durability of our love in the face of our active but separate social lives. Without renouncing our fundamental "spiritual" fidelity, we even confessed to one another late in the first term that we each were now dating only one person. But sometime after Christmas, the correspondence stopped.

I do not want to give the impression that I surrendered to the erosive power of time and space. My maturity forced me to allow Janice Martin the right to a new steady boyfriend, just as it granted me a similar privilege. But I refused to stop loving her or believing that she would always love me. The fact that she had not acknowledged my letter announcing my visit in no way rocked my conviction of my primacy in her life. It merely underscored the problem my brief presence in New Orleans would pose for her new relationship. As I dialed her number from the motel room that April day of my first hangover, I ached with love for her just as I had when we first kissed and then squeezed each other fiercely as if we could squeeze time to a standstill and make that moment last forever. It was an ache of love that I can still conjure up for Janice Martin as I sit writing this now, wherever, whoever she may be.

"Hi," I said when Janice came to the phone, "This is Rich."

"Richie," she exclaimed, "where are you?"

"In town," I said. "It's my Easter break." I wanted to ask if she hadn't gotten my letter but sensed the awkward turn that could force on the conversation.

"How long are you going to be here?" she asked.

"Only till tomorrow," I said. "I'd like to see you."

"Gosh, Richie, I've got a date tonight. I told you about Joe."

"I was thinking about this afternoon," I said.

"My parents aren't home," Janice pointed out, referring to a policy that she wasn't able to have male guests in her house without supervision.

"Excellent," I said.

She laughed. "Come on over, Rich. But you have to promise to leave so that I can get ready to go out."

I made tentative plans with Bubba and Wayne to meet them after their return from the beach. "But don't count on me," I warned them, "because I just may wangle much better company for the evening than the two of you could ever provide."

I caught the Elysian Fields bus and rode out toward Gentilly. Near the lakefront, at Robert E. Lee, I disembarked and walked the remaining blocks to Janice's house. I felt a surge of contradictory emotion: that I was about to claim something I deserved and that I was about to taste something forbidden.

When Janice opened her front door in a spaghetti strap sun dress that revealed the cleavage between her breasts, when she shook her long dark brown hair off her face and smiled to show her two front teeth, which overlapped ever so slightly, it was as if I had never gone away.

The afternoon passed in a light-speed exchange of anecdotes and reminiscences and future hopes, punctuated with fleeting, familiar touches: her hand, while she giggled, on my arm, my hand, remembering, on her knee. I kept expecting that she'd volunteer to break her date. My conviction of her right to protect the life she had forged without me kept me from asking her to. Finally, she looked at a clock on her living room mantel and informed me gently that it was getting late.

I embraced and kissed her, first tenderly, then with unfeigned passion. Two years before we had sexually initiated one another with a silly game called baseball. A kiss was first base, a French kiss second, I stole third now when Janice let me slip my hand down the top of her dress and grope at each large breast. She allowed herself to be laid back on her living room couch, and she only gasped when I brought my hand up under her dress to the moist vertex between her thighs. She did not resist even when I cupped in my hand the entire dampening, silky crotch of her panties. But when I tried to slip my fingers underneath the elastic, Janice firmly pushed my hand away, sat up, and with a dismissing kiss on the forehead said, "I'm sorry, Richie, but you can't go home anymore."

Janice Martin kept her date that night. And I once more went down Bourbon Street. I met Bubba and Wayne at Pat O' Brien's. We started with gin and tonics and tried mint juleps. We laughed and told each other lies and became good friends. Wayne now claimed to have slept with Terry two nights before. He described his conquest in detail, and Bubba and I pretended to believe him. In the pink-misted blear of hurricanes, I forgot about Janice Martin and her rejection of me.

Wayne said to me, "And what about you, Richie, studboy? Give with today, how about it? Get any of that little Southern belle stuff on you?"

I replied, holding my hand over the center of the table, "Just sniff on that a while, baby." And we all slapped our index fingers against our thumbs and threw back our heads and howled.

We walked back to the motel with our arms around one another singing, "When the Saints Go Marching In." It was years before I knew the term, but that night we had the El Cholo Feeling.

Our camaraderie did not last. I wrecked Bubba's car driving home the following night, and even though it wasn't my fault, his parents were so angry with him that he could barely forgive me. Wayne asked out my Chicago girlfriend, claiming he thought that I was in love with Janice Martin, which was true but no excuse. And Wayne, of course, later joined the Marines.

The El Cholo Feeling passes.

4

1969

Though spring had arrived in Lancaster, it was that hesitant, insecure, Midwestern spring—sunny afternoons when for several hours you can be comfortable outside in your shirt sleeves, brisk damp nights when you have to put your gloves back on.

Faith Cleaver came into the lounge of her sorority house, where Richard Janus sat reading *Newsweek*, waiting for her. Her unwashed, dark red hair was tied back in a blue bandana. She had on jeans and a sorority sweatshirt turned inside out. On her feet were fuzzy athletic socks and a pair of black, low-cut tennis shoes. On her face were rectangular-shaped, tortoise-shell glasses.

Janus glanced up casually when he sensed Faith coming toward him. Briefly recognizing that she had finally come down, he looked back to his magazine to finish the article he had been reading. Faith stood in front of him for a long moment before finally saying, "Yeah, so what do you want?"

Still he did not look up but glanced at his watch and after studying it said, "You're prompt, but at least you're pleasant to boot." He returned his eyes to the magazine.

Faith sat down on the deep, square love seat beside him with her back against the arm. She drew her knees up against her chest and laid her head back against the cushion. "Shall we fight in here or try to get outside first?" she sighed, staring at the ceiling.

Janus laid the magazine down on the clear plastic coffee table and said, "What the hell, it's a nice day. Why don't we just skip the fight altogether." Her head was still back and her eyes were closed. "Hey," Janus exclaimed, "you're wearing glasses."

Faith sat up quickly and snatched the glasses off her nose, folded them up and covered them with her hands. Janus laughed out loud. Staring hard at him, Faith deliberately unfolded the glasses and stabbed them back on her face. Janus laughed still harder.

"It's *not* funny," she said.

"I agree," Janus answered, struggling to control himself.

"Then stop laughing at me."

"Okay," he snickered. "Tell me, Faith, why are you wearing glasses?"

"Because I'm practically blind without them." She took the glasses off and screwed her face into an exaggerated squint.

Perhaps she expected her response to spark a renewed outburst from Janus, but it didn't. Instead, he said seriously, "But I've never seen you with them before."

"I usually wear my contacts. I bet you even thought my eyes were green."

"Aren't they?" Janus said, astonished. He reached and pulled her face near his, but she squeezed her eyes tightly shut. "Open up," he commanded.

"No."

"Come on, open up," he cajoled.

"No!"

Janus reached down and began fiddling with the laces on Faith's sneakers. "You better open up," he advised, "or I'm going to tie your shoe strings together."

"Ha," Faith said. "You think I can't hop to wherever I need to go?"

"Okay." He began to inch her sweatshirt up. "If you don't open your eyes, I'm going to tickle you until you wet your pants."

"And what makes you think I can't go places in wet pants?" she said. But she opened her eyes wide and drew her chin back to make a vulture-like peer. Without the tinted contacts, Faith's eyes were hazel and flecked with spots of steel gray. "I'll bet you even thought I was a natural redhead," she said in a voice made low and gravelly by the contorted position of her head and neck.

"What evidence I've seen," Janus replied with a leer, "would indicate that to be the case."

With an absolutely expressionless face, like a chalkboard which has not only been erased but also washed clean, Faith responded, "You have a filthy, disgusting mind. How dare you come here, to my home, and humiliate me with such vulgar, suggestive talk in front of my sorority sisters, the only people in the whole world who truly love me."

Janus looked around the lounge. Not another soul was in the room. Shaking his head with a breathy, laughlike sound, he asked, "How long have you been wearing glasses, anyway?"

"Since third grade."

"Were they those weird light blue things shaped like cats' eyes with rhinestones on the corners?"

"They did not have rhinestones on the corners." Faith still maintained her automatonic face. Only when she occasionally blinked did any part of her face move.

"But they were light blue and funny-looking?"

"Yes."

Janus attempted to ape Faith's blank expression but succeeded only in parodying it. He shook his head slightly side-to-side instead of keeping it perfectly still, and rather than keeping his jaw firm, he let it go a little slack, causing his mouth to hang partially open. "God, I bet you were ugly," he said.

"I was not," Faith said. "I was cute." She struck him hard on the shoulder for emphasis. One, two, three, four times. "Cute as a button. All the boys liked me."

Janus rubbed his arm. "I'm sure you were cute. If I'd been in your class I'd have surely liked you."

"I was not cute," Faith said with a protruding lower lip. "I was an ugly mudpie. I had to wear weird blue glasses with rhinestones on the corners." Janus laughed. "And none of the boys liked me because I could throw a curve ball and none of them could."

"You could throw a curve ball in the third grade?"

"Yes...or the sixth grade anyway. My dad taught me. I'm a good athlete. I really am." It seemed important to Faith that Janus take her last assertion seriously.

"I believe you are," Janus assured her. "I watched you play basketball for the sorority in intramurals last week. You didn't see me, but I saw you in your little blue uniform and black Keds. You were terrific. Darting in and out, stealing the ball, shouting, 'Hey! Hey!' all the time. I wish my defense were as effective as yours. You *should* learn to pass off a little more. But I love that little one-handed push shot you launch from your stomach."

"Don't make fun of me," Faith said quietly.

"I'm not. I thought you were clearly the best...."

"You *are* too. I *am* a good athlete. Not as good as you maybe, but I might have been if I hadn't been a girl. Nobody ever coached me, but when I was twelve, I was the best athlete in my neighborhood, boy or girl." She turned away from him.

"I'm sure you were, Faith," Janus said. He tugged at the cuff of her jeans and patted at her firm calf. She was looking out the large picture window at three of her sorority sisters talking on the front lawn, trying unsuccessfully to keep their dresses down in the gusty spring wind. "Look at me. I'm sure you were. And I was serious about watching you play the other day." He tugged again on her jeans to get her to turn back to him, as if her head were connected to a string which ran down her pants. "I watched the whole game. And I enjoyed it. You were a regular blue darter."

Faith turned back to him, listlessly, as if she had not been listening to him. "Richie," she said, "when we're married, will you protect me?"

Janus had learned that Faith had a way occasionally of steering conversations in abruptly different directions, but he was still somewhat dumbfounded when she did it. "I don't know exactly how to answer that," he said. "I've always thought of marriage as a partnership. You know, you support and protect, I guess, one another. Is that what you had in mind?"

"No."

"Well, what then?" Janus shifted himself around and put his legs, splayed wide, up on the coffee table.

"I don't know," Faith said. "I want to be sure I'll be safe. Don't you understand?"

"Sure," Janus said, "I think so." He looked at her intently.

"No, you don't." She smacked the sofa with a flat hand, raising a tiny cloud of dust. Janus watched the motes swirl in a shaft of sunlight which sliced through the picture window like a laser and landed between his legs on the coffee table.

"Okay, I don't," Janus admitted. "But I'm sure I can. Explain it to me."

With her lower jaw thrust out, Faith stared at him rather than replying. Finally, she said, "I can't. Don't you see? You ought to just understand." She looked away from him then back outside. "I *can't* explain it. What did you come over here for, anyway?"

Janus considered trying to pursue Faith's feelings about marriage further but decided that there was an abraded quality to her today that was perhaps best left alone. He consciously brightened his tone and said, as if he'd just arrived, "There's going to be a co-ed softball game this afternoon. I came to get you to play."

"I can't," Faith said.

"Why not?" Janus implored, not really believing that she couldn't or even that she didn't want to. "We'd let you throw your curve ball." He meant this as a fond and gentle encouragement. He never suspected that she would read it as a challenge. But her eyes turned to dry ice and the hard little muscle in her jaw twitched. "You don't think I *can* throw a curve ball, do you?" She spoke without moving her lips.

Janus hadn't thought about it at all, but now that he did, the fact of the matter was that he *didn't* think she could throw a curve ball. Forced to make a conscious judgment, he didn't even think she knew what a curve ball was. He believed without question that Faith's father at some point must have told her she could throw a curve ball, and so he was certain that Faith believed she possessed this skill, or at least had believed it until she misperceived Janus's remark as the bait to a trap. Most of all Janus didn't care. Sandy Koufax himself wouldn't have thrown curve balls at a Sunday afternoon softball game. And whether or not Faith understood the finer points of pitching mattered to him not in the slightest. All these thoughts passed through his mind in seconds, but he felt like a man caught in quicksand nonetheless.

He opted for strategic dishonesty. Arranging his face into an expression of earnestness, he said, nodding his head, "Sure I do. And sometime I want you to show me. I'll bring a couple of gloves over, and we'll play catch. You wouldn't really get the chance today, of course; we're just going to play slow pitch."

"I have my own glove," Faith said.

"Great. Run and get it, and let's go."

"Nah." She began to pick at pieces of lint on her jeans. "It's not very good. It's pretty old."

"Come on. It can't be that bad, or you wouldn't have brought it to school with you. Besides, we're always short of gloves, so anything is better than nothing." Faith got up slowly, without responding, and went to her room.

She returned with the glove on her left hand and sat down again next to Janus, her leg touching his. "This is it," she said. She pounded her fist into an ancient first-baseman's mitt. The leather was cracked on the outside; the meager cotton stuffing was beginning to fall out of the worn inside. A fraying gray shoestring had long since replaced the leather thong to hold the webbing in place. "My dad gave it to me when I was eight." She pounded the pocket of the glove again. It was a gesture very nearly like that of a thousand Little Leaguers on any summer morning, except that instead of driving her fist into the mitt straight on like a punch, she smacked it with the back of her closed hand. "He got one for my sister, too, only he forgot she was left-handed, so hers never worked very well."

Janus put his arm around her and squeezed her shoulder. "It's a nifty glove," he said.

"You think it's dumb," she said quietly.

"No, I had one a lot like it. My first glove. It didn't even have a strap to hold the fingers together. I took it to play catch with B.F. Johnson right after I got it. The first ball he threw went right between the fingers and hit me on my cheekbone. Gave me a world-record shiner and turned me into the school celebrity." A silent moment followed, a moment in which Janus assumed that his story had wedded their separate memories. Finally, he said with deliberate gentleness, removing his arm from around her and laying it on her knee, "We better get going. Otherwise we'll both have to play right field." He stood up and extended his hand to her to pull her up as well.

"I'm not going," she said, ignoring his hand.

"What?"

"You heard me. I'm not going. I told you that before. You never listen to me."

"Why did you go get your glove?"

"I'm not going to play softball, Janus, okay?" Faith said.

"Then why did you go get your glove?"

Faith cocked her jaw and wedged her tongue between her teeth, then said, "I went to get my glove to show it to you, but I am not going to play softball. Are we clear on that yet?"

"Let's see. You're not going to play softball. Is that it?"

Faith was not amused. "I don't have time to stand around in the wind and watch you swill beer all afternoon while all of your groupies tell you how wonderful you are."

Janus shook his head like a fighter trying to clear it following an unseen blow. "Huh?" he said and sat back down on the love seat. He brushed his fingers through his hair, which hadn't been cut since basketball season. "Christ, Faith. What's this all about?"

"Don't swear at me."

"Who's swearing?"

"You don't call saying *Christ* swearing?"

Janus raised his hands, chest high, palms up. "Okay, I'm sorry. I'll try to stop swearing around you."

"Why don't you stop it, period. It doesn't make you sound very intelligent, you know."

"I'll try to stop it, period," Janus promised.

"I hate it," Faith said.

Again Janus raised his hands. "I said I was sorry."

"Go on to your softball game."

"Look, Faith. I really am sorry I've made you mad. I don't quite know how I've done it, but I certainly didn't mean to. It's such a pretty day. I just wanted to spend it with you."

"I think you ought to see other girls, Rich."

"What?"

"You heard what I said. You always make me repeat when you don't like what you hear."

"Why should I see other girls?" Janus raked again at his hair with his finger tips.

"Because I'm not sure I'm right for you." Faith sat forward, bringing her face close to his. She was very intense. "You ought to date some other girls to make sure I'm the one you want."

"Don't I get a voice about which girl I want?"

"Maybe you don't know what girl you really want. Maybe you've got senioritis or...."

"How could I have senioritis? I'm only a junior. I was sure I had a year of eligibility left." Janus ventured a smile.

Faith sat back away from him. When she spoke again, she was looking at the ceiling. "Why do you always interrupt me? You know I didn't mean that literally." She didn't continue, but Janus thought that perhaps she was testing to see how long he could sit silent. He decided to wait her out. Finally, she lowered her gaze back to his and said, "What I'm trying to say is that there are girls on this campus who might be better suited for you than I am. Girls who are smarter than I am. And better looking. Girls whose wardrobes don't consist of Villager skirts and monogrammed sweaters."

"Like you're wearing right now," Janus said.

Faith looked at herself suddenly as if someone else had dressed her. "I never went around like this before I started going out with you," she said.

"See," Janus said. "Give me a chance and I can turn you into a slob." Faith didn't respond, and Janus reached over and cupped his hand behind her neck. "Faith, if I wanted to ask out other girls, I would. But obviously I don't want to." He pulled on her head, and she allowed herself to be rearranged with her head in his lap.

"What's this all about?" he asked.

Faith closed her eyes. "Nothing," she sighed.

Janus took her glasses off and placed them on her chest. He laid his open hand along her moist cheek. "Much ado about nothing," he said.

Faith opened her eyes wide and shook her head. She sat back up and put her glasses on as she did so. "Will you go to your softball game already?"

"You're sure you don't want to break down and come?"

"I've got to study," she said.

Janus looked a her suspiciously. "You got a test tomorrow?"

"No, I don't have a test tomorrow. Do *you* only study on the day before a test?"

"No, but you do," Janus pointed out.

"Not anymore, smart guy."

"Since when are you such a grind?"

"Since now."

"Is that what this whole song and dance has been about since I got here? You think you have to study this afternoon?"

"I *do* have to study this afternoon. There's no thinking about it."

Janus's look of devilment played across his face for an instant before he let it pass. He didn't know what was bothering Faith and had begun to believe he wasn't going to figure it out. Not today, anyway. He determined to forgo the wisecracks and excuse himself casually, as if things hadn't been tense at all, as if he had only stopped in for a brief and cheery hello. "Well," he said, standing up to leave, "if you're gonna be a bookworm...." He patted her knees and said, "If I don't see you before Friday, I'll be by at seven." When Faith didn't confirm their date, he added, "Okay?"

"I can't see you Friday, Rich," Faith said. "I have to study then, too."

A jumble of thoughts crowded into Janus's mind. Unable to sort them quickly enough to grasp for sure what Faith was telling him, he forced himself to say calmly, "Oh? All right. Do you mind if I study with you?"

She hesitated before answering long enough that he knew her answer would be negative. He prepared himself to hear her pronouncement that their relationship was at an end. It had been that kind of day. Nothing quite added up. That she had decided to break up with him seemed reasonably on the agenda. He felt himself steel to take the blow. Finally, she said, "I kind of promised I'd study with Cassie on Friday. I don't think three of us would work out. I think maybe you ought to make other plans."

Cassie Sears was Faith's striking blond roommate and sorority sister. She was a long-legged, California rich girl with frosty green eyes, a yellow Corvette and a wild reputation. At one time or another she had dated most of the men at Lancaster, including Richard Janus. He had taken her out in the fall of their freshman year but had not succeeded in sowing any of his wild oats by reaping any of hers. Driving home on their lone date, she had made a point of smoking a joint in front of him, an act still considered questionable and dangerous at that time in the Midwest. Janus felt certain she intended to shock him and determined not to give her the satisfaction, though in fact she succeeded, something Janus remembered now with a twinge of private embarrassment. She had offered Janus tokes, of course, but he had refused on the grounds that he was in training.

Still, he was generally lusty enough that he had gotten light-headed himself at the thought that she might be filling herself with an aromatic aphrodisiac. When the joint had been smoked and the roach deposited back into the Sucrets tin from which it had been taken, Janus pulled Cassie against him and kissed her. After only a moment, he knew something was wrong. She was opening her mouth with her lips rolled back so far that she gave him only her teeth to kiss. And though she moved herself about, panted and even moaned a little, it all seemed unnatural to Janus, altogether studied and passionless.

When he took her to the door of her dorm, he didn't kiss her goodnight. And he never asked her out again. He had seen her around campus often since then but had always found her cool. In the months since he had started going out with Faith, Cassie had not warmed to him at all. More than once the two women had shared a joint in their room before Faith went out and had come giggling down the stairs with their arms around one another. But Cassie would kiss Faith lightly on the cheek and send her into the lounge to meet Janus alone. Janus had never given a lot of thought to Cassie's standoffishness. He assumed that it derived from her lingering awkwardness over their long ago date.

"So what you mean," Janus said to Faith now, "is that Cassie would just as soon I wasn't included."

Faith shrugged.

Janus stared at her hard. "I don't like having my dates broken," he said.

With her eyes on the floor, Faith said, "No, I didn't expect that you would." But then she looked up and raised her arm out to him like a drowning swimmer. "I wish I could make you understand," she said. She took his hand and pulled herself up on it. When she was standing, she squeezed his hand a little and said, "I've really got to study now, Rich. You've got to go play ball, and I've got to study." She stood on her tiptoes and kissed him quickly on the chin. "We'll work this out probably."

Then she bent and picked up her old baseball glove, folded both arms across it as if she were holding an infant, turned and ran from the room in long stiff strides.

For two weeks after the Sunday softball game, Faith thwarted all of Janus's attempts to spend time with her. She and Cassie, she said, had made a pact to make the dean's list and were enforcing it by supervising one another's study habits. They had decided to eliminate all social activities until after midsemester exams. She would accept Janus's calls but quickly hurry him off the phone. When he tried to complain about the abrupt turn their relationship had taken, she admonished him with the argument that she had never interfered with his studying and that he must honor her program now.

Several times Janus encountered her between classes. She always lingered a moment to talk, but she seemed distracted and showed none of her characteristic flirtatious wit. She would interrupt his small talk with questions about material in her courses and would sometimes flip open a notebook to jot down some aspect of his answers. And Janus imagined that she was forever checking behind herself as if she were afraid that someone was sneaking up behind her. Twice, in fact, Janus spotted Cassie standing in the hall a short distance away. Neither time did she approach them. And both times Faith broke away from him as soon as she noticed her roommate nearby.

In the middle of the second week, Janus dropped by Faith's sorority house unannounced at dinner time. He hadn't talked to her in several days. Midterms were underway, and he had decided to try to catch Faith at dinner, so that he could wish her well and point out both that he was thinking of her and that his thoughtfulness extended to not calling her later and interrupting her study.

Faith and Cassie were sitting at a small square table on the far side of the sorority dining room as he entered. They were wearing identical sweatshirts with their sorority's coat of arms offset on the left side. They had finished eating and were smoking cigarettes, flicking ashes into the saucer Cassie had slid out from under her coffee cup.

As Janus approached, Cassie exhaled a plume of smoke and said something Janus was too far away to hear. She crushed out her cigarette, reached across the table and drew Faith's hand toward her. She patted it quickly and left her hand lying on Faith's. When Janus reached the table, Cassie snatched her hand away as quickly as the smile disappeared from her lips. She picked up the pack of Winstons lying on the table between them and took out a fresh smoke.

"Hi, Rich," Faith said.

"Hi. Mind if I sit a minute?" He looked at Cassie, who shrugged in reply.

"No, sit down," Faith said. "But you can only...."

"I know," Janus interjected. "A minute is all I can sit."

"Well, we may tolerate two," Faith said. "If you're good."

Janus started fiddling with the Winstons, but Faith took them away from him.

"Now, don't try to act sophisticated and smoke," she said.

Janus was heartened by her tone. Perhaps her distant mood was about to pass. "How's all the booking going?" he asked. He turned his head to include Cassie in the question.

Cassie took a drag on her cigarette and exhaled an "All right." She looked at her watch. Janus turned back to Faith.

"Oh, I don't know," she said. "I wish I hadn't been such a goof-off all my life. But I'm gonna do better. For once I know what the courses are about, at least."

"You'll both do fine, I'm sure," Janus said. "And I hope that after this marathon is over you'll be able to relax over spring break and then go about your studying less frenetically for the rest of the year. I'd sure like to see you more often than I've managed recently."

Faith took out a cigarette and shook her hair back as she lit it. "Cassie has just asked me to spend break with her at her parents' cottage in Big Sur," she said. She tilted her head and smiled in her roommate's direction.

"California?" Janus said to Cassie. He was shocked. He and Faith had made no firm plans, but they had talked both about visiting her parents in St. Louis and about trying to rent a cabin on Michigan's northern peninsula.

"Is there another Big Sur I don't know about?" Cassie said in a low voice. She licked her lips.

Janus searched his mind for some retort that would deny Cassie her victory. He felt damp. And he could come up with nothing. So instead, he said to Faith, "Well, if you haven't made a decision yet, I'll tell you why, in addition to my well-wishing, I stopped by. I, too, have a spring break proposal. I managed to get the north Michigan cabin we talked about." It was a lie, of course, but Janus felt desperate.

Cassie blew a stream of smoke that was nearly, though not quite, aimed at Janus's face. "Come on now, Richard," she said. "I'm sure Faith is flattered that you want to take her into the woods. But surely you can't think that some musty Michigan cabin compares with a week at Big Sur."

Janus said to Faith, "You can afford airfare round trip to California?"

Cassie answered, "My parents are taking care of that. This isn't going to cost Faith anything."

Janus turned slightly in his chair to face Faith more directly. It was as if he were on the court, attempting to screen Cassie away from the basket. "I'm gonna feel stood up," he said under his breath, almost whispering.

Cassie laid icy fingers on his arm. He fought off the impulse to shake her hand away rudely. "You're really looking at this from the wrong angle, Richard," she said. "I'm offering Faith two days in San Francisco on either end of a week at Big Sur. That is obviously glorious. Especially for someone like Faith, who has never been to California before. There's just no way your suggestion can compete with that." She licked her lips again and smiled and gave Janus's forearm a dismissive squeeze and pat.

"Compete," Janus said. He turned slowly back to face Cassie. "*Compete*," he repeated. He was like a butterfly emerging from a cocoon. "You're right, Cassie. Competition is the American way. It's what has made this a great country. Our forefathers competed with the Indians in order to leave us this land. They competed with the French to get the Midwest for us. And they competed with dirty, greasy Mexicans to get us Texas, the sunny Southwest and golden California. Now, a little friendly competition between classmates for desirable companionship should be just exactly the right thing to do."

Janus suddenly recognized how nasty his tone had become. Simultaneously he realized how much he disliked Cassie Sears and everything he assumed she represented: money and privilege, breeding, incessant opportunity. Cassie was one of those people who was born rich and was incapable of actions grand enough to prevent her from dying that way. She could toy with drugs. And she could try on, like clothing at a ready-to-wear, a variety of lifestyles without ever having to commit herself to one. At any crossroads in her life, she could choose a course without foreclosing the paths she rejected. Her good fortune was irksome to Janus. Her attempt now to cut him off from Faith incensed him. He was being nasty to her, and he was not sorry in the least.

Cassie began to move dishes about and stir in her purse in preparation to leave. "Well...."

But Janus was not done with her. "You're not leaving, are you?" he said. "You can't *leave*. The competition has only just begun. Surely we aren't going to quit after the openers."

"Cut it out, Rich," Faith said.

"Cut what out?" Janus replied. "Am I doing something wrong? I was only trying to accommodate your roomie. Both Cassie and I would like to spend spring break with you, and it seems only fitting, only American, that we should resolve our mutually exclusive desires on the field of competition. I'm confident that our heiress of the great Sears family approves heartily. Am I mistaken that it was she who introduced the very notion of competition into our little difficulty? And why shouldn't she? She comes from a long line of highly successful competitors. Just who was it you Searses defeated to gain your successes, your Corvette Stingrays and fancy clothes, your cottages on Big Sur and townhouses in San Francisco? And isn't there a ski lodge in Aspen? And what about numbered Swiss bank accounts? Surely there are numbered Swiss bank accounts."

Cassie stood up and said, "Faith, I'll...."

But Janus cut her off. "No, Cassie, you can't go. We haven't even decided what the competition should be. You're not going to demand that we quit after the first round just because you won it, are you? That wouldn't be terribly sporting. And really, in the final analysis, competition needs a personal aspect to remain interesting. I'm sure you agree. So? Basketballs at fifteen feet? No, that's not fair, is it? I'm too tall. How about sarcasm at two inches. If we talked fast enough we could even spray each other with spit. Now, that sounds good and kinky."

"Shut up, Janus," Faith said.

Janus picked up a dirty fork from one of their plates. "I've got it," he announced. "Forks. Forks at choose your distance." He turned to Faith and said, "This forker likes you."

"You're repulsive," Cassie said.

"Now, watch your mouth," Janus said. "When we rejected sarcasm for the competition, I think we implicitly set aside direct insults as well." Cassie stared at him with a look of utter loathing. She started to move away, but Janus began to wave the fork in her path. He feinted with it toward the insignia emblazoned on the bulge of her left breast. "Better get yourself a weapon, Cassie girl. Gotta protect yourself." Cassie took a short step forward and slapped him so hard that she knocked him over backwards out of his chair.

"I'll be waiting upstairs," she said to Faith. She stepped over Janus and walked out of the room without looking back.

"Lucky bitch," Janus said from the floor, still waving his fork. "I was just about to let her have it in her sorority crest."

When Faith walked out of the dining room before he could get back to his feet, Janus assumed that his shenanigans had put his relationship with her to an end. In her mail box near the front door, he left a two-word note: "I'm sorry." And that was it. He didn't even bother to call to try to patch things up. He was surprised, then, when Faith called him a week later and invited him to her parents' for the break. She said that she assumed he had already cancelled the reservation for the cabin, but that she would really like him to meet her folks, anyway.

Janus asked her what had happened to Big Sur. At first she would only say that she had decided not to go. She would never say more than that she and Cassie had a disagreement which had soured their plans.

Janus responded to Faith's invitation with more hesitance than he would have expected. He was not sure that he wanted to let a visit to Faith's parents serve to smooth over their problems. But she wooed him, and he agreed to go with her. He would remain objective, he told himself. He would make the trip a test of his potential to get along with Faith in an environment outside of Lancaster.

It was a bright and unseasonably warm Saturday afternoon when Janus picked up Faith for the four-hour drive to St. Louis. She climbed into his scratched and rusty VW bus, wearing her tennis shoes, blue hiking shorts, a blue and white striped blouse without a bra underneath and dark glasses. As Janus navigated the van through the elm-lined streets of the small college town, Faith unreeled a complicated apology for "mistreating and neglecting him." He pulled the bus onto the four-lane highway leading south and reiterated his apology for his outrageous behavior to Cassie. Faith said that though his actions weren't excusable, they nonetheless made her see that he must really care for her.

"I really love you, Tricks," she concluded. "But lots of the time I can't see why you might love me, so I don't believe that you do. You're so good at everything, and I just want to be good at something, too, so that I can always be sure you'll respect me."

Janus told her that she worried needlessly, that love was something one couldn't earn by accumulating items for a resume, and that what he felt for her could never be altered by either accomplishments or the lack of them. At the same time, he acknowledged that he basically approved of any determination she might exert toward becoming a more serious student or attaining any other goal she might set for herself. A need for a sense of achievement, he emphasized, was something he certainly understood. Janus lifted his right arm up around Faith's shoulders and pulled her over against him.

She took her sunglasses off and turned her face full against his chest and said in a muffled whisper, "But you didn't say it, Richie. You didn't say it."

"Say what, Faith?" Janus squeezed her and kissed the top of her head. He could feel her body quiver, and he knew she had begun to cry.

"You didn't say that you still love me."

Janus felt that same trapped sensation he had felt the first time he and Faith had made love. He waited longer than he should have before answering. He knew the pause was hurting her, but he couldn't make himself speak sooner. He didn't like the partial lie he knew he was going to have to tell. Finally, compromising, he said, "But I do, Faith. Of course, I still do."

"You still didn't say it," Faith said into his shirt.

Janus swallowed and said quietly, "I still love you, Faith."

"I hope it's true," Faith said. She cried harder for a while. And they rode along in silence. Finally, Faith sat back up. She wiped her face with the back of her hand. "Puffy eyes," she said to Janus, laughing a little and pointing to her eyelids which were red and swollen from her tears. Janus looked at her and smiled. "Ha, ha," she said. "You can't laugh at my puffy eyes because *I* brought *my* sunglasses." She put the glasses on and leaned over and switched on the radio. They were not yet too far south to be out of the range of Chicago's WLS. As a rock tune began to fill the car, Faith began to move in gentle rhythm with its beat.

"God, I'm hot," Faith said. She stuck her arm out of the window and tried to direct a stream of wind onto her body. "Aren't you hot, Richie?"

"Right warm," Janus concurred.

Faith reached down and untied her tennis shoes, kicked them off and rolled off her socks. She unbuttoned the two top buttons on her blouse and fanned herself. She looked at Janus from under the left side of her glasses and then unbuttoned her shirt completely.

"What are you doing?" Janus said.

"I told you. I'm hot," Faith said.

"You're gonna flash the truck drivers," Janus said, laughing and checking the rear view mirrors to see if anyone was on the road near them.

"I'll just have to risk it. I'm really hot. Besides, they won't recognize me because I'm wearing dark glasses." She hunched up in the seat, snaked an arm behind herself, unzipped her shorts and pulled them off.

"Faith!"

"I'm just burning up, Richie." She hooked her thumbs inside her bikini pants and pushed them down to her ankles, then curled one knee, leaving the panties dangling from her right foot.

"Faith!" Janus was laughing again. "What in the hell are you doing?"

Faith put her mouth up to Janus's ear and said in a breathy whisper, "I want you to eat me." She sat back against the door and lifted her foot and with it laid her underwear on his lap. He looked at her slender, half-naked body, her smooth, flat stomach, her sparse pubic hair. It struck him that her body could have been that of a fourteen-year-old. She opened her shirt and tucked it back under her arms so that her small firm breasts were fully exposed. "*Richie,*" Faith said. She brought her right foot up under herself, spreading her legs as widely as possible. "I want you to eat me." She moved her finger tips, slowly, lightly between her legs.

"Have you gone crazy?" Janus said. He was still laughing. And he was turned on. But he was also enormously worried that someone would drive alongside of them and see her. He tried at once to look at Faith and keep his eyes on the road and the mirrors.

"I want it now, Richie," Faith said breathlessly.

"Can't you wait until we get there?"

"I want it right now."

"You want me to pull over?"

Faith shook her head. "I want you to," she said, "but my parents are waiting." She licked her fingers and returned her hand to its slow, swirling motion between her legs.

"You're driving me crazy!" Janus screamed.

Faith smiled. She reversed her position, putting her back against her boyfriend. She pulled his right hand off the wheel, around her, down into her lap.

5

The El Cholo Feeling is a complicated thing. I have been afflicted with versions of it almost all my life. It takes on many guises and employs many props. It has also worn such disparate costumes as beach balls, gold stars, Mahatma Gandhi and hell. And it was waiting for me as early as first grade, where the fate of my whole life was probably determined on my very first day of school.

My teacher gave each member of the class a dittoed drawing of a multipanelled ball. "Boys and girls," she said, holding one of the sheets neck high, the top just at the bottom of her chin. "This is a beach ball. How many of you have been to the beach and seen a ball like this before? Raise your hands. Most of you. That's good. What colors are a beach ball? Red. Yes. And yellow? Yes. And green? Sometimes they're green. Black? I don't think I've ever seen a black one. Yes, and some are blue. Beach balls are lots of colors. They're any color you want to make them. And that's what I want you to do right now. Take out your crayons and color the balls any way that you like. When you're finished, I'm going to put every one of them up on the board. So be careful and do a good job."

We all knew how to color, or thought we did, and so were not intimidated by the first task of our education. But it wasn't easy for me. Was it true that we could make the balls any color we liked? Or should we try to make them look like beach balls that we'd actually seen? I wanted to color mine green and black, but I figured that what the teacher wanted was a ball colored like real ones. So I traced the pale blue lines with my black crayon, then colored alternate panels red and yellow. Smooth and light, all in the same direction, just as my mother had taught me.

The teacher thumbtacked the finished sheets to the bulletin board. "Oh nice. Very good. Very, very good. Pretty." We felt wonderful. When all the sheets were attached in a long row to the strip of cork which stretched the width of the room above the blackboard, she turned to the class and announced, "These are so good I'm going to give every one of you a star." Standing before each ball, she contemplated which star to select. Some papers she awarded green stars, others blue. For a few she selected gold stars.

My paper was at the end. As she neared it, I became anxious. When she pasted a gold star on my work, I felt very wise for having colored it red and yellow instead of green and black. For a long time thereafter, life for me was like that beach ball: red and yellow and rolling downhill faster and faster toward more gold stars.

But then between my ninth- and tenth-grade years in school, my parents moved. My father had received his tenure, a promotion to full professor and a tidy raise. It was American Dream time. Mom and Dad sold the little frame prefab in which I had grown up and built themselves a French provincial near the Lakefront. Although we had not really made it into a posh neighborhood, we had gotten close, and in my parents' view, they had achieved the ultimate. But for my parents, one must remember, the ultimate in fashion, for instance, was a banlon shirt with a trout over the left breast. Such a shirt was just as nice, they pointed out, and sold for $2.50 less than one with an alligator on it.

It wasn't a move of any great distance, only a couple of miles or so across town, but for me it might as well have been a move to another planet. We had changed school districts. All my lifelong pals went on to Thomas Jefferson High, a seedy, run-down place with a reputation as being tougher than reform school. I had to attend the brand-new Earl K. Long, a school which drew the bulk of its student body from the affluent Lakefront and Uptown sections of the city. I was instantly out of sync. All my male classmates dressed in oxford-cloth, buttoned-down shirts made by Gant; I was forced to wear my inevitably limp banlons with a little trout on the left side.

At Jefferson, or T.J., as everyone called it, my maturity would have been viewed as admirable; among the young snobs at Long, I was seen as, well, a kind of goody-goody. For example, I had always made a policy of getting to class early enough to claim the middle seat in the front row, the one immediately in front of the teacher's desk. I did so in order to impress the teacher with my rapt attention and my diligence at writing down all that was said. In the past such a policy had always resulted in my being quickly spotted as a committed, mature student, which inevitably led to good grades. At Long it more quickly led to my being regarded as a loathsome brown-nose, which in turn produced few new friends.

This proved a real obstacle to my social life. I did meet several nice girls who rode the bus with me out to my new part of town, but I was hesitant to ask any of them out for fear the one I chose might be suffering from some terminal social disease. I figured that in the long run it was better to be thought of as a shy brown-nose than to make a blunderous misstep which would wreck me at Long forever. I knew a precedent. In eighth grade, Ronald Demart ruined himself forever by asking Karen Mert to the Halloween Dance. Ronald was new in our school that fall and had no inkling of Karen's sordid past. But he found out the day of the dance when B.F. Johnson rose at the end of our lunch period, walked over and stood behind Ronald's chair, rested his hand lightly on Ronald's shoulder, and announced, "Our fine new student, Ronald Demart, has graciously asked our dearly beloved Karen Mert to tonight's dance. And Booga has enthusiastically accepted." Most everyone except Ronald and Karen stood up and cheered.

What Booga lurked in the halls of Long High, waiting to entice me into total humiliation? I didn't know, so I bided my time.

"I think you're very wise," consoled my mother. "There are all sizes of fish in the sea. Some are big and some are little. You could catch yourself some sweet little guppie now. But if you wait until basketball season starts and everyone gets to see how good you are, you can catch a nice, big, juicy fish." She was right, of course, that what I wanted was a nice, big, juicy one.

And once basketball season started, I worked up the nerve to ask for a date with Sandy Wilkerson, who was soon to be voted the most beautiful girl in the sophomore class. I had the best of reasons for choosing her: I had determined beyond a doubt that she was the most beautiful girl in the sophomore class. I asked her out two weeks in advance so she couldn't tell me she already had another date. Even so, it took some courage. Sandy was an Uptown girl, and I wasn't even really a Lakefront boy. Uptown New Orleans is that part of the city upriver from Canal Street. This is sometimes hard for non-natives to grasp since, as it happens, Uptown is the southern part of the city, while Downtown, everything downriver from Canal Street, is largely north of Uptown. It's a strange city. But be that as it may, Uptown New Orleans is where the old money lives. Lakefront New Orleans is the only other part of town where any self-respecting affluent person would deign to reside. It is the home of the city's new money. I now lived near the Lakefront. In other words, I was still a Downtown kid.

Significantly, Sandy and I had different telephone prefixes. She was a SUnset girl. I was a PRescott boy. For the most part, interprefix dating was frowned upon. But since I was a good student and an important basketball player, I asked Sandy Wilkerson out anyway. She accepted, so perhaps she came from a family of Uptown liberals.

I was chagrined nonetheless at having to take her out in my family's five-year-old Dodge station wagon. I felt certain that all Sandy's other boyfriends arrived in recent model automobiles built by General Motors. I tend to forget how important cars were to us in those days. For countless hours my peers could stand around and enthuse about "four barrel carburetors with two deuces." I didn't even know what they meant. I discovered, though, that real car knowledge was far less important than the mastery of several phrases of jargon. I found I could pretty much hold my own in a car conversation with three well-timed questions, not one of which I understood: "Does that come with an overhead cam?" "Has that baby got fuel injection?" And, "How many cubes you sittin' behind there?"

Unfortunately, I was planning on taking Sandy Wilkerson *out* in a car, not having a conversation with her *about* cars. And ignorant as I was of car engines, I knew what kinds of cars had status and what kinds didn't. Sports cars were cool. Fast cars were cool. Most anything by General Motors was cool. Dodge station wagons were not cool. And my one alternative was bleak: the family's other car was a faded red Volkswagen. Volkswagens had not attained the youth cult status they were to have only a few years later. At the time, they were even less cool than Dodge station wagons. And furthermore, Volkswagens had bucket seats which would have denied Sandy Wilkerson the opportunity to sit close to me in the car should she become so inclined.

Getting her to sit close to me in the car was a major priority, and I needed a plan for accomplishing that. More immediately, though, I needed a plan for how to behave toward her in the two weeks before we had our date. I considered an extended case of diarrhea but couldn't afford to miss basketball practice. Fortunately, we had only biology class together and didn't sit anywhere near each other, so I figured I could handle biology with a smile and "Hi."

Lunch was another problem. Lunch for a new kid is always a problem. Save at lunch, your time is scheduled; there is always something with which you can keep busy. But at lunch you're naked. Where should you sit? With whom? You're conspicuous if you sit by yourself, but what if the group you choose to sit with thinks you're a drip?

I hated lunch. I hated lunch all the more after I asked Sandy Wilkerson for a date, because we had the same lunch period. Should I sit with her now that we were going out? Were we *going out*? We hadn't gone out yet. What about the boy or boys who were taking her out this weekend? Should I perhaps sit with her at lunch next week but not this one? And what should I say to her? I had never said much of anything to her before. If I had to speak to her, should I refer to our date? "See you a week from Friday at seven" didn't seem very catchy. What if she didn't want her friends to know? I wanted my friends to know, but I didn't have any friends at Long. I finally solved my lunch conundrum by deciding to spend my eating periods in the library in hopes of avoiding her completely.

I have never been a very lucky person. On the Monday of the week we were to go out, I had hidden from Sandy all lunch with a book about Charles de Gaulle. But near the end of the period when I opened the door and went rushing into the hall, I knocked someone down. By the time I realized it was Sandy Wilkerson, she was shaking the long black hair from her face and smoothing her green and white checkered dress back over her knees. Like a zombie, I made no effort to help her up. I was so astonished at what I had done that I could barely speak. I was also mesmerized by what I could *see*. As she drew her legs up under her, attempting to rise, her dress fell back toward her waist, revealing the pale bulge of thigh between each stocking top and her white panties. From the blunted nylon V of her crotch, a few wisps of pubic hair escaped.

I thought I was going to die. I could feel the redness of a blush creep up from the collar of my black banlon shirt all the way into my scalp. "Wha—what are you doing here?" I stammered. My eyes were locked on her underpants. I might as well have said, "Gee, you have a great-looking snatch."

"I think you just knocked me down," she said.

"What I meant was, why are you in the hall? Why are all these people in the hall?" Why, in other words, wasn't it empty like it should have been so that I could have come crashing into it without knocking someone over?

"It's raining," she said with a funny smile. "Didn't you know?"

I didn't. But I looked across the hall through the glass doors and into the courtyard where everyone *should* have been gathered. Beyond the courtyard I could see the headlights of cars creeping cautiously along Wisner Boulevard. I felt as if I were lost in a time warp. I looked back at her tilted, pretty face with its speculative smile, but I couldn't force my eyes to linger on hers. She noticed them dart to her splayed legs and moved her dress to cover herself again. The gesture was free of irritation, not quite as if she were pleased to catch me staring between her legs but not at all as if she thought me ungentlemanly. She kept one hand on her dress at her knees and extended the other upward toward me.

"Help?" she asked.

"Oh, sure." I pulled her to her feet and restrained the urge I felt to begin dusting her off. "Well…," I said. I was so awkward that I'm surprised I didn't stumble from just the effort of talking.

The bell ending the lunch period rang, and we began walking with the throng of other students towards our afternoon classes. "Do you always," Sandy Wilkerson laughed to me, "sweep your dates, so to speak, off their feet this way?"

"Right," I said. "Ha ha. Of course. All the time."

I needed a lobotomy.

Why couldn't I be cool? Why couldn't I have said something like, "No, but on rainy days I always try to run over girls in green checkered dresses"? But by the time I thought of that response, I was twenty-eight years old and writing this note.

"Don't get wet," Sandy Wilkerson said as she turned away from me to go to her class. "Remember, it's raining."

"Right," I said, ever the master of the clever riposte.

Convinced that Sandy had discovered me a bumbling nitwit, I formed two plans of action for Friday night. The grander plan was to try to capitalize on my lunch period awkwardness by pretending to be a nascent intellectual, deep and unorthodoxly charming if absent-minded and clumsy—the kind of man, in other words, a smart Uptown girl should latch onto early, the kind of man who made up in long-term potential what he lacked in current cool.

The second plan was to get things off to a nice cozy start by trapping Sandy into sitting close to me on the Dodge's flat front seat. The second plan, of course, went into operation first. When I arrived at Sandy's river-side home on Perrier Street, I pulled my car up heading east, or toward Audubon Park. That meant the driver's side of the car was next to the curb. When she came out of the house, I let her into the car on my side. That way she had to slide all the way across the seat in order *not* to sit close to me. This strategy, I figured, might circumvent any hesitation she might have had at sliding across the seat *in order* to sit close to me.

The plan half worked. She did not slide *all* the way across the car to sit by the door, but she didn't exactly snuggle up to me either. I didn't know how to judge her response. Had I let her in the passenger's side of the car to begin with, I'd have been pleased had she ended up in her present position. It would have meant a deliberate movement toward me and away from the safety of the outside. But as things had developed, her present position had resulted from a movement away from me greater than was necessary.

I felt like a jerk, but I nonetheless managed to drive us to a small seafood restaurant at the marina.

"You're really quite mature," Sandy Wilkerson told me when we had been seated at a lakeside table. She really did tell me that, and as she did her green eyes sparkled in the yellow light of the large candle that sat between us.

Was my grand plan working so soon? "Why do you say that?" I grinned as suavely as is possible for someone sporting a new crewcut.

"No one has ever taken me to dinner before."

This revelation disturbed me. "Oh, really," I said off-handedly. Did she find this pretentious? Did she think I was just trying to impress her? Hell, I *was* trying to impress her.

"Oh, you know. I've gone out with a guy to a drive-in after a show or something. To get a Coke, or maybe a hamburger. But no on has ever taken me out to dinner like this."

"Oh, really," I said.

I could talk up a storm when I got started.

A silence followed in which we both pretended to study the menu, though I already knew I was ordering fried oysters, and I bet she was, too.

When the waitress was slow in appearing, Sandy said, "This is just like going out to dinner with my dad." Was that a compliment? I didn't know, and I couldn't think of a single thing to say in response. I'd used up my quota of "Oh, really's." After a while, when I hadn't said anything and was still hiding inside my menu, Sandy said, "I think I'll have the fried oysters."

"Me too," I agreed.

It was not the most stimulating dinner.

Afterwards, though, we drove downtown, left the car in a parking garage on Rampart Street just off Canal, and walked over to the R.K.O. Orpheum across the street from the Roosevelt Hotel. The theater was crowded, mostly with a lot of other teen-agers on dates. In those days, the Downtown movie houses were still the *in* places to be. A tuxedo-clad usher informed us we'd find seating more easily upstairs.

It was hot in the balcony, so I took off my multicolored sports jacket of which I was very proud because, as my father pointed out when he bought it for me, "It will go with anything." It was, of course, the only sports coat I owned. When you've got one that will go with anything, you don't much need another one.

Under normal circumstances, I would have left my coat on despite the heat, but I wanted to display my fashionable short-sleeved white dress shirt with the snap tab on the collar which fastened underneath my narrow red tie and forced it out at a jaunty angle. I may have been merely a Downtown boy, but I wanted her to notice that I knew a thing or two about style. I don't think she ever did, though. We made small talk about God-knows-what, and then the house lights went down.

The movie was *Sunday in New York* with Jane Fonda, Rod Taylor, Cliff Robertson and some voluptuous redhead whose name I don't remember. The film was about fucking. Rather, it was about *not* fucking. Which may be the story of my life. Robertson wanted to fuck the redhead, but she wasn't sure. By the time she was sure, they couldn't find a place. When they found a place, they couldn't arrange a time. Meanwhile, Rod Taylor wanted to fuck

Jane Fonda. Then he found out she was a virgin and decided to be a gentleman. That made Jane mad, and she decided she'd fuck Rod Taylor. He tried to hold out, but then he gave in. Jane Fonda is awfully seductive. But once Rod quit being a gentleman, she wasn't so sure she really wanted to get fucked. She began to hold out again. Then her brother, who was still another character, came in and punched Rod Taylor in the face. In the end, nobody got fucked. Except me, which unfortunately was true only in a metaphorical sense, and at any rate that had happened some time earlier.

On the way out of the theater, Sandy Wilkerson encountered two of her girlfriends who were there with boys I didn't know.

"How'd you like the movie?" Sandy asked.

"It was darling," one of the girlfriends said.

"Wasn't it cute?" said the other.

"I really liked it, too," Sandy said.

The boys and I didn't comment. We were busy sizing each other up. I was sure her Uptown friends were wondering what she was doing out with someone like me. Then I remembered that being from Downtown was not a racial condition.

I was rather stimulated that Sandy Wilkerson was so taken by a movie about a lot of unmarried people trying to hump each other. And as I reflected upon the brief conversation she'd had with her friends, I began to feel good. She hadn't shown any signs of being embarrassed about being seen with me. I began to consider sort of slipping my arm casually about her waist as we walked back towards the parking garage. Regrettably, I toyed with this notion for too long. We arrived at the parking structure before I actually made my move, and by then it was too late, of course. Even *I* knew how foolish it would be to put my around her in the waiting room.

But my good feeling resurfaced after I let Sandy into the passenger side of the car and she slid across the seat toward me, locating herself perhaps a little closer even than she had earlier. I pulled the car out of the garage and worked my way over to St. Charles Avenue and headed back toward Sandy's house. It was nearly 11:30, and I was supposed to be home by midnight. But as I pondered anew the fact that Sandy liked *Sunday in New York*, I began to nurse the outrageous hope that she'd be interested in necking. For that I'd gladly have incurred my parents' wrath.

Before I'd left home, my mother had reminded me not to be out late. She had straightened my tie and held me by the shoulders at arm's length to make sure that I was presentable. "Look at my big high school boy," she said. "Almost all grown up now. My little minnow has become as big as a whale." She hugged me, and while she was squeezing us together, she whispered into my jacket pocket, "Are you kissing your girlfriends now, Richie?" And after

I'd replied, "Come on, Mom," she said, "Well it's perfectly okay, honey. Just remember, on the lips or the cheek only." She pulled her head away from my chest to look me in the face. "Never kiss a girl on her neck. And never, ever on her ear. That can make a girl crazy."

I learned two things from that piece of advice. The first was that my mother must have had very erogenous ears. The second was that I'd adopt even the most ridiculous poses for the chance to put my lips on Sandy Wilkerson's neck and ears.

As we headed up St. Charles, I thought I'd sort of casually suggest to Sandy that we drive out to the Point where I could make her crazy in the complete privacy of several hundred other necking teen-agers. But I couldn't quite figure out how to put it. "Wanna make out?" seemed a tad abrupt. We hadn't spoken for several minutes, but I figured that meshed well enough with the absent-minded intellectual role I was playing. Still, when I stopped the car at a traffic light, I put my arm up on the back of the seat behind Sandy. I didn't quite touch her, but I thought the move must have seemed affectionate and familiar, altogether better than mere conversation. When she seemed to settle back a little in the seat, I could see us as practically married.

Opposite us a dark brown 1957 Chevrolet with the rear end jacked up pulled up to the light. The driver had his radio playing so loudly we could hear it in our car. As we waited for the light, he kept revving his motor. When the light finally turned green, he roared toward and past us, screeching his tires clear across the intersection. Sandy turned her head to watch the car rocket down the street. I watched in my mirror. We could hear the Chevy grind through its gears even after its red taillights disappeared in the galaxy of city lights behind us.

I looked at my watch as I slowly pulled the Dodge into the intersection. I had forgotten the hot rodder instantly. "Well, what now?" I said. I had decided that maybe Sandy would suggest the Point.

But, as Yeats has mentioned, things fall apart. Sandy was still turned backwards watching the trail of the souped-up Chevy. She turned to me and said, "Wow, what a cool car!" She looked out the back window again, hoping to catch one last glimpse. "Wouldn't you like to have a car like that?"

I have to admit I was put off—not so much because I might not have liked to have a fast, cool car, but because I was trying to turn her on with my silent, brainy act, and here she was getting wet pants over A.J. Foyt. So I said, affecting boredom, "Not really."

She was surprised. "No? Why not?"

"I just think that kind of thing is rather juvenile. Don't you?"

Even back then I had an instinct for my own jugular.

"Oh," she said. "Yes. I guess so."

She was just being nice, of course. Southern girls are trained to agree with their dates even if they decide to defend infanticide. I should have finished off my lunatic priggishness by yawning and announcing, "Quite," but by now I sniffed the acrid odor of disaster. I quickly asked if she'd like to stop at a drive-in for a Coke or something, but she said she guessed I better take her on home.

"I turn into a pumpkin at twelve o'clock," she said.

"That's okay," I should have said, "I turn into an asshole at 11:30."

I drove her home and walked her to the door. We chatted for a minute on her porch until I said, "Would you mind if I kissed you good night?" It was hard for me to say, but I was trying to dredge up the confidence I had possessed earlier when visions of necks and ears danced in my head.

"Rich," she said, "if a girl wants to be kissed, then she doesn't want to be asked."

What I should have done then was say, "Who's askin'?" and simply smiled and kissed her, but instead I said, "Oh, really?" and tried to fathom what she meant. In other words, I stood staring like a mongoloid. I stood there so long that she finally leaned forward and kissed me delicately on the lips and said, "Good night, Rich, and thank you for a very nice evening." She looked at me then as if debating what to say next: "When a girl kisses you, remember to put your arms around her."

"Right," I said. She smiled and went inside.

I have always remembered, but I never asked Sandy Wilkerson out again. How could I after that performance? I was convinced she'd turn me down, and I didn't want to find out for sure. But clinging to a developing adolescent cynicism, alone in my room, I used to think of her often. I'd draw back my curtains with their montage of athletic heroes and stare out at the night. And I would practice protective cynicism with a shallow laugh I thought sophisticated and sneer at the fate which had landed me on this new street two long blocks from Elysian Fields.

Struggling with the Earl K. Long version of the El Cholo Feeling, I dedicated myself especially to my studies. The encouragement my instructors gave me was the attention, I guess, that I very much needed, and I was motivated to work all that much harder in order to get as much as possible. My peers, of course, still saw me as the ass-kissing jerk, but it was part of my cynical defiance act to work harder just because it enhanced my alienation.

Pleasing my world history teacher was particularly unpopular since the other kids at Long didn't like her. With an M.A. in European history from Yale, Almak Acen was a flamboyant Yankee and an especially hard grader. Around school, students made fun of her mannerisms. Whenever in lecture she came to something that needed to be enclosed in quotation marks, she would raise her arms from the elbow to shoulder height, and with the index and middle fingers of each hand, flick in the needed punctuation. And whenever someone asked her a question that she couldn't answer, she would throw back her head, roll her eyes and announce in her New England accent, "I really haven't the foggiest."

She was a homely, fortyish woman of Balkan parentage, whose pronounced overbite and tight-skinned face gave her visage a skeletal quality, like that in a child's Halloween mask, which is amusing rather than gruesome. She was short, abnormally thin and loose-jointed, tawny-colored with black eyes that gleamed when she looked at me and made me feel as if we were sharing some private joke. There was a pixieish quality in the herky-jerky, strobe light way she moved her tiny body. She seemed never to be in motion but always to have just arrived.

Almak Acen made world history interesting and challenging. And when I received an A in her class for the first six-week grading period, I felt a sense of real accomplishment, a sense that had seldom accompanied the hundreds of A's I had received in the past.

When the second grading period began, Mrs. Acen announced to the class, "I am no longer going to award honors to students solely on the basis of superior performance on assigned work." (She always referred to an A as "honors.") "Beginning this term, those of you who aspire to honors must submit a paper on some topic related to our course of study. It must be five to seven pages long, typed, and have its assertions documented by footnotes in the proper form. This is to be regarded as a research paper. Please do not confuse this project with a book report."

I did not confuse the assignment with a book report. When I decided to write a paper on Charles de Gaulle for our unit on France, I checked out all the books on de Gaulle in our school library. It was the shortest of these I was reading the day I knocked Sandy Wilkerson down in the hall. By the time I finished the book, basketball season was in full swing, I was feeling somewhat less alienated, and world history was no longer quite so important. So I wrote my paper on de Gaulle without reading any of the other books. Then came the tricky part: using the index of the book I had read and the indices of those I had not, I ran down enough page references to specific points in my paper to provide myself with a set of footnotes. I knew I was giving the impression that I had drawn material from several sources, but on the other hand I was hardly inclined to read the other books on de Gaulle since I was sure they all contained basically the same information. I assumed I had behaved properly enough when Mrs. Acen graded both my paper and my term work A.

When the third term was getting underway, Mrs. Acen asked me to come see her after school. Though it was an unusually cold day in December, the city's stubborn greenery still could be seen through Mrs. Acen's classroom windows and through the yellow haze of late afternoon.

"Hi, Rich," she greeted me as I entered her room. "Sit down." She indicated a chair she had placed near her desk. It was pleasant to talk with her without having to sit in one of the student seats. "I wanted to talk to you about your de Gaulle paper."

It instantly stopped being pleasant. Good God, had she somehow detected that I had forged my footnotes from a bogus bibliography? I started to sweat, beads of perspiration breaking out first on my lower back just above my belt and spreading from there up toward my armpits. What was I going to do?

Mrs. Acen took my paper out of a desk drawer and spread it open in front of her, glancing quickly at certain passages she had marked and rereading her own comments. She must have detected that I thought something was wrong when she looked up at me, because she quickly said, "Your paper was fine, I want you to understand. You presented your information on de Gaulle in a nice, straightforward manner." She glanced back at the paper again, brushing its top page lightly with her palms. "I think your writing is good. You have an eye for dramatic detail."

This was all very nice. For an infinite instant I had thought I was in indescribable trouble, and now all this praise. Surely no one in the history of the race craved praise more than I did, but I knew she was leading up to a *but*. There have always been *buts* in my life.

"But," Mrs. Acen said, "the paper does not really attain the level of sophistication of which you are capable."

Looking past her and out the window as she spoke, I watched the last rays of the afternoon sun shrink and disappear, merging the school's lawn and the asphalt parking lot behind it into one massive black shadow.

"Yes, ma'am," I said, confused. I could just as well have said "No, ma'am." Or nothing. I didn't really grasp what it was she was driving at. I wanted her approval. I did the paper for her. She had given me an A. She said the paper was good. What more was there?

For me there were thirteen years, from then to now. But as clearly now as I can see back to then, then I could see very little at all.

Mrs. Acen smiled at me. "In your paper on de Gaulle, you have provided only a narrative," she said. She put her hands flat on my paper and gradually leaned on them across her desk toward me as she continued, "And narrative, even one as good as this one, is not adequate." She smiled again and shook her head gently. "I know you don't altogether grasp what I'm telling you, but you will with time, Rich. You see, in this paper you have posed no problems for yourself as an historian." Why *an* historian? Why not *a* historian? Besides, I was neither. I was just a high school basketball player who admired his teacher and wanted to please her.

When I didn't say anything, Mrs. Acen went on. "In the paper you will write for the present grading period, I want you to start the process of becoming an historian. I want you to pose questions for yourself about your material, questions which your paper will address and attempt to answer from your assessment of the historical data. In other words, I want analysis. You're an exceptionally mature young man with as much potential as any student I've ever had. If you're going to be good at something, you should start training for it early. You're capable of the kind of work I'm asking for right now. And I want to see you doing it. Do you understand?"

"Yes, ma'am," I said.

I understood that it was going to be a lot more difficult from now on getting an A in world history.

"Good," she concluded. "I will be willing to help you in any way that I can, Rich. Never hesitate to ask me or stop by after school." Her expression was very intense, and in the dim light I thought she was beautiful. When I got up, she asked me to turn her classroom lights on as I left. But with my back to the window, I couldn't locate the switch. She saw me groping at the dark wall, got up from her desk and came over toward me. "You're looking in the wrong place, Rich," she said. She found the switch on the opposite side of the door and flicked the lights on. I smiled sheepishly and left her there bathed in the strangeness of fluorescent illumination. The hall was dark, and I had to make my way out of the school slowly.

I thought I was in love with Almak Acen, and so I was determined to write her a sophisticated paper more in line with my capabilities. A paper which would pose some questions and suggest some answers based upon my unique analysis of the historical data.

I decided to write my paper on Mahatma Gandhi. We were studying India that term in a unit on Asia. My father suggested the idea. He had been reading Martin Luther King and was interested in Gandhi's thinking on the politics of civil disobedience. He offered to buy me a book on Gandhi that he was anxious to read.

One Saturday we went to the bookstore at his college. He bought me Louis Fischer's *Life of Gandhi* and for himself another of Martin Luther King's works and Will Campbell's *Race and Renewal of the Church*. As we were leaving the bookstore, he did something he hadn't done in a long time: he put his arm around me. Joined together, father and son, we were two scholars, each with limitlessly promising futures. Neither of us could foresee for an instant that in little more than four years neither of us would any longer be in

New Orleans, but in Chicago—I with long hair and a summer's growth of beard in the streets outside the Democratic National Convention; and he, after having lost his job over his stance on the race issue and my mother over his inability to handle his firing, with no prospects in a furnished bachelor apartment without dishes, save for one empty plastic ice cream container from which he drank water and into which he poured his Scotch. And Martin Luther King would be dead.

To research my paper, I checked out all the books on Gandhi from the school library and from the public college libraries as well. There were seven or eight in all. I didn't read any of them. I read the book my dad had bought me.

Reading about the career of Mahatma Gandhi had an impact on me that transcended my desire to succeed in world history. It affected me like nothing else I had ever read. Gandhi was unlike any man who ever lived, it seemed. But if my fundamentalist religious training was correct, then Gandhi must have gone to hell. I couldn't bear the thought, not when I considered all the creeps that had probably crowded into heaven on the basis of deathbed conversions.

I brought the issue up for consideration in my Sunday School class. My teacher had urged us to bring up any matter that we found troubling. Ned Marasmus was a wiry man with an unwieldy shock of dirty brown hair. A big-time building contractor when he wasn't teaching Sunday School, he specialized in erecting entire prefabricated subdivisions into which, among others, black people were not allowed to move. "Don't let old Satan get you into a game of one-on-one," he warned. "Bring your troubles here to the House of the Lord where your brothers in Christ can help you give the Devil the beating of his life."

"Mr. Marasmus," I asked, "do you think that Mahatma Gandhi went to hell?"

"Gandhi? The Indian fella? He wasn't a Christian, was he?"

"No," I said.

"Well then, Rich, what do you think?"

"I think Gandhi lived a very Christlike life."

"But you remember, Rich, that in John 3:16 the scripture says, 'Whosoever believeth in me shall not perish, but have everlasting life.'"

"Yes, sir. But Jesus didn't say whosoever does *not* believeth in me *shall* perish and *not* have everlasting life."

Ned Marasmus was astounded. "See here now, Richard Janus," he said, biting off each word. "'None cometh unto the Father but by *me*.' This Gandhi was no Christian. He was a socialist or something. And you better make no mistake about it, Mahatma Gandhi went to hell. If I believed otherwise, I'd be risking my own immortal soul. And so will you. I'm sorry for Gandhi, but he knew of Jesus and he rejected him. Of course he went to hell. Do you understand?"

I understood why Gandhi said that he *would* have become a Christian except for one thing: Christians.

Troubled by my concern for Gandhi's soul, I set about writing my world history paper. I posed a question for myself (I figured one was sufficient for a tenth grader): Was Mahatma Gandhi's leadership crucial to the Indian independence movement? Subscribing to the great man theory of history, which has since gone out of fashion, I answered yes. Of course, I was careful to argue that only the particular climate of British foreign policy in the post-World War II period would have allowed such a movement as Gandhi's to succeed, based as it was on the politics of pacifism. In other words, the question I asked, I begged. But the begging sustained an ambitiously long twelve pages. Using the technique I had mastered earlier, I fashioned a set of footnotes.

I entitled the paper "Mohandas K. Gandhi: Enigma of the East." Without realizing it, I had adopted the common style for academic titles. With colons.

Almak Acen loved it. "This is just what I was looking for," she told me. "It is truly superior work. It is well-researched, well-organized and well-written. Rich, you have a real future as an historian." And she was right, of course. I had a real future as an historian who would write an ambitious twelve-page prospectus but never a dissertation.

6

1970

The first time Janus was in Faith's parents' house, he had arrived, in B.F. Johnson's phrase, "as horny as a twelve-point buck."

That was the previous year at spring break. Faith had taken off all her clothes in the car on the way down and had proceeded to drive him crazy. Even after she had come and had rebuttoned her blouse, so as not to attract the stares of passersby, she refused to put her pants back on. And after a short while she began to complain of the heat again. But there was no lewd display or sexy talk this time. She simply nestled against her boyfriend and brought his hand between her legs. "Do me again," she commanded.

And Janus did her again, and still she left her lower half naked. Not until St. Louis's Gateway Arch came into view did she wiggle back into her shorts. Janus, of course, was out of his mind with lust, but all of his pleas for reciprocation were met with firm rejection. "Not while you're driving, Richie. I'm sure you don't want us to have an accident."

"I'll control myself," Janus promised.

"Well, if you control yourself," Faith argued, "it wouldn't be much fun, would it?"

"Then you drive," Janus begged.

"But I have to drive with two hands. I'm not a confident driver like you are."

"We'll pull over then," Janus offered.

"No," Faith said. "My parents will be looking for us, and I don't want to be late."

The flat landscape on either side of the car seemed one continuous farm, the black soil still visible under an endless row of short green stalks of corn. They seemed not to move at all. Each solitary, majestic silo they passed, rising proud and certain beside the road, seemed surely the same one they had passed a moment ago.

"Please," Janus pleaded.

"You'll be okay, honey," Faith said. "I'll take care of you when we get home."

Janus wasn't sure he believed it. And when they got there he quickly became sure he *didn't* believe it. Faith's mother met them at the door and, after introductions, informed Faith that she'd be in her own room upstairs and that Richard would sleep in the guest room on the first floor. This was no particular surprise, but when Janus carried Faith's suitcase to her room, he discovered that the master bedroom was at the head of a creaky staircase and that even the greatest stealth might not succeed in concealing movement between the floors.

When the suitcases were stowed, Janus was taken to the kitchen where Mrs. Cleaver was making dinner. She offered the travelers something to drink. When Faith opted for Coke, Janus did likewise. Mrs. Cleaver asked him questions about his family, and he answered them as honestly as possible without revealing that his parents were divorced. He wanted to make a good impression. Knowing that Mr. Cleaver was chairman of the psychology department at Washington University, Janus talked about his father's academic background.

After ten minutes or so, Professor Cleaver came into the kitchen wearing an open-collared plaid shirt and baggy, pleated pants. He was a short, slight, bald man. Janus started to rise to shake hands, but, without speaking to his guest, Mr. Cleaver went to a cupboard under the sink and brought out a bottle of Southern Comfort. He poured several ounces into a stained plastic glass and ran tap water on top. He added a single ice cube from the refrigerator and swirled it around in his drink with his finger. After he had sipped from the drink twice, he set the glass on the counter next to the sink and began to swing his arms back and forth, clapping his hands in front.

When he had clapped half a dozen times, Professor Cleaver said to the refrigerator, "What kind of name is Janus, anyway?"

Janus ached for someone in the room to say, like the chaplain in *Catch-22*, "It's Janus's name, sir." But no one did, of course. So Janus said, after clearing his throat, "I'm English on my father's side, German on my mother's."

Professor Cleaver acknowledged this response with a nod at the ice box, turned and drank from his glass again and resumed swinging his arms and clapping his hands. "Your major's history, huh?" Clap. Swing, clap. "Okay." Swing, clap. Suddenly he looked at Janus for the first time, tilted his head and squinted at him over the top of his glasses. "Okay.

What was Booker T. Washington's middle name?"

Janus looked at Faith, who said, "Do you know?" Mrs. Cleaver continued to slice vegetables for the salad.

Janus cleared his throat again. "Taliaferro, sir," he said.

Professor Cleaver continued to stare at him over the top of his glasses long enough for Janus to begin entertaining the queer idea that Washington's middle name had somehow changed. But then Mr. Cleaver raised a clenched fist and made a deliberate twisting motion with it. "Right," he announced. "Right you are." He shook his head and pursed his lips in approval, turned and picked up his drink and left the room. For the rest of the visit, Mr. Cleaver did not speak directly to Janus.

For dinner that night, Faith and Janus cleaned up and changed out of their traveling clothes. Janus put on a knit shirt and a reasonably new pair of jeans, but Faith put on Janus's favorite dress, one so short that he worried her parents might be scandalized. Neither seemed to notice, however.

Faith's father did not make his appearance at the table until everyone else was seated. When he had taken his place at the head of the table, the dishes were served. Aside from compliments by Faith and Janus on the quality of the meal, there was little conversation while they ate.

Though Mrs. Cleaver had done nothing more than open a can and melt butter over the contents, Janus commended the lima beans in particular. "I was a freshman in college before I discovered that lima beans didn't have a natural kind of bitter, toasty taste," he explained. "My mother never enjoyed cooking very much and had the habit of scorching all vegetables." When no one found this brief anecdote amusing, Janus decided against elaborating. He had a whole routine on his mother's ability to burn assorted foods, but opted not to try to entertain the Cleavers with it.

At intervals through the meal, Mrs. Cleaver asked Faith and Janus if they cared for additional portions of each dish. Occasionally, she would simply hand a bowl of corn or greens or a basket of rolls to Janus and say, "Help yourself."

Nervously Janus would take a little more or would say, "No thank you, ma'am," or "Not just yet, but thank you very much," and pass the bowl or basket on to Faith, who set it back in the middle of the table without extending it toward her father.

Mr. Cleaver gobbled his food in silence. He finished well before the others and pushed his dishes to the center of the table. Rising from his chair with a quiet but unmuted belch, he went into the kitchen and returned with a bowl of ice cream and a jar of Karo syrup. With a large spoon, he ladled the syrup into his bowl as a topping. He licked the spoon and used it to eat his odd sundae in four large bites. Mrs. Cleaver seemed to watch him from under her eyebrows. She remarked to Janus that she'd very much like to read his father's book on communion rites in the first-century Christian church. Janus promised he'd send her a copy, a promise he forgot instantly. He wanted to exchange glances of amused wonderment with Faith, but he didn't dare it.

When he had scraped all the syrup from his bowl, Mr. Cleaver cleared a space on the table by sliding the bowl and syrup jar against his other dishes. He took a volume of World Book from the shelf behind his chair and spread it open in front of him. Without an introduction, he began reading aloud a passage on the Adriatic Sea. When he finished, he leaned back in his chair and said, as best Janus was able to tell, to the chandelier, "I was in Italy at the end of the war. We were down at the beach one day in Brindisi." He began to chortle. "Some Italian boys were out swimming beyond this roped off area they had there. You know the sort: long greasy black hair, like some of those motorcycle fellas you used to see a few years ago." He got up from the table. "Well, one of those guys' hair was so long it got in his face, and he drowned." Mr. Cleaver smacked his hands together and burst into a guffaw.

He started from the room, but Faith said, "Dad, is that supposed to be a comment on the length of Rich's hair?"

"Well, now, I don't know," he replied and began to cackle again. "It depends on whether or not your young man here ever goes swimming." He clapped his hands one more time and was gone.

After the Cleavers retired, Faith made drinks and brought them to Janus, who was sitting on the living room sofa. She sat next to him, kicked off her shoes and twisted her legs onto the couch. When Faith had finished about half her gin and tonic, she said, "Damn, I'm dying for a cigarette."

"Are you out?" Janus asked. "I could run get you some."

"No, I'm not out."

"Ah, your parents don't know you smoke," he said, laughing.

She punched him on the arm. "No, they don't. And don't you dare let it drop that I do."

"Never," he said, raising his hand palm outward. "I swear on all my favorite books." He took a sip of his Scotch and water.

"Besides, I'm going to quit."

"Right," Janus said. "When?"

"I don't know. When I get pregnant."

"Let's hope you keep on puffing away for some time then."

She punched him on the arm again. "I want a cigarette, and all you do is make jokes."

"Hey," he said, "tell your parents I smoked them. How are they to know?"

"Nah," Faith said. "Won't work. They know you're a basketball hero. If they thought you smoked, it would ruin your image. Then we'd have to listen to Dad make more comments about your hair."

Janus balled the hair on the back of his neck into his fist. He liked it long, felt more comfortable about his looks when the season was over and he could let it grow. Pondering the little he had seen of Faith's father that day, he laid a hand on her leg, which was naked in her short dress higher than mid-thigh. She squirmed seductively when he touched her. "Your father's kind of a weirdo, isn't he?"

"Sssh," Faith said.

"Oh, they can't hear me," Janus whispered. "I wasn't talking loud at all."

Faith shifted up onto her knees to face him. Slowly, she kissed his lips. "No," she said. "Don't talk about him. I don't want you to hurt my feelings." She kissed him again.

"Okay," Janus said. "I didn't mean any disrespect."

"Sssh now," Faith said. "I really need a cigarette. I've got an oral fixation." She smiled, and her tinted green eyes glinted in the silver street light that spilled into the room through the window behind the sofa. "You've got something that could help me. I've just got to suck on something." She giggled and started groping at the front of Janus's pants. She got his belt unbuckled and began to work the zipper down.

Janus took a swallow of his drink and set the glass on the lamp stand beside him. He put his arms around her and ran his hands down the thin nylon of her dress to the curve of her hips. "Have you been running around all evening without your underpants on?" he asked.

"Uh huh. I was supposed to tell you, though. To drive you crazy. But I didn't get a chance with you alone after I changed. I read it in a book." She began to claw at the elastic waistband on his jockey shorts.

Janus laughed and shook his head. "Well, since early this afternoon, as B.F. Johnson would say, you've had me as horny as a…."

"Hush that filthy talk," Faith interrupted. She kissed him again and slipped her hand inside his shorts.

"Hey," he gasped. "I don't think it's fair to fool around like this."

Faith was unsuccessfully trying to work Janus's pants down. "Who's fooling? I mean to gratify my oral fixation. Lift your butt up so I can get your pants off." She lifted his shirt and kissed his stomach just below the navel.

"Faith," Janus said in a croaky whisper. "We can't do this in here. They'll hear us."

"They're heavy sleepers," she said. She lifted his underwear and kissed the head of his penis. Janus raised himself up on his hands and let her pull his pants down around his knees. She pushed him down on the couch and arranged him lengthwise so that his head was propped up on the arm.

"You're not really gonna do this," Janus said. She licked at him, and he gasped again. "You know that when I come I bellow like an elephant."

Faith handed him a throw pillow from the other end of the sofa. "Put this over your face," she said as she knelt on the floor beside him.

That was the beginning of what Janus would remember for many years as the most sex-filled week of his life. Faith was as fearless as she was insatiable. She would enter his room with orange juice in the morning and fellate him while her mother made breakfast just down the hall. She would close the door to her room as if she were dressing and follow him into the shower. She would take him into the third story attic with the excuse of looking at her high school yearbooks and demand that they make love amid the jumble of her abandoned childhood possessions. The very idea of being in her parents' house seemed to turn her on.

It was during this first visit to Faith's parents' that Janus asserted to himself that his feeling for Faith had become love and that his love was unreserved. The entire week was wonderful. Faith and Janus climbed the tree in the back yard and played catch in the front. And while she couldn't really throw a curve ball, Faith proved herself remarkably agile, fielding gracefully, throwing with a fluid overhand motion that delivered a pitch hard and accurate. They played tennis and Faith exhibited the hand-eye coordination and the natural instincts that would one day turn her into a superb player. They went to films. And when they had sex, Janus no longer felt uneasy about declaring his love for her. He did love her, and it made him happy that he did. And it made him happy that Faith could tell and was so pleased.

It was semester break of his senior year when Janus went to St. Louis for a second visit. Faith had already been home for a week. Because of basketball practice, he had had to remain in a deserted Lancaster the last bleak week in January. He drove down on a Saturday morning and had to return the next day.

The trip was hurried but important. Faith wanted him present when she informed her parents that they had finally settled on a wedding date in mid-March instead of the expected time in June after graduation. Janus and Faith had announced their engagement to her parents in the late fall when Mr. and Mrs. Cleaver were in Chicago for a convention of family counsellors. Neither had shown surprise, and Mrs. Cleaver observed that they were wise to finish their educations before shouldering the responsibilities of marriage. Faith was nervous that the planned shift would not meet with her parents' approval.

When Janus arrived, frazzled from six hours of driving over snow-slicked highways, Faith greeted him at the door. She kissed him quickly, as if he had just come in from a day at the office, and followed him into the guest room, where he dumped the knapsack in which he had brought a change of clothes and his shaving kit. He embraced her, and as he touched his lips to her face, the memories of last spring's revelry came rushing back. Instantly, he was aroused. He squeezed her tight against him and kissed her hard on the mouth.

"Oh, I've missed you, babe," he said.

"I missed you, too." Janus started to kiss her again, but holding onto his arm, she pulled away and led him toward the door. "My parents are due home any minute. Let's not get caught in your bedroom."

"Okay by me," Janus said. "Let's go make out on the sofa and get caught in the living room."

But Faith led Janus into the kitchen where she asked him if he'd like something to drink. "How about an Irish coffee," he said. "A little nip to take the chill off."

"How about hot chocolate?" Faith said. "I'd really like you sober when we confront Mom and Dad."

Janus started to protest that he wasn't really likely to get tanked on one Irish coffee, but he could tell that Faith was edgy and said, "Hot chocolate will be fine."

Faith fixed the cocoa, and they sat at the kitchen table to drink it. Janus asked if she was still worried about her parents' reaction to their news. She said yes, that she didn't even want to bring the matter up. Janus offered to do it, and Faith seemed relieved that he was willing.

"Why should they care?" Janus argued. "We're getting married sooner, not putting it off or calling it off." Faith did not look comforted, so Janus began to tell her exaggerated tales about the thousand times he nearly died in auto accidents on the trip down. In the middle of these yarns Faith's parents came in, Mrs. Cleaver toting a bag of groceries, which, after a greeting and a kiss on Janus's cheek, she proceeded to unpack. Mr. Cleaver went under the sink for his Southern Comfort.

"Rich was just telling me about how bad the roads are between here and Lancaster," Faith said.

"I don't want you kids starting back tomorrow if things don't clear up," Mrs. Cleaver said.

"Maniacs," Mr. Cleaver said. He poured his drink, watered it and plunked in his ice cube. They all waited for him to elaborate.

Finally Faith said, "Is there any more to that observation?"

Her father took a drink and said, "Yep. Too many of 'em. They're all over the place. Just like these maniacs on college campuses. Can't see but one direction at a time."

Janus bristled inwardly. He wondered if Mr. Cleaver was trying deliberately to irritate him, but he made no response and tried to manifest no visible reaction. He knew better than to get into a discussion of student politics and the antiwar movement. These issues touched him too deeply to be certain of remaining dispassionate.

"We were taking about the weather, Dad," Faith said.

"So am I. Maniacs make it worse. When they ought to slow down, they speed up."

Mrs. Cleaver had unwrapped a ham and placed it on a cutting board. She shifted the board from the counter to the table, brought out a carving knife and began slicing. "We're so glad to have you with us again, Rich," she said without looking up from her work. She was very methodical, never hurrying, never ceasing. "We had hoped to have you here at Christmas, but I know you were traveling with your team. We'd really like to see more of you."

Janus decided to make the plunge. Faith had counselled him to wait until the "right moment" to reveal their change of plans, but to Janus the moment seemed as right as it was going to get. "Well actually, Mrs. Cleaver," he said, "Faith and I have some news which should result in your seeing me again sooner than you expect." Everything seemed suddenly to go still; the refrigerator seemed to stop churning, the wall clock to stop whirring. But Mrs. Cleaver's hand continued to saw back and forth, pulling the knife through the meat. "We've decided to move our wedding date from June to March." Now Mrs. Cleaver's hand stopped moving, though she continued to clutch the knife. Janus laughed. "You can keep on slicing the ham," he said, patting at her wrist. "We have good reasons."

Mr. Cleaver came over and stood by the table. Janus began to explain that he and Faith felt they should share the decision-making process that was facing them during the last months of school. "As I'm sure Faith has told you, I've got a very low draft number and must deal with Selective Service instantly upon graduation. In addition, I have to decide whether to go on to graduate school next fall or find work until the whole business with the draft is ultimately settled. The decision I make on these issues will obviously affect Faith, too. Where to go. What to do. I think it's only fair that she play a part in making these decisions."

Mr. Cleaver set his drink glass down on the table and looked at Janus over the top of his glasses. "What else is in the works here?" Faith got up from the table and began washing the hot chocolate cups.

Janus looked Mr. Cleaver square in the face. "I think I've explained it as best I can, sir. It's better for us this way. That's really all there is to it."

"No *other* reason, huh?" Mr. Cleaver said.

"I'm not pregnant, Dad," Faith said without turning around from the sink.

Janus continued to look at Faith's father, trying to extract with his stare some statement of blessing. Mrs. Cleaver got up from the table and busied herself rewrapping the ham.

Mr. Cleaver drained his drink and moved back to the counter to make a new one. Finally, he said, "Okay, I just hope you got money in the bank, Hank. I hope you got bread for the bed, Fred." He took a large swig of his whiskey and ambled to the kitchen door. Before walking out he said, "You gotta have grits for the bowl, Joel." He cackled and left the room.

"Some guy your father is," Janus said that night after the Cleavers had gone to bed. He was angry.

"Sssh," Faith said.

"I'm not talking loud, damn it. We come down here to explain something perfectly reasonable to him, and he responds with cryptic doggerel. What *is* all this 'money in the bank, Hank' B.S. anyway?"

"I don't know," Faith said. "He'll be all right once he gets adjusted to the idea. It *is* a change. And getting married before school is out *is* unusual. So he's suspicious. Just be patient."

Janus started to say something more about Faith's father, but instead he took a deep breath and blew air noisily up past his nose. He locked his fingers behind his head and squeezed with the heels of his hands at the back of his neck. "I've got it!" he said suddenly. "Let's kill the funk. Let's will it away. Let's have a beer. And then," Janus paused and leered at Faith, wagging his tongue across his lips, "let's have each other."

"Not tonight, Rich," Faith said quietly.

Janus was sure she could be wooed. "Hey, I haven't seen you for a week," he said. "Let's do it again like we did last summer, ba-yay-bee. Even if it was last spring. Tell me 'ssh' and raise the hairs on the backs of my arms."

Faith shook her head. She was looking away from Janus out toward the hall and the foot of the stairs. "Not here. Not now."

"How about the attic then? My room? The bathroom? The basement? Now that's a good idea. Wet and clammy."

"I don't want to run any risks now," Faith said as if Janus weren't there talking to her.

"Faith!" Janus said. "You're the girl who tried to transform my brains into cottage cheese in this house last year. Surely you remember. You weren't afraid of getting caught then."

Faith turned back to look at Janus. "Well, it's a lot more important not to get caught now. Don't you understand?"

No, he didn't understand. And he was hurt that Faith didn't want him. But he reasoned that she was upset by her father's behavior. Why that should dampen her usually torrid sexual fires, he didn't know, but he put his arm around her and kissed the top of her head. "Okay, party pooper.

Break my lustful heart." He had decided immediately to forgive her.

Janus felt ill. The stubborn Lancaster winter had retrenched instead of waning as March replaced February. The frigid temperatures outside had prevented him from opening a window, and the fumes from the paint and the thinner had given him a headache that was spreading down to his stomach. It was late, and he was tired.

"I've got to go home, Rich," Faith said.

"Just a minute," Janus said without looking at her. He was leaning out trying to put one more swipe on the wall before he got down to move his stepladder.

"I've got to go home *now*."

"I'll be finished with this wall in just a minute. If you want to go home any sooner, why don't you pick up a brush and help me?"

"There's no use in getting paint on my hands when I want to go home. And anyway, pretty soon, you'll just be trying to get me to stay all night. That's your usual procedure." Faith slung her purse onto her shoulder and moved to stand in the doorway.

"No, I won't," Janus said with a hint of irritation creeping into his voice. He got down from the ladder, moved it several feet, readjusted his paint bucket and climbed back up. "I just want to finish this wall; then I'll take you home." He dipped his brush and leaned out away from the ladder again. A blob of paint dripped and spattered on the floor. He had neglected to reposition his dropcloth. He cursed under his breath and hurried off the ladder to wipe at the one large spot and its countless satellites. As he was soaking a rag with thinner, he said to Faith without looking at her, "You could take more interest, you know. A week from now this place will be *your* home."

"How long is this going to take?" Faith sighed. "I'd really like to go."

"Fifteen minutes, maybe twenty." He looked up at Faith as he squatted to his work. She had propped herself against the doorjamb and folded her arms across her chest.

"You mean an hour," she said. "You always underestimate when it's to your advantage." Janus wiped without complete success at the spot on the floor. Resigned that he could remove no more of the spot, he got back up on the ladder again, dipped his brush and carefully wiped it. He had forgotten once more to move the dropcloth.

"Faith, move the cloth over under me, will you?" he said.

"No," Faith said. "I'm not an apprentice, and you're not a foreman. I'm tired of taking orders from you as if you were my boss. Give me your keys, and I'll drive myself home." She walked over to the ladder with her hand stuck out.

Janus continued his painting without acknowledging her. When he spoke, he struggled to make his voice sound controlled. "Then I wouldn't have a car, would I?"

"What do you need a car for? It's after eleven. I'll come over and pick you up in the morning. You *are* going to church with me like you promised, aren't you?"

He balanced his brush carefully across the lip of the paint can and turned on his ladder to face her. "Yes, I'm going to church with you like I promised, but I need the car tonight. I'm supposed to meet a couple of the guys at the Frank House when I'm finished painting this room."

"Have one of your sodden friends pick you up."

"Hey, don't put down my friends, how about it. You didn't like it when I made jokes about your sorority sisters, and I quit doing it." Janus looked back at the stretch of wall which remained unpainted. "If you'd let me work instead of arguing, I'd finish this, take you home and we could forget about the whole thing."

Janus began the clumsy process of turning himself back to his work, but Faith stopped him when she said, "Of course, your friends probably wouldn't want to come pick you up, because they're already too drunk."

"Damnit, Faith," Janus said. "I told you to lay off my friends. And while you're at it, lay off me, too. I'm doing this whole sorry business for you. You're the one who's too good to live in this place until it's painted. So I'm painting it. Do I have to be your chauffeur as well?"

"Don't you swear at me with your filthy mouth. Who do you think you are to swear at me?"

Janus looked at the ceiling. He breathed deeply, exhaled and said, "I wasn't swearing at *you*, Faith. I was just swearing. There really is a difference."

"And don't raise your voice to me, either."

"I didn't raise my voice."

"You were almost screaming," she said.

"I wasn't screaming," Janus responded with an amazed chuckle.

"*You* were screaming," Faith said through gritted teeth. Her face was so venomous that Janus briefly wondered how he could ever have found her attractive.

"I was not screaming!" he screamed. "*Now* I'm screaming. Now maybe you'll understand what screaming is like. And get this through your head: I'll fucking scream at you whenever you fucking bitch at me long enough."

Very quietly and with something like a smile on her lips, Faith said, "You disgust me. You're a maniac." She turned and started back toward the door.

"Where do you think you're going?" Janus said, coming quickly down the ladder.

"I'm walking home. To *my* home. This place will never be my home now. You've ruined it."

Janus felt all his fury drain out of him, replaced instantly by a sad resignation. The backs of his eyes ached. He felt tired in a way that was utterly unrelated to the healthy fatigue he felt at the end of a practice session or a close game. He quickly rubbed his hands with the turpentine cloth, closed the apartment door and followed Faith down the stairs. "Okay, Faith," he called out to her, "I'll take you home." Aloud, but only to himself, he said, "You win."

After a five-minute ride in tense silence, Janus pulled the black VW up in front of the dorm where Faith was a counsellor. He crossed his arms on the top of the steering wheel and rested his head against them. "Hey, Faith," he said, "let's...."

"No," Faith interjected, "I don't want to hear what you're going to say. You were going to apologize or something. It's too late for that. I'm not going through with it, Rich. I'm not going to marry you." She put her hand on the door handle and pulled it.

"Come on, Faith. Don't...."

"I mean it, Rich. Listen to me now. I mean it."

Janus turned his head and looked at her. She was still clutching the handle but had not yet shouldered the door open. A streetlight in front of them bathed one side of her face in light, leaving the other side dark.

"I mean it. I want you to believe that," Faith said.

Janus turned his head to stare out the windshield. "You're crazy," he said.

"You're the one who's crazy. But I'd *be* crazy if I married you."

Janus shook his head slowly side to side. He did not turn back to look at her. "You're crazy," he repeated.

"That's your response to everything. Call people names. Just like my old man. Anyone who doesn't agree with you is crazy. You think practically everyone in the world is crazy."

"Not true," Janus said. He turned to look at her again. "I think some people are bullshitters. Others, I think, are assholes."

If Faith almost smiled, she fought it off. "You think I'm not serious, but I am," she said after a moment.

"Oh come on, Faith," Janus said as he reached over and squeezed her knee. "Look, I'm sorry. It's late. I'm tired. I blew up, and I shouldn't have. But it's no big deal. Let's just forget it, okay?"

Faith grabbed Janus's arm at the wrist and put his hand back on the steering wheel. "*I am not going to marry you.* Get it?"

Janus smiled and lifted his eyebrows. "Not even if I admit to being an asshole?"

"Hey, listen to me," Faith said. She grabbed his head and turned it fully toward her, touching him only with her finger tips. She didn't scratch or even apply pressure, but Janus could feel the hard touch of her nails. "Listen to me. We are *not* getting married. Understand?"

Janus stared at her and did not try to free his head from her grasp. "Okay. I believe you. We're not getting married. Does that make you happy?" She dropped her hands, and he began shaking his head again. "Why aren't we getting married? This afternoon you loved me. We have a fight and I disgust you. So you're not going to marry me. Is that it?" He looked out the windshield again. At the front door of the dorm one of the freshman women was kissing her date good night. The boy slowly slid his hand down from the small of her back until he had it cupped under the curve of her ass. They seemed so young. "Your emotions are a little too goddamned mercurial for me," Janus said.

"Everything with you is a curse word. Can't you ever talk without cursing?"

"You and your prissy Puritanism. Your mouth isn't so clean either, you know."

"You're right," Faith said and began to cry. "It isn't anymore. But it was before I met you. Being *with* you, I'm getting to be *like* you. I don't even know who you are. Do I really? Soon I'm afraid I won't know who I am, either." Faith sniffled and brushed at the drops on her cheeks. "I'm getting lost in the shadow of your big toe."

Janus didn't respond. He was trying to grasp Faith's last remark, and he thought her tears signaled that the worst of the storm was past. He laid his hand gently on her leg again. But before he could speak, Faith screamed, "Don't touch me! You can't touch me anymore!"

Janus jerked his hand away and waited a while before saying calmly, "Faith, you're not serious about this. We're getting married in a week. The invitations are all sent out. The announcement has appeared in the papers."

"I'm not marrying you!" she screamed. She shook her whole body like a four-year-old in a tantrum.

Janus waited again. Finally, he said in a very soft voice, "You know how hurt your mother was when your sister jilted Paul. She was humiliated. You told me so yourself. You don't want to put her through all that again."

Faith laughed derisively. "I knew you'd resort to the guilt-trip approach, but I have to admit I didn't think you'd pull that out of your trick bag so soon. Well, it won't work!" She banged her fist against the window. "I have to think about me now, not my parents. I have to think about what I need and what I want." She balled both hands into fists. "And I neither need nor want to marry you. I have to be strong. I am not a bitch. I won't let you turn me into one." She quickly pushed the door open and fled.

Janus called after her as she ran inside, but she didn't answer.

Early the next morning, Janus called her to ask if she'd changed her mind.

"No," she said.

"Can I convince you to change your mind?"

"No."

"Have you told anyone yet?"

"No." Janus heard irritation in her voice.

"Why not?"

"I don't know. Who is there to tell?"

"Well, to start with there are your parents. And then there are my parents. And the people in the wedding and those who were planning to attend."

"Okay, okay," she said. "There are people to tell."

"Can I come over to talk to you?"

"I have to go to church."

"Church doesn't start for three hours. Why don't we go somewhere and have breakfast?"

"It won't do any good, Rich. You think because I haven't told anyone that I have second thoughts. I don't."

"I just want to talk to you, Faith."

"No, you want to talk me out of calling the wedding off."

"Doesn't that seem normal in my circumstances?"

"Well, I don't want you to talk me out of it. I'm doing the right thing."

"How can I get you to at least see me?"

"Promise not to try to change my mind?"

"I could promise to try not to try. That's the best I can do."

Faith and Janus talked in a corner booth at the House of Pancakes. Despite his promise, he urged her to go through with the wedding. When she refused to consider it, he argued that a subsequent divorce could hardly be worse, that it would at the least put off hurting people. "And who knows," he said, "it might even work out." He laid his hand outstretched on the table, wanting her to take it in hers, but she did not. "Your mother already has all the dresses made," he said. He gulped at a knot at the base of his throat that was choking him.

"You don't give a shit about my mother, you hypocrite. You're only worried about yourself. *You* don't want to be embarrassed. That's what this is really all about. Big man on campus doesn't want to be scorned by a dingbat sorority girl."

"Why are you doing this to me?" Janus said. "Surely nothing I've done to you merits this."

"I told you last night."

"Tell me again. I don't understand anything from last night. And I want to understand. I need to understand."

"Why? You're just going to hate me. You're already preparing yourself for it. No one bests Richard Janus and gets away with it." Janus tried to remember where he had established this reputation for vindictiveness. "Pretty soon you'll be telling all your friends what an asshole I am. And they'll believe it, have no fear," Faith snorted.

Janus's voice broke. He gave up trying to hold back tears. "I love you," he said. "You've said you love me. Why are you being so cruel? What in the world have I done? Tell me, and I'll fix it."

Faith finally took his hand. She turned it over and began to stroke it. "You can't fix it, Rich. Don't you see? You always think you can fix things up, but you can't do it this time."

"I could try," he said.

Faith shook her head but continued stroking his hand. "Why should you change for me, Rich? You're fine the way you are. I…I just don't love you."

"How could you love me yesterday but not today?"

Faith withdrew her hand, fumbled in her purse and found a cigarette. "I didn't love you yesterday. Or ever."

"Why ever did you tell me that you did? Why did you let us come to the brink of marriage?"

She lit the cigarette and took a deep puff. "I did *think* that I loved you, but I saw last night that I was mistaken. We're too different." Faith paused as if expecting some response. When Janus made none, she said, "I'm terribly attracted to you, Richie. I think you're smart. I think you're handsome. And very sexy. More than that, I think you're a good person."

"Don't I sound like a good catch?" Janus said.

"Yes, but I also think you're tough in a way that scares me. You're so damn loyal that if you ever figured out I wasn't the right woman for you, you wouldn't do anything about it. Today you want to marry me. And if I don't do it, you'll be hurt. But you'll see the uselessness of the hurting, and you'll will it away. You're just that strong. But if we got married, the hurting would be different and would last a lot longer."

Janus had stopped listening to her. When she finished speaking, he wiped at his cheeks with the back of each hand and said, "But what have I *done*, babe? I didn't mean it. I won't do it anymore. I promise. I'll change, you'll see." Faith sucked on her cigarette. "I don't even know what this is all about. I yelled at you. I won't yell at you ever again. I curse too much. I agree that's a bad habit. I ought to stop. So I will, not even for you, but for me. People *can* change, Faith. I already have in some ways. I used to get pissed when you'd fall asleep. Remember? That doesn't even bother me anymore."

Faith blew twin streams of smoke out of her nostrils. "I can't help it that I fall asleep. I've got narcolepsy. Why do you always bring that up?"

"Faith, you don't have narcolepsy. The doctor only.... Anyway, that's beside.... Look. People can't change their parents or the places they were born. But they can change the way they act. And I'm especially uptight now. The damned draft. I don't even know where I'm going to be after June. Canada? Jail? That's why we decided to get married now instead of waiting. Maybe I'm a little screwed up now, but I won't always be."

Janus reached out to take Faith's cigarette. "You don't need this," she said. He shrugged his compliance, and she stubbed it out.

"After I went home last night, I finished painting the apartment. You'll like it. A week from now, we won't even remember this, huh?"

"I wish I believed that, Richie. I tried to think that things would work out, but I discovered that I really don't."

Janus took her hand, and she let him fold it into both of his. "If you really want them to, they will. Marriages have to be worked at, you know."

"You got that notion from your father. Look what happened to his marriage. You *shouldn't* have to work at marriage. You shouldn't have to *try* to get along. You should just get along."

Janus released her hand, leaned back in his seat and ran both hands through his hair. The hard, dried paint at the base of his fingers scratched against his forehead. "Come on, babe. Don't throw my parents' divorce at me. You shouldn't try to hurt me like that. Maybe my parents just didn't work hard enough at their marriage."

Faith leaned across the table toward him. "Listen to me, Rich. Marriages ought to *work*. You shouldn't have to work *at* them. Why won't you accept that? And why do you want to go through with a marriage that you think from the outset will require working at?"

"Because I love you," Janus said. He picked up a package he had secreted on the floor under the table and placed it between them. "See, I'm working at our marriage already. Even though we're not married yet. You know how you complained once that I'm not as thoughtful of you as your other boyfriends? I'm going to be from now on." He took a small item from the bag and handed it to Faith. "You mentioned you needed a new pen." He took another item from the bag. "And I know you could use this nifty new purse. But mostly I wanted to buy you this." He took a dark floppy hat from the bag. "It's a witch hat. Not a bitch hat. You take this hat, and when I'm mad at you, I'll call you a witch and make you put your hat on."

Faith covered her face with her hands. Janus got out of his side of the booth. He put the hat on her head and moved to sit beside her.

7

I've been writing this note for days, but I don't think I'm getting it all right.

Rereading what I've written so far, I realize, for instance, that in the fifth grade we did things other than square dance over broken shuffleboard courts and call Karen Mert "Booga." We also collected baseball cards and played marbles for keeps, which my father would not allow.

Collecting baseball cards was a marvelous pastime which made me feel guilty. I'm not even certain how I got all the baseball cards I ultimately owned, but at the time it seemed that the cards reproduced themselves biologically. I certainly didn't buy the boxes of well-organized cards I kept stored under my bed. I wouldn't have had enough money even if my father had regularly paid me my fifty cents allowance. And when, after falling several weeks into arrears, he would finally bestow a small fortune on me, I did not immediately convert my windfall into baseball cards. Rather, I promptly placed it in a small manila envelope to be held for deposit in my school savings account, which was collected in a large manila envelope every Wednesday. The school savings plan was a promotion of a local bank in cooperation with the public school system. Its goal was to teach New Orleans's youth the benefits of a regular program of federally insured savings. As in every learning situation, I strove to be a standout. Just as I led my class in books read, words spelled, and A's made, I wanted to lead in money saved. Saving was further polish for my badge of maturity.

Hence, I rather liked my father's habit of not paying me my allowance weekly. It facilitated the growth of my fifty cents pittances into sums of several dollars without my having to handle the money. And since I am constitutionally conservative with large sums of money, his habit removed any temptation that might have arisen for me to spend my allowance on such trifles as baseball cards.

Today I treat the Internal Revenue Service much like I used to treat my father. I never claim the exemptions to which I am entitled, and every May I receive a large refund check from the federal government. A friend has pointed out the idiocy of this habit, that in effect I allow the government to hold my money for a year without paying me interest, but my friend just does not understand the peace of mind I derive from not being tempted to dribble this extra money away. I have, for example, not purchased a baseball card in years.

When I get my government refund check every May, I promptly place it in a small manila envelope to be deposited in my savings account. Hibernia National Bank and the New Orleans public school system would be proud. Unfortunately, I am no longer on the school savings plan. Since I began actively not writing my doctoral dissertation, I don't go to school anymore. Not writing my doctoral dissertation makes me afraid that the life I must lead as a result soon will require that I *spend* the money in my savings account. I have an idea that watching my account dwindle will be less fun than watching it grow.

My father never much liked the idea of my collecting baseball cards in the first place. He considered it an extravagance which the income level in our family could ill afford. This wasn't really true, but my father had grown up during the Depression and liked to tell people that when he was a kid, extravagance was an extra corn cob in the outhouse. My father could be disgusting sometimes.

Once he came into my room and found me sitting on the floor surrounded by piles of baseball cards. "Are all these yours?" he asked. When I nodded affirmatively, he added, "How in the world can you have all these baseball cards when you put all your money in your school savings account?"

"They come free," I said.

"What do you mean they come free?" He looked at me sharply. "Don't be impertinent. Nothing in life is free." And I've learned he was right, of course, since I've not been able to get a Ph.D. without writing a dissertation.

"They *are* free," I insisted impertinently. "They come free in packages of bubble gum."

"Oh," my father said, not having really listened and already thinking again about whatever new piece of Biblical scholarship he was involved in. I made a note never to let him have a glimpse of my entire collection again for fear that next time his interrogation might not be so easily satisfied.

I need not have bothered. At dinner that night, as if there hadn't been a two-hour interval, as if he had just begun his questioning, he said, "But where do you get the money for all the bubble gum?"

"What bubble gum?" I said. My father's temples, which bulged on either side when he chewed, froze in the puffed position. He hated it when I acted cute. "Oh, you mean the bubble gum that comes with…I mean the bubble gum that you get baseball cards with."

"Precisely," my father said and began chewing again.

"I don't buy so much," I said.

"Then how do you have so many baseball cards?"

"Well, I don't know. I guess I do have pretty many, huh. You see, at school we kind of trade them back and forth. I gave up five players for Duke Snider and Billy Buck gave me twenty for Mickey Mantle."

My father studied the pieces of bland meat and scorched lima beans on his plate. He moved the food from place to place on the dish. Finally, he said, "I suppose there's nothing wrong then."

But deep in his heart, my father believed that there *was* something sinister about the practice of trading baseball cards. He was disturbed that his son was learning the evils of capitalism by parlaying a few baseball cards, procured free in mysteriously purchased packages of bubble gum, into a sizable collection. Unlike Max Weber, Billy Graham and most of America's political leaders, my father did not regard Jesus as a disciple of Adam Smith. Though he by no means would have donned the label, my father was something of a Christian socialist.

After stirring his food a moment more, he finally speared a piece of gray sirloin and brought it halfway to his mouth before he stopped and said, "But I don't want you taking advantage of your friends. Just because you can get twenty cards for one your friend wants badly doesn't mean you should. You're a lot smarter than the other boys, and that imposes upon you the responsibility to look out for their interests as well as your own. Do you understand?"

I understood that parents could be truly incredible sometimes.

And I also understood that I was not quite the capitalist piglet that my father suspected I was. Most of the cards in my collection had been gathered not by skillful trading, but by skillful gambling. Like pitching pennies, in someone's hushed room or in a deserted school yard, we would squat and spin our cards several feet toward a wall. The kid who managed to stand his card highest against the wall kept all the other cards in the contest. A master of this game, I was something significantly worse than the ruthless trader my father thought. I was a baseball card shark.

Often when my parents punished me by confining me to my room, I practiced spinning cards up against the wall, practiced until I could stand them up straight, so high the bottom of the card was nearly flush. My parents were frustrated that I entertained myself so successfully during my incarceration. They even considered confiscating my baseball cards to insure my confinement would produce a larger dose of misery. But they knew that my room was too full of potential sources of amusement for this plan to work. Had they taken my baseball cards, I'd still have had my marbles.

In fact, I played with my marbles while being punished almost as often as I played with my baseball cards. I didn't play marbles, of course. It's no fun playing marbles by yourself. And you can't control where they'll roll on a hardwood floor. Pretty soon most of them end up under the bed. So I took the surviving members of my toy soldiers, preserved expressly for this purpose, and the players from both teams of my electric football set and lined them up under my desk. Then I shot them down with my marbles. This game was passably fun and had the additional advantage of creating rolling and wall-banging noises to irritate my parents.

Undoubtedly my father disliked my marbles for this reason alone, but he had a more deep-seated reason too: as a child he had lost all his marbles. Furthermore, as a Biblical scholar, he had scruples against playing for keeps.

Noticing the ample bulge in his old sock which served as my marble bag, he asked me to come into his study one night. When I followed him in, he closed the door and sat in his chair and pressed the tips of his fingers together. He stared over his desk lamp at the wall behind it. "Son, I notice your marble collection is growing."

"Yes, sir," I said.

"Have you been playing for keeps?"

Actually I had been playing "keepsies." "Well," I said. My father let his fingers mesh and dropped his hands into his lap. He looked at me for the first time. "Yes, sir," I said.

"I thought we had agreed when I bought you the marbles that you wouldn't play for keeps."

"We say keepsies."

"Keepsies, then," my father said without distaste. "But did we agree or not?"

We had agreed. The evening my father brought the marbles home. It was the same evening he tried to teach me how to play.

"I already know how to play," I had replied to his offer of instruction.

"Well, you can let your old dad show you something, now can't you? If you already know how to play, that's fine. But maybe I can show you a trick or two that will make you better. How's that?" As always, he was gentle and patient.

In a grassless place in the back yard that was normally home plate, my father drew a circle in the dust with his finger and placed all but two of the marbles inside. The kids in the neighborhood never did that. All they ever did was shoot their marbles at their opponents' marbles. Whatever they hit, they kept.

"The object of the game," my father explained, "is to knock all the marbles out of the ring without letting your shooter go out. When you fail to knock a marble out, or when your shooter does go out, then your turn is over. It's simple. Got it?" I nodded. "Okay, let's play a game then. You go first."

I squatted in the ebbing light, picked up my shooter and rolled it adroitly between my fingers, positioning it to shoot between the tip of my index finger and the knuckle of my thumb.

My father grabbed my hand. "Here now. That's not right," he said. "Let me show you how to shoot. Look here." He cupped the marble inside the knuckle of his index finger, holding his hand near my face for me to see. Then he lowered his hand and pushed the marble away with a thrust of his thumbnail. My father was a cunny-thumber.

"I like to shoot this way," I said. I aimed and shot, knocking a marble out of the ring, leaving my shooter in perfect position.

"Pretty good," my father said, "but in the long run you'd be more accurate my way." He was wrong, of course. And it was no wonder he had lost all his marbles as a kid. That evening, just ahead of darkness, I won the only two games we ever played.

When we had finished playing, my father helped me pick up the marbles. And when we stood, he rolled those he had gathered into my hand and put his arm around my shoulders. "You're a good one, son," he said. "Not like your old dad."

And he was right, of course. I'm not like him. He finished a dissertation and became a college professor. I never will.

"I guess we agreed," I said to his interrogation now. "But I win lots more than I lose. Look how many I have." I held up the black sock to show him that it was bursting with ten times the number of marbles he had originally bought me.

"Have a seat over there, Richie. I want to have a serious talk with you." He motioned me toward his battered, wing-back reading chair. When I was seated, he turned his chair so that he was facing me. He bent forward, resting his elbows on his knees. His hands were flat together, pointing at the floor. "The extra marbles in that sock once belonged to someone else." He took a deep breath. "Let me tell you a story about a young boy during the Depression whose father gave him six nice marbles like you have there." I shifted the sock to a position between my legs, and my father seemed to study it for a moment. "Whose sock is that, anyway?" He suddenly sat back in his chair.

"It was yours, sir. Mother said I could have it. Lots of guys have real marble bags, but I think this sock is just as good." I hoped to impress him with the humbleness of my needs in life.

But he called out to my mother, who was taking a bath, "Honey, did you give Richie my sock for a marble bag?" For all of his willed generosity, my father's fundamental instincts were conservative. He did not want to see socks become marble bags until he was fully satisfied that their usefulness as socks had been exhausted.

We could hear my mother sloshing around in the tub. She was happiest, I think, when she was bathing, and she was not to be riled by the rancor which registered in my father's voice. She reported that the sock was old and mateless and of more use as a marble bag than as a dust collector in my father's dresser drawer.

He twisted half away from me, and I thought for an instant that he was going to begin his speech on the mysterious disappearance of his possessions, a speech that sometimes ended with my mother in tears after he accused her of slipshod homemaking and pointed out that *his* mother had probably never lost a sock mate in her entire life, because if she had, her husband and children would have had to go barefoot.

But this time my father resisted the impulse to lecture my mother so that he could continue the parable he had begun to me. "Anyway," he said, twisting back to face me, "this young boy had only five or six glass marbles that his aunt had given him. He didn't have very many, but they were the prettiest marbles in the whole neighborhood. All the other boys owned only rolled clay marbles they had baked themselves in a skillet over the fireplace. This was during the Depression. Do you know what the Depression was?"

I nodded. The Depression was my state of mind after he told me stories about his childhood.

"Well, during the Depression," he continued, "to own five glass marbles was really something. I took them to school the day after I got them. I was only in the third grade. This sixth grader came up who wanted to play. He won, of course, because he was older. Then he took all my marbles, claiming that we had been playing for keeps. That young boy, son, was your old dad. I had those nice glass marbles for only one day. Now, do you understand?"

I understood that my father was a cunny-thumber, too unskilled to keep from losing all his marbles. And I was suspicious that this was just another of my father's fishy stories designed to get me to abide by his prejudice against playing for keeps.

So I continued playing keepsies until my marble collection spilled out of my father's sock and into the Roy Rogers lunch box that I had kept stored under my bed since the time that all the other fifth graders began taking their lunches to school in brown paper bags. I continued until the day I played keepsies with a third grader who began to cry when he lost all his marbles and wouldn't take them when I tried to give them back.

Marbles wasn't much fun after that.

Recently I realized that the lunch box full of marbles, like the toy soldiers and electric football players and the desk under which I played with them, has disappeared. I have no notion where they've gone.

Fifth grade began for me a year after the Russians knocked out the Eisenhower quiescence by launching Sputnik. My grammar school officials counter-punched by staging a First Annual Science Fair. They wanted to provide stimulation for any of us who might secretly have been Wernher von Braun. Every kid in school was required to design a project for the fair, and every teacher in school decided to base the term's science grade on the quality of the project. This was a neat ploy which eliminated the need for them to teach us any science.

Even as a kid I hated science, and I had immense difficulty arriving at an idea for the fair. But with the project deadline approaching, I decided to build an electromagnet. I got this idea while watching Mr. Wizard on television one Sunday morning when I was sick and therefore not in church. Coincidentally, Mr. Wizard happened to construct an electromagnet on his program that day. Why, you ask, was a science-hating kid watching a science show? Because not much appears on Sunday morning TV except for church programs, which were of even less interest to me as a kid than science. I should have gotten sick enough to have missed the entire science fair, but as a fifth grader I didn't have my sickness under control.

So instead, I constructed a wizardly electromagnet by wrapping a large nail with the center section of a piece of wire from which the insulation had been stripped. The ends of the wire were connected to an electric switch which in turn was wired to a dry cell battery. When the switch was thrown on, presto, the nail became an electromagnet and could be used to pick up any number of smaller nails I had wisely provided for that express purpose. My science project undoubtedly dispelled any notions my teachers might have harbored that I was the Wernher von Braun for whom they were searching. On the other hand, the project should have been adequate to earn me my usual A in science.

But it wasn't. I was the victim of scientific plagiarism. My friend Stevie Essel stole my idea for building an electromagnet. Granted, I stole the idea from Mr. Wizard, but Mr. Wizard was not in our fifth-grade class.

Standing alone, my electromagnet might have looked simple but perhaps also direct and efficient, or even elegant. But beside the one Stevie Essel built, mine looked primitive and hasty. He built his with his erector set, an expensive toy which my parents never gave me largely because I never wanted one. Stevie Essel's electromagnet was fastened to the end of a nifty crane, which was positioned in the midst of a miniature city. And his electromagnet picked up toy cars instead of small nails.

When Stevie Essel got my A in science that term, it occurred to me to beat him up for his treachery. But even as a kid I knew that violence was wrong. I decided instead to humiliate him in geography. And I annihilated him with a hundred percent on my state capitals test, despite misspelling Bismarck, which I mistakenly thought was spelled Bismarc*h*.

I got a hundred percent because even as a kid I had poor penmanship. It was probably the best talent I had for becoming a doctor. Poor penmanship was my ally on the state capitals test. There was no question in my teacher's mind that her most mature pupil knew how to spell Bismarck. So when she saw the scrawl next to North Dakota beginning with a B, she counted the answer correct. With a guilty conscience, I informed her of the error. She showed me the test. I could tell no better than she if the final letter was an *h* or a *k*. So with noticeable indifference, she let my perfect grade stand. Stevie Essel was vanquished, and my teacher even praised my integrity for bringing the matter to her attention. For some people, it's just hard to get behind.

I learned two lessons from that experience. First I learned that few people deeply care how you spell the capital of North Dakota. The utility of this lesson I demonstrated years later when my friend Johnnie Golden covered North Dakota politics for the Associated Press. I repeatedly wrote to him in Bismarc*h*. He never complained of failing to receive my letters.

The more important second lesson I learned was that appearances often are more important than realities. Ernest Chiron once said that there is no such thing as genius, only hard work, good luck and reputation. I might add that the greatest of these is reputation. I applied this lesson throughout the rest of my schooling. Whenever I found myself ill-prepared for an in-class exam, I deliberately wrote illegibly but at great length. My teachers always graded my work A.

Now if only I could submit my doctoral thesis longhand.

Fifth grade was also the year I met Carter Percy. That's when he and his family moved into my Gentilly neighborhood. I was too skinny, and he was too fat, and his name was Fred. And we did not become best friends right away.

Carter Percy's full name was Fred Carter Percy IV. Even as a kid, I envied his numerals. On the first day of school, our teacher called him Fred, so we all followed suit. Except for B.F. Johnson, who initially called him Fats. No one thought to ask what name he wanted to be called, and he was far too shy to correct either the teacher or any of the rest of us. Already he was the strong silent type.

Carter would ultimately teach me so much about friendship that I was grateful he never learned that I first regarded him as a rival. Friendship, Carter demonstrated, was not a situation; it was a definition. A devastating blocker, he was an All-City tackle for Thomas Jefferson High School even as a sophomore. At my new school, I was a third-string quarterback who didn't play enough even to letter. But Carter never let me forget that I was his best friend. During basketball season, though it cost him friends at his own school, he became my team's most enthusiastic fan. He mourned the loss of our high school years together and was vociferously adamant that at T.J. I would have been a football starter. He was wrong, of course, but he was loyal, and I loved him.

It is embarrassing to remember that when he first moved to town I wished him ill. Or, more precisely, I wished him defeat. By the end of the first couple of months of fifth grade, Carter was our class's leading math student. He had the most stars beside his name on the math chart. We had timed arithmetic tests every morning. Something like two minutes to solve ten to fifteen multiplication or division problems. If you finished under the time limit and if you solved all the problems correctly, you were entitled to a star beside your name on the big MATH chart which hung on the cork board in the front of the room.

Today's teachers have progressed beyond the status-anxious techniques of the 1950's, which did such things as award stars for excellence. Relying on the principles of behavior modification instead, they award Snickers, Hershey bars or malted milk balls. Perhaps adults of the 1990's will be obese instead of neurotic. At any rate, I was accustomed in such contests to emerging first. So I found Carter's lead in this one bothersome. Bothersome enough that I shamefully appealed for help to higher powers. I prayed.

But prayer in this situation could not be straightforward. One did not pray for another's misfortune. I knew better than to ask God to visit Fred Percy with a case of the dumbs, so I only requested that all my papers be perfect. I was certain that Fred Percy couldn't do perfect work all the time and that if I did, I would overcome his lead. Whatever sort of god would pay heed to such a frivolous request, some god granted it.

I have since been concerned that gods grant men only so many wishes in their lives, and that I wasted one of mine on a fifth-grade math contest.

Perhaps because of our math rivalry, Carter Percy did not immediately replace Billy Buck as my best friend. Billy Buck was another emblem of my maturity. He was two years older than I, in a neighborhood large enough and rife enough with Baby Boom youngsters for most best friends to be chosen from among classmates. But I chose Billy Buck, two years my senior. Or better, I allowed Billy Buck to choose me.

Billy Buck was a nice, quiet kid who should have become a painter when he grew up but became a doctor instead. Even as a kid he hated science. And even while he was my best friend, he hated me. This last fact I only partially understood at the time.

Billy Buck and I were such good friends that we always sat in church together every Sunday morning. Because we were well-behaved (mature) young men, our parents allowed us to sit apart from them. Like the congregation's adults, we had our regular pew in which no one else ever sat. Ours was the second, right behind the deacons' pew. I envied Billy Buck more than he ever knew. I envied his longish black hair which his mother never made him get cut into a flattop and on which his mother let him put some gluelike substance which made it shine like record album plastic. I also envied the fact that his mother let him wear white socks with his loafers. My mother wouldn't even let me wear the loafers.

"Billy Buck gets to wear loafers," I would point out to my mother when begging her to buy me a pair.

"And so does your Uncle Bob," my mother would retort. This was a winning argument. Uncle Bob was the black sheep of my father's family. All Dad's other siblings were self-made persons, rising to solid middle-class respectability despite their impoverished rural roots. But Uncle Bob had turned down a scholarship to Louisiana Tech in favor of marrying his childhood sweetheart and getting right away into lifelong indolence. He quickly sired several thousand ragamuffin little cousins of mine and began to collect welfare checks. Sometimes he worked in a gas station. Mostly he didn't. When I did anything my parents wanted to humiliate me for, they compared my action with some similar one of Uncle Bob's. If Uncle Bob wore loafers, the options left to me were tie shoes, sandals and barefoot.

White socks were another matter. Uncle Bob didn't wear them, so I could not be precluded from wearing them on those grounds. My mother's was not, however, a single weapon arsenal. When I argued that, "Billy Buck wears white socks. His mother even lets him wear them to church," she fired her marine analogy at me.

"And if Billy Buck's mother let him go jump in Lake Pontchartrain, would you want to do that, too?" When I shook my head trying to grasp her point, she continued. "Billy Buck's mother knows about as much about fashion as I know about fishin'. Or fission," she added. "Or fusion, for that matter."

My mom could get carried away sometimes.

But for all his white socks and nifty plastic hair, I mostly envied Billy Buck's ability to draw. As we would sit in our pew every Sunday, not required to be stirred by the preacher's dreary and droning observations about the wages of sin, but only to be quiet, Billy would sketch, first trains and cars, later people. He had genuine talent, and by the time he reached high school, he was one of the city's most promising young artists.

But something in Billy made him undervalue this skill. I was awed by it, but he was never pleased when I complimented him. "It's easy," he would always shrug. What wasn't easy for Billy Buck was what he wanted most: being a better athlete than Richie Janus. He figured this was not an unreasonable desire in a just universe. He was bigger and stronger, and he was two years older.

Billy Buck and I were always captains in our neighborhood games of football and baseball. But no matter how we chose sides, my teams always won. He fumed and bullied his teammates in trying to spur them to victory. He screamed and he schemed. He smashed his baseball glove to the ground and punted the football over the fence and into the next yard in his fury. And always his side lost. Which drove Billy Buck crazy. And made him hate his own best friend.

He was no more successful at individual athletics than he was at team sports. Whether we pitched horseshoes or played ping-pong or shot baskets, the result was always the same. Sometimes Billy Buck would get ahead, but he never won. With a lead, he could never make the shots it took to win. When behind, I could never miss the shots it took to lose.

But Billy Buck was nothing if not persistent. He had hope and placed it in tennis. He had his older brother teach him the game on the sly, and when he had learned, he invited me to play with him. He borrowed his brother's rackets and a can of balls, and we rode the bus to City Park. I remember particularly Billy's cheery mood on the way. He took one of the tennis balls from the can and bounced it repeatedly on the floorboard until the driver made him stop.

When we got to the courts, Billy patiently showed me how to grip the racket and how to keep my arm out when hitting the ball. He carefully explained the game's baroque scoring rules. He showed only one snideful moment of joy as he took the first three games. His confidence began to ebb, however, when he dropped the next three games. And his boiling sullenness began to show when he lost the set 4-6. His fury became rage at love-4 of the second set after he blew a 40-love lead and double-faulted at add-out.

Carrying the three balls and the racket under his arm, Billy strode briskly from the court without speaking to me. He marched past the clubhouse and across the street with me trailing slowly behind him. Standing in the high weeds on the bank, he deliberately pounded all three balls into the green algae slime of City Park Lagoon. We both knew that it was my face, not tennis balls, that he really wanted to smash. As the last of the concentric ripples began to fade from the water, Billy turned and smiled at me as I approached him, shaking my head. It was an eerie and dangerous smile. Then he turned back to the pond and sailed the tennis racket, backhand, as if it were a frisbee, out and down into the center of the lagoon.

We didn't talk on the bus ride home, though to himself, through heavy sighs, Billy muttered over and over, "It's no use. It's just no use. It's no use."

And he was right, of course. Billy Buck was snake-bitten. What neither of us then understood, however, was that I was not the snake. And that victory anesthetized the certain fact that I was bitten, too.

8

1971

By the time Richard Janus emerged from the rear entrance of the gymnasium, darkness hung on the St. Louis winter like a shroud. It seemed to drape from the edges of buildings and sag into the gaps between light poles. Janus zipped up his down jacket and smoothed his wet hair inside the hood. He tied the hood snugly under his chin, strapped his briefcase onto the rear of the motorcycle and pulled on his visored helmet.

Blowing a sigh over his face, Janus straddled his bike and cautiously edged it into the homebound traffic. He had come to hate the motorcycle. The euphoric sense of daring he had felt when he bought it had long ago disappeared. Notions about the joy of carefree, wind-in-the-face cruising had evanesced in the reality of freezing, exhaust-sucking rides to work and back on a daily basis. In addition, he had fallen twice on rain-slicked streets, and though he had escaped unhurt both times, he now was terrified whenever he climbed aboard. But his daily terror was unavoidable. Faith needed the Volkswagen to get to the classes she was taking for her teaching credential and out to the school where she practice taught. And they couldn't afford a second car.

When Janus reached the old brown brick apartment complex on Skinker near Forest Park, the fronts of his thighs had gone numb from the stinging wind, and he had only tingling sensations in the little fingers on each hand. He worried about frostbite. Wasn't it enough that maniacs tried to run him off the road? Did he have to get frostbite, too? There was a saving feature, he laughed to himself: if frostbite resulted in the amputation of most any of his parts, he'd at least be saved ever having to ride the goddamned motorcycle again.

Janus chained the bike to a telephone pole in the alley behind the apartments and made his way through the basement and up the stairs. Faith was sitting on the ugly naugahyde sofa in their living room reading her educational psychology text. "Hi, honey," he said as he dumped his briefcase and helmet and went into the kitchen.

He came back with a can of beer and slumped into the faded wing-back chair which once had resided in his father's study. He cracked the beer open and took a large swallow with his eyes closed, then held the can for a moment against the center of his forehead. Resting the can in one hand on his knee, he laid his head against the chair back. Then he belched and looked over, somewhat sheepishly, at Faith. "Ah, the good life," he said. "Where's me paper and slippers, Mother, and me good faithful dog, Spot?"

Faith did not look up from her book, so Janus closed his eyes and settled back in the chair again. Finally, she said, "Do you have to open a beer first thing when you get home?"

"I didn't open it *first* thing," Janus said. "I opened it *second* thing. First, I took off my coat and gloves and ran warm water over my hands. I'm very clean, you know." He raised his eyebrows and smiled.

Faith peered at her husband over the top of her glasses. Her lower lip seemed to stretch as she shifted her jaw slightly to the left. "If you're thirsty, why don't you drink a Coke? Drinking beer like that is a bad habit."

"I'm not so much thirsty as tired."

"Then you really shouldn't drink beer. Alcohol is…."

"Aw, come on, Faith, millions of people come home from work and open a can of beer. Why can't I?"

"Millions of people are alcoholics." Faith closed the textbook on top of one finger to mark the place and adjusted her glasses higher on her nose.

"For Christ's sake, I'm not an alcoholic."

She pursed her lips and moved her head up and down. "You're developing the habits of one, buddy."

"Jesus." Janus shook his head and closed his eyes. He slid down in the chair, opened his eyes and stared at the ceiling, and shook his head again. He took a sip of the beer, but it didn't cool the boil of anger he felt rising inside. "You know, I leave for work at seven o'clock in the morning. I teach all day. I ass kiss the principal so he won't fire me for being a dirty hippie. By the time I get done with practice, it's long since dark, and by the time I've scared myself silly on that death machine I have to ride home, I'm exhausted. I'm worried sick about the goddamned draft and where we're going to get your next tuition payment. You'd think I could peacefully drink a beer when I get home without having to endure a hassle from you. Why do you feel the need to pick on me?"

Faith reopened her book and spread the pages smooth with the flats of each hand. She looked at the book, but under her breath she muttered, easily loud enough for Janus to hear, "Goddamned this, goddamned that. Christ, Christ, Christ, *Christ!*" she exploded, slamming the book shut. "Why can't you learn to stop swearing?"

Janus let out a long breath and slowly stood up from his chair. He went back into the tiny kitchen with its half-size stove and rusting metal cabinets and poured the remainder of his beer into the sink. When he returned to the living room, he said, "Hey, Faith. You're sick, you know. As if the world isn't full enough of trouble, you have to create trouble where it doesn't exist."

Faith got up and went to the scarred dining room table on which her school materials were scattered and began to pack the large cloth purse she used as a book satchel. Her back was to Janus, but he could tell she was crying.

He started to move across the room toward her. "Honey," he said.

"Don't," Faith said. "Don't start being nice to me."

"Why?" Janus asked with a small, breathy laugh.

"Because," she said, turning to face him, "I hate you."

Janus stopped dead still. He felt as if he'd been struck. He felt himself twitch and dimly recognized that the involuntary motion could have been the beginning of a real one, a raised hand to strike back.

"Dig it, Janus. I hate you. You make me marry you, and you've done nothing but make me miserable ever since." Tears began to rush down Faith's cheeks again. "God, I hate you. You tell me I'm sick. You're the one who's sick. You ought to get help."

He returned to his chair in the living room and watched Faith busy herself at the table. He was surprised at the immediate absence of his anger. He was tired. He didn't want to squabble. "What is this all about?" he called over to her. "What are we fighting about now? I never quite seem to know."

"Shut up. I'm not talking to you."

"You just talked," Janus pointed out.

"I said shut up."

Janus slammed his hand down on the chair so hard that Faith jumped. "No, I won't shut up." He got up and began to move back toward his wife. Faith, as if fleeing, moved around to the far side of the table. Janus put both hands flat on the plastic tablecloth and leaned across the table toward her. "You piss me off, Faith. You piss me off so bad I can't believe it. You're nuts, you know. Totally, inconceivably, irredeemably nuts."

"Garbage mouth," Faith said.

"You know what's wrong with you, Faith? You're a prude. A pusillanimous Puritan pussy." The words burst from Janus's mouth as if authored by someone else, and he smiled suddenly at the unwilled alliteration. In a soft, laughing voice, he said, "Hey, I outdid myself with that putdown, didn't I?"

"You think you're so cute. I think you're disgusting," Faith said.

"Hey, I was trying to cool it." Janus began a little uncoordinated soft-shoe accompanied by the atonal singing of, "You cool some. Then I cool some more. Pretty soon we'll have it made in the sha-ay-ade. Ta da." He clapped his hands and stretched one arm out toward her.

Tight-lipped, Faith said, "I don't think you're funny. Booze hound."

"Oh, fuck you," Janus said.

Faith's eyes widened and now she was the one to rest her hands on the table and lean across it. "Fuck you. That's it, isn't it? Always the final level. A woman is nothing but a cunt to you, so the ultimate putdown is *fuck you.*"

Janus smiled malignantly at his wife. "I'd say that given the frequency with which we have sex that you're not even that to me." He spun around and walked to the door. Before opening it, he clicked his heels together and saluted Faith with a pantomime hat tip. "Adieu, my dear."

"Where are you going?" she screamed.

"Out," Janus said. He slammed the door and walked downstairs. But when he reached the foyer, he merely checked the mailbox. He didn't really expect to find anything, but by nervous habit he looked into the box even when he was certain there was nothing there. Finding it empty, he closed the little windowed door, spun the combination lock and slowly headed back upstairs. When he reentered the apartment, he shut the door with exaggerated gentleness.

"Hi," he said. "I want to interrupt this argument for an important political announcement. I shouldn't have called you a pussy. It was a sexist thing to say. I'm ashamed." He stared at Faith, who was seated again on the couch bent over an open book on her lap. She looked up at him without speaking. "The pusillanimous Puritan part still stands, of course. It's not as impressive an alliteration, I know. On the way upstairs I considered substituting prick, but that isn't really applicable, is it? And besides, it would probably be sexist, too. Is that right? Anyway, I really am sorry." Janus snapped his fingers. "How does pusillanimous puritan piece of shit grab you? I wish I could have been that heady in the heat of battle."

"You shouldn't call me a pussy," Faith said. "It's sexist."

Janus looked around the room, mugging to an invisible audience his disbelief at Faith's having flatly repeated his point as if it were being made for the first time. He feigned a shiver. "I know. That's the reason I interrupted our argument. To apologize."

"And you shouldn't drink beer every night, either. It's a bad habit, and it's dangerous."

Janus slumped down into the old wing-back chair. "Come on, Faith, don't start up again. Can't you see I'm trying to defuse things?"

"I don't want you to become an alcoholic. Besides, beer is fattening and you're starting to get fat."

Janus looked down at himself and sucked in his gut a little. He shrugged and said, "Well, you're no longer Slenderella yourself, you know."

"I don't have a spare tire around my belly, do I? Anyway, if you didn't keep all the beer and other stuff around the house, I wouldn't eat and drink it. I never buy that shit."

"What stuff?" He pulled his shirt tight around his middle to demonstrate that he wasn't fat.

"What does it matter?" Faith said. "You buy beer, and I end up drinking a bunch of it. But not anymore. I quit. You can get to be a fat alcoholic all by yourself."

Janus was suddenly angry again. Why wouldn't she let it drop? "Oh, go to hell," he muttered. He looked at his watch. Not yet eight and he was exhausted.

"Go to hell. Fuck you. It's always the same with you, Janus. We have an argument, and you just resort to obscenities."

"That's because we never argue about anything that makes any sense."

"It makes plenty of sense, Janus. You're just too dull to understand it."

"Yeah, well why don't you just explain it to me then, Lady Clarity."

Faith watched her husband for a long moment as a slow smile edged into his face. He was pleased with the name he had fashioned for her. "You're revolting," she said.

"I just realized," Janus responded, "that if you are Lady Clarity, then we should stop this hassling and immediately engage in sex." He arched his eyebrows to exaggerate the smile into a smirk. "Because that way I would become Lady Clarity's lover."

Faith placed her book into the satchel she had brought with her to the couch. When she had shifted its position several times and stood the entire bag upright against the back of the sofa, she turned and opened her small leather purse, which was sitting on the other side of her. Searching through the purse, she said, "You're not funny, you know."

"Some people think I'm a stitch."

"I've got news for you, Janus. You left your groupies behind at Lancaster."

"Ah, my groupies. How I miss them. How I wish I'd known them better. Just their names would have been nice. For memory's sake."

"You're despicable, you know," Faith said. She pulled a set of keys from her purse.

"What'd I do now?"

"You're alive. You breathe. You're here."

"Hey, that's not very nice, you know." All the bounce was gone from his voice.

"I find you repulsive," Faith said matter-of-factly.

"And that's not very nice, either," he said in a menacing voice. It was the flatness of Faith's tone that had succeeded in irritating him.

She stood up, keys in hand, and slung her purse onto her shoulder. "Well, you aren't going to have to put up with me not being nice any longer."

"Where are you going?"

"To work, remember? And it's just as well. The drunks *there* don't call me names."

Janus stood up too. "You think you're just going to end this ridiculous argument about God-knows-what and go to your two-bit barmaid's job?"

"That is precisely what I'm going to do."

He folded his arms across his chest. "And just how do you think you're going to get there?"

"How do I normally get there?" Faith walked to the large closet beside the front door, opened it and disappeared inside. When she came out she had her overcoat draped over an arm.

"Normally you take the V.W.," he said.

"Such a memory."

"That's the problem, you see." Janus propped himself against the front door. "I need the bus tonight myself."

"For what? Besides, you can ride your goddamned motorcycle."

"No, this time I think I'll let *you* ride my goddamned motorcycle. I'm sick of freezing my ass off, and I'm sick of being scared to death. I'd like to give the opportunity to you."

"You're crazy. You see these keys?" Faith jingled them at her husband. "They operate that white van down there. And right this minute I'm going to go put them in that car and drive it to work."

"That white van just happens to belong to me."

"Big deal."

"At this moment it is a big deal. You're always so big on keeping straight whose possessions are whose. Let me remind you that the bus was mine before we married. It stands to reason then that it is still mine."

"Don't pull that shit on me. I've got to go to work. Get out of my way."

Janus did not move. Faith put a hand on his shoulder to shove him aside, but he made himself rigid and leaned against her hand to resist the pressure. "Move!" Faith screamed and pushed against him harder. He wouldn't budge. "You goddamned bully! God, I hate you!" She hammered him once in the chest with her fist.

"Watch your mouth now," Janus said. "You don't want to lose your reputation as Prudence Purity."

Faith instantly slapped him. And when he grinned at her, she slapped him again. He laughed out loud, and she hit him in rapid succession, once, twice, three times. The third time Janus's arm instinctively jerked up, but he caught himself and laughed again.

Faith backed off then. "You nearly hit me, Janus. Do you know that? You nearly hit me. I think you'd really like to hit me. Why don't you do it?" She screwed her face into an aged mask and shoved it up to his chin. "Come on, bully boy," she rasped. "Hit me. HIT ME!" she screamed.

Janus didn't hit her, but neither did he move from in front of the door. He struggled to keep the smile of derision fastened on his face, but it slipped away, carrying the heat of anger with it. His eyes burned, and he recognized in his fatigue a dismal loneliness.

"Are you going to move?" Faith said.

Energyless, Janus shook his head. It was as if his motion was not meant as an answer, but Faith spun around and strode across the room to the phone, which she picked up and dialed. "This is Faith Janus," she said into the receiver. "I can't come to work tonight. No. My husband is holding me forcibly in the house. No, don't worry; he doesn't have the guts."

Janus moved then and sat back in his chair. Staring at the floor, he said, "Did you have to do that, Faith? I know that woman. How will I ever be able to look her straight in the face again?"

"What am I supposed to do, lie to her? Make up some phony excuse she's sure not to believe?"

"I'd have let you go. Don't you know that? Can't you see that…?" There was no need to finish the thought. Faith had snatched her purse from the phone table and was gone.

Janus forced himself to stay up until Faith got home. He wanted to apologize for blocking the doorway. But when she refused to acknowledge his greeting when she came in, he was reluctant to force a conversation with her. Still, he waited in his living room chair as he heard her changing her clothes and cleaning up in the bathroom. Finally, there was silence, and he knew that she had gone to bed. He undressed in the living room so that he would not bother her with a light. He slipped into bed beside her, crowding himself to the edge so that they wouldn't touch. He listened to the sound of her breathing in the dark. Finally, not expecting a reply and as much to himself as to her, he said, "I'm sorry, babe."

"I want my own car," Faith replied. Though his eyes had not yet adjusted to the dark enough for him to see her, he could feel her roll onto her side to face him. "I thought about this all night at work. The VW is your car. You bought and paid for it. I want you to lend me enough money to buy my own car. One that you can never tell me I can't use."

"The bus isn't the issue, Faith," Janus said.

"It's the issue now. Are you going to lend me the money or not?"

"Babe, we don't need a second car. What I did was wrong. I won't ever tell you that you can't use the bus again. I promise."

"Yes, you will," Faith said. "You'll do it again the next time you're mad and the occasion arises."

"I promise, I won't."

"I don't believe you."

"I promise, babe." Janus tried to place his hand over Faith's, but she moved hers away.

"You will. But it doesn't matter anyway. I want a car of my own."

"Faith, I'd like an airplane, but I can't have it. I can't have it because we don't have the money. And the same principle applies to your desire for a car. We don't have all the money for your next tuition installment yet, much less enough for another car. And what conceivably is the sense? You have nigh exclusive use of the car we do own. Or do I just fantasize about riding a motorcycle all the time?"

"I'll take the tuition money," Faith said.

"Fine. And what will you use to *pay* the tuition?"

"I'll drop out."

"You're crazy."

"I'm serious."

Janus sat up in bed and switched on the reading lamp. "If you're serious, you really are crazy. You've spent this entire year working for that credential, and now you're talking about chucking it for a car we don't need." Janus splayed his fingers and raked the hair off Faith's face. "Is that it?"

"Yes."

"Come on, Faith."

"It's only fair. You have a car. I should have one."

"And even at the price of your teaching credential?"

"Yes."

Janus stared at his wife. Unblinking, she stared back. Finally he smacked the bed with his hand. "Damnit, I can't believe you. You tell me that more than anything in the world you want to be a high school psychology teacher. You rant and rave at a sexist society that gives me a job without a credential because I can coach. You tell me that you can't possibly be happy unless you get to teach. So how do I react? Do I support you? Of course I do. I support you completely. We scrimp and save and borrow money. I offer myself daily as a rolling target for the homicidal drivers in this town on a motor vehicle that gives me about as much protection as a soap bubble. Why? So you can get to school. But now all this is meaningless. Now you're going to just pitch it in the junkyard. So that you can have your own car. So that the next time you pick an idiotic fight with me I can't possibly tell you that you can't use the car we have now. Is that the goddamned picture, Faith?"

She rolled away from him to face the wall. "Yes," she said.

"You're nuts. You know that. You're really nuts. But okay. Goddamnit, if that's what you want to do, then go ahead. I said the money was in the bank for you. If you want to try to buy a car with it, be my guest."

"Maybe I could get a loan at the bank," Faith said. Her voice was small and far away.

"You need collateral for a bank loan, babe. What do you have? You don't even have a job."

"I have a job."

"Come on. You work eight hours a week."

Faith turned back to face Janus again. "You're just like my drunken bastard old man. He wouldn't even teach my mother to drive. Just so he could keep her chained at home and lord it over her."

It was a long moment before Janus could respond. "You know, whenever you're mad at me, you compare me to your father. When will you figure out that I'm absolutely nothing like that crazy old fart and that I never will be?"

"Don't call him an old fart."

"Oh, Jesus." Janus stared at the ceiling in supplication. "Who brought this up?"

"Just don't call him names like that."

"Oh, my God. Oh, my God." There was a slight tremor in Janus's voice that he willed as a parody and then lost control of. He felt himself actually on the verge of crying. He took a deep breath and finally said. "Can we go back to the top? Why do you want your own car?"

Faith sat up in bed facing him. She drew her feet up underneath her and spread her long flannel nightgown out over her knees. "You really don't understand?" Janus shook his head. "That comes from being a man, I guess. From having a car all your life."

"I haven't had a car all my life."

"Will you listen?"

"Go ahead," Janus sighed.

"Let me tell you something. I know you worked during high school. I know you didn't get the bus until your second year at Lancaster. I remember you told me all that. Okay? But I worked all during high school, too. And you know what I did with the money I earned? I didn't save up for a car. No, I took the money home and gave it to my father. Like a good little girl, I dutifully endorsed every check I ever earned over to him. He took it 'against my room and board.'"

"What an asshole."

"Don't!" Faith screeched. She squeezed her hands into fists and her whole body shook. "Just listen to me for once, will you? Without commenting?" Janus raised his palms toward her in assent. "Now, you have a car, and I don't. Whenever you want to go somewhere, you can. You don't have to check it out with anybody. You can just go. Just get in your bus and go. Don't you see, Rich? You have a freedom that I don't have."

"But Faith, when do I ever go anywhere without checking with you? And how often do I use the V.W., anyway? Don't you mostly have it?"

She began to cry then, and she bent over so that her face was between her knees. In a voice muffled by the hem of her nightgown, she said, "But you *could* go, Rich. Don't you see how important it is that you *could.*"

Janus didn't see exactly, but he recognized that Faith was trying to express something of considerable importance to her. He stroked the back of her head, lifted the damp hair away from her face and mopped at her tears with the back of his hand. "Keep trying to tell me, babe," he said. "Maybe I'll finally get it."

Faith sat up and looked at him. Her hair fell back across her face and stuck to her wet cheeks. "If you ever got so pissed at me that you decided to leave me, Richie, you could just get in your bus and go anywhere you wanted. You could do it because you wouldn't be taking anything that was mine. But if I wanted to leave you, I couldn't do it. I'd be stealing your car. Wouldn't you feel terrible if the situation were reversed? For you it would maybe be like depending on your parents, or having to depend on them. Think about it, Richie. You've never had to depend on anybody for anything. You got a scholarship to college, and now you have a job to support yourself. If you were in my shoes, wouldn't you be miserable?"

Janus lay back against his pillow. He ground the heels of his hands into his aching eyes. "Yeah," he said with a sigh. Faith shifted her position on the bed so that she was facing him, and when Janus opened his eyes, she was staring at him curiously. He breathed deeply and puffed out his cheeks. "I'd feel miserable," he said quietly, looking away from his wife. "I'd feel all caged up and crazy."

Faith put her head down on Janus's chest, and he put his arm around her shoulders. Neither one spoke for a while. Finally, Janus said, "What if I sell you the V.W.? Legally, I mean. You pay me ten dollars or something out of your tip money, and we get the title transferred to your name. Then, it would really be your car, and if you took it to leave me, you wouldn't be ripping me off."

"If I had my own car, Richie," she said, "then I wouldn't want to leave you."

Janus laughed softly. "Then by all means, let's find ourselves a notary tomorrow."

Faith looked up and kissed him on the chin. "You're good to me, Richie. Sometimes it seems like I forget it, but deep down I always know it." Janus kissed her on the forehead, right at the hairline. She nuzzled her head against his neck, but he pulled her face back to him and kissed her on the eyes and the bridge of her nose and gently on the lips. And even though it was a week night and very late, they made love.

Afterwards they lay curled together like spoons, his head nestled in her hair. Janus was on the verge of falling asleep when Faith suddenly said, "I wish my father was like yours."

"Divorced?" Janus said, his breath hot against her cheek.

"Why do you always have to be so flippant?" Faith said. But her voice was without rancor.

"Just a born smartass, I guess." He yawned. "Why do you wish your father was like mine?"

"I wish he had paid attention to us when we were kids. Your dad went to all your ball games. But in all the years I was a cheerleader in high school, my father never came to watch me cheer. 'Too busy,' he said. He was so busy on his family counseling textbooks, he never had time for his own family."

"I'm sorry, babe," Janus said.

"Finally, when I was a senior, Mother got him to come to a basketball game. I was so excited. I was as nervous as I had been for my first junior varsity game as a freshman. I was sure I was going to do one of the routines wrong. I even put on a Kotex because I was afraid I would start my period and have to leave the floor or else bleed on my uniform and humiliate myself. Isn't that just crazy? I kept asking the other girls if I looked all right, and I kept trying to get them to stay in the locker room until it was getting really late." Faith laughed breathily. "He left at half time. 'You weren't gonna do anything any different in the second half, were you?' he told me. When I said he could have watched the game, he said, 'Who cares about a bunch of guys running around in their underwear? Anybody fool enough can do that.' He never said one thing about my cheers."

Faith sniffled, and Janus could tell that she was crying. With the arm that was lying on the side of her body, he added pressure, hoping to convey his desire to comfort her. "You deserved better," he said.

"I wish *you* had been my father."

Janus laughed and squeezed the top of her thigh with his hand. "I don't mind being your sugar daddy."

"I'm not as dumb as I seem, you know. I just didn't work in college. But I really studied in high school. I wasn't the smartest kid in my class or anything, but I made the National Honor Society." Again the wet, breathy laugh. "I thought I'd finally done something he'd approve of, something he'd get enthused about. He had some meeting the night of the installation ceremony. Afterwards I brought the medal home in its little jewelry box. He was sitting in the living room, reading. He had a glass of ice on the arm of his chair and his bottle of Southern Comfort on the floor beside him. I gave him the box to look at. 'What's this, kid?' he said. 'Open it up,' I said. 'It's my National Honor Society medal. It means I'm one of the best students in my class.' But he just handed the box back to me and grinned. Then he snapped his fingers and said, 'Nah, kid, it's just a piece of tin. Just an old hunk of scrap metal.'" Janus felt Faith sob, and she said in a choking voice, "My old man was really an asshole."

He turned her over so that she was facing him and dabbed at the tears with the end of a pillow slip. "But it isn't his fault," she added finally. "He just never learned how to love anybody."

Janus pulled her against him so that he could hold her with both arms.

9

Yes, I was bitten, too. And perhaps the most terrifying bite was inflicted by an oriental hydra named Vietnam, often shortened to an effectively terrifying THE WAR. The war in Vietnam, as I tended ponderously to address it when I started college in 1966, was a lower case conflict that held a distant kind of intellectual curiosity for me. I was against it, of course. My family were liberals. My father was a creeping Christian socialistic pacifist. He had lost his job at New Orleans Baptist College for daring to suggest that Jesus really did love the little children of the world, red and yellow, *black* and white. But he was no agitated opponent of the war at the time, only one of the armchair variety. Without strict leadership from Dad, I was left to assess the matter more or less on my own.

The news magazines I began to read when I started college predicted that the war would end in a matter of months, so Vietnam did not loom as something with the potential to affect me directly. It was just another "issue" on which I was obliged to adopt a position if I wanted to regard myself as a "serious" person. Should capital punishment be abolished? Should drug use be treated as a crime? Was God dead?

My years in college would, of course, see the war in Vietnam become a decidedly upper case catastrophe and my opposition to THE WAR move from intellectual to emotional, from casual to ardent to frantic. By the time I was a senior, the war which long ago should have been over had become THE WAR which might never be over.

In the first draft lottery, I drew a lucky number seven. It was very lucky for anyone who didn't share my birthday.

Though I was not to graduate until June, my number was called in January. Uncle Sam gave me permission to get my diploma, but he was waiting. At first I tried not to worry. I applied the force of reason (deductive): for more than twenty years I had avoided truly bad things happening to me; this must be the result of God's loving me a lot; if God loved me a lot, he would continue to protect me from truly bad things; therefore, THE WAR would surely end before I graduated.

A month passed without THE WAR ending.

I applied the force of reason anew (inductive): all of my friends had found a vehicle for avoiding the draft; one was headed for divinity school; another had wrecked his knee playing football; one was underweight, another too fat; a bunch of my basketball teammates were too tall; two guys I knew had even contracted epididymitis, each losing a testicle but gaining a I-Y; therefore, something bad enough to cause a deferment would surely happen to anyone who didn't want to go to Vietnam. I certainly didn't want to go to Vietnam; hence, something bad enough to cause a deferment would shortly happen to me.

Another month passed, and I continued to feel depressingly fine.

I began to make plans. Neither obesity nor anorexia was attractive. The seminary was unthinkable. I might *say* I'd give up my right nut to avoid the draft, but I wasn't *about* to inject it with shriveling disease. So I applied for conscientious objector status. In the same envelope that my draft board notified me of my CO's rejection, they informed me that I must report to Chicago for a pre-induction physical.

That night I questioned my friend Paul Taylor about his leg injury. We were getting drunk in his seedy one-room apartment with its gritty floor, naked light bulb dangling from the ceiling by a frayed cord and giant wall posters of Elvis, Jean-Paul Belmondo and Bob Dylan. Paul had one fairly comfortable chair in the room, but out of an ingrained politeness he sat with me in the hard, straight-backed chairs at the "kitchen" table. Paul threw his leg up on the table, rolled up his jeans leg and showed me the thick, faint blue scars which ran up either side of his knee.

"Still hurt?" I asked.

He rubbed his beer can against each of the scars, then tilted the can to his lips and stared over it at me. "Only when I'm movin'," he drawled. "Or when I ain't."

Paul Taylor had arrived at Lancaster from Cairo, Illinois, without so much as one letter of encouragement from the football coaching staff. He was small and lacked natural footspeed. But he was tough and so savvy that he earned the nickname "Nose," for hard-nosed, and became a starting halfback in his sophomore year. He hardly missed a down until his knee was torn apart in the last game of his junior season.

Paul took another drink from his beer and grinned at me. "I shore missed knockin' heads this year." He seldom referred to football by any other name than "knockin' heads." "But this old knee's worth 'bout a million bucks now. Now that the big hurtin's over, I suspect I could find quite a few fellas willin' to trade for her." He laughed, slung his leg off the table and bent to yank down his pants leg. When he sat back up, he brushed at his short brown hair, which had fallen across his freckled forehead.

"I'd trade you," I said. I crushed my empty beer can against my knee and then aimed it toward the metal trash can in the corner. The beer can rattled in the receptacle like a bell with a broken clapper.

"Sure you would," Paul said. He got up from his chair and went to the refrigerator, returning with two unopened cans of Schlitz. He clicked mine down on the table in front of me and tore the tab off his. "Sure you would, Tricks." Paul sucked at the foam oozing from his can.

"I sure as *fuck* would," I said, my voice heated. Somehow I thought he was making fun of me, that he was insensitive to the fact that I was already scared shitless and was getting more desperate with every passing day.

"Man," Paul grinned at me, "what kinda guard you gonna make with only one wheel? Your defense ain't so much as it is."

"You redneck hillbilly," I said. "You know about as much about my defense as Westmoreland knows about defensing the Cong."

"*You* callin' *me* a redneck is about like Rose callin' Scarlet, Crimson. You may think you've Yankeed up that accent of yours, Tricks, but we all know that underneath you're still just as Southern as grits."

"Fuck you," I said, laughing.

"Buddy, I'd do *most* anything in the world to help you beat this draft thing. But if you want out on a homo, you better find yourself some other cracker."

"Shit," I said.

Paul looked at me and shook his head, "Tricks, man, you gotta getta hold of yourself. You gotta keep things in perspective."

"Yeah. I just don't want my perspective to be blurred by a goddamned translucent body bag."

"That's morbid, man," Paul said.

"That's *real*, man. That's what I'm facing."

Paul did not respond. We finished our beers, and he got us another round. We drank them in silence, Paul occasionally shaking his head, me staring at the light bulb trying to decide whether it was actually moving ever so slightly back and forth.

Finally, when Paul brought us still two more beers, he said, "I could fix it, you know. I mean, if I got drunk enough, I think I could."

"Fix what?" I said.

"We could prop your leg up on the table here, and I could just fall on it.

That's sort of what happened to me." He stood up. "My cleats were stuck in the grass, like this, see." He planted his foot and grabbed his leg to demonstrate its inflexibility. "I was straightened up by this big guy from behind. He had me by the shoulders and was driving me forward. Then my cleats stuck. And when the safety came in low from the front, he just buckled my knee backwards. At first I didn't even feel it."

In his description of his injury, which I had heard many times before, Paul seemed to have forgotten his proposition. He looked at me intently. "It'd hurt ya like hell, Tricks. But I'd do it."

"That's crazy, man," I said.

"Yeah," he said. "I know." He got us more beers, and we drank on.

Somewhere well into my second six-pack, I said, "Would you really do it, Nose?"

"I'd hate it. I'd hate it," he said.

"But you'd do it?"

"I'd do it. I'd have to love ya awfully much. But I'd do it."

I drank off about half a beer at a draught. "Then let's do it."

"Now?" Somehow his tone was only half-questioning. It was as if he wasn't asking a question at all, but only resigning himself to some preordained fate.

"One more beer," I said. Paul brought fresh ones, and we averted our eyes from one another. When the beers were done, I rolled my pants leg up in a tight knot above my knee, which I rubbed with my palms. Paul looked at me, not in the eyes but at my face just out of eye contact. I propped my leg up on the table.

"Now," I said.

Paul rose. He came and stood behind my chair and rested his hands on my shoulders.

"I'm ready," I said.

"Okay," he said.

He moved around alongside my leg so that he could bring his full weight down on me. One hand on my thigh, the other on my shin, he tested the leg's give.

"Tricks," he said, "I can't do it."

"No?"

"No," he said. "I'm sorry."

"Thank God," I said.

And so spared by Paul Taylor's cowardice from the gift of his awful compassion, I was forced to endure the pre-induction physical. Y'all probably know the procedure. Dr. Burden, I remember, was in the Navy. First comes the mental exam. Since I was apprised of all the modes of resistance, I knew that one was attempting to answer every question on the mental test wrong. Hadn't something of that nature worked a while for Muhammad Ali? Sure, but Army types were anxious to believe that he *was* an imbecile. A competing view held that messing up the mental exam only identified you as a troublemaker and did nothing to get you out. So I took the exam half-assed. I figured that you had to do mighty poorly to fail to qualify as cannon fodder, but success might mean officer candidate school. Who knows how well I did? Who knows if the Army ever scored those tests?

Next was taking off all your clothes except your skivvies. Nothing convinces a man that he's a worthless hunk of shit like being made to walk around most of the day in his inevitably stained underwear, following a bunch of other men in their inevitably stained underwear, all clutching a sheaf of papers with their whole futures on it in their right hands and their wallets in their lefts. The same inept Army that couldn't defeat a determined little Asian nation the size of New Mexico also couldn't protect a luckless draftee's personal possessions for a few hours.

Once declothed, we were marched off to various stations. At one we were asked to distinguish figures of numbers disguised in fields of polka dots. Here a wonderfully hostile potential inductee asked the examiner if this test was to determine our "jungle vision." He hadn't realized, he said, that Southeast Asia jungles were polka-dotted. When the examiner answered him with only a glare, he said, "Oh, now I get it. These Cong guys we're gonna kill wear numbers on their helmets like football players."

The examiner stated matter-of-factly, "The test is for color-blindness."

"Are we for or against it?" the potential inductee asked.

"Those who are severely color-blind are eligible for deferment."

"Then we're agin it, huh?" the future inductee said. "That's a real good policy as far as I can see." He leaned close to the examiner and added in a feigned whisper, "'Cause I understand a lot of these gooks over there are yella."

At a subsequent station, we were asked to surrender the insides of our arms for blood samples. Here a bunch of my cohorts fainted. I thought that was marvelously strategic of them, but as far as I could tell the Army took only momentary notice.

At another post we were told to fill out a little gummed label with all our vital data and to stick it on a little jar into which we were to pee. At the pee gathering place, an enlisted man dressed in hospital whites announced loudly every three minutes or so: "All of the men unable to produce the fluid at the urinal should wait in line for one of the stalls." Years of pre-game peeing in front of my teammates enabled me to deliver at the urinal and avoid the indignity of having to wait in line with the stall men.

After urination came hernia and asshole checking. This, unquestionably, was the high point of the whole physical.

Marched into a long room in groups of twenty, we were ordered to toe a rancid yellow line and step out of our BVD's. First was hernias. "Spread legs," croaked some toady orderly. The doctor moved quickly down the line. His hand reached up under our scrotums. "Turn your head and cough." We turned our heads and coughed, and he had his hands on the next guy's balls before our chests stopped heaving.

Did the Army ever discover some lucky guy with a hernia? Would a doctor whose entire job seemed to be to fondle a thousand sets of testicles a day have even noticed? Our doctor did notice the wonderfully hostile guy who was standing next to me. He had written, "Hi, soldier guy," in ball point pen on the head of his penis. It was a nifty job, too, since the letters read facing out toward the doctor. I wondered if part of the effect was to raise the suspicion that he'd gotten help with his lettering.

A similar notion evidently occurred to the doc, who said as he probed under the guy's testicles, "Get your pal to lend a hand in this, soldier?"

The hostile inductee attempted to snap to attention, which was difficult with that hand still between his legs. But he did manage to salute and say, "I'm not a soldier yet, SIR."

"But you will be, sonny," the doc said. "This Army's even drafting faggots nowadays. Now, turn your head and cough."

By the time the fellow had coughed and said, "Oh doctor, dearie, could I just get you to write that faggot business on my form here?" the doctor had his hand on me.

When the doc reached the end of the line, the orderly called out, "Recruits, about-face." And when we had turned around, he ordered us to bend over and grasp our ankles. The doctor moved back down the line, spreading our cheeks with his finger tips. Whatever he was looking for, he didn't find. We were all ordered to get back into our underwear and report for hearing tests.

This was my big chance, I had decided. I'd always considered myself hard of hearing, and I saw no harm in enhancing my case for deferable deafness. So every time I heard the little tone ping in my earphones, I waiting a second or two before pressing my acknowledgment button. It worked. I failed.

The enlisted man who reviewed my chart shook his head slowly when he looked at my hearing graph. "Why do you guys do this?" he asked me.

"What's that?" I said, meaning, what do you mean by that. Instantly, though, I hoped he interpreted my question to mean that I hadn't quite heard what he said.

But he just shook his head at me and said, "You're gonna have to take the hearing test over again." He jerked his thumb toward a small, glass-enclosed booth, half-filled with half-naked guys holding their wallets in their left hands and a sheaf of papers in their rights. The room I entered was divided in the middle by a long console sprouting vines of headphones. I took a seat wondering if falsifying data on a hearing test was a felony offense.

When the room was filled, a Marine came in and spoke to us in a very quiet voice. "Men," he said, "there's been a little problem with your hearing tests. From what your graphs indicate, you're all as deaf as Helen Keller. This leads us to the conclusion that we've either had an outbreak of a monstrous epidemic, or that you men have attempted to perpetrate an act of fraud against the United States government. Now, to determine which, we're gonna repeat the test you had a while ago. This time I'd advise you to push down your buttons just as soon as you hear the tone." He turned as if to leave the room but then slowly turned back as if he'd forgotten to finish his droning speech. "In case some of you were considering just waiting a while to make your responses, I should warn you that we will consider fraudulent any graph which fails to match the first. That is, unless you pass the test this time. Should that happen, we'll just tear up the first chart and forget about it."

Could they really prosecute me for cheating on a hearing test? I had no idea. But I suspected that if they could send me to die in a war they'd never declared, they could do just about anything they wanted. And I figured if I was going to let them put me in jail, I'd just as soon it be for draft evasion as for cheating. So the second time, I passed the test. Cheaters, I learned anew, never gain.

At the end of the physical, I tried to convince an interviewing physician of a lifelong problem with several diseases, most notably diarrhea. But lacking documented medical evidence, I didn't get very far. By five o'clock, I was back on the gray school bus headed for Lancaster. In my pocket was a document informing me that I was fit for military service. In my heart was an icy dagger of terror.

As you might imagine, the circumstances called for drastic action. I certainly got countless pieces of drastic advice. "Move to Oakland, California," one acquaintance urged me. "The Oakland Induction Center is notorious for screwing things up. Some people even believe they do it on purpose. And if you eventually have to refuse induction, there's no place like Oakland because northern California judges always go easy on you."

"Get braces on your teeth," someone else told me. "Tell 'em you're planning on being an actor or something. A lawyer maybe. The Army ain't gonna fuck with braces, man. Just keep 'em on your teeth until you're twenty-six and in the clear."

"Take a fistful of speed right before your induction physical."

"Shave off your pubic hair and wear a bra on the day you get sworn in."

"Find yourself a doctor who'll swear you have some exotic disease which is especially aggravated by warm, wet climates."

"Join the National Guard. No question it's a military trip and a bummer, but it beats hell out of Nam."

"Move to Canada."

"Move to Sweden; the girls in Sweden are outasight, man."

I never hurt for advice. My Marxist friends were the most consistently imaginative. "Fuck 'em, Tricks," they said. "Just fuck 'em. I mean, blow something up and go underground." Or better, "Move to Cuba, man. Help Castro bring this pig nation of ours down." I loved my Marxist friends, but they could never agree with one another on what it was I should blow up. Nor could they tell me exactly where underground was or why Castro needed *my* help to bring our pig nation down.

So I devised drastic action peculiar probably only to me: I abandoned my immediate plans for graduate school. Somewhere in those hazy days between my preinduction physical and the invasion of Cambodia, I had won a Fortran Graduate Fellowship which would support me for four years of graduate study in history. I had intended to head off for UCLA, but I was afraid of trying to tackle school and play hooky from the draft all at the same time. And fortunately the Fortran would wait.

Somewhere in there Faith and I got married, too. It was mature of us to do so, of course, before school ended so that she could participate in whatever decision I made concerning the draft and my career. Poor Faith: basketball teammates for groomsmen and sorority sisters for bridesmaids. And the next day back in school and nothing was changed. Except that now we slept in the same bed every night, and everybody said it was okay.

I was still out of town for my remaining road games and at the Frank House with my drinking buddies and in such a state of perpetual agitation over the draft that I was impossible to live with. But she pitched in. She convinced her father to wangle me a coaching job at a high school in St. Louis. One of his buddies was on the school board. That job not only provided me with some of the most satisfying moments in my adult life, but also helped me formulate a new strategy vis-a-vis Uncle Sam and General Hershey.

In the good old days, a wife and a teaching job would have turned me golden. But LBJ had withdrawn marriage as a draft deferment back in the dark ages of THE WAR, when I was still in high school. And about five minutes before I signed my contract as J.V. basketball coach and social studies teacher, it seemed that Tricky Dicky Pricky Nixon abolished occupational deferments.

What Nixon hadn't done, however, was remove a draft registrant's right to "request" an occupational deferment. None was any longer granted, but technically the classification still existed. And local draft boards had to follow their whole elaborate bureaucratic procedure before they could deny such requests. Due process, it's called. I loved it. Wonderfully, draft boards met only one night per month. So a well-timed deferment petition could buy thirty days, often more. And after the local board rejected a petition, there was appeal to the state board. That could take half a year to get dismissed.

By the time of Kent State, I understood: the name of the game was delay. It was the draft dodger's version of peace with honor. The alternative was to refuse induction and serve a jail term or leave the country. I lacked the martyr drive necessary for jail, and Canadian sports pages were undoubtedly filled with ice hockey scores. I didn't even understand hockey. Blue lines, red lines? Offsides doesn't even cost five yards. So the name of the game for me was delay and pray for THE WAR to end. Stay in the country, stay out of prison and stay on your toes. Make the system work for you. In basketball terms, it was the four corners. Don't try to score. Just try to keep your opponent from getting the ball.

I started my stall by convincing a sympathetic Lancaster registrar to delay my official graduation until the end of summer school. Selective Service regulations allowed me four full years to get my college degree, and I couldn't afford to waste a single day of that 2-S deferment. Actually, I got my diploma in early August, but I bought the rest of the month before the start of my teaching job by moving to St. Louis immediately and forcing my draft board to process my change of address.

Once I started teaching, I had the St. Louis School Board on my side. It was obviously in their interest to keep me out of fatigues so that they wouldn't have to go searching for someone else they could underpay. Both the board and my principal wrote letters in support of my application for a nonexistent occupational deferment. It was hardly a surprise when the application was rejected, first at the local and then at the state appeals levels. What was surprising was how quickly the system was working. By the middle of November, I was in very deep shit.

Timing became incredibly crucial. I had to get another delaying action underway before my board sent out my induction notice. Once sent, induction letters were practically impossible to get withdrawn. The slightest error now could mean Saigon. As coaches of the four corners know, it takes great patience to play the delay game, great discipline and great nerve.

I wrote my draft board a letter acknowledging that my occupational deferment had been denied and that I understood they were now likely engaged in the process of preparing my induction orders. However, I pointed out, to draft me immediately would deprive my employer of a teacher he could not easily replace in the middle of the year. I appended to my letter still another one from my principal, in which he attested to my indispensability.

The draft board wrote back, emphasizing its sympathy with the situation and announcing its willingness to delay my draft notice—until January. January? This ploy was supposed to get me all the way to June. But no. The board argued that my indispensability ended with the fall term.

I began to feel the stagnant water of rice paddies dampening my socks. Then in December I became miraculously ill. O God, who saves his suffering for the needy. Everything I ate reacted in my stomach like a spoonful of nitroglycerine. Even milk, which was purported to be a stomach soother, only seemed to fuel the fire which raged in my gut. So for the last two weeks before New Year's, I ate as much gastronomic garbage as I could stand: pizza, tacos, doughnuts, beer, chili and Coke. It worked wonderfully. I felt absolutely wretched and confident I could confront a physician.

The doctor told me exactly what I wanted to hear: I had an ulcer. It was the sweetest irony. I had worried so much about the draft that I had managed to worry myself out of it. The doc put me in the hospital and had me drink chalk so that he could ascertain the extent of my disease and determine the nature of my treatment. But the traitorous chalk revealed that I didn't have an ulcer after all, only some undeferable malady called hyperacidity. What that meant, the doc informed me, was that my stomach burned after I ate and that I could make it feel better if I munched some Rolaids. For this I paid $500.

As soon as I was out of the hospital, I appealed my CO rejection to the state board. The fall term was ending, and I was really up against it. This appeal appeared to be the last card in what had become a very weak hand. The strategy now was to lock the system up once more for as long as possible. By the time the state board rejected the CO, I hoped to be well into the second semester. That would reopen the indispensability argument and, I hoped, protect me until June. After June? Panic.

The first half of the strategy worked. My new appeal *did* hang the system up long enough to enable me to start teaching in the spring term. And it gave me time to find myself a so-called "peace doctor," an antiwar physician who'd examine me for the express purpose of discovering that my first doctor was guilty of uncontrollable quackery or something. The peace doctor listened to the story of my non-ulcer diagnosis with great patience and sympathy and suggested that I buy Rolaids in the large economy size. He then subjected me to a thorough, professional and committed inspection and detection. Which resulted in my utter dejection. There was, he told me, nothing wrong with me that was deferable. On the other hand, he pointed out, I was guilty of non-deferable hemorrhoids.

The final result of my peace doctor experience: acute embarrassment.

Remarkably, by late March I still had not heard from the state board on my CO appeal. Dangerously, I began to hope that the state board wouldn't reach a decision until September, when I could begin arguing that they had to let me teach another year. More realistically, though no less dangerously, I began to hope that the board might grant the CO appeal. Faith and I even began to speculate about alternative service employment. She was finishing her teaching credential and was excited about a non-traditional school in Chicago where her friend Cassie Sears was working.

I agreed that CO work would be no more odious in Chicago than in any other place, so I contacted Paul Taylor, who was working for the state employment office in Chicago and was a volunteer at the Chicago Draft Resisters' Union. I asked him to investigate alternative service opportunities in the Chicago area for me. His news was not too encouraging: CO work in the area likely meant assignment as an orderly at the state mental hospital in Elgin.

This depressing news was not unexpected, though. Draft boards were notorious for trying to make alternative service as miserable as possible. What the hell, I told myself. Maybe I wouldn't have to do alternative service after all. Maybe I'd be lucky and get drafted.

Then it happened. Or I should say, it happened again. I was playing in the faculty basketball league. Midway in the second half of our game against Lindberg, I snared a rebound only to come down flush on the chunky foot of their driver education teacher. The clicks in my ankle as it turned over sounded like the winding stem on a gigantic watch. The pain wasn't new, but it was instant and horrible. I was a professional ankle sprainer, having sprained each of mine perhaps half a dozen times. This one I could tell immediately was bad, the kind that would leave me hobbling three weeks later, the kind I had iced, whirlpooled and played on within two days several times in the past.

But this time I was wrong. I was still hobbling five weeks later when I finally decided to consult a physician. Up to that point, I was confident that a doctor would only help to lighten my wallet. But none of my sundry earlier sprains had taken so long to heal. The orthopedic surgeon I saw, Dr. James Keaton, ordered x-rays, of course. That always tacked a few extra shekels onto your bill. Naturally, the x-rays showed that I had sprained my ankle.

"I just love modern medicine," I mumbled when Dr. Keaton presented me with his findings.

"Pardon me?" he said.

"Well, doc," I said, attempting to mask my irritation, "I sort of *knew* I'd sprained my ankle. I've done it a hundred times."

"Really?"

"I'm the Picasso of sprained ankles. What I'm worried about here is why it's taking so long to heal this time."

Dr. Keaton nodded understandingly and ordered me back to the lab for a new set of x-rays. I resigned myself to the proposition that my purpose in life was to keep doctors in Jaguars. The technician explained to me that the second set of x-rays would be shot in the stress position, which meant that he would hold and turn my ankle as the new photos were taken. This also meant that medical science had found still another way to inflict pain.

Or so I thought, until the doctor told me after analyzing the new pictures, "Your left ankle is unstable, Richard. Whether this latest injury rendered it so or whether some earlier one did, we can't tell until we operate."

"Operate?" I said. "Operate?"

"It's the only way we can approximate normal use of the ankle. You've torn so many ligaments that there are several bone chips which need to be removed. And without reattaching the ligaments, your ankle will never be stable."

The extent and implications of my injury were finally dawning on me. "What do you mean by normal? I mean, will it continue to be like it is now? The soreness? The limp?"

The doc explained that the limp was just a reaction to the pain and that it would gradually disappear, but that the ankle's instability meant that reinjury was almost guaranteed. "You could step on a pebble and reinjure it leaving the office," he said. If I were forty, he might settle for a special support shoe. But given my coaching and interest in athletics, he recommended surgery.

"If I forgo the surgery," I asked, "what kind of risks do I run?"

"Well, in the first place, as I say, you risk spraining the ankle just walking on it. More seriously, you risk tendon damage which may not be reparable.

"Doc," I said slowly, choosing my words carefully. "I'm supposed to go into the service sometime this summer. How does this injury affect that?"

In a tone of consolation, Keaton answered, "Right now, I'm afraid that's out of the question. Your ankle is so weakened that you couldn't possibly attain the kind of mobility you'd need for basic training. Every day would bring the danger of permanent injury." I wanted to shout "hot damn." HOT DAMN! I wanted to kiss the man full on his mouth. He went on talking, but I heard little that he said. My rotted stomach was doing flip flops. I wondered if he noticed the difficulty I was having breathing. I wanted to thrust my arms in the air like a victorious athlete and dance around on top of his desk. I was awash in the El Cholo Feeling. "Mr. Janus?" the doctor said.

"Yes, sir. Excuse me." He had evidently asked me a question to which I had failed to respond.

"When would it be convenient for us to schedule surgery?" He looked at his watch as if he planned on doing it within the hour.

"Uh huh," I said. "Well…." What could I say? Surgery? I didn't want surgery. Surgery would make me better when I had only just gotten properly hurt. I had a million dollar injury here. The last thing in the world I wanted was to be made well. "You see," I said, "this thing with the draft has sort of got me hung up. I mean, I couldn't very well take time off for a hospital stay between now and June when school ends. And I'm certain to be called up shortly after that."

"Well, of course, I'll supply you with a letter to the effect that you're presently unfit to serve."

"What about after the operation?"

"We can never be certain, of course. But I should think if you still want to serve after your convalescence that we can probably render you fit. I'd say perhaps by the end of the year. Not before."

How about fixing my leg so I could still play ball but not fix it enough for Uncle Sam, I wanted to ask. But I didn't risk that. Instead I said, "Terrific. Why don't you write a letter for my draft board now, and let me contact you later concerning a surgery appointment. I'd hate to commit to a date now and have to change it later."

He agreed with that plan, and I returned to his waiting room while he wrote the letter and had his secretary type it. As I sat in his outer office, surrounded by year-old magazines and the pervasive smell of rubbing alcohol, I felt like a marathon runner who had finished twenty-four miles. I was tired but exhilarated. And I wanted to sprint the remaining two miles. I wanted it all over with at once.

Dr. Keaton brought the letter out to me himself. "Be sure to call for your appointment as soon as possible," he urged.

"I will," I promised. And it was no lie. Surgery just was not possible until I turned twenty-six or THE WAR ended. "See you soon," I said. This was the lie. I never saw that man again.

Faith was not as excited as I had anticipated when I got home. She counselled me not to count my chickens before they hatched, and she pleaded with me not to be disappointed if the physical deferment didn't materialize. "I really think the CO is going to come through," she said. "I can take that job in Chicago. And even if Paul's right that your service will be at the Elgin hospital, you'll adjust to it. Just getting the CO at all is more than we dared hope for only a few weeks ago. *This* may be too much to hope for."

But I knew what I had. I had an ankle made of gold, all bruised and swollen and beautiful. I had a ticket to freedom, and it was going to get me out of the Army and out of Elgin State Hospital as well. The next day I called my local board and told them that I wanted a new physical. In doing so, I broke the cardinal rule of draft evasion: never appeal to your board about more than one matter at a time. The corollary to this rule went: if you haven't heard from your board in some time, count your blessings.

But I was on a hot streak, and I wanted the physical I-Y deferment before the miraculous forces that had injured me miraculously healed me.

It took some concerted explaining, but the board finally agreed to schedule me an "orthopedic consultation" at the St. Louis Induction Center.

On the appointed day I was ushered into the office of Dr. Nörd Pederlieben, orthopedist. He was sixtyish, German, red-faced and grotesquely fat. His tight clinical smock appeared to have lasted the duration of THE WAR without benefit of laundry. The doctor was at his cluttered desk, his back to the door as I entered. Without turning, he stuck out his left arm toward me and said, "Papers."

I handed him the forms my local board had forwarded to St. Louis. He glanced at them, set them on top of another pile of papers and went back to the writing he had been working on when I entered. I shifted my weight from my good leg to my bad one and wondered if it was possible to limp while standing still.

When he finished writing, he shoved his work roughly aside and spun on his wheeled chair to face me. He looked me up and down slowly. Leaning back against his desk like an obese viper about to strike, he suddenly slammed his hand down on the forms I'd given him. "Your papers," he hissed.

I lifted my arm to point out that he had his hand on them, but before I could, he snapped, "A doctor's letter. You've got a doctor's letter? No doctor's letter? You're wasting my time?"

"Oh, no *sir.* No sir, not at all," I said. I stepped forward, forgetting to limp, and gave him my sacred envelope. "I'm sorry, sir. I didn't understand what…."

"Hmph," he announced and swung back to face his desk where he spread my letter open and read it. "We'll need the x-rays," he said with his back to me. This surprised me somewhat because I had assumed that Dr. Keaton's letter would suffice. But okay, I thought, I can do another x-ray. THE WAR was now, and cancer wasn't likely to strike me for years. I stood waiting for instructions. Moments passed. He swung around on me again. "You understand? We must have the x-rays." I looked at him blankly, an expression he undoubtedly took for stupidity.

Finally I said, "Uh, where do I go, sir? Do I, uh, report to the x-ray room now?"

"Six six six," he said, which I took to be the room number.

"X-ray is room 666, sir?" He did not reply. "Thank you, sir," I said, to which he also did not reply.

In room 666 I found an x-ray machine and a soldier sitting in a steel folding chair reading a comic book. He was munching on a toothpick and had on one of those long black aprons that supposedly impedes an x-ray technician's job from killing him.

I told the guy I was there for an ankle x-ray and, once I'd climbed up on the table, tried to explain that he needed to shoot one in the "stress position." But he wasn't exactly receptive to my instructions.

"I don't know nuthin' about this stress shit," he maintained. "And I ain't stickin' my hands under this machine till some officer says I gotta."

"Pederlieben will just have to send me back," I contended.

"May be," he grinned, shifting his toothpick from side to side. "If so, I'll still be here."

Ten minutes later I was at the orthopedist's door with a manila envelope containing two x-rays of my injured ankle, neither taken in the stress position. "Sit over there," Pederlieben told me when I gave him the package. He pointed to a high metal stool beside his examining table. He took the two pictures from the envelope and fastened them side by side to the viewer on the wall next to the door. I could hear his tongue clucking as he studied them.

"I don't think those x-rays will show that...."

"Take your clothes off," he said.

"I can just roll my pants up," I said, and began to pull at a shoestring. "I think you're gonna have to order another...."

He turned abruptly to face me. "You must take off the clothes."

"It's just my ankle," I said. I thrust my leg toward him to demonstrate what part of me needed examination.

"The clothes. Please."

I shrugged and unbuckled my jeans and stepped out of them, stripped off my left sock and sat back on the stool. "Those x-rays you've...."

"All the clothes, please," he said.

"Shirt, too?"

"Please."

I began unbuttoning my shirt. "It's only my left ankle that's hurt, you understand." He just stared at me like a mule. I slipped my T-shirt over my head. "You want me to sit up on the table?"

"Undertrousers also, please," he said. That's when I began to suspect I was dealing with some sort of war-mongering voyeur masquerading as a human being. But what was I going to do? This certainly wasn't working out as planned. I thought I was getting the draft off my back, but instead I was getting to serve as a live centerfold for a goddamned pervert.

"I have to take off my shorts so you can examine my ankle?"

"Please," he said.

O God, I thought, is this what I have to pay for your miracle? Pain doesn't count? Pain just comes with this particular miracle, but I pay with humiliation?

I took off my shorts.

"Now," Pederlieben said, "touch your toes." I touched my toes. What touching my toes had to do with an ankle injury, I never discovered. "Rise on your toes, please." As I did so, I was delighted to note that my left ankle gave a distinct pop. I hoped he heard. But I didn't look at his face to find out for fear I'd discover him staring at my pecker, which no doubt by then had shriveled up to the size of a peanut.

"You will duck-walk to my desk and back, please, now," Pederlieben said.

That did it. "Look," I said. "What in the hell has duck-walking got to do with my ankle? For a knee I could maybe see it. But *my* problem is a bum *ankle.*"

"You want to be trouble to me?"

"Of course not."

"Then you will duck-walk to the desk and back."

What was there to lose now? My dignity? That was a laugh. I'd been standing naked in front of this degenerate for minutes.

I duck-walked over to his desk and back. I felt like a fool, of course, but I'd have quacked for him too if it would have helped. It's very difficult to limp while duck-walking, if you've never thought about it.

"On the table now," he instructed.

When I was up on the table, Pederlieben ordered me to lie back. Wanting him to think I was oblivious to how weird this all was, I resisted the urge to cover myself. He came over and took hold of my foot. I flinched. Foot he could touch, I told myself, but if he made the slightest move toward any of the rest of me, this orthopedic consultation was history.

But Pederlieben was content with visual jollies, I guess. He may have held on to my ankle a little long as he turned it this way and that, but he made no attempt to venture from his foothold.

That's not to say he didn't screw me, however. The sonofabitch screwed me good.

After he had felt enough of my ankle and finally let me get dressed while he went back to his desk, I mentioned the business of the stress x-ray again. He just kept marking on my forms. "I have seen enough," he said. "This should take care of you." Misunderstanding him utterly, I fled his office thinking myself victorious, only to have the ensign who processed my final papers announce that Dr. Nörd Pederlieben had found me fit for military service.

"There must be some mistake," I suggested.

The ensign reread my form carefully, then looked at me sympathetically. "No, I'm afraid there's no mistake. The orthopedist says you've suffered an ankle sprain, but there's nothing more serious than that."

"What about the opinion I brought from my own orthopedist?"

"Dr. Pederlieben refers to a letter from Dr. Keaton, who, he says, has greatly exaggerated the nature of your injury."

"Pederlieben doesn't know what he's doing," I said. "He didn't bother to order a stress x-ray, which is the only way the extent of my injury can be determined."

"A stress x-ray?" the ensign said.

"Right," I started to explain the procedure, but the ensign cut me off.

"Look, I don't know anything about this. You were entitled to an orthopedic consultation, and now you've had one. We can't do anything but rely on Dr. Pederlieben's judgment."

"I'm trying to tell you that Pederlieben didn't...."

"And I'm trying to tell you that as far as Selective Service is concerned, you are fit to be drafted." It was clear that I had exhausted the ensign's patience.

"I want to see your commanding officer," I said.

"I'm afraid that's not possible," the ensign said with exaggerated calmness.

"I have a right to see your commanding officer," I said, matching him calm for calm. I had no idea if I possessed such a right or not.

"Now look, mister," the ensign said, standing up from behind his desk, "don't try to start trouble. I don't want to have to call the M.P.'s in here."

Calmness was over. Now was the time for screaming. "I WANT TO SEE YOUR GODDAMN COMMANDING OFFICER AND YOU EITHER LET ME SEE HIM OR YOU BETTER GET THE M.P.'S IN HERE AND YOU BETTER GET ONE WHOLE BIG BUNCH OF 'EM, AND YOU AND ANY FUCKING M.P. WHO LAYS SO MUCH AS HIS HOT BREATH ON ME BETTER GET READY TO GO BACK TO WHATEVER IN THE WORLD IS LOWER THAN AN ASS-SUCKING M.P. OR A DESK JOCKEY ENSIGN, BECAUSE I'M GETTING FUCKED HERE AND I'M NOT GONNA GODDAMNED PUT UP WITH IT! YOU GOT ME, MISTER?"

The ensign got me an interview with his commanding officer.

Looking back, I can muster some sympathy for Col. Robert Slure, who was surely just trying to do a job when he was confronted late one afternoon by a raving maniac in the throes of draft evasion. He was probably a career man, a West Pointer in his starched uniform and spit-shined shoes, glad to be out of a war zone, dreaming of making general one day, perhaps. I remember the photograph on his desk of a woman and two blond-headed little girls. He probably just wanted to get home that day to be with them.

But at the moment I burst into his office, a step ahead of the ensign carrying my traitorous papers, I had no inclination to sympathy toward Colonel Slure. At that moment I was into screaming.

"ARE YOU COMMANDING OFFICER OF THIS IMPRESSMENT OUTFIT?" I still think that little display of my historical knowledge was an inspired thrust.

"If you want to talk to me, you'll calm yourself down, young man," the colonel advised.

"Okay," I said, my reasonableness belied only by my artificial smile.

The colonel motioned me toward a chair and sat back in his. "Now, what can I do for you?" he asked me with only the faintest whiff of patronization.

"You and the rest of the bastards in the Selective Shanghai System can stop buggering me; that's what you can do for me." My plastic smile didn't crack a smidgen. "Isn't it enough that you guys are running an illegal war? Do you have to break your own fucking rules to get me to fight it for you?"

The colonel put his elbows on his desk and leaned across it toward me. He ran one finger across his bottom lip before he said, "What's your beef, mister?"

"My beef is you've got a goddamned quack pervert pretending to be an orthopedic surgeon."

The ensign stepped nervously forward now, placed my papers in front of the colonel, and said, "Mr. Janus, uh, objects to the determination of his orthopedic consultation."

"Not at all," I corrected, my face beginning to ache from its enraged smiling. "I didn't get an orthopedic consultation. That's what I object to. Granted, I was pawed by a pederast with latent medical tendencies. But I object to that, too."

"Pederlieben examined him," the ensign explained.

The colonel paged quickly through my papers, came to something, probably Pederlieben's opinion, and read it through. When he'd finished, he breathed deeply, rubbed a thumb across an eyelid and said to me, "Dr. Pederlieben has examined you and found you fit, Mr. Janus. I'm afraid we've no recourse but to rely on his professional judgment."

Calmness had failed. It was obviously time for more screaming. "THE HELL YOU DON'T!" I suggested. "WHAT YOU'VE GOT NO RECOURSE ABOUT IS OVERRIDING THAT NAZI IMPOSTOR AND DECLARING ME UNFIT TO SERVE!" I was on my feet and at the colonel's desk. I slapped my hands on the sheaf of my papers and the colonel vaulted out of his chair. "ONE DR. JAMES KEATON SAYS I'M UNFIT!

AND IF YOU KNOW WHAT'S GOOD FOR YOU, COLONEL ROBERT S. SLURE, YOU'LL TAKE HIS WORD FOR IT."

The colonel didn't quite scream back, but there was unmistakable menace in his reply: "You raise your voice in this office one more time, mister, and you're gonna be in so much trouble that Nam'd be a picnic by comparison."

I was all out of breath. I stabbed with a finger at my papers. "Dr. James Keaton, one of the leading orthopedists in this city, says I've got a seriously unstable ankle attached to my left leg here. Do you understand that?" The colonel didn't confirm that he did. "He says that sometime during basic training I'm likely to injure that ankle, and that injury could well disable me for life. Can you understand what I'm telling you?"

It was Colonel Slure's turn to stab a finger at the papers now. "Can you understand that our orthopedist disputes those findings?"

I had become convinced that the Army could only hear me when I raised my voice. "I'M GONNA SUE YOU, YOU BASTARD! YOU DRAFT ME AND I'M GONNA TEAR UP MY LEG WITHIN A WEEK AND I'M GONNA LET EVERY CONGRESSMAN AND NEWSPAPER IN THIS COUNTRY KNOW THAT SOME COLONEL ROBERT SLURE NOT ONLY DECLARED ME FIT BUT REFUSED TO GRANT ME A PROPER MEDICAL EXAMINATION, AND THAT THE FAT ARMY PENSION I'LL DRAW IN ADDITION TO MY COURT SETTLEMENT SHOULD BE ATTRIBUTED TO YOUR PERSISTENT NEGLIGENCE!"

When I'd finally exhausted myself, the colonel looked at the ensign, who had plastered himself to the wall in embarrassment. "Don't you have some duties to attend to?" Slure said. After the ensign had saluted and fled, the colonel looked back at me and muttered under his breath, "Jesus, I hate this war." He asked me what I wanted him to do, and I explained about the stress x-rays Keaton's office had taken. He said that if I could secure those x-rays from Keaton's office, he'd order Pederlieben to have a look at them.

I thanked him, genuinely grateful. But before I left his office, he counselled me in a tired voice. "Those x-rays better show what you claim they do, Mr. Janus." He stared at me hard but without expression. "Or else your ass is mine."

10

1971

It wasn't until mid-May that Richard Janus discovered it had become spring. The signs were all around him, of course. Forest Park had long since molted its white skin of snow, and the brown stubbly grass had gradually become a deep green, darkened by the shade from renascent oaks and elms. But Janus was oblivious. It was still brisk enough each morning when he climbed on his motorcycle that he continued to wear his down jacket over a sweater. And though he was in shorts every afternoon with his tennis team, the chilly ride home each evening, his wet hair never fully tucked inside his helmet, kept him thinking that somehow it was still winter.

But then Janus missed a second consecutive day of school to procure a set of ankle x-rays from the office of Dr. James Keaton, orthopedic surgeon, and to deliver them to the St. Louis draft induction center. The ensign he had intimidated the day before took them without expression of even visible recognition.

"What now?" Janus asked.

"You'll be hearing from us," he said.

"I shouldn't hang around?"

"It'd be a long wait. The doc doesn't come in again until next week."

"Then I won't know anything until next week?" Janus looked at his watch as if it might register the specific number of hours. It was 10:34. Somehow he had thought he would know by noon.

"At least," the ensign said.

"At least?" Janus asked.

"There's no guarantee that he can get to your file the next time he's in."

"At least next week," Janus repeated. The ensign turned away to put the x-rays into a wire basket on a table behind his desk. From the basket, Janus hoped they would be expeditiously and accurately moved into the hands of some intelligent person who was capable of reading and understanding what they meant: that Richard A. Janus should be henceforth left alone. He stared at the wire basket. Attached to the front was a little sign which read: IN. Janus tried to imagine what hidden message that sign carried. *In* the army? He shuddered. Of course not, he suddenly understood. *In* luck. *In* the chips. *In high cotton.* That was the message. He studied the table on which the basket rested. How long would it take for his x-rays to move from the IN basket to the OUT basket next to it? He felt a surge of confidence. He could read the messages now, all the messages. When his papers arrived in the next basket, he would be *out* of the army, *out* of harm's way. Next week seemed not so long to wait.

Still, Janus lingered, reluctant to let the x-rays which he was sure would save him pass from his sight. The ensign turned back to him and said, "Do sumthin' else for ya?"

"No," Janus shrugged. He smiled at the sailor, but the man looked away and busied himself shuffling papers. When the ensign raised his eyes to look at him once more, Janus finally began to move out of the large room, down the long dark hall. The brilliant morning light outside hurt his eyes, but they adjusted to the brightness on the way to his car. As he looked about himself, he suddenly realized it was spring.

Janus's buoyance ebbed back into anxiety as quickly as that St. Louis spring became summer. After two weeks he had heard nothing. When he called the induction center to make inquiries, he was told that no decision had been reached. A week later he called again. The news was terrifying: no one had ever heard of him; no record could be found that he had submitted x-rays. But not to worry, he was assured. If indeed he *had* left x-rays for examination, they would be found and processed in due course.

Janus rejected both a murderous rampage and suicide as conduct unbecoming a conscientious objector.

By the last week of school in early June, he had come to believe that draft fighting for him was to be a lifelong occupation. Selective Service would never quite get him, but he would never be free of their pursuit.

His finals were graded, and Janus was putting in one last day restoring order to his classroom. That morning the principal had asked him again if he would be returning next fall, explaining that he'd like to get staffing matters settled as soon as possible. Janus had asked for just a few more days' grace, assuring his boss that the news from the draft just had to be positive. The conversation had been amiable enough but had left Janus depressed nonetheless. His principal was patient, he knew, and the man wanted to retain him. But he couldn't and wouldn't wait much longer.

Janus stacked the last of his world history textbooks back on their dusty storage shelves, gathered his belongings and made his way wearily to the parking lot. He slipped on his gloves, but in concession to the heat strapped his jacket to the seat behind him. Riding home in his short sleeves, he shouted warnings to other drivers. He was convinced that his naked arms rendered him particularly vulnerable and especially attractive to some lunatic whose pleasure in life was running over motorcyclists. Inside his helmet he sweated, and the sweat dripped from his eyebrows and the end of his nose.

At home, he parked and chained his bike and made his way to the front foyer of his apartment building to check his mailbox, habitually, hope long since jettisoned.

It was there.

The Selective Service return address lurked in the upper left-hand corner like an assassin. Janus took two deep breaths. He set his helmet on the tile floor and turned the envelope over as if its message might be written on the back. Somehow he knew that the end had finally come, that whatever verdict was contained inside was final. He had hope. He had good cause to hope, he told himself. He was scared breathless.

Just as he was about to tear the envelope open, Faith appeared at the top of the stairs. "Hey, you're home," she said. "What're ya doin'?"

"Checkin' the mail," Janus said. He picked up his helmet, tossed the envelope casually inside it and started up the stairs.

"What'd ya get?" she asked.

Janus moved past her into the apartment. "Just a letter," he said, dropping his helmet on the black naugahyde couch.

"To you?"

"Yeah." He peeled off his gloves and threw them into the helmet on top of the envelope. He started toward the bathroom.

"Who's it from?"

"General Hershey," he said over his shoulder. He closed the bathroom door behind him.

"Oh, my God," Faith said. "What are you doing?"

"I think I'm doing what you do when you use the bathroom. What *do* you do in here all the time?"

He flushed the toilet and came back into the apartment's tiny hall where Faith was standing waiting for him. "Are you just trying to torture me?" she asked.

"What are you talking about?"

"Why are you peeing when you should be opening this letter?" She handed him the envelope. Janus took it, walked into the kitchen, where he opened himself a Coke. Faith followed him, and he asked if she wanted something to drink, too. "I want you to stop this and go open that letter. You *are* doing this to torture me, aren't you?"

"Nope," Janus said. He grinned at her.

"What are you doing then?"

"I'm cooking up some good news."

"You're crazy," she said.

"Just superstitious. Remember when I got my Rhodes letter? I tore it open instantly, and what did I find? Sorry, we love you immensely but you're just not for us. On the other hand, I let my Fortran letter simmer, and I won." He left the kitchen with Faith behind him, picked up the envelope and sat down in his living room chair.

"Open the goddamn letter!" Faith screamed.

"Do you think it's ready?" Janus shook the envelope back and forth as if it were a frying pan.

"Open it," Faith said.

He took out his pocketknife and slid the blade inside the envelope's flap. He looked at his wife. "This is for the ball game," he said to her quietly.

He moved the knife though the paper. Inside was a small rectangular card. His eyes quickly found the all-important notation. Without change of expression, he handed the card to Faith. As she read it, without uttering a sound he rose from his chair and began the victory strut of a boxer who has just won a championship.

When Faith had read the card and put it aside, Janus began to scream as if the sound on the television set had suddenly been turned up. "Hot damn!" he yelled. "Hot double damn! O God, where are all the words I need to express how I feel. Jesus. O God." He stepped across the room and swept Faith off her feet, twirling her in a circle. "Can you believe it, baby? We won!" He set his wife down and gripped his hands around her shoulders, holding her at arm's length. He closed his eyes and said, "O thank you, god of basketball ankles, O god of perseverance, of terror, of blind luck, of whatever it is that brings this moment." He opened his eyes and pulled Faith against him. Into her hair he said, "We're set, babe." Then he squeezed her, kissed the top of her head and began doing his victory dance again. Faith sat on the couch, her hands in her lap.

Janus danced in front of her and chanted, "We are set. We won big. Want to bet? We'll dance a jig." Then he said, "Gimme a W!" His intent was to spell out his whole jingle. His intent was to act totally silly for days. But Faith did not respond to his request for a W, so he said, "Come on, gang, let's let those Army mules know we came to play. Gimme a D!" Now his intent was to spell out draft resister, but Faith just studied the draft card which she had placed in her lap.

"What's the matter?" Janus asked her.

"Nothing," she said.

"Nothing? Well then let's take off all our clothes and race out to Skinker and back. Let's eat goldfish. Let's stuff a telephone booth." Faith rubbed her thumbs over the card from the center to the edges, as if perhaps she was trying to wipe away a smudge. Janus knelt in front of her and placed his arms along her legs. He bowed his head so that he could bring his eyes into her downward gaze. "What's the matter, babe?"

"Nothing."

"You're not acting very happy. Isn't this a time for joy?"

"I'm happy," Faith said. "I'm very relieved."

Janus laid his head on her knees. "Can you believe this? We won everything. No Vietnam, no jail, no Canada. I won't even have to do alternative service." He looked up at her again. "Hey, no bed pans!" He squeezed the outside of her thighs. "Baby, no nothing. We won everything. The fucking World Series Super Bowl of my life. We've got to celebrate, kid." He pulled Faith to her feet and began to dance in front of her, but she walked away and pulled back a curtain at the window to stare into the courtyard in front of their apartment, where the setting sun was casting a sepia glow like the color of an old photograph.

"Hey, I'm dancing by myself," Janus said.

"I know," she said.

He stopped, walked to her, turned her gently to face him. "What's wrong?"

"Nothing."

"We both know that's bullshit. Out with it, old spot." He petted his hand across the top of her head and down her springy hair to her shoulders.

"I said nothing's wrong."

"Come on, babe. I've been sweating this fucking draft thing since just after Columbus landed, and now after several hundred years I've beaten it. I'm not even going to have to do CO work. You've finished school. With both of us working next year, we'll commence being rich. A year later I'll start graduate school. All of this has just come true. Where's the old capacity for ecstasy?"

"I couldn't be happier for you," Faith said.

"For me? Not for us?"

Faith shrugged.

"What's the rub here?" Janus said.

"I guess I just never thought this I-Y would come through."

"So?"

"So I was planning on being in Chicago next year. I like that job at Cassie's

school. I figured you'd finally get the CO and work at the Elgin hospital."
Faith went back to the couch. She splayed her legs out and leaned her head
against the back, staring at the ceiling.

Janus stared at her. Finally, he said, "Are you *sorry* that's not going to
happen?"

Without looking at him, she said, "I guess I had sort of counted on it."

"You counted on my working as an orderly at the state mental hospital?"
Faith didn't say anything. "You *counted* on my spending two years emptying
bed pans?"

"I'm glad you don't have to do that. You'd have hated it."

"You say that like some people might enjoy it. Anyone would hate it. Why
do you think they make CO's do it?"

Faith sat up a little and finally looked at him. "Don't get pissed off," she
said.

"Pissed off? Pissed *on* is what I'd get if you had your way." Faith sighed,
shook her head and resumed her position staring at the ceiling. "Jesus," Janus
said. "I've just gotten the best news I've had in my whole life and you're
pining after a fourth-grade teaching job."

"I like that school in Chicago," she said. "Cassie's there and...."

Janus closed his eyes and blew out a big breath. "Look, babe, I know you
like the school in Chicago. I know you're fascinated by the open classroom
business they use. But Cassie.... Now she's your friend again. Last year she
wasn't. It's hard to keep up with. But the point is, who knows how long being
near Cassie is an advantage and when it becomes a drawback?"

"Cassie has always been my friend," Faith said.

"That's why she was in our wedding."

"She was out of town."

"Convenient, wasn't it?"

"Oh, drop dead."

"I won't have to. I just got a draft deferment."

"I know," Faith said, still staring at the ceiling.

Janus was totally surprised by the insane coolness of Faith's reaction to his
news. He had anticipated this moment for years, dreamt about it, prayed for
it. The moment he would finally be free. He couldn't believe she found
reason for disappointment. He was confused and hurt and angry. He felt
himself about to launch into one of his storming lectures, but he was
determined to remain calm, to try to understand Faith's response.

He went and sat on the floor at her feet, his back against the couch seat.
Encircling her legs with his right arm, he stroked his hand up and down her
shin, feeling the rough stubble of hair. Under other circumstances, he would
have teased her for shaving so infrequently, but he knew better than to do so

now. "Hey, kid," he said, "don't forget you've got a job offer here, too. It pays more. And it's a higher grade level. That should be a factor."

Faith laughed. "I *want* to teach high school. That's what I *want*. What difference does it make between fourth and fifth grade?"

"That argument cuts both ways, doesn't it? I mean, neither job is what you really want. But the one here pays more and has the added advantage of being located in a town where I have a job that I like."

"If I can't teach high school, I want at least to teach in an open classroom."

"You don't listen to me."

"I know," Faith said. "You think the open classroom is for the birds."

"I tried it. And what I got for my trouble was a bunch of kids choosing to sit on the floor instead of in their desks and choosing to screw off instead of trying to learn something."

"Yeah, and you gave it about a three-week trial."

"Three weeks too long. The purpose of school is education. And contrary to what Herbert Kohl may think, education is not always fun. Learning takes discipline. Most kids don't have self-discipline, so they need someone to impose it on them."

"Some draft protesting radical you turn out to be," Faith said. She moved her legs away from her husband and pulled them up under her on the couch. "In another five years you'll be voting Republican."

"I can't believe you," Janus said quietly. "On this night, you say something like that to me."

"You just don't understand," Faith said.

Janus exploded, slamming the cheap green carpet with his hand. "You're goddamned right I don't understand." He stood up and began to pace back and forth in front of her. "I get good news; no, I get great news, wonderful news, life-changing news. But are you happy? No, you choose that as an occasion to say something record-settingly shitty to me, something totally baseless. You're right, I don't understand." Faith just stared at him. He softened his tone and implored her, "Come on, Faith, why don't you explain this to me? Explain to me, why, on this night, you say something like that."

"You wouldn't understand," she answered.

"Christ, you're unbelievable."

"Always swearing," Faith said. She wasn't looking at him anymore.

Janus walked into the kitchen to get a beer, thought better of it and decided on a Coke instead. But there weren't any more Cokes, so he grabbed one of Faith's Tabs instead. He hated Tab. He brought the diet soft drink back into the living room and sat down in the chair facing her to drink it.

She was crying.

Janus took a large swallow of his cola and looked around the room. The rug was fraying and dirty in a half-moon around the front door. The heavy green curtain that had once hung in his mother's living room sagged where one of its hooks had slipped away from the rod. He looked back at Faith; she was staring at the ceiling again, tears streaming down her face. He took another swallow from his drink, set the can on the floor, and moved to sit next to her on the couch, resting his hand on her knee. "Talk to me," he said. "I'll never understand what's bothering you if you don't talk to me."

Faith sniffled and mopped at her cheeks with the back of a closed fist. Still staring at the ceiling, she said, "I wanted that job in Chicago real bad, Rich. I got it all on my own. Cassie spoke up for me, of course. And that helped. But when I interviewed, I could tell that the principal really liked me. He said he had several dozen applicants but wanted to be sure he found just the right person. And he chose me."

"The principal here chose you too, babe. And there must have been other applicants for this job as well."

"It's not the same."

"Why not?"

"The principal here is a friend of my father's. The first thing he asked when he saw my maiden name was whether I was one of Paul Cleaver's daughters. When I said yes, he decided to hire me right then. He didn't give a shit about any qualifications I might have."

Janus wiggled his legs and ran a hand over his face. "Want some of my Tab? I don't think I'm gonna finish it." She shrugged no. "Faith, you can't try to get out from under your father's thumb at your own expense. You can't cut off your nose to spite your face." He reached and grabbed her chin and turned her face toward him. He smiled and said, "You could use a nose job, though. Maybe you should put your shoulder to the wheel and your nose to the grindstone."

Faith snapped her head away from him. "Don't clown. Please!"

"Okay," Janus said. "I just wanted to cheer you up. On this day, of all days, I would have thought we could be happy."

"Yeah," Faith said.

"Look, I'm really sorry that you feel so bad. Let me cheer you up. Okay! Ask me for anything."

"Move to Chicago anyway."

She had really caught him off guard. "Come on," he said.

"I'm serious."

"Can't you see that it makes absolutely no sense to move to Chicago, if we don't have to, for you to take a job for less money in a place where I don't have a job at all?"

"It obviously makes no sense to you."

"It *obviously* makes no sense, period. Christ, Faith, anything we do is only for one year. I'm going to graduate school the year after."

"I know," she said.

"What's that supposed to mean?"

"What do you think it's supposed to mean? It means I know."

"Christ. Sometimes I think you and I are characters in something by Ionesco." Janus moved to sit back in his chair. "Of course, I get my best lines from John Osborne. I've got it. We have all the absurdity of Ionesco and all the hostility of Osborne." He took a sip of Tab. "God, this stuff is awful. How can you drink it?"

"You could go to the University of Chicago," Faith said quietly.

"Why would I want to do that?"

"It's a good school."

"I'm going to UCLA to work with Warren Burden. I've been planning that for years. You've known that for years."

Faith started to cry again.

"Right?" he said.

"Yeah," Faith said. Or would have said if her voice had not broken and put the sound out more like a groan than a word.

"I thought you always wanted to live in California." Faith didn't respond, so Janus added, "Right?" When she still didn't respond, he said, "Well, have you said that or not?"

"I guess I've said that."

"Guess?"

"Yes, I've said that, goddamnit. What choice have I ever had? You've always planned on going to UCLA as soon as you could. So since we're gonna go, I think I ought to try to like the idea."

"But the idea has never genuinely appealed to you?" Faith began to fiddle with objects on the lamp table next to the couch. She put a cap back on a pen, closed a book, put the pen on top of it and moved both to the table's edge. "The notion of living in Los Angeles never once really appealed to you?" Janus repeated.

"Of course, it does. Sometimes it sounds really exciting. Other times it just scares me. I don't know anybody in California. But that's not really the point."

"What is really the point?"

"The point is that the plans are yours. The plans are always yours. I just get included. If I like it fine. Otherwise.... But you always get what you want."

"That's just nonsense."

"No, it's not," Faith said.

"Bullshit."

"When did I ever get my way about anything important?"

"How about a list?" Janus said. "Let's start with our wedding. Who chose the day, the time, the setting? Who decided she didn't want my father to preside? Who picked her theology prof instead?"

"Oh, shut up," Faith said.

"Who has picked out our apartments? And who decides what goes where in them, and what gets done and when?"

"And who," Faith screeched between clenched teeth, "has to raise hell to keep you from turning them into pigsties?"

"Damn, you have an amazing ability to leap from one argument into another. But since we're having so much fun, let's explore this little tangent for a while. If you were half-rational, Faith, you'd admit that I do half the work in this house. And don't misunderstand me, I think that's fair. On the other hand, if you were wholly rational, you'd admit that I do more than half. But that's more than I can expect. I don't even want to contest it. I'll gladly accept an admission that I do half. The *point* is that you get your way plenty. Because whatever share of the housework I do, and we could argue about the percentage endlessly, I'm sure, I do it to your standards, on your schedule."

"You made me quit counselling," Faith said.

Janus was flabbergasted. She had done it to him again. A thousand times in their thousand arguments, it seemed, she had leveled him with her non sequiturs. He could almost count on her doing it. Yet, she disarmed him every time. "What?" he said.

"You heard me."

Janus got up and began to stalk around the room. He spun on his heel to face her. "*I* made you quit counselling?"

"Yes," she said.

"You remember that you quit counselling to get married?"

"How could I ever forget?"

Janus began pacing again. He went to the curtain and attempted to fix the hook which had slipped away from the rod. He succeeded only in loosening two more. "Christ," he said. He felt like smashing his foot into the wall below the window but resisted doing it, knowing that he'd only feel worse. He went back to his overstuffed chair and sat down so hard that the chair groaned and tore at the carpet. He stared at Faith and struggled for control of himself. As if by their own volition, his balled fists hammered at the tattered arms of his chair. He took a deep breath and stretched his fingers out until the backs of his hands ached. Speaking deliberately, he said, "What in hell has counselling and your quitting got to do with any of this?"

"I didn't want to quit. I liked counselling." Faith's eyes were down, and she was brushing at her skirt with her fingernails.

"What you're saying is that you didn't want to get married."

"You made me. I did it for you."

"Oh, God," Janus said. His voice rumbled so slow that it seemed to come from his chest rather than his throat. "Damn, you suffer from a bad case of convenient memory." His voice pitch jumped two octaves. "Oh, it's true that you put me through hell the week before we married. It's true you said then that you didn't want to go through with it. It's true that you made me crawl. But if you'll try to remember things *before* that week, you might remember that you and Cassie had quit speaking to one another and that you were desperate for an excuse to get out of her room. Counselling with Cassie— your grand scheme—had turned into a nightmare. Was Suzy Sugartits *your* counsellee or was she Cassie's? How could Cassie tell Fawn Freshbottom she could do whatever it was when you had explicitly told Fawn she couldn't?"

"That's not the way it was!" Faith screamed. Now it was her turn for clenched fists.

"Oh, no?"

"You're twisting things for your own argument."

"Me, twisting things?" Janus laughed. "You're the Chubby Checker of domestic disharmony. You've never mentioned this I-made-you-quit-counselling business before. If it's such a big deal, why have you never brought it up before? Why have you waited a year and half before mentioning it?"

Faith didn't answer.

"Why, Faith, if it's so important?"

"Because I knew it wouldn't do any good. I knew you'd just argue with me and twist things around. I knew it would just make you mad." Faith's head was down again. She rotated it slightly and looked at Janus sideways. "Clearly I was right."

He shook his head and began to rub his face with an open hand. Then abruptly the motion stopped and both head and hand were still. He began to tap at the bridge of his nose with a forefinger, finishing the gesture by pointing at Faith and slinging his hand and finger as if he had burned himself. "You know what it is, Faith. I know what it is. You and Cassie were on the outs for a long time. Then she arranges this job for you, and suddenly I'm the bad guy for splitting the two of you up. That's the gist of it, isn't it? All that was necessary was a little surgery on the old memory, and I'm the bad guy."

"Shut up," Faith said.

But Janus was not about to shut up. He was sure he had found the connection and determined to provide the wrap-up.

"Why in hell should I shut up?" he said. "I finally get the draft off my back. I'm free for the first time since I was eighteen years old. Hell, maybe I'm free for the first time in my life. So this is a big moment, huh? And we should be celebrating. Right? No, not Faith and Rich. We're not celebrating. We're fighting. I used to think we only fought because times were bad. Because I was under pressure and wasn't patient enough. Because I was uptight and unintentionally made you uptight, too. But this proves that we're just instinctive fighters. We can fight over good news just as well as over bad news. Probably better. Now we can fight without letting anything external complicate and intrude on our fundamental argument. Now, that's the truth of it, isn't it, Faith?"

Janus rose and went to the couch and stood over Faith, speaking down to the top of her head. "Right, Faith? In fact, it took good news this time, didn't it? If I had just learned that my physical appeal had been turned down, and that I had to do alternative service, we wouldn't be having this fight. I'd still have figured myself plenty lucky to have gotten the CO. We'd have packed our bags and headed for Chicago. You for your dream job in your dream reunion with Cassie Sears. Me to stick my thumbs in buckets of piss."

Faith looked up at him, eyes wide, nostrils flared. "You're disgusting," she said. She bit off the word so hard that a spray of saliva hit Janus in the face.

He smiled derisively and wiped his face with the back of his hand. "I guess I am disgusting. I have the disgusting habit of expecting my wife to rejoice with me at good news, the disgusting habit of wanting to celebrate something wonderful." Janus had nearly talked his anger out. He felt himself on the verge of tears. He sat in his chair, his head against the high back. An arm, raised as if to ward off a blow, propped against a wing and fell across his face.

"You don't understand," Faith said.

From behind his arm Janus said, "We've been here before, I think."

Faith sat forward, elbows on knees, and leaned toward her husband. "Rich, I do everything you want." Janus responded with a breathy laugh. "We do everything because of your plans. We do. If we hadn't gotten married, I'd have kept counselling. After graduation, I'd have traveled or gone into VISTA or something."

"Where does all this come from?" Janus asked. He still hadn't lowered his arm. "I've never heard any of this before. You're the one who arranged for us to come to St. Louis. Your father got me the job here. You wanted to get your teaching credential, and that's what you're doing."

"You don't understand," Faith said, sitting back on the couch.

Janus dropped his arm and looked at her. "That seems to be the refrain to this disharmonic musical."

As if he hadn't spoken, Faith said again, "You just don't understand."

She started to cry again. Her eyes were trained on the ceiling. Every blink pushed large tears onto her cheeks. Janus studied her. She was right. He didn't understand. Faith's mind seemed to work in a manner alien to his comprehension. It was never true that he didn't want to understand her, but he knew there were moments in their arguments when he was less interested in understanding her than he was in getting her to submit. But those were angry moments. As he looked at her now, it was without anger. What he felt was sadness that they had gotten along so poorly, a sadness born of the dawning fear that they would never get along. He didn't know what to say to her. Only beginnings of sentences occurred to him. He wanted to comfort her now, recognized that his own agony could be eased only by trying to ease hers. But he didn't know what to say.

Finally, Faith said, "Marriage didn't change anything for you, Rich. You were going to do something to earn money while fighting the draft, and you've done it. Year after next you'll be going to graduate school. And I'm expected to go wherever you go. When you finish school, you'll take a job, and again I'll be expected to relocate with you. That's the way things work in this world. But you'd never do such things for me. It has never occurred to you that *our plans* doesn't translate *your plans.*"

In the silence that followed, Faith's crying became audible for the first time. She bent over, and her whole body shook with the sobs. "I just wanted this one year," she said. "Just this one lousy year."

Janus's response was rather awesome to him. He felt as if he had been feeling his way along a dark, narrow hallway when suddenly the lights came on, and he found himself in the middle of a strange room. The sudden bright light blinded him, and he could not really make out the extent of the space. But in the edges of the glare, he could hear voices, some of which sounded familiar, others which were altogether foreign. He was shaken and confused. He felt like the victim of some elaborate practical joke. But of one thing he was abruptly, frighteningly certain: she was right. Marriage had meant something largely different to her than it had for him. What was fair in this situation, he didn't know. But "one lousy year" was hardly much to ask.

Janus began to yank on the mane of hair on the back of his head. "Hey, Faith," he said. "You think I need a haircut?" She looked over at him as if he had said something terribly insulting. He twisted his torso away from her and raked his hair upward from his shirt collar. "What do you think?" he said.

"I don't know what you're talking about," Faith said. Her voice was as cold as a northern Illinois dawn in January.

"I'm talking about whether or not I need a haircut. If I'm going to interview for jobs in Chicago, maybe I ought to get one."

Janus intended to smile at his wife, but somewhere between the intention and execution, he began to cry. Faith got up from the couch and sat on the arm of the chair. She put her arm around him and pulled his head against her breast.

11

The year after I finally got my draft deferment was the period I recall as my dope and religion phase. I smoked dope religiously and practiced religion dopily.

It was not so good a year. I think I had concentrated my energies on the draft for so long that I expected life to be perfect the instant I was free from its threat. But life started not being perfect immediately. Poor Faith was so set on taking a job at a non-traditional school in Chicago that she sort of forgot that it wasn't to my advantage to have to do CO work. We got into one of our all-too-frequent arguments, and I accused her of being self-centered. She accused me, in so many words, of being a male chauvinist pig. To my horror, she managed to convince me that she was right. Faith's like that; she has the disarming habit sometimes of making sense just when I least expect it.

The upshot was that we should move to Chicago so she could take her job. It was awfully important to her. So I cut my hair and got out my three-piece suit and got turned down for every teaching job I applied for. The problem was that I didn't have a teaching certificate, and Faith's father didn't have any friends on the board of education in Chicago. Goes to show you what pull will do. The year before I had nothing going for me except a background in athletics and Paul Cleaver's dialing the right numbers. This time out I had a year's experience, good recommendations from my department chairman, principal and athletic director, and a junior varsity basketball team that had gone twenty-one and two. I was without Paul Cleaver in Chicago, though, and I never stood a chance.

Faith was so despondent when I called her with the bad news after my last interview that I dreaded facing her. I was staying with Paul Taylor, who was still handling claims at the state employment office and working as a counsellor for the Chicago Draft Resisters' Union. We had been in contact throughout the year since our graduation from Lancaster, and I usually bunked at his apartment whenever I was in town. Faith always stayed with Cassie Sears. My wife found Paul Taylor too crude for her tastes, but he was always solicitous toward her. He wanted both of us to join him for dinner that night, but Faith told him she'd prefer to eat with Cassie. To which Paul replied good naturedly, "Then fuck ya, girl, if ya lack good sense." He was unaware of how much sexual references made Faith cringe.

When I arrived back at Paul's, he had a pot of spaghetti sauce on the stove, the Beatles's *Abbey Road* on his stereo and a joint in his teeth. I accosted him for acting like a hippie when the sixties were so obviously long gone. "Why don't you grow up, man?" I told him. "When are you gonna settle down, move to the suburbs and go into debt?"

"Have a jay," Paul grinned, pushing a little white stick toward me. "At my house, every man has his own private jay. None of this passing dope back and forth, letting the ends get all soggy with everybody's disgustingly mingled spittle."

I took the joint but made no attempt to light it. I wasn't then really much of a dope smoker. "I've got a problem, Nose," I said.

"It's good to know you're still alive, Tricks," Paul replied. "Can I help?" He took a drag on his joint and talked in a squeaking voice because he was holding all the air in his lungs to keep the smoke down. "I love to help you, Tricks. I love to help you because I love you like a brother. I love you so much. I'd have squashed your leg for you. You know that, don't you? I'd have done it. But I didn't have to. You took those lousy, spongy ankles of yours, on which you never could jump over a dog turd anyway, and beat the goddamned draft without my help, you perseverant son of a bitch. Where's that no-good wife of yours? Too stuck-up to break bread with a redneck? Light your jay, man."

"You're stoned," I said.

"Thank God," he answered. "I was afraid I had lost my mind." We both laughed.

I told Paul the story of my dismal day. He listened with his eyes closed, patting his hand on his thigh in quiet rhythm with Ringo's drums.

"The bottom line is," I concluded, "that I feel real bad, Paul. I told her we'd move up here, but I haven't been able to come up with a teacher's aide position in a kindergarten."

He opened his eyes and stared at me for a second before fitting the stub of his joint into a roach clip. "How bad you want to make this move, Tricks?"

"I don't want to make this move at all. I'm in love with the job I've got.

What can I say? I love it. Sometimes I think I shouldn't give it up next year to go to graduate school."

"Maybe you shouldn't," Paul said. He lit the roach and waved it under his nose.

"Well, that's a crazy thought, of course. I mean, I've got this Fortran Fellowship waiting for me and all. And I'm sure I'd prefer to teach at the college level. But damn, I like the coaching. It's kind of wonderful, you know. I can teach a kid something and watch him put it into practice. Before my very eyes, I can watch someone grow good at something."

"I hear you," Paul said.

"But Faith's right, of course. I'm gonna determine where we live *after* next year. So it's only fair that she get to choose where we live now."

Paul nodded his head and then began to shake it. "Marriage is a bitch, man," he said. "I think I'll avoid it."

"No, you won't."

"No, I won't," he agreed, and we laughed. "You want to let her make this move bad enough to work some shit job for a year before you become a fucking golden-haired, California beach bum?"

"Christ, I don't know. Why ain't life ever easy?"

"There's a job open in my office," Paul said.

"You're shittin' me."

"I'm shit-faced," Paul said. "And you better smoke your goddamn jay or you won't be able to follow what I'm gonna tell you about how to get this job."

He was serious. He wouldn't tell me anything until I lit the joint and puffed on it. "Hold the smoke down," he ordered. "No info from the Nose until you hold the smoke down. I need some company out here in the twilight zone."

So I held the smoke down and learned that there was a civil service exam the next morning, which, if I took it, would make me eligible for the job in Paul's office. He promised he could take care of the rest.

"I owe you, Tricks. I wouldn't bust your knee for you, so maybe I can save your marriage."

He broke out a bottle of cheap red wine, and we drank it while we got stoned. By the middle of the evening, we decided to dispense with the spaghetti. We shared the sauce directly from the pan. We listened to all the Beatles's albums and some Stones and some more Beatles. When we found we were hungry again, we decided to go for ice cream. We snorted a couple of roaches to tide us over for the trip. Paul drove us in his pickup to a Baskin-Robbins he claimed was close by but seemed to me to have been located in another state. On the way, I hung my head out the window and read the numbers on the license plates of all the parked cars as we whizzed by them.

"934 M 278. 752 B 945. 123 K 911."

"You are some fucked up, Tricks," Paul said.

"821 F 967," I said.

Full of ice cream and back at Paul's, we were just about asleep when he said, "Tricks, you sure you want to take this job?"

"Course I'm sure, Nose. Why?"

"'Cause you're gonna hate this job. I hate it. What you do at this job is hand out checks to a lot of people, some of whom don't need it. But mostly what you do at this job is tell people who really do need money that you don't have any for them." There was a long silence in which I thought he'd dropped off to sleep. Then he added, "I'd sure like havin' you around every day, but it's a real shit job. I don't wish it on ya. I wouldn't wish it on an enemy."

As it turned out, I didn't have to take the job. I did take the civil service exam the next morning, and even though I was still stoned when I took it, I did well enough that the job was mine for the taking. But suddenly Faith's ardor to move to Chicago cooled. I knew what the problem was, though she would never admit it: something had once again gone wrong in her relationship with Cassie.

So we stayed another year in St. Louis, and I was enormously relieved. Paul was right: I'd have hated the job in his office.

Thus my first year free from the draft became my St. Louis year of dope and religion. I found that I liked smoking dope. No longer in training and no longer too worried about the draft to do anything else, I felt free to do it. It was kind of wonderful. I felt like I was getting to be the hippie that basketball had kept me from being in college.

But as much as I enjoyed getting stoned, I could never quite get over the feeling that it must be bad for me. Surely, I reasoned, there were better things that I should be doing with my time. Oughtn't I to begin working on my history studies? Much of the time I spent stoned, in fact, I spent contemplating the merits of dope smoking. When I would recall all the good times I had while smoking, when I argued with myself that I never appreciated music until I sucked my first joint, I would conclude that I had adopted a beneficial habit.

But when I thought of the miserable mornings I awoke still stoned and the general social and intellectual incompetence that marijuana smoking bred, I concluded that the habit was bad. But no sooner would such a negative thought register than would it be supplanted in my fogged brain by the contention that even if dope smoking was bad, to discover it bad required dope smoking; so, dope smoking mustn't be bad if it could reveal to the dope smoker such important truths.

Such is the crystalline logic of a dope smoker.

Applying this logic one night while I listened to record albums, watched Perry Mason reruns on TV, ate Eskimo pies and worried that I should be reading some history book, I wrote on a piece of notebook paper the following startling observation:

> If pleasure is good
> And one smokes dope for pleasure,
> Then if he finds pleasure in dope
> Dope must be good.
> I know work is good.
> Hence, work must be dope.

There may be some distorted truth in this observation for the so-called workaholic, but finding the piece of notebook paper the next morning convinced me that I needed to reduce my intake of marijuana.

My dope-smoking phase was followed by my religion phase. Mostly this had to do with developments in Faith's life, but some of it arose from concerns uniquely my own. I had put away my religious beliefs around the time of my parents' divorce. I read *Catch-22* and under Yossarian's guidance became an atheist who didn't believe in the God who invented things like tornadoes, cancer, pain and phlegm, none of which seemed very useful for mankind.

I know it's somewhat out of fashion in intellectual circles to have religious beliefs, other than TM or some other oriental kind which possesses an eccentric acceptability, but since I have been owning up to everything else in this memo, I might as well own up to religious beliefs as well.

Actually, the resurrection of my religious beliefs is not nearly as sinister as most of my intellectual friends seem to believe. I learned from Martin Buber that they had never really been dead. All along in my atheist period I was guilty of religion. I cried out in pain; I called on God to relieve my anguish; I wished for Him to be there. These are the first elements of religion. Furthermore, I always had trouble denying Mr. Jesus of Nazareth, who, it seemed to me, could no more be held accountable for the actions of Christians than Gandhi could be held accountable for India's having built the nuclear bomb. When I confess these notions to my Marxist friends, they almost visibly shudder. But so be it. We all have our heroes. I just happen to be more comfortable with Jesus and Gandhi and Martin Luther King than with Marx or Lenin or Mao.

The end of my dope phase and the beginning of my religion phase overlapped a little. Faith brought home an album of the rock opera *Jesus*

Christ Superstar. The teaching job she took was at a parochial school (Lutheran), and thus she was associating with a lot of religious types in those days. She wanted me to listen to the album while she was at a PTA meeting and tell her what I thought when she got home. I was rather afraid of the assignment. We were getting along so well at the time that I was sure whatever I thought would be the most horrible thing she had ever encountered. But I had no choice but to listen to it. Not to have done so would have been rebellion, a crime worse than mere heresy.

So I rolled myself a jay, smoked up and gave the album my thoughtful consideration. What struck me about it was the composers' efforts to emphasize the humanity of Jesus. Matthew, Mark, Luke and John had the opposite problem. When they were writing, everyone took Jesus's humanity for granted. The gospel writers had to convince their readers that He was God. *Jesus Christ Superstar* was written, I gathered, for people, like me, whose fundamentalist religious training practically ignored the part of Jesus that was the man. I mean, the guy liked to drink, for Hissake. And it wasn't grape juice like my Sunday School teachers had always tried to tell me.

My drugged brain began to speculate. Did Jesus ever masturbate? Did He ever make it with one of the gals who were always following him around? Why did I know that Faith and almost anyone else who took his Christianity seriously would be aghast and scream blasphemy at just the asking of these questions?

Then I remembered a sermon I had heard as a teen-ager, delivered by a young apprentice preacher. "He didn't have to," the young preacher kept repeating, meaning Christ didn't have to die. He didn't have to die because He was God and could have pulled some miracle at Calvary that would have really wowed them.

I got pretty excited in the midst of this sermon because I figured the young preacher was going to solve one of the problems that had been bothering me: why didn't Christ show up the taunting Roman soldier and come down from the cross as he was challenged to do? He could have put the soldier in his place and then climbed back on the cross and died if that was in the cards. Or He could have worked it the other way: He could have gone ahead and died right away, as it seemed important for Him to do, and then sprung back to life while the big crowd was still around. That would have scared a lifetime's worth of meanness out of the cruel soldier.

But the young preacher never got around to any of these concerns of mine. He was content just to repeat, "He didn't have to. He was God, and He didn't have to die. But He was also a man like you and me, and like a man, He was scared of death; but like no other man, He died when the power to live was in His hands." The preacher left me with the conclusion that Jesus was a pretty inscrutable fellow. Years later I discovered that Milton and Luther, among others, had reached the same conclusion.

But I shouldn't carp. You can only crowd so much into one sermon, particularly if you're only an apprentice preacher. Still, I felt that the young preacher was on to something. I have wondered since whether he ever developed his idea. And whether he ever had another one. Scott Fitzgerald said that most men have only one idea per lifetime. Even great men. Maybe he's right. After all, didn't Einstein stop after E equals MC squared?

I wonder if my one idea is not to write my dissertation.

When Faith got home, I was bright enough not to share with her most of the reactions I had to the album, bright enough to let her do most of the talking, bright enough to indicate agreement wherever possible. I gathered that she liked it but was concerned that the story contained no reference to the Resurrection, an omission she found troubling.

I would have expected that my religious musings would have ended with my acquiescence to Faith's concerns about *Jesus Christ Superstar.* They didn't, however, and they were piqued anew when I read Philip George's book *The First Americans: An Ethnohistorical Survey.* I was gathering material I wanted to use for a unit in my history class I called "The Peoples of Early America," and I became fascinated by George's presentation on Indian revitalization movements. Those of you on the committee unfamiliar with ethnohistory are perhaps not acquainted with these phenomena.

Revitalization movements are religious responses that occur in communities under stress. Such stress can arise from developments wholly internal to a society, but normally it is a response to an external pressure. Anthropologists have studied these movements in all parts of the world in sundry different time periods.

American Indian history is replete with revitalization movements. This is hardly remarkable when one reflects that from the first coming of the white man, one Indian community after another came under externally exerted stress. Jack of the Feather started perhaps the first revitalization movement in what is now the United States, among the Virginia Powhatan within years of the founding of Jamestown. Neolin led one among the Delaware; Tecumseh's brother led one among the Shawnee. Handsome Lake had disciples in all six Iroquois tribes, and Wovoka's teachings about the Ghost Dance attracted followers throughout the tribes of the Great Plains. In each case, the leader suggested a religious solution to community problems that were essentially political and military. Each taught that a religious awakening, a return to a lost purity, would provide relief from the reality of Euro-American aggression. Each leader wrapped his ideas in the cloak of conservatism. That is, he sold his new and radical doctrine as a return to the old ways.

On the day I finished my lectures on all this to my class, I was seeking to construct a bridge of understanding for my students when suddenly I announced, without preparing to do so, "You know, there are some who think that similar transformations can be found in so-called modern peoples as well, for example, among American colonists during the Great Awakening about which we have talked earlier. Think of all the comparisons." *I* had not even thought of all the comparisons myself. In fact, I had made up the fact that anyone had ever thought of such comparisons before. Of course, someone might well have had such thoughts, but I certainly wasn't aware of it. One way or another, I liked the idea. I judged it a good one. You can't expect much more from the end of a lecture. But I wasn't done. No, there was more.

Bonanza.

"And there are others," I continued making things up, "who think that perhaps such a transformation, such a revitalization movement model, typifies the career of Jesus Christ." Jesus Christ, what an idea to throw out right at the end of a lecture. Especially when it was my second idea of the day. In less than a minute, I doubled my life's quota. Was Scott Fitzgerald wrong? "I don't intend these remarks as a challenge or rebuke to anyone's religious faith," I added in conclusion, "but once again, just contemplate the comparisons. I think you'll find them fascinating. I know I do."

And I still did when Faith got me to begin taking adult confirmation classes at the church with which her school was associated. This was one of the more sordid episodes in the sordid story of my life. And it just goes to show you how the road to hell is paved with good intentions.

I had absolutely no hankering to take up church attendance again. As a result of my parents' religious convictions, I had been a faithful attender right through high school, but I had never gotten much out of it—other than sleepy during long-winded sermons. The first Sunday I was in college, my roommate asked me to go to church with him. I decided to skip it just this once. And I didn't go again until Faith harassed me into going to the interdenominational chapel several times in Lancaster.

Faith had a much lower threshold of guilt about church attendance than I did. She too had always been a regular churchgoer, and she largely sustained the habit during her Lancaster years. The first year we spent in St. Louis, however, we didn't go to church much. Faith managed to feel mighty guilty for this backsliding, and she later managed to blame me for it. When she took her teaching job at the Lutheran church school, she began going to church every Sunday again.

This caused problems.

I think Faith must not have liked church very much because she was always insisting that I go with her. It wasn't like she was worried about my soul or anything, not at the beginning, anyway. It was more like misery loves company: if she had to go because of her job, then by cracky I had to go because of our marriage. I think things would have been easier on us if she'd have just admitted that she hated going to church. But she wouldn't do that, of course.

I didn't think the whole thing was very fair. It was her job and her responsibility, and if she'd have just told her employers that she was married to a hostile heathen, they would have clucked in concern for the cross she had to bear and been extra nice to her. But no, I had to go to church with her and smile and shuffle around her principal and pastor and assorted other religious fanatics. I had to nod and pretend to love Jesus, which was true enough, I guess, but none of their business that I could ever see.

But the main reason I didn't think the whole thing was fair was that I was being forced to go to a Lutheran church. I don't have anything against Lutherans, understand. I'm sure they're as fine a group of institutional Christians as there is. (I don't care for *any* institutional Christians a whole bunch, of course. I tend to look at things as my friend Paul Taylor does. Once when we were drinking beer and shooting the bull, our discussion turned to serious matters, and we ended up trying to analyze why it was that both of us, after strong church rearings, had given it up. Paul laid that big hammy hand of his on my knee and said, "We don't go to church anymore, Tricks, because *this* is church.") It was just that I was raised a Southern Baptist. All of us Southern boys are either Southern Baptist or black. And the blacks might have been Southern Baptist, too, but we wouldn't let them. Southern Baptists have a certain body of hymns and a certain way of doing things that I was familiar with. The Lutheran service was like a foreign language to me. I didn't understand it, and I couldn't function in it.

Faith, on the other hand, was raised a Lutheran. She knew the liturgy and all the hymns. And at the end of the service she could march forward with all the other faithful and take part in Communion. Communion was the bad time for me. Baptists had Communion four times a year. They sat in their pews, and the deacons passed out Welch's and tiny saltines. But these Lutherans had Communion every blessed week at the end of the rest of the service. Each of the parishioners would go to the altar to receive the bread and wine. One part of me sort of liked the ritual. I could imagine that it could come to represent a special, spiritual moment in every week. But the foremost part of me felt uncomfortably conspicuous at having to remain in the pew while Faith and everyone else received the Sacrament. I felt like I was wearing the Star of Baptist sewn onto the fabric of my suit.

That's what led to the adult confirmation classes. I made the mistake of complaining of my sense of isolation (I might have called it the El Cholo Feeling, but I hadn't yet learned the term), and she seized on the complaint as a lever to get me to become a church member. Our marriage wasn't working terribly well, and I figured that if I was going to have to go to church with her anyway, I might as well do the utmost to please her and become a church member and take Communion like the rest of them.

I was leery of embarking upon a program of religious instruction, but Faith convinced me that the pastor, the Revered William Burnside, was a liberal-minded sort who would want to teach me about the tenets of Lutheranism, not test me for orthodoxy.

Boy, was she wrong.

I'll have to admit, though, that Pastor Burnside was an amiable kind of guy. He had mastered that ministerial obsequiousness that parishioners often confuse with saintliness. He seemed always just on the verge of committing a good deed, for which he would quickly thank God. The good deed he committed in my case was to fail me in his adult confirmation class. It was the first class I have ever failed, but it was not for lack of trying. I just made the mistake of honesty. I should have memorized the confirmation book and told him what Lutherans believed on all the important issues. Instead, I tried to talk theology with the guy. I learned an important lesson from this experience: don't ever talk theology with a person who takes it seriously.

I think Pastor Burnside had suspicions about me on repeated occasions. I was weak in the belief department on several matters of Old Testament—the parting of the Red Sea, for instance, and particularly the part I jokingly referred to as Jonah's swallowing the whale. The pastor was not amused. But I really got in trouble over the issue of Communion. He was completely in favor of it, and I was in favor of its being completely different.

My position was one I'd learned from my father, who saw the Communion rite as one which historically limited the fellowship of Christ when it should have been used, oppositely, as a gesture of openness. Dad's contention was that by including in the Communion service only those who were "saved," Christians practiced a policy of exclusion which was very unChristlike. And after the one church was split into a hundred different denominations, things got a whole lot worse. At that point Christians began to refuse to commune with any but a small group who agreed with them on narrow issues of theology. My father, you see, among his other failings, was a die-hard ecumenist.

When I confided my Communion beliefs to Pastor Burnside, he quoted me some scripture and said that benign as my sentiments were, they were impossible to implement because, "the Sacrament of Communion involved ingestion of the body and blood of our Saviour."

I should have seen the handwriting on the altar at that point and humbly acknowledged my error, but I was still discussing. "In the symbolic sense," I said.

"In an actual, immediate sense," he corrected.

"Uh huh," I said, confused. "But that's Catholicism, isn't it? That's transubstantiation."

"Not at all," Burnside said. "Luther's position here is one of the fundamental differences between our faith and that of the Roman church."

"Uh huh," I said, more confused.

"A Catholic believes that in the hands of the priest, the bread and wine actually turn into the body and blood. We do not believe that. Baptists believe that the bread and wine are consecrated symbols of the body and blood." He was clearly short on information about Baptists if he thought they saw *wine* as anything other than the consecrated symbol of damnation. "We do not believe this, either."

"Lutherans believe something somewhere in between," I guessed.

"Precisely. Lutherans believe that the bread and wine do not become the actual body and blood, but are nonetheless the actual body and blood."

"I may have some trouble with that," I said.

"You should pray for the grace to understand that which transcends understanding."

I should have prayed for the grace not to tell the man that I had even more radical religious notions. Studying Indians, as I had begun to do, I discovered a capacity for ecumenicity which would have challenged even my father. At our last adult confirmation class, I told Pastor Burnside, "I've been thinking of Jesus in terms of revitalization movements." He didn't know what I was talking about, so I quickly explained the revitalization phenomenon to him and gave him a couple of examples from Indian history. "Now, to make the connection to Jesus," I said, "think of the situation in the Middle East during His time. The Jews were under the thumb of Rome in much the same way that American Indians were dominated by whites. Jesus criticized the Jewish leadership for failing to be faithful to scripture, cloaking, in other words, His radical message in a mantle of conservatism. But wasn't He suggesting a religious solution to a political and military problem?"

"Surely you aren't suggesting that Jesus's message was limited to a narrow band of territory at the eastern end of the Mediterranean two thousand years ago."

"No more than would a Marxist be trying to limit the application of his creed by recognizing that Marx himself was foremostly concerned with the problems of the British working class."

"But you're making human comparisons," Burnside said.

"Jesus was a man. Why are human comparisons faulty?"

Pastor Burnside shook his head and began to move things about on his desk. "You know," he said, "it seems to me that you are foundering at the same point as the authors of *Jesus Christ Superstar.*"

I acknowledged their role at the inception of my thoughts, omitting the part about smoking dope, of course.

Pastor Burnside responded, "I think you have become so fascinated with the humanity of Jesus that you have lost sight of His divinity."

"Well," I said, "I guess what I find most interesting about Jesus was His humanity. It seems to me that most Christians are really clear about His divinity but are forever forgetting that He was a man." I really didn't have an inkling of what hot water I was getting into. I was still thinking of me and William Burnside as two cerebral types who got together twice a month on Wednesday nights to share some ideas about religion.

I am capable sometimes of a stunning capacity for perceptual blindness.

"What do you do with the miracles, son?" Burnside said. His voice was very somber.

"I fit them right in," I said with anachronistic buoyance. "The Indian leaders performed miracles, also."

"And you regard the feats of the Indian leaders as something more than sleight of hand, as something more than primitive trickery, preserved and enhanced by myth?"

"Well," I said, still unaware of what we had come to, "I have prayed for the grace to understand that which transcends understanding."

I laughed. William Burnside did not.

"Richard," he said. Have you ever noticed how you can always tell that someone is about to say something important to you when he uses your formal first name? "Do you believe in the divinity of Jesus?"

I didn't get any further in giving him an answer than a little joke about transcendentalism before Burnside cut me off. What I was going to tell him was that, well, I sometimes believed in Jesus's divinity, and I usually *wanted* to believe in his divinity, and I definitely believed in a god whose presence was no less absurd than the alternative of his non-presence, but that, no, I didn't always believe in the divinity of Jesus as he was using the term, though I certainly *always* regarded Jesus as a pretty godly example of a man, and I also always believed that if we all tried to be like Jesus that we could turn the world around; and though I was completely cynical about ever turning the world around, trying to be like Jesus was a personal, existential notion of which I was more than passingly fond.

But as I said, he didn't wait to hear my circumlocution. He cut me off in a sad whisper. "I can't confirm you, you know. You've really misled me from the beginning. To think that…. Poor Faith is going to be so very disappointed."

Well, I disagree that I misled him. My motives were always pure. But he was right about one thing, of course. Faith was very disappointed.

12

1972

Richard Janus had started counting. He was an inveterate list maker and record keeper. In high school and college, he kept detailed statistics on his basketball performances. His J.V. basketball squads were given dittoed sheets of statistics for every game, a practice even the varsity coach did not follow. He wrote down every movie he saw, every book he read. But until now he had not turned his accountant's quirk on his marriage.

Since the first of the year, Faith had threatened to leave him thirteen different times. He hadn't tried counting the number of times she had said, "I hate you." And trying to place a number on the fights they had would have been practically impossible. Sometimes fights lasted a week or more. They seemed usually to start over something wholly inconsequential, but once begun, he and Faith could deny each other a pleasant word for days. The fighting commenced shortly after their wedding and had recurred regularly during their more than two years together.

Not all the reasons for the fighting were puzzling to Janus. He recognized that however much he might have argued otherwise at the time, he had brought certain sexist notions to his marriage. And he knew, particularly early on, that a significant element in his marital difficulties was Faith's attempt to achieve a legitimate measure of equality in their relationship.

But there seemed another element in their disharmony which lay beyond Janus's grasp, something deeper than his eroding (he hoped) male chauvinism, something far deeper than the natural friction that two people encounter when they begin sharing a life together. Janus loved his wife, and he remained committed to making his marriage work. But he had begun to fear that there was something inherently wrong in their relationship, something that made Faith fight him when there was no need.

Until he began to count, Janus would later surmise, his capacity for being shocked by Faith's threats of separation was undiminished. Until he began to count, his willingness to entertain the possibility of all fault being his remained intact. So the counting represented a change, a change that was perceived even by Janus at the time. It was the registration of a terrible resentment which was growing inside of him like molten rock grows inside a volcano for years until the moment of its eruption.

That second year as a high-school teacher and coach was an anxious time for Janus for reasons outside his marriage as well. His splendid first basketball team won its last twenty games in a row. His '71-'72 team went nineteen and five, a fine record to be sure, and a record accomplished with less talent than the '70-'71 squad. But poor coaching, Janus believed, had cost his team one win outright and had nearly cost another. At the end of the second year, he was far more awed and challenged by the coaching profession. It was with a growing sense of loss that he acknowledged the second team would be his last. It was with a smoldering sense of regret that he chided himself for not having studied the sport more, for having so blithely relied on his own natural skill and enthusiasm for the game and on his fondness for his young players to pull him through. It wasn't chagrin over the lost game that bothered him, but a gnawing feeling that, without even knowing it, he had given less than all of himself and that he'd never have another chance.

Janus's job—teaching, coaching, preparing, grading—took most of his waking hours. He used what little spare time he had to begin a program of reading history. Since he felt himself to be two years behind others his age, he wanted to hit graduate school in the fall with a running start. He was occasionally disturbed that his reading captivated him so seldom. A book on Indian history he found engrossing, but much of what he read was so barren in terms of narrative that he was very nearly bored by it.

More than once he experienced a wave of self-doubt over his decision to enter UCLA's history graduate program in the autumn, but each time he dismissed such thoughts as natural nervousness about the unknown. He was an honors student in history, wasn't he? He'd won a Fortran Fellowship to study history, hadn't he? Of course his reading wasn't so interesting now. He was doing it in a vacuum. Once in graduate school, he was sure it would turn fascinating.

Years later he would remember these thoughts and remark to a friend, "Boy, was I wrong."

Late on Wednesday afternoon in April, after supervising tennis practice, Janus got in his V.W. bus to drive from south St. Louis, where he taught, up to the Forest Park area, where he and Faith lived. But instead of heading directly home, he decided impulsively to take the freeway north along the river to a new downtown bookstore he had discovered. He had finished a book the night before on urban politics in the 1890's, Dailey Turnbull's *The Big City Machines: Reformers or Recidivists?,* and wanted something else to read. Even more, he knew, he wanted to delay getting home. For the last several Wednesday nights, Faith had been attending special prayer meetings at her church and had been fervently urging Janus to go with her. But he had been just as fervently resisting. He knew that the pressure would start the moment he walked into the apartment, and he was eager to postpone that moment as long as possible.

Driving north on I-55, Janus felt a fatigue that was unrelated to either the time of day or his tennis workout. He stuck his head out the window of the Volkswagen and let the wind blow in his face. The gritty air stung his eyes as he craned his neck to follow the smog line, which rose all around him like a cathedral ceiling to a smutty yellow pinnacle overhead. He could taste the acrid air on his lips, and as he turned off the highway away from the river and the towering silver arch, he suddenly knew what it felt like to be old.

At the bookstore he browsed in the history section but could find nothing that he wanted to read. Knowing that he risked Faith's wrath if he lingered long, he wandered quickly through the fiction section and picked up a copy of Ken Kesey's *One Flew Over the Cuckoo's Nest.* He had been meaning to read the book for a long while but somehow had never made the time. He paid for the book and went back to his car.

Driving home, he felt a rush of energy. His improved spirits were as inexplicable as his earlier fatigue, but when he went inside his apartment building, he was whistling.

Faith wasn't whistling, unfortunately, when Janus arrived. She was banging pots and pans around in the kitchen; Janus thought the banging had an angry tone. He actually felt he could perceive Faith's demeanor by listening to her move. When she was content, she rustled like a kitten moving through long grass. But when she was angry, all her movements were clipped and punctuated with little explosions, like the hammering of a manual typewriter.

He entered the kitchen and said, "Hi, honey," in a forlorn attempt to head off what he now felt was a certainty. She didn't answer him. He opened the refrigerator door, took out a Fresca, went to the pantry and said to a jar of Honey Bee, "Hi, honey."

The Honey Bee jar said in a squeaky voice that came from Janus's throat, "Hi, Rich. Gee, I'm glad you're home. Did you have a tough day? Did anything exciting happen?"

Before Janus could reply to the jar, Faith said, "Why are you late?"

The Honey Bee jar said, "I don't think he's so late, Faith. Remember, he has tennis practice after school."

"Cut the crap," she said.

"Yeah, cut the crap," Janus said to the Honey Bee jar and shut it up in the pantry for punishment. Through a small crack where the pantry door didn't fully close, Janus admonished the jar, "Here Faith's been working hard all day, and all you want to do is fool around." He took a drink from the Fresca bottle and sagged into a chair at the kitchen table. But only for the briefest second. Instantly he was back on his feet and headed for the refrigerator. He almost made it.

"You planning on helping with supper, or shall I start charging you for domestic service?"

Faith had become rather big on shared house duties.

"I was just getting some onions to chop," he said, taking the shallots from a plastic bag in the vegetable drawer and getting out a block of cheese. He brought the cutting board down from its hook on the wall and the grater from its drawer of kitchen utensils and began to work on the salad.

"Why are you late?" Faith asked as she fried hamburgers in a skillet.

"I didn't realize I was. I stopped off at a bookstore to get a book, but that couldn't have taken me more than fifteen minutes."

"You promised to be home early."

"I did? When?"

"Last Wednesday. You said if you got home early and got some work done before supper that you might go to prayer meeting with me."

"I did?" Janus said. "I'm sorry; I guess I just forgot." The truth was that he didn't remember promising her such a thing, but he guessed he might have said anything last Wednesday to keep from going to prayer meeting that night. Too bad this Wednesday had arrived so soon. "I'm pretty tired," he said.

"Yeah," Faith said.

"Yeah," Janus echoed. "Wednesdays are bad nights for these things, don't you think? School night and all?"

"Why won't you go with me, Rich?"

"I was kind of planning on reading. I just bought a copy of *One Flew Over the Cuckoo's Nest*. I've been wanting to read it for a long time."

"What are you reading that trash for?"

Janus laughed. "I wouldn't exactly call it trash."

"Why aren't you reading some history book?"

"I don't know. I'm tired of reading history."

"That's a great attitude for someone who's going to become this great historian." Faith flipped the two hamburger patties onto a paper towel. Janus got a head of lettuce out of the refrigerator and tore off leaves for their salads. He washed the lettuce, shook it in a colander and divided it into two bowls, sprinkling the onions and cheese on top. "You really gonna read tonight?" Faith said.

"Planning on it."

"You aren't going to watch some garbage on television?" They each brought their food to the table and sat down to eat.

"How often do I watch television?" Janus said.

"All day on Sunday."

"Besides sports, how often do I watch television?"

"You watch the news. Sometimes you watch Perry Mason reruns. How do I know *what* you do when I'm not here?"

"Faith, I'm going to read tonight. I just bought a copy of *One Flew Over the Cuckoo's Nest,* and I'm planning on starting it. But what if I were going to watch TV? Don't I have the right to do whatever I want? I work twelve hours a day to earn the privilege."

"That's an exaggeration."

"Barely."

"If you work so hard, how come you spend so little time on it at night anymore? It makes me wonder whether you really work so hard or just pretend to."

Janus looked at her over a forkful of salad raised halfway between his bowl and his mouth. "I'm not going to a prayer meeting with you," he said. "And you won't get me to go by trying to either pick a fight or lay some crazy guilt trip on me."

"Last year you brought work home every night," Faith said. "You always worked after supper, and lots of mornings you got up early to work before school. Last year there wasn't any reading novels. There wasn't even time for your history books."

Janus chewed his salad slowly and took a big swallow of Fresca before responding. "And last year was my first year of teaching. This year *you* work after supper and before school. This is *your* first year of teaching. Next year won't be quite so tough for you. See any parallels?"

"I'll always have to work this hard," Faith said.

"Then that's because you must be stupid," he said, regretting it immediately.

"Don't call me stupid, you son of a bitch," Faith retorted. She got up and scraped the remains of her half-eaten supper into a garbage sack.

"I'm sorry," Janus said.

"Shut up."

"I shouldn't call you stupid. I didn't mean it. You're not stupid, and I have never thought you were."

"Yes you do, Rich. You think I'm stupid."

"No, I don't, babe."

The fork Faith was using to scrape her plate slipped from her hand and fell into the garbage. She bent to retrieve it, but before grasping it she suddenly sent the plastic plate crashing against a cabinet. "I hate you!" she screamed. She turned on her husband with clenched fists stiffly at her side and screamed again, "I hate you!" She began pacing back and forth in front of the counter. "If you ever call me stupid again I'll…." Her hand fell on the paring knife Janus had used to chop onion. She picked it up and pointed it at him. "I'll kill you," she said.

Janus jumped to his feet, as much astonished as enraged. But he felt the urge to rush over and wrench the knife from her hand, even if he had to break her wrist to do it. With a tremendous exercise of control, he made himself sit back down. He was shaking when he said, "Don't be ridiculous, Faith. Put that knife down. I've said that I'm sorry and that I didn't mean it."

Faith put the knife back on the counter and returned to the table. She put her face in her hands and began to cry.

Janus took a deep breath, assuming this particular storm had passed. He placed his hand on his wife's thigh and said in a soft voice, "I don't think for a moment that you're stupid, Faith, okay?" He withdrew his hand and said aloud as much to himself as to her, "I don't think we were even really talking about your intelligence, though I think I stupidly steered the conversation in that direction."

Faith shuddered as she screamed at him with renewed energy, "When are you ever going to shut up with your dumb, stinking jokes?"

Janus slammed his hand down on the formica table with such force that his fork clattered to the floor. "Cool it, goddamnit," he yelled. "I'm not so dumb either, you know. I think that whatever all the dinner conversation has *not* been about, it *has* been about whether I'm gonna go with you to some fucking prayer meeting. Well, get this straight: I'm not. Not tonight. Not ever." Janus stood up. Now it was his turn to pace the kitchen. "I'm on to your games, you know. And the game tonight was to make me uncomfortable. If I'm not working, then somehow I maybe ought to go with you to a prayer meeting. Hence you merely had to make me feel guilty about not working. Well, understand something. Last year was so hard for me because I had never taught before. I had new preparations to do every day. But this year I have all of last year's preparations to call upon. I carefully saved all the material that I used last year in neat, organized manila folders."

Janus suddenly realized that Faith had succeeded once again in making him earnestly address one of the issues in an argument which was entirely beside the point. He smiled and said, "Which leads me to ask, do you happen to know just why folders of that particular variety are called 'manila'? For instance, do you think that they were first produced in Philippine coolie sweat shops?"

Faith looked up at him with red eyes. "Is everything with you a joke?"

Janus sat back at the table and smiled at her. "Not funny, huh? Well, you can't ever be funny if you never try, I guess."

"And you won't ever be ridiculous if you never try to be funny either," she said.

"True," Janus nodded his head. "But it's such a small price."

"Why don't you just finish your lecture?"

"Ah, yes. My lecture. Now, where was I? Manila folders, I believe. Now, as I remember, we had just decided to leave open the question of their Philippine origins. The point, I believe I was about to make, was that I saved last year's material, along with my notes on what worked well and what didn't, and this year I have all that to draw on. I have a vast supply of these manila folders, and I'll gladly give you some so that you too can escape the ogre of ongoing preparations. I can see that we have exhausted our time for today, so class dismissed."

"You really think I'm stupid, though," Faith said.

"You don't listen to me. Why do I bother giving you my wonderful lectures?" Janus reached over and touched her face. "Hey, babe, I'm really sorry. I'll never call you stupid again."

"But you think all the people at the prayer meeting are stupid, don't you? That's why you won't go with me."

Janus shook his head and leaned back in his chair. "Faith," he said, "I can't even believe *you're* going, that you've already gone and want to go again."

"It's beautiful, Rich."

"It's bullshit, babe."

"You don't know anything about it."

"I know plenty about tongue speakers," Janus said. His voice was growing heated again. "I know they're divisive. I know they're self-righteous. I know that I have not a smidgen of desire to become one of them."

"Then you have nothing to worry about. Glossolalia is a gift. No one receives the gift who doesn't seek it." Faith softened her tone. "Rich, you could at least come. The people are really kind and gentle."

"Kind and gentle, my ever lovin' ass. It was a bunch of segregationist, Biblical inerrancy, tongue-speaking assholes who drove my father out of his job. Those people are about as kind and gentle as a nest of rattlesnakes. They think they're God's anointed. They think they're the only ones who are saved, who are really Christian. No thanks, Faith. You can keep your tongue-speakers. And kindly keep them away from me."

"These people have nothing to do with your father," Faith said. "They're Lutheran, not Baptist. They don't believe the gift of tongues is the only gift, or even God's supreme gift. It's just one of many gifts. These people are supporting our church, not attacking it."

"And Hitler was supporting Germany, not attacking it."

"Don't talk like that."

"I'll tell you, Faith, God's gift to me tonight is Ken Kesey. I've heard his book is a very beautiful gift, too. I'm thankful to God for His gift, and I'd like to show my gratitude by reading and enjoying Kesey's book."

Faith got up from the table and picked up her plate, which was lying upside down on the floor where she'd thrown it. She also picked up the fork Janus had knocked to the floor, gathered the other dishes from the table and put them in the sink. "You're a blasphemer, Janus," she said. "You speak of God, but you don't even believe in God."

"You've come to know me so well in three years, Faith. What do I have to do? Short of speaking in tongues, that is. I believe in God. I believe in a lot of incredible things. Like this marriage, for instance. I believe in God, and I believe in marriage, and even though I think church is pretty antithetical to God, for the sake of this marriage I go to church. Every Sunday I go to church with you. Or have you forgotten?"

Faith didn't respond.

"I even went to adult confirmation class for the sake of this marriage," Janus added.

"Yeah, and you flunked," she said.

"I flunked because your hypocrite pastor told me to be perfectly honest with him."

"You know, you pat yourself on the back all the time for going to church with me. And you congratulate yourself even more for going to that confirmation class. But it doesn't mean anything. Not to me. And not to you. And for the same reason. You just did it to get along with me. That's a lousy, insincere reason." Faith took a sponge from the sink and began to wipe the table with it. With crumbs in her left hand and the sponge in her right, she said, "I know that secretly you're glad you flunked confirmation. I can just hear you telling the story to your friends. Have you written Paul about it? Have you called him some night when I'm not here? If you haven't, you will. What I really believe is that you flunked the class on purpose."

"Right," Janus said. "What was I supposed to do? Lie? Now, that's an admirable way to get accepted by the church."

Faith dumped her collection of crumbs back on the table and leaned on it with both hands. "Do you know how humiliating it is for me to be married to a man who flunked adult confirmation?"

"I didn't do it on purpose, Faith."

Pushing with her hands on the table, she began to rock back and forth, heel to toe. "You did," she said. "You did it on purpose." She pushed herself away from the table and went into the living room, where she gathered her purse and a cotton jacket. Janus followed.

"I didn't do it on purpose, Faith. I didn't."

"You did," she said. "YOU DID."

"I didn't. We're like two little kids. I didn't, but whatever you believe isn't going to get me to go to your prayer meeting."

Faith moved to the front door. She opened it and looked back at her husband. "I know. But while I'm gone, you could try going to hell." She stepped into the hall and slammed the door behind her.

"Life with you," Janus said to the empty apartment, "is a more than adequate simulation."

Spring ebbed into summer. Faith stopped going to her prayer meetings some time before school ended. And even with occasional enthusiasm, Faith and Janus began to make plans for moving to Los Angeles.

By the second week of June, their apartment was a chaos of preparation. Nearing midnight and alone, Janus worked amidst the disarray: sorting, discarding, dismantling, cleaning, boxing. His dark blue T-shirt was drenched with perspiration, and his hands and face were dirty with two years' accumulated dust. He and Faith had to pay rent for the entire month, even though they were leaving on the fifteenth, and in a foolish attempt to save money, they had opted not to pay the extra twenty-five dollars per month their landlord charged for the use of an air-conditioner. An evening-long rain had forced Janus to close the apartment windows and had denied him even the little breeze that might have stirred past the screens. Sticky and uncomfortable, he had been sipping beers since noon.

Afterwards, as he looked back on what happened, he would decide that his drinking was the crucial element. He was not drunk, but the alcohol had definitely affected him. It cost him that extra measure of control that had never failed him before.

Throughout the afternoon, Cassie Sears—who was in town to bid farewell—Faith, and her St. Louis friend, Ellen, had worked with Janus. But they had gone out for the night with his blessings. There were parties with his friends in the nights just ahead, and he could understand that the three women wanted a time just for themselves.

What he didn't understand was Faith's coming home from a night of conspiratorial drinking and saying within moments of arriving, "I'm not going to Los Angeles with you, Rich."

"Okay," Janus said. He didn't believe her for a second. He was very tired.

"Okay?" Faith said. "That's all you have to say: Okay?"

"What do you want me to say? You write my lines and I'll speak them."

Inaudibly Faith began to drum her fingers on the naugahyde seat cushion of the sofa where she sat. "I'm telling you that I'm going back to Chicago tomorrow with Cassie and that you'll never see me again."

"You're drunk," Janus said.

"Ha! Living with you for two years, I must've been drunk. And you're one to talk anyway. How many beers have you had today?"

He picked up the can of Busch next to his chair and took a swallow. It was warm. "A million," he said. "A million, two hundred forty-three thousand, six hundred and nine, to be precise. But who's counting?"

"Your ceaseless sarcasm is one reason I'm leaving you."

"Right," Janus said.

"You don't believe I'm serious, do you?"

"I believe you are a serious asshole." He rubbed his eyes with his finger tips and took another sip of his beer.

"God, I hate you," Faith hissed.

"Now, *that* I am coming to believe."

"I can't even talk to you. Don't you even want to know why I'm leaving?"

"I'd like to know why you decided to wait until I had packed all of our stuff together to decide that you're leaving. If you'd just had the foresight to decide a couple of days ago, we could have divided things into two piles, and I'd have had only half as much to pack."

"Are you just going to be mean, or are we going to talk about this? I want you to understand that I'm leaving in the morning."

Janus closed his eyes and scratched at his hair. "How can you leave in the morning? All your stuff is in these boxes here."

"You just take what you'll need in L.A. and leave the rest. I'm going to stay with Cassie until you're gone. After that I'll come back and decide whether to salvage this place or find a new apartment. I'm calling my principal before I leave in the morning to tell him not to replace me, that I'll be coming back in the fall."

"Sounds like you've got your plans all made." Janus was slowly coming to realize that Faith was serious, or at least that she was more serious than she had ever been in her threats before. He got up and went to the kitchen, bringing back a cold beer. "You're really wonderful, you know. First you let me pack all this stuff. Then you leave me to unpack all of it. What's the matter with you anyway, Faith? Explain to me for once how your brain operates."

"I want to have a baby," Faith said.

Janus was so flabbergasted he almost laughed. "What?" he said.

"You heard me. You always say 'what?' like you don't hear what I know damned well you do."

"What does having a baby have to do with any of this? We'll have a baby. We've always agreed that we'll have a baby just as soon as I'm through with graduate school."

"And when will that be? We have no idea. I want to have a child now. I don't want to wait."

"That's typical Faith reasoning if I ever heard it. You want to have a baby, but you don't want to live with your husband. You thinking perhaps of artificial insemination? Or is there someone you haven't told me about? Is Cassie Sears going to be the daddy?"

"Shut up, you son of a bitch!" Faith screamed. "God, I hate you; God, I wish you were dead. You've blown it this time, Janus. You might have talked me out of this like you've talked me out of everything else in this rotten relationship. But you're too drunk and too basically a shit. And you've blown it now, buster. God, I should have known what a drip you were the first time we went out. All your flip sarcasm and Southern hick charm. You could barely get another date. You told me that for a while in high school you *couldn't* get a date. You shouldn't have told me that story, Janus, because it let me see you for what you really are: a loser. A loser I had the misfortune to get stuck with. But I'm gettin' unstuck now, baby, and you better believe it." Faith was on her feet, walking about the living room, occasionally kicking at one of the boxes Janus had spent the evening closing with tape and tying up with cord.

"You're a maniac," Janus said.

"I'd be a maniac if I went to L.A. with you. Why should I go to L.A.? I don't even know anybody there."

"I don't know anybody there either," Janus pointed out.

"Yeah, but you *want* to go there. It's what you've been waiting for. You're finally going to graduate school. But I have no such reason for moving to California. I have a job here that I like and people I like to work with."

Janus took a long drink from his beer. He hoped that by delaying his response, Faith's anger would cool. But he was getting angry himself. And what he did not need at that point was more alcohol. "Remember, Faith, that a year ago you didn't even want to take the job here at all. You wanted to take that job in Chicago. Don't you think that you'll find a job in Los Angeles that you'll like just as well with people you'll like just as much?"

"Why should I go to Los Angeles with you when you wouldn't go to Chicago with me?"

That thrust brought Janus to his feet. "That's not true, goddamnit, and you know it. I was willing to go to Chicago with you. I busted my ass to find a teaching job, and when I couldn't, I landed that job as an unemployment claims officer."

"Yeah, with your Southern hick soulmate, Paul Taylor." Faith walked over to a bookshelf that remained to be dismantled and picked up the large red piggy bank that Paul had given them as a wedding present; it had come with the advice to put a penny in every time they had sex the first year of their marriage and the promise that if they took a penny out every time they had sex after the first year, they'd never get the bank empty. "Crude, disgusting Paul Taylor, who had the polish to give us this vile item for a wedding present."

"You keep your rotten mouth off my friends," Janus said. "And you better put that bank down before I take it away from you and shove it up your ass."

"You can't tell me what to do anymore!" Faith screamed. "You can't ever tell me what to do any more." She lifted the piggy bank high above her head and sent it smashing to pieces against one of the bricks at the bottom of the bookshelf. Hundreds of pennies scattered all over the room.

Janus knelt on the rug with his fingers in the shards of the destroyed bank. He looked up at Faith and said in a voice that was a growl, "Fuck you, bitch."

"Fuck me. Fuck me. That's always it, isn't it." Faith, who was wearing a plaid wrap-around skirt that fastened with an oversized safety pin, unhooked the pin and pulled the skirt across her body and off as if she were drawing a sword. She pressed down on the heel of each shoe with her opposite foot and then kicked each loafer across the room toward Janus.

He stood up and started moving toward her. He had never before been so mad.

"Fuck me. You wanna fuck me, Janus?" She yanked her underpants down around her knees and thrust her pelvis toward her husband, who stopped desperately still in the middle of the living room. "Come on, Janus," Faith croaked, "fuck me. If that's what you want. FUCK ME. Do something so finally horrid that I'll never be able to forgive you for it and won't have to care anymore that I hate your guts. FUCK ME." She bent and pulled her underpants all the way off, again thrust her pelvis forward and began walking swaybacked toward him. She began to chant in a whisper as she approached, "Fuck me, Janus; fuck me. Fuck me, Janus; fuck me." When she was right in front of him, she spit on him, and when he didn't flinch, she threw her panties in his face.

From his side, Janus's arm jumped out at Faith. His fist was balled tight and meant to land on her venomous face, but not all his control was lost. As the arm moved, the fist unraveled into an open hand. And as it moved, the target shifted. Instead of landing on her face, a blow that might have knocked out teeth or broken her nose, the hand circled behind her and cuffed the back of her head. Awful remorse began even as he felt the contact. He prayed instantly that he had not hurt her. But Janus was a large and powerful man, and Faith dropped as if she'd been hit by a blackjack. He could not believe he had actually hit her, much less that he had knocked her down. Yet, sorry as he was, his fury was not entirely spent.

"Get up, Faith. I didn't hurt you," he demanded. She lay on her right side, her arms in funny positions, one trapped underneath her, the other flung over her head. Her eyes were closed. Janus stood over her. "Okay, Sarah Bernhardt. Good show. Now get up." Faith didn't move.

Janus walked away from her. He went into the bathroom and looked at his strange, blotched face in the mirror. He turned on the tap and rubbed his face with cold water. He dried himself with a towel and looked again in the mirror. His eyes were very red. There were faint lines in his forehead he had never noticed before.

When he returned to the living room, Faith still lay on the floor. If she had moved, he could not detect it. He knelt beside her and examined her quietly for a moment. "Come on, Faith," he said softly. "I didn't hurt you. I'm sorry I hit you. But I couldn't have hurt you." When she still didn't respond, Janus began finally to worry. He brushed his finger tips across her forehead and temples, lifting her damp hair away from her head. "Babe?" he said. He felt a rush of panic that was as scary as any moment he had ever experienced. What if he *had* hurt her badly? What in the world should he do? "Oh, my God," he said. He picked her up, carried her to their bedroom and brought back a wet washcloth, which he put over the top of her face. When that did not revive her, he squeezed drops of cold water from the rag onto her forehead and gently mopped them up again.

When Faith finally began to move, Janus started crying. He buried his face into the crescent of bed between her head and shoulders. His hot breath against her neck, he said in a broken voice, "I'm sorry, Faith. Oh, Jesus, I'm sorry." Faith threw her arm over him and laid her hand flat against his face, and he repeated his sorrow. He neither moved nor attempted to stop her when her fingernail burrowed its way into his flesh.

Later he would tell people that he had gotten the two-inch scratch on his right cheek when someone tried to slap the ball away from him after he had pulled down a rebound. It was a story he would never alter, even years later after the scratch had healed into the faint scar that sometimes he thought wasn't visible at all. But to Faith he said, "Does that make us even?"

He pulled away and sat on the edge of the bed. His face did not bleed much, but it stung as he dabbed at it with the wet washcloth. "We'll never be even," Faith said. "When a man hits a woman, there's nothing she can do to make it even."

Janus left. He got into his car, drove downtown and parked in the lot for visitors to the Gateway Arch. It was very late, and the whole world seemed deserted. He walked under the arch, beyond it, up over the levee and down to the muddy water of the Mississippi. There he sat on an outcropping of broken cement blocks and relished the indiscriminate bite of the jagged concrete as it dug into his legs. He salvaged a stick of wood which he found wedged between two of the blocks and sailed it as far as he could out into the river. He saw it splash and thought he could see it for a while as it began its southward journey. He marveled, as if the notion were peculiarly his, that something thrown in the water at St. Louis might actually float all the way to New Orleans.

Janus and Faith didn't break up then, of course. They moved to Los Angeles and resumed the odd battle that was their marriage. In future arguments, Faith would taunt her husband about his having once struck her and would challenge him to do it again. He never did. And after a time he was sure that he never would. But despite her taunts, Faith never shared his confidence. And Janus could never say that he blamed her.

In future years, when he thought back about that night, he could judge it the moment that something happened to his love for Faith. He felt that she was absolutely right, that there was no excuse for his having struck her, that there was no provocation that justified what he did. He was too large, and she was too powerless to defend herself. But he felt that a part of him began to hate her that night—not because she had taunted him so obscenely, and certainly not because she had scratched him. But he began to hate her because she had driven him to do something for which he would never be able to forgive himself.

13

Johnnie Golden first took me to L.A.'s popular Mexican restaurant, El Cholo, in December of 1972. Most of you on the committee probably don't remember Johnnie. Even if he enrolled for your classes, it's unlikely he attended long enough for you to get to know him. Johnnie was my friend. He still is my friend. I haven't talked to him in a long time, but he's still my friend.

A native of Atlanta, Johnnie was a Harvard grad a couple of years my senior. He claimed he did well at Harvard because he took only lecture classes where the graders assumed from his name that he must be a black woman. "They assumed they were helpin' out the niggers, when in fact they were just givin' breaks to another kike." Johnnie was his given first name. He was not a Jonathan or even a John. Unusual in most parts of the country, it was fairly common for Southern families to name their sons with the childhood diminutive permanently attached.

Blessed with horribly poor eyesight, Johnnie escaped the Vietnam draft and did a master's degree in journalism at Columbia right after college. That credential landed him a job in Minneapolis working the night shift for the Associate Press. But the AP experience turned out to be a disappointment. He referred to his time in Minneapolis as "the three years I was a typist." Belatedly, he decided to try a career in history. He later referred to his term as a graduate student at UCLA as "the year I was a very large asshole."

You can perhaps see why we became friends.

Johnnie was a strange looking person with long coarse hair, which he was not terribly good about keeping clean. He almost always wore it pulled back in a ponytail. He also almost always wore a leather, snap-brim cap which was several centuries old and whose bill he had creased so severely that it looked like the roof of an A-frame house. With his contacts in, he was bug-eyed as a frog. He was better looking when he wore his incredibly thick glasses. But not much. His most striking physical trait, though, was his agonizing thinness. Spurting a full eight inches after he entered college, he was nearly six feet tall, but his weight never topped 120. His thinness was almost dictated by his misshapen frame, narrow hips and even narrower shoulders, but sitting on top of that body was a normal-sized head, or perhaps an even larger than normal one. If he had ever known that I was going to write this about him, he would have told me his hat size so that I could be precise. Despite his frail appearance, however, Johnnie was surprisingly hardy, well-coordinated, and an excellent, though modest, guitarist.

Johnnie's unusual shape led his high school mates to call him "Odd Body" with as much derision as their adolescent sadism could muster, a fact that he confided to me with considerable solemnity after we had become friends. He related that tale along with several other horror stories of his childhood. Since he was late to mature sexually, gym class was an awful time for him. His daily showers there revealed not only that his penis was undersized, but that he lacked a single strand of pubic hair. The other boys in his school delighted in calling him "Hairless," particularly when they caught him talking to a girl.

But the crowning indignity they perpetrated on him occurred at the homecoming football game his senior year in high school. Far too small to participate in athletics, Johnnie was in the process of winning a coveted school letter by serving the football team as its manager. To show their appreciation for the fact that Johnnie had not lost a single piece of equipment all year, the team members stuffed him into a large duffel bag and dumped him at the fifty-yard line at half time. As the band members marched all around him, he struggled to free himself. When he was finally able to wriggle out of his canvas prison, he was greeted with a humiliating standing ovation.

Johnnie related these stories with such evident pain that I reciprocated by telling him of my experience with Sandy Wilkerson, the night I got turned down for dates by twelve different girls and how my singing voice was so rotten I was asked to be a mouther in the church choir. They were not equivalent stories, I knew, so I waited several days before I referred to Johnnie as Odd Body myself.

Of course, I avoided calling Johnnie Odd Body in public, but he accepted my occasionally calling him that in private as a sign of our bond of friendship. In public I called him Johnnie (most everyone else called him John) or just Asshole for short. He normally referred to me as LALA, a melodic acronym for "Largest Asshole in Los Angeles."

While Johnnie was at Columbia, he had fallen in love with a woman who was a senior at Barnard College. Diane, it seems, looked like a cross between

Catherine Deneuve and Candice Bergen, and Johnnie was incredulous that such a creature could love him in return. The problem, I think, was that because of his looks, Johnnie tended to underestimate his attractiveness to women. But the fact was that many were drawn to him. He had a certain vulnerability that women responded to. And furthermore, he was an incomparable good time. He was knowledgeable about most every field of human endeavor and a side-splitting storyteller.

After they married, Johnnie rapturously paid Diane's way through law school at the University of Minnesota, where she proved that in addition to the face of a goddess, she had the legal mind of Perry Mason. Unfortunately, it developed that she also had the loyalty of Benedict Arnold. When she graduated from law school, she left Johnnie for a partner in the firm where she took her first job doing insurance defense work.

When people suggested that if Diane was the kind of person who chose to do insurance defense work that she was hardly the woman for Johnnie anyway, he would respond, "Not true, not true. You'd just have to know Diane. I'm sure all the little people she screwed just loved it. I'm a little people, and I sure as hell loved it when she screwed me." Despite his habitual flippancy, it was painfully obvious that he was heartbroken over his divorce. And it was at least partially a desire to get away from Minneapolis that led him to become my classmate.

We entered UCLA in 1972. He had come to study nineteenth-century intellectual history under your renowned colleague, Dr. Richard Boeotian. It was a typical miscalculation. Richard Boeotian was on leave for the academic year 1972-73. The following year Boeotian offered no courses for which Johnnie was eligible. But by that time it didn't matter because Johnnie was no longer in school.

"Maybe some work with Boeotian would have made a difference," I suggested when he informed me of his decision to quit.

"Nah," he replied. "Boeotian's just an asshole like the rest of them. Larger, in fact, because he's more successful."

In general, Johnnie subscribed to a self-developed theory owing its origins to the Peter Principle, which for those of you who don't know, maintains that a person is normally promoted one step beyond his competence level to a position where his incompetence allows him a lifetime of misery. Johnnie called his maxim the "Asshole Axiom."

The "Asshole Axiom" maintained that the larger an asshole a person was, the more successful that person became. "But the 'Asshole Axiom,'" Johnnie warned, "must not be confused with the 'Bulbous Tit Theory of History,' of which it is only a corollary, and which holds that the whole world sucks. Nor must it be confused with the 'Puckered Pink Premise,' which states that all the world's inhabitants are assholes save for a gravely small percentage, including myself and several others who either are or could be my friends. And among that gravely small percentage there are those, namely myself and one Richard A. Janus, about whom there remain very serious suspicions."

The nifty thing about Johnnie's proclamations on the state of the human condition was that he never applied his theories to his relations with other people. He was the farthest thing in the world from a snob. "Remember, *mein Freund*," he often counselled me, particularly if I had taken some stance with which he disagreed, "there's an awful lot of asshole in the goodest of us, and at least some good in the assholest of us."

Via his escape clause, he allowed sundry sorts to avoid fundamental damnation—sorts, he urged, that included him and me, several other graduate students, even an occasional professor, and most of the eight-ball pool crew at the now defunct LoDaMar bowling alley in Santa Monica, where he spent those evenings he should have spent finishing the seminar papers that he never bothered to begin. Though he vehemently denied it, Johnnie Golden was one of the warmest, most genuinely friendly people I have ever known.

"Eat shit," he responded when I shared the fact that I held this opinion of him.

During the year that Johnnie spent in L.A., I saw him almost every day. Only once, though, the night he told me he was quitting graduate school, was I inside his apartment. He lived alone in a cheerless one-room flat on Gayley Street, which separates UCLA's western boundary from residential Westwood. The room was large but oppressively dark. A two-burner hot plate constituted the kitchen. A bed and a desk against opposite walls were the room's entire furnishings, discounting a shelf of concrete blocks and boards on which he had his surprisingly few books.

Johnnie's room had no chair for reading, no table for eating. A large empty space in the room's center dominated its appearance. Johnnie was a person of such frenetic habits and moods that I remember being struck by his apartment's neatness. The papers on the small desk were organized into precise piles; the bed was made.

Most of our social visits took place at my apartment on Fourth Street in Santa Monica, three blocks north of Wilshire. We met within weeks of my arrival in L.A., when each of us enrolled in a summer German class to help prepare us for the language exam we had to pass on the way to our Ph.D.'s. We fell into casual conversation one day after class, and I ended up inviting him over that weekend for dinner. Faith and I made spaghetti, and Johnnie brought along a bottle of Italian Swiss Colony Pink Chablis. We were all boycotting Gallo in those days, of course. Faith complained that she didn't really like wine and Johnnie suggested that she mix it with Seven-Up or ginger ale and make herself a wine cooler. Faith and I were trying to save money in those days, so all we had was Bubble Up, which we bought in quart bottles whenever they were on sale at the Food Giant. Johnnie told her that Bubble Up would probably do just fine and that he'd really like a wine cooler himself. Somehow that pleased Faith, a little gesture on Johnnie's part that showed he shared some peculiarity with her. After he went home that night, she said she thought he was nice. I remember feeling very happy because we were so newly arrived in L.A. and already we had made a friend, someone special because he was liked by both of us.

For the next six months, Johnnie ate with us probably once a weekend. He would come over early and help us cook, sometimes providing the ingredients, always providing a large jug of Italian Swiss Colony, which he mixed with our Bubble Up in a glass pitcher Faith and I had received as a wedding present.

Faith grew nearly as fond of Johnnie as I was. She marvelled at how funny he was and often commented on his sensitivity. Once, however, she remarked that she thought Johnnie was a bad influence on me. "He doesn't know what he's doing," she said. "And I'm afraid he's going to convince you that you don't either." Another time she opined that Johnnie hated women. I asked her what evidence she had to support that judgment. She was silent for a while but finally said, "None. But it's true anyway. He would never admit it, but I know it's true."

Usually, though, Faith and Johnnie got along well. He teased her and flirted with her, and she enjoyed the attention. I even experienced a moment of jealousy about the closeness of their relationship. We were fixing a chicken dish that called for crushed garlic. When we discovered that our last clove was moldy, I made a trip to the Food Giant for more. When I returned, Johnnie was sitting in my chair, and Faith was perched on his lap. They made no attempt to separate when I came in the front door.

"I see you two are getting better acquainted," I said and laughed. I admit it was a sort of strained laugh.

Faith twisted her head around to look at me and said, "Darn, you're back. We were just about to run away together to South America."

"Not true at all," Johnnie said. "I was just promising her Brazil so I could cop a few feels."

Faith looked at him. "You mean you were only interested in the sex?"

"What do you mean *only?*" Johnnie said.

I assumed it was all innocent enough, though after Johnnie went home I brought up the incident to Faith. "Were you jealous?" she asked, her voice registering surprise.

"No," I said. Isn't that what I was supposed to say? "On the other hand, yes," I added.

"You ought to be ashamed," Faith said. "Your wife and your best friend. That's incredible."

"I'm ashamed."

"Good," she said. "You're kind of cute that way."

Despite her liking Johnnie, though, Faith seldom stayed up late when he came to visit. She was a committed nine-hour-per-night sleeper, a total she almost never got during the work week. To recoup her losses, it was not at all uncommon for Faith to sleep eleven or twelve hours on Friday and Saturday nights.

After she made her usual early departure to bed, Johnnie and I would imbibe wine coolers until we killed the large bottle of wine. Sometimes we would begin bleary-eyed games of chess, not one of which we ever finished. After school started in the fall, we began the habit of watching taped replays of UCLA football games and later the rebroadcasts of the great Bill Walton as he led the Bruins to still another national basketball championship. While we watched the games and the Basil Rathbone/Sherlock Holmes movies that followed, we talked, became closer and confided the apprehensions each of us had begun to feel about our lives. We had hoped to become men of broad knowledge but found ourselves being trained as very narrow specialists. We were determined, nonetheless, we told one another, to succeed in this profession.

We were capable of great self-deception.

On weeknights while Faith was grading papers, or after she had gone to bed, I would occasionally join Johnnie in his favorite haunt, the bar at the LoDaMar bowling alley. After ten o'clock on any night, I could count on finding him hunched over the pool table. Our eight-ball matches were competitive, though we tended to dominate each other in alternating streaks which came and went without explanation. For a while we even got into bowling. Then one night, cheering madly for one another, with enough beer in our bloodstreams to smooth out the jerks in our followthroughs, we each rolled a six hundred series. We photocopied the score sheet, got it attested by the alley manager and agreed never to go bowling again.

The thing I suppose that succeeded in cementing our friendship was the German exam we had to pass. Though it was perfectly senseless to force American history students to master a foreign language, we were required to do so all the same. Johnnie and I made a pact to get the exam out of the way at the beginning of our careers instead of letting it hang around to delay our degrees, as some graduate students inevitably did. In September we agreed to study German together for at least an hour, five days a week. Johnnie would arrive at my apartment by eight o'clock, and we would drill each other on vocabulary and grammar. As the December exam date neared, the sessions became increasingly longer. First two hours, then four, sometimes even six. I had difficulty keeping up with my other classes. Johnnie, as it happened, didn't keep up. We were working hard on the language, but sharing it, we even enjoyed ourselves.

Late on weeknights we still occasionally drank *ein Bier* at the LoDaMar. Always on the weekends we had our *rot Wein mit Boobel Über* (red wine with Bubble Up). And as often as possible, we found reasons to call one another *Eselloch.* We might have used *Mastdarm* or *Afterschliessen,* but since those words really meant "anus" or "rectum," we preferred *Eselloch.* Even though we had concocted it ourselves, we figured it had to be translated as "asshole."

Our German never was the greatest.

But we would study, and when one of us knew an answer that the other didn't, he would deride the other's *Ich weiss nicht* with: *"Du weiss nicht? Was ein Dumkopf. Was ein Eselloch."*

Incredibly, we both managed to pass the exam. It was clearly not very important to the makers of the system that we really know anything about a foreign language, just that we pass an exam and thereby give the appearance of knowing something.

About thirty minutes after the mailman brought my test results, my phone rang. Johnnie's voice said, *"Ist dies mein Freund, Eselloch?"*

"Freund, ja," I replied. *"Eselloch, nein."* A short silence followed in which neither of us wanted to ask the inevitable question for fear the other's news was bad. Finally, I said, "So, my German test scores came a little while ago. What about yours?"

"Yop," he said, putting a *p* on the German *ja.*

"So I'm pretty *glücklich* right now. *Bist du glücklich?"*

"I'm so fucking *glücklich,* I could make nice remarks about Richard Nixon," Johnnie said. "Do you know we never have to *sprechen Deutsch* again as long as we live? Our *Pferdscheiss* German period is over."

"I can't believe it," I said.

"Me neither," Johnnie said.

"I just can't believe it."

"You've already said that, asshole."

"I tend toward redundancy at moments of ecstasy."

"I will tolerate no redundancy today," Johnnie said. "I want to do something new. I want to take you and Faith to a Mexican restaurant downtown."

"I can't believe it."

"I'll forgive you, *mein Freund,"* he said. "But only because I've got the El Cholo Feeling."

That night Johnnie took us to El Cholo, a small restaurant on Western Avenue several blocks south of Wilshire. It had four small dining rooms, a total seating capacity of perhaps 125, a bar with six stools and two tiny waiting rooms crammed with people standing shoulder to shoulder. It reminded me of a late nineteenth-century scene from Ellis Island. Only El Cholo, not America, was the promised land.

The L.A. night was as unusually clear as our spirits when we entered. Squeezing against the white, wrought-iron fence, we edged our way by the crowd of people standing on the awning-covered porch, past a sign which warned that consumption of alcoholic beverages outside El Cholo was illegal. Inside the waiting room we squirmed through the throng waiting for tables and up one step to a tiny, jammed hallway, where a young chicana recorded the names of the people on the waiting list. As we reached her, she said into a microphone built into the wall over her desk, "MacMurphy. Party of four. MacMurphy. Party of four."

Johnnie said to her, "A table for Golden please, party of three."

"MacMurphy. Party of four," she replied. "Last call for MacMurphy, party of four."

"Golden, three," Johnnie repeated when she looked at him.

"Thank you, señor." She wrote his name in the ledger.

"How long is the wait?" I asked.

"An hour and a half, señor."

"An hour and a half?" I looked at Johnnie with one of those looks that says, are you sure this is worth it?

The ledger lady saw the look and said, "This is your first time at El Cholo, no?"

"Yes," I said.

She smiled and said to Johnnie, "And you, señor?"

"I've been here before."

"Your friend must have liked El Cholo, for he has brought you this time," she said to me.

I laughed and said, "An hour and a half."

She laughed, too. "Be patient, señor. At El Cholo the waiting is part of the fun."

"I'll buy you a drink, LALA," Johnnie said.

"Lala?" the ledger lady said. "That is your name, señor?"

"Nickname," I said.

She smiled broadly. Her teeth were very white against her coffee-colored skin. "That is an unusual nickname, señor. What does it mean?"

I had no idea what I was going to tell her. I think I might have just stammered until our table was ready if Johnnie hadn't quickly spoken up. "It's because he's a singer, lalalala."

"You are a famous singer?"

"No, no," I said.

"It's a cruel nickname," Johnnie said. "He's such a bad singer he was kicked out of a church choir."

The ledger lady smiled again. "I think you are putting me on, señor, but I will forgive you. Enjoy El Cholo, Mr. Golden, and you, too, Mr. Lala."

Johnnie just loved her saying that. Laughing delightedly, he led me and Faith down the narrow hallway, past a window where the waitresses picked up their bar orders and into the interior waiting room. We shouldered our way through another crowd until we reached a spot in the corner. There we stood and talked. Mostly, Faith and I marvelled at this place's amazing popularity. When the ledger lady called out another name, four people sitting near us on one of the battered, plastic couches that lined the walls of the room arose to eat. We took their seats. Johnnie grabbed a fat but marvelously graceful waitress, whose job it was to bring drinks to the mob in this room. "A pitcher of margaritas," he ordered. "Three glasses."

"A pitcher of margaritas?" Faith said.

"It's a special occasion," Johnnie reminded her.

"I'm not sure I like margaritas," she said.

The waitress reappeared with the tray of booze held high above the heads of the crowd. Johnnie paid four dollars for the drinks, tipped the waitress another dollar and refused to take any money from me as he passed out the salt-rimmed glasses.

"If you've never drunk margaritas before," he explained to Faith while he poured the foamy liquid into our glasses, "pull the salt into your mouth as you sip the drink and mix the salt with the drink in your mouth before you swallow."

Faith wrinkled her nose. "I don't like it," she said.

"They're wonderful," I said.

"I don't like the salt," she explained.

"I can get you a clean glass," Johnnie offered. "They have glasses without salt, but without the salt you won't be getting the real McDoogle."

Faith took another sip from her glass. "I don't really like hard drinks very much. Maybe I should just get a wine cooler."

"Just try it," I said. "It's no stronger than lemonade."

Faith swirled her finger around the drink, lifted some of the foam from the glass and licked it off her finger. Johnnie and I drained our glasses, and he got up and disappeared into the crowd, returning soon with two freshly salted glasses and a wine cooler for Faith. "It's okay if you don't like them," he consoled her. "That leaves more for me and LALA." He filled the two new glasses from the pitcher, handed one to me and raised his. "To my good friends," he said as we clinked our glasses together. "May the success we've had today be only the beginning of many successes in our long careers."

He wasn't even being ironic.

"To the El Cholo Feeling," I said.

By the time the ledger lady announced, "Golden. Party of three. Golden. Party of three," Johnnie and I were halfway through our second pitcher of margaritas and all the way through with being sober.

For dinner, Johnnie recommended we try chile rellenos. For two dollars I had mine with an enchilada. For $1.50 Faith had hers by itself. Johnnie ordered the El Cholo Dinner, a feast at $2.95 that included an enchilada, taco and relleno. Despite his small frame, he finished all of it. I struggled to get through less. Faith didn't finish hers, though she claimed to have liked it quite a bit.

Stuffed and drunk, we fought our way back into the cool L.A. night. The fog had rolled in from the ocean. The sky, which only hours earlier had been clear enough to see stars, was now gray and murky. Beside me in the front seat of the Volkswagen as we drove home, Johnnie held his stuffed stomach and moaned.

"You okay?" I asked.

"Fine," he grunted.

"What's the matter with you?" Faith said from the back seat.

"I've just got the El Cholo Feeling," he replied.

The trip to El Cholo became our new ritual. Few weekends passed without at least one outing to the Western Avenue restaurant. And soon we began to include a fourth, Danielle LeBlanc, a neighbor Faith and I idly tried to pair with Johnnie.

Danielle was thirty years old, a large woman at five-feet-nine and perhaps 135 pounds. She was obsessed with the notion that she was fat and was forever on one crash diet or another. One week she would eat nothing but celery, another just grapefruit, but every weekend she would enthusiastically break whatever regimen she'd been maintaining to accompany us to El Cholo.

Danielle was an actress. She had managed to get an agent who occasionally landed her roles in cheap commercials that only ran on non-network television stations late at night between advertisements for Cal Worthington Used Cars and spots offering special collections of old record albums that weren't available in retail stores. The commercials brought her little income but made it possible for her to collect unemployment insurance for a time afterwards. When unemployment money ran out, she sustained herself by working as a Kelly Girl.

By the winter of 1973, Danielle had come to understand that she likely would never make it in her chosen profession. In the eight years since she had graduated from the University of California at San Diego, she had not landed even the smallest role in a professional theater or film production, save as an extra. But she kept on. She was a senior member of the semiprofessional company at West L.A.'s Odyssey Theater, but even there she seldom landed a leading role. Still, few plays were cast without her. She was always someone's mother or someone's sister or a nurse or a maid. And she claimed that the opportunity to perform, in however small a part, was enough to keep her going. She kept hoping, a hope beyond believing, beyond even conscious dreaming, that soon, perhaps tomorrow, a miracle would occur.

Aside from her professional failure, Danielle's life was in disarray. She had had her first date as a junior in college. Two months later she married the only man who had ever asked her out. Two years later she divorced him when a fellow actor at the Odyssey flirted with her. The new man bedded her for a while and allayed her insecurity about her size by assuring her that he liked his women large. And it may even have been true. When he left her, it wasn't for a petite woman but for a delicate man. Later, Danielle and Johnnie would argue about the definition of the word *cuckold,* a term Johnnie frequently applied to himself. Because her lover had left her for another man, Danielle wanted Johnnie to agree that she was a cuckold, too.

After breaking up with her actor friend, Danielle guarded against rejection with a conflicting pair of strategies. When she met a man to whom she was genuinely attracted, she acted haughty and abusive. With other men she hopped into bed as soon as possible and made marriage noises as soon as they hopped out. Both strategies kept her lonely, full of self-contempt and single.

Toward Johnnie, Danielle used the first approach, but it didn't altogether work. "You know why I like you so much, Danielle?" he constantly asked her. "Because I've got a real soft spot in my heart for obnoxious people."

Danielle and Johnnie never became an item, but our El Cholo foursome thrived anyway, mainly because of Johnnie's ability to communicate to Danielle how much he liked her even though he didn't want to sleep with her. The only thing that really aggravated Johnnie about Danielle was her habitual lying. "I don't know," was an expression foreign to her. Smart but notoriously ill-informed on most every topic, Danielle was a knee-jerk bullshitter. She seldom missed an opportunity to imply that she'd read the book or seen the film someone might mention. One El Cholo night while discussing *Cabaret,* Johnnie was awash in margaritas and this habit succeeded in getting under his skin. He turned on her and snapped, "Goddamnit, Danielle, how can you say that when I know goddamn well that you haven't read Isherwood's book?"

She was very cool. She took a drag on her cigarette and blew smoke out slowly. "I've never found that a particular problem before," she said. "What I offer are my opinions, and those opinions are only coincidentally based on information. I normally share the opinions of the last person I talked to who had any." She took another puff at her Salem as we all stared at her. "So if you'll kindly continue, Mr. Golden, I can discover what it is I think about *The Berlin Stories.*"

There was a moment of silence followed by a burst of laughter all around. By embracing Johnnie's accusation and making light of it instead of taking offense, Danielle had saved not only our party but had saved Johnnie a heavy dose of self-recrimination. Ever after that night, he regarded her with a new respect.

Danielle was a good sport and an excellent audience. She could take teasing and rewarded any attempt at humor with a warm laugh. She stood in sharp contrast to Faith, who often ignored or even scorned efforts at witticism. But Danielle's best trait was her neighborliness: you could count on her. If furniture needed moving or an apartment needed painting, if plants needed watering or if just a thirst needed slaking, Danielle was available. She knew what it meant to be a friend. And we all liked her very much.

One Friday in March, at the end of our second academic quarter, I was in a particularly festive mood when we made our El Cholo jaunt. The Sunday before, my wasted ankles wrapped as always in a cast of athletic tape that stretched from toe to calf, I had shared with my recreation basketball teammates that special joy of victory in our league championship game. And that morning I had turned in a seminar paper to you, Dr. Burden. It was my first piece on King Philip's War, and I was rather excited by it. I still had my doubts about becoming an historian, of course, but for once I felt fulfilled by having written a little bit of history. And with a week of vacation coming, it was time for celebration.

In the crowded El Cholo hallway, the ledger lady greeted me warmly and by name. "A table for four, Señor Lala?"

I think Johnnie paid her to address me that way.

"Si, señorita," I said.

She wrote "Lala" in her book, then looked at me, smiling, and said, "You and your friends are very fond of El Cholo, no? Is Señor Johnnie with you tonight?" I explained that he and the others were parking the car and had dropped me off to get our name on the waiting list. It was so crowded in the hallway that I could barely move and was forced to stand practically brushing up against her. Forced by circumstances into conversation, I asked her about the derivation of El Cholo's name. I had always presumed that it stemmed from the family name of the original owners. She seemed surprised that I was not acquainted with the term *cholo* but explained that it was a Mexican-American slang word.

When the others came in and we ordered a pitcher of margaritas, three glasses and a wine cooler, I asked Johnnie if he knew what *cholo* meant.

"Nigger," he said, getting the expected giggle from Danielle.

"Come on," Faith said.

"All I know," Johnnie explained, "is that in *The Long Goodbye,* Marlowe calls a chicano houseboy 'cholo' and almost gets handed his head."

"It means wetback," I said. "But Johnnie's kind of right. The ledger lady said it's not a name you usually call a friend. Do you think that's right, Cholo?" I said to Johnnie.

"Absolutely, Señor Lala," he said, affecting a Mexican accent.

We were in such a festive mood that night that we drank and ate even more than usual. Johnnie ordered nachos as an appetizer and insisted that we all not only eat the cheese and chips but the jalapeño peppers as well. Everyone was game but Faith, who pronounced that she thought the whole idea was "macho."

"Not if I'm gonna do it, too," Danielle said.

"For you it's 'macha.'" Faith said, getting her best laugh of the night.

The primary impact of eating jalapeño peppers, we shortly discovered, was that we were required to drink whole vats of margaritas to extinguish the inferno the peppers lit on our tongues.

"Good existentialist fare," Johnnie said, holding a pepper before us like a scepter. "You suffer. But in an act of pure defiance, you enjoy it anyway."

I thought I was totally stuffed when I finished the El Cholo Dinner Johnnie required me to order that night. But when he ordered green corn tamales to finish, I managed to pack away my share of that special sweet dish, too. Finally, I told him, "If you order one more item, you're going to have to eat it alone."

"Have no fear, *mein Freund,"* he said. "We have eaten it all."

When the check came, Johnnie grabbed it and tried to pay it. But the rest of us stuffed money into his pockets and threatened to kill him if he tried to give it back to us.

As we were preparing to leave, Faith laid her hands on my stomach, which felt as taut and swollen as a basketball. "Now, this is what I call the El Cholo Feeling," she said.

She patted me lightly, and I responded to her touch with a melodious "um."

Johnnie patted his own stomach twice and answered me with an "um umph."

Faith got up, rolling her eyes toward Danielle. "I'm getting out of here before these two guys get arrested for impersonating human beings," she said.

"Um umph," Johnnie and I groaned in reply, pushing ourselves out of the booth.

When we got to the Toyota we'd bought for Faith our seccnd year in St. Louis, Johnnie moaned, "uuuumph" and climbed into the back seat. I started to get behind the wheel—I often drove home from El Cholo, even if we had taken Faith's car—but she blocked me away from the driver's side. "You're too drunk to drive a tricycle," she pointed out.

"Uuumph umph," I agreed and got in the back seat beside Johnnie.

"Aren't they charming?" Faith said to Danielle as the two of them got into the car.

"They aren't gonna belch and fart at us all the way home, are they?" Danielle said.

"The first one who belches, walks," Faith threatened.

Danielle looked into the back seat menacingly. "And the first one who farts, dies," she said. "You two understand?"

"Um um um um," we said in unison.

"What's that?" Danielle asked Faith.

"Rich is studying Indians now," she said. "Johnnie's probably decided to become one."

The women shook their heads, and Faith pulled the car into traffic. Danielle suggested that we head home along Mulholland Drive, a scenic road atop the Hollywood Hills which affords views of the L.A. basin and the San Fernando Valley. It was one of the rituals the four of us had adopted in association with our trips to El Cholo. Somehow the sight of a nearly endless expanse of light never grew old to us.

Forty-five minutes later, as we were coming into Santa Monica, Johnnie asked Faith to stop at Baskin-Robbins.

"What in the world for?" she asked.

"Ice cream," he said. "At least a pint, maybe a quart of pralines 'n' cream. You can get some too if you want."

Danielle and I laughed, but Faith said, "How on earth can you even think about ice cream after all you've had to eat? An hour ago you were too stuffed to talk."

"Ah, Faith, but you forget," Johnnie said. "The El Cholo Feeling passes."

14

1973

When Faith finally decided that she'd move to Los Angeles with her husband, she insisted on keeping the battered old Toyota they'd purchased for her at the beginning of the school year. That meant driving west in two cars and at Faith's pace, which meant a slower and shorter day. But once Janus accepted the certainty of this, he adjusted, and it caused few problems. Their only moment of tension on the trip occurred at a gas station in Oklahoma. While Faith was in the restroom, Janus jawed with the attendant about Sooner football. He did not break away instantly when she returned and got in her car. On a note of laughter at one of the man's anecdotes about a Sooner win over Texas, Janus finally paid for the gasoline and stuck his head through the passenger side of Faith's car to discuss how far they would try to get before they stopped again. She was crying.

"What's the matter, babe?" he asked.

"Nothing," she said.

Janus was tempted to get in beside her and try to coax out of her whatever was wrong, but he resisted the impulse. That kind of talk with Faith, he knew, could last for hours, could unearth unimagined ills, could prove terrifyingly explosive. Such a talk might end with her deciding to turn back. So he just sighed and clucked at her and said, "You sure?"

"Yeah," she said. "Go get in your car and let's go."

"Okay," he said, and started to move away.

"Listening to you talk to that guy made me realize how Southern you really are. You should hear yourself when your accent comes out."

Janus could feel the rush of anger rising over him, but he fought it down. When he and Faith decided to stay together after their last, horrible fight in St. Louis, he had promised himself that he'd never fight with her again. It was a promise he'd been unable to keep forever, but it produced an attitude on his part that unquestionably benefitted their relationship. In this instance, it saved a needless squabble. Had he shown anger and demanded that Faith explain her remark, a fight would likely have followed. By merely nodding and walking away to his car, he prevented it. At the motel that night in Amarillo, Texas, Faith voluntarily clarified what she had been thinking earlier in the day.

"I know it's not true, of course," she said, "but I kind of think of us as having been together always. Like you were a kid in my neighborhood when I was growing up, or my brother or something. Then when I hear your accent sometimes, I realize that inside of you is a little boy that I'll never know."

The next day they crossed into New Mexico and the enveloping heat seemed to function in their lives as a purge. By the time they were searching for an apartment two days later in the bracing ocean breezes of Santa Monica, they felt like newlyweds enjoying the honeymoon they had never had.

They were all alone with a whole new world to explore together. They made a special joint enterprise of decorating the tiny apartment they had selected on Fourth Street. Faith spent an entire morning arranging and rearranging the few pieces of furniture they had shipped from St. Louis. Janus did the manual labor for her and could not imagine why he had ever been so impatient with such duties in the past. She found an old ship's hatch cover at a lumberyard, and he invested in an electric sander and made it into a dining room table for her. What it lacked in skilled workmanship, it made up in natural beauty.

In a stroke of amazing good fortune, in less than a week of searching, Faith found a job teaching sixth grade at a public school in nearby Mar Vista. They were hardly going to be well-to-do, but their immediate financial future was secure. With Janus's Fortran Fellowship stipend and now Faith's job paying substantially more than she had made in Missouri, the coming fall loomed as a time of new challenge, not of uncertainty and fear. For the present they were still drawing checks from their schools in St. Louis, so the rest of that long, springlike California summer became a joyous vacation.

They went swimming daily on the Santa Monica beach. Janus learned to body surf and teased Faith for being so afraid of the water. He began to teach her to play tennis, a sport at which she quickly became very skilled. They took the Universal Studios tour and made the long drive to Disneyland. Janus registered for a German course to prepare him for one of the doctoral language exams he had to pass. And in the course he met Johnnie Golden, who became their first California friend.

They became fond of a little Italian restaurant not far from their house. The Piece of Pizza on Wilshire was just another in L.A.'s countless chain restaurants, not at all endowed with the romantic qualities that Faith and Janus found in it. But it was the first place in L.A., other than McDonald's or The All-American Burger, in which they ate out. And for that reason, it was special to them. Even when they'd eaten elsewhere, they often went there late at night or after a movie to share a carafe or two of red wine, to talk, to laugh, to speculate about the future. Afterwards, a little tipsy, they would make love. Other nights they would stay home, lie in bed together and read. Janus would place his hand on top of hers, and she would scrunch closer to him and hook her arm around his so that she could have a hand free to turn pages, but they could remain intertwined.

That summer, Faith and Janus fell in love all over again.

In the fall that followed, Janus discovered frightening misgivings about his graduate career, but in the interest of marital harmony, he kept them to himself. Freed from the shackles of parochial education, Faith, on the other hand, was delighted by her new situation. She still made occasional noises about how sixth grade was not exactly where she'd like to spend her working life, but the public school was a welcome change from her initial experience in the Lutheran school. She no longer had to teach religion; she wasn't presumed to be pious; she wasn't expected to be a regular church attender. Furthermore, she was surrounded by a faculty of bright young colleagues, mostly female, to whom Faith quickly became attached.

Around the turn of the year, led by Kate Banford, one of the third-grade teachers, several of the women at Faith's school started a "consciousness raising group" which Faith eagerly joined. One part of Janus was not thrilled and was even threatened by this development. For the first time in their marriage, really, he and Faith had been getting along, and he was fearful of any and all changes.

When he confided his apprehension to Johnnie Golden, his acerbic friend said, "Women are like dogs. They have to sniff each other's behinds once in a while to make sure they're all still bitches."

Janus laughed, but he felt guilty doing so. "I wouldn't lay that line on Faith."

"You kiddin'?" Johnnie said, "I'm kind of partial to my balls, you know."

"And Faith thinks you're so sensitive."

"Shit," Johnnie said.

The better part of Janus was sympathetic to the women's movement in general and to Faith's legitimate need to become a part of it. He told Johnnie so, and his friend said, "Man, I understand what the women have to do. I'm just not fond of being a man in the midst of it."

As time passed, it seemed that Janus's worries about Faith's women's group were altogether needless. She spent her Wednesday evenings out, but she brought home with her no animosities that he could detect.

"We have fun at our meetings," Faith explained. "We drink wine and just talk about different things. It's important for us to share our experiences with one another. But it would be hard for me to say that anyone's consciousness has really been raised. We all have the same problems: men dominate us, and we lack the confidence and courage to do anything about it. But we all knew that before we started meeting. I think the big thing is for us to realize that we're all basically in the same boat."

Janus wondered if Faith felt that he still dominated her. He knew she had felt that way in the past. He wondered, but he didn't want to bring it up.

"If anything, my consciousness has been raised in reverse, Bubba," Faith added. Since their arrival in California, Faith had mysteriously taken to calling him "Bubba," as a term of endearment. He cherished the tone with which she always uttered it but inevitably wished she'd chosen some other name.

"How's that?" he asked.

"It's made me realize what a bargain you are, basically. You're the only husband in the group who really shares the house duties. And you may be the only one without hostilities toward the very idea of our group. Kate Banford's husband has gotten so mad on Wednesday nights that he's threatened to lock her in the house. I think they may get a divorce."

"You really think I'm a bargain?"

Faith flipped her skirt at him as if she were shaking a blanket. "I think you're a cheap lay."

"I love it when you talk dirty," he said.

When Faith announced her intention to change her last name back to Cleaver, Janus felt some of the concerns he had experienced when her group first started meeting. Why she preferred her father's name to his escaped him at first, but she explained her feelings very clearly. The issue was not where the name came from; in a patriarchal society, all names derived from men. The issue was the habit of changing names. She was *really* Faith Cleaver because she'd been a Cleaver considerably longer than she'd been a Janus. A man would *never* change his name to that of his wife, so why should a wife be expected to take her husband's name? What she argued made sense to Janus, and he had to admit that he'd never really thought of the name Janus as properly belonging to Faith anyway.

But he wouldn't have resisted her even had he failed to understand. He had adopted a firm policy of accommodation toward her, and to the best of his ability to judge, it was working. If there were clouds on the horizon of their relationship, he did not perceive them. Miraculously, it seemed that he and

Faith were happy, a development which had deepened Janus's belief in God. In the desperate last moments in St. Louis, he had prayed. He hadn't known whether Faith would finally choose to stay with him. He wasn't at all sure that she should. But he prayed that if she did decide to stay, that he would find a way to make her happy. He prayed that he would discover a source of patience so great that Faith would never again make him angry. In that first year in Los Angeles, it seemed that God had chosen to answer those prayers.

Janus held fast to his commitment to restraint and forbearance, but this new approach on his part hardly altogether explained the success his marriage suddenly began to enjoy. However much he contributed to Faith's happiness, he did not create it. Her new contentedness derived extensively from her new job and her new colleagues and her excitement at living in a new place.

And Faith and Janus did not live in perfect harmony, of course. Like any couple, they had their periods of friction. But unlike their years in St. Louis, those periods were short and seemed caused by normal problems of overwork and fatigue. What spats they had no longer seemed to arise out of some deep-seated ill will.

Ever the perfectionist, Janus kept trying to eliminate even the briefest moments of tension. He thought Faith worked too hard and that she failed to organize herself properly.

One night shortly after their first warm L.A. Christmas, Janus was reading Richard Hofstadter's *Age of Reform* for a course in twentieth-century historiography. It was nearly midnight. He was working in his father's old reading chair, which was the only comfortable spot in the living room. The naugahyde couch had been abandoned in St. Louis, replaced in their tiny Santa Monica apartment with two canvas-seated director's chairs. Faith was at the new dining table, which occupied a space in the living room-dining room-kitchen just over Janus's shoulder. She got up and began rattling pans at the stove behind him. He asked what she was up to.

"Just making coffee," she said. "Want some?"

"You kiddin'?"

Faith did not answer. He could hear her yawning.

"Hadn't you better be going to bed now instead of drinking coffee?" he asked. He got up and went into the kitchen, put his arms around her waist and hooked his chin over her shoulder as she sleepily tried to strike a match to light the stove.

"I've got to finish grading these papers." She finally got the burner lit under the coffee pot.

"Do them tomorrow," Janus advised. Faith turned around and kissed him quickly on his chin. When he didn't move out of her way, she put her hands flat against his chest and shoved him.

"Move, you big whale," she said. "I've got work to do. I've got to hand these papers back tomorrow. I've had them for a week."

Janus followed her back to the table and stopped to hook his chin over her shoulder again after she sat down. When she placed another spelling test in front of her to mark, he tried to take it out of her hands. "If you've had these papers for a week, what's one more day when sleep is at stake?"

Faith brushed at his hands as if they were annoying insects. "I have to give another test tomorrow, and I need to give these back first." She yawned again. "What's it to you anyway?"

"You know how miserable you are when you don't get enough sleep."

"Yeah," she said, "some of us don't have to rush out for a seminar by the crack of noon. Some of us can sleep to six A.M. almost every day. What time did you get up today, Rip Van Winkle?"

"Ten."

"Tough life being a graduate student, isn't it?"

"Hey," Janus said. He moved from behind her and plopped into a chair at the end of the table. "I don't sleep any more than you do. I *did* sleep until ten this morning, but I was up reading last night until four. In fact, counting all the sleeping you do on the weekends, I don't sleep nearly as much as you do."

Faith rubbed her face with both hands and then tried to find the column in her grade book to record a spelling score. "Don't you think there's a difference between our two situations? I *have* to get up early every morning, and you don't."

"I'm not saying I want to trade places with you."

Without looking up from the papers in front of her, Faith laughed. "I guess not."

"What's that mean?"

"It means, Janus jerko, that you're doing what you want to do, and I'm not."

Janus was feeling tired himself. He could sense that this discussion was sliding into uncharted and dangerous seas. "I thought you liked your job."

"I'm not saying that I don't, but I sure don't have a ball grading spelling tests."

"Which is exactly what I'm trying to get you to stop doing." Janus smiled, glad to have discovered an escape from Charybdis.

"Will you leave me alone so I can finish this before dawn?"

"I'm just trying to help," he protested.

"If you want to help, pour my coffee." Faith pulled another spelling test in front of her.

"I've got a better idea. Let me grade the papers for you."

"No," Faith said.

"Why?"

"You'll just get pissed." She looked at him like a criminal about to make a confession. "I just gave twenty-two spelling words last week. You're just gonna yell at me and tell me I'm stupid."

Janus put his hand on her arm and held it down as she tried to rearrange the papers in front of her. "When was the last time I said you were stupid, babe? I don't think you're stupid. And I *do* think you're a superior teacher, imaginative and dedicated. Your students are very lucky to have someone like you."

"So why didn't I give twenty or twenty-five words like you told me so that I could figure the grades quickly?"

"Because you forgot."

"No. It was because I'm stupid."

Janus picked up her hand and kissed it. "Hey. Stop that. This whole business here was just to get you to go to bed. Let's not turn it into Dr. Freud's sofa. Give me those papers and go get ready for bed. I'll leave them on the table for you."

"You love me, don't you, Bubba." Her remark was a statement, not a question. "Next time I'll give them either twenty or twenty-five words. I promise."

"Okay," Janus laughed. She got up from the table and hugged him on her way out of the room. "And don't call me Bubba," he warned her.

Faith took a shower and brushed her teeth while Janus worked on the spelling tests at the table. When she had gotten into bed and turned out the light, she called into the other room to him, "Good night, Bubba. I love you."

From his place at the dining room table, he could hear her marvelously silly giggle.

Janus's seminar the next afternoon ran from three until six. He did not chain the bicycle he rode daily to UCLA to the palm tree in their apartment courtyard until after 6:30. Inside, he slung off his canvas backpack and called out, "Hello Faith, I'm home."

"How'd you know I was home?" she giggled from the bedroom.

"Is it supposed to be a secret?"

"How'd you know I was home?" she repeated in her silly, winsome voice, as if he'd not answered the first time.

"I saw the car on the street. What are you doing?"

"Waiting for Bubba. Come in here."

"Not if you're gonna call me Bubba," Janus said.

"Okay, Bubba, I won't."

He walked into the tiny, cramped bedroom. Faith was lying on the bed with a sheet pulled up under her nose. "See anything new?" she giggled. She kept rolling her eyes to the right toward Janus's desk so that he knew whatever she had done to surprise him lay in that direction. Deliberately he began to look on the other side of the room. "No," she said, tilting her whole head to the right, "I said, did you see anything new?" Janus inspected the side of the room away from his desk with greater care.

"Something the matter with your neck?" he asked.

Faith rearranged the sheet around her so that her naked right breast was exposed. Cupping it, she thrust her chest toward Janus's desk. "See anything new?" she said.

"You finally decided to go ahead and have that tit transplant?"

Faith re-covered herself and placed a pillow over her head. As if her voice were coming from far away, she said, "You're impossible."

Finally, Janus walked over to his desk. On it was a framed photograph taken when he was twelve years old, on the day of his first Biddy League basketball game. He was wearing his green number thirty-four jersey and holding a basketball which looked much too large for him. Faith had discovered the old picture in a photo album at his mother's. He was very touched that she had gone to the trouble of having it framed. He sat down on the bed and wormed his way under the sheet beside her. "You framed my picture," he said.

"Do you like it, Bubba?"

"Very much."

"I framed it because you graded all my papers for me last night. I hurried home from school and went right up to Westwood. I spent a lot of money."

Janus laughed. "You don't have a lot of money. How did you raise it?"

"I had to sell my body on the street, but I did it because I love my Bubba so. Bubba means brother, and that picture is of the brother I didn't ever have."

Janus scrunched himself closer to her and put his head up under the pillow that covered her face. He threw his leg over the top of her naked body and laid his cheek next to hers.

"You have to fuck me now," Faith whispered into his ear. "You think I'm all naked for nothing?" Janus kicked off his sandals and let them drop over the side of the bed. He rolled on his back to unbuckle his belt. "Don't take your pants all the way off," Faith whispered. "You have to fuck me quick, like you haven't been laid in six months."

When Janus entered her, she gasped. "Harder," she demanded. "Faster. Harder." When Janus came, Faith, who normally liked for sex to be long and languorous, cried out as if she had, too.

Collapsed on top of her, he nuzzled her neck. She alternately stroked and twined her fingers in the long hair on the back of his head. After a long time she said, "You're not going to fall in love with any of those smart girls in your graduate school, are you, Bubba?"

On a sunny February morning, as was their Saturday routine, Janus crept out of bed without disturbing his wife. He washed his face and brushed his teeth, got the *L.A. Times* from the front stoop and settled into his chair to read the sports section.

When he finished, he went into the kitchen to prepare an orange beverage to take to Faith when he woke her. She had gotten the basic recipe from her friend Kate Banford, who called it Orange Julius, but Janus had added the touch of mixing the frozen orange juice, milk and honey with two trays of ice cubes. Once crushed in the blender, the tiny ice crystals glistened throughout the drink and led Faith to dub the concoction Orange Jewels.

Janus poured her a glass and, as a special gesture, cut up an orange and hung a slice from the lip of the glass.

"You are my sunshine, my only sunshine," Janus sang as he carried the garnished drink into the bedroom.

"No Gene Autry," Faith said, pulling her pillow over her head.

Janus put the drink on the night table and sat on the bed next to her. He pulled the pillow off her face and said, "I thought Governor Jimmy Davis recorded that song."

"No Jimmy Davis," Faith said, pulling the pillow back over her.

"It's time to get up, Faith." He grabbed the pillow and held it out of reach as she groped for it, eyes squeezed shut, like a player in blind man's bluff. "You've been sleeping now for twelve hours, and that's enough."

"No," Faith said, refusing to open her eyes. She shook her head violently, like an impudent five-year-old, and slid down toward the foot of the bed, pulling the sheet up over her head.

"Oh, you gotta get up, you gotta get, you gotta get up in the morning," Janus sang. "I've brought your Orange Jewels."

Faith sprang from under the covers as if she were getting a surprise treat. "Thanks, Bubba," she said. She took a long drink from the glass, coating her freckled upper lip with orange. Giggling as she wiped her face, she handed the glass back to Janus and slid down under the covers as if she were attached to a string and were being pulled by the feet. From under the covers, she called out, "Good night."

"Get up, Faith, and we'll go to the pancake house."

She didn't answer, so Janus got into bed beside her, the sheet pulled over his head, too. In a conspiratorial whisper, he said, "Are you afraid of the great out of bed?"

"Yes," she whispered back. "No one knows what lurks in the great out of bed. I'm a denizen of the great *in* bed. It's so wonderful in bed.

Warm and toasty."

"Hot and sweaty," Janus said in a normal tone of voice and pulled the sheet down around his shoulders.

Faith's head popped out beside him. "It is *not* hot. And it *can't* be sweaty if I'm around. *I* never sweat. Feel me, I'm cool and smooth."

"If you're cool and smooth, it's because you drool while you sleep. One of these mornings I'm going to wake up drowned."

"Ha ha," she said. "Shows what you know. You can't drown; you're a whale. Bubba the Magic Whale."

"Ha ha," Janus retorted. "Shows what you know. Whales are mammals, and they can drown if they want to."

"Intellectual snob. Do I really want to go to the pancake house with an intellectual snob whale?"

"Yes," Janus said.

"I'll have to shower first. My hair feels like I massaged it with Crisco."

He turned on his side and stroked his hand down his wife's frizzy, dark red hair. "Your hair's not so bad, babe. I'd say it's only like you massaged it with Wesson Oil." Faith stuck out her tongue at him and turned away, hiding her head under a pillow again. "You're just my little Sleeping Greasy," he cooed. "Should I kiss you and turn you into a frog to go with your long tongue?"

"I'll never be a frog," Faith said. "I'm much too greasy ever to wrinkle. That's why you hate me, isn't it? Because you want a wife with dry skin who wakes up looking like the perfect sleeper."

"I don't want any wife but you." Janus put an arm over her and stuck his head up under her pillow. "Give us a kiss, Sleeping Greasy."

"Okay," she said but made no effort to turn her face toward him.

"Okay what?" Janus said.

"Okay, you can kiss me. But you better move fast."

Janus shifted up onto his knees so as to bend around and kiss her, but as he did so she darted out of bed cackling, "Ha ha ha, you big whale. I told you you better move fast, because I'm so slippery I'll get away just when you think you've got me."

15

I have failed to mention, I think, that I have taken to writing this note on a picnic table in Palisades Park at the corner of Wilshire and Ocean Boulevard. I don't want this to be seen as a symbol that I think writing is a picnic or even that I think memo writing is a picnic compared to dissertation writing. (Do memo writers even employ symbols?) On the contrary, I've begun to work at this picnic table because working outside forces me to write longhand. Then when I type things up, I can make changes and try to express myself better. I guess I've begun to take pride in my work. I know that being a memo writer is hardly a job in much demand, but it's what I do, so I should try to do it to the best of my ability.

During the several weeks that I've made this picnic table my daytime office, I have watched a painter who works a short distance up the palisades from me. I'd guess he's American Indian, though I have no clue to the identity of his tribe. He's swarthy and high-cheekboned. But his regular outfit, fringed leather jacket, short braids and a beaded headband, seems to owe more to Jay Silverheels than to any Indian group with which I am acquainted.

Tonto, which I call him for the want of any other name, is a seascape painter. I don't know diddly about art, but I think he's pretty good. His gulls in flight have a desperate energy about them, not at all lazy like the hovering gulls we tend to think about. And his renderings of Santa Monica Bay at night, with the light from the pier spilling over the black waves across an abandoned rowboat, can almost make me smell the slimy pool of water which glints in the boat's bottom.

Every morning Tonto arrives a short while after I do and hangs a number of paintings on the fence that keeps the skateboarders and the moonstruck strollers from falling down the cliff onto the Pacific Coast Highway. What he hopes to do is sell the pictures to passersby. I notice him haggling with people once or twice a day. I think he's asking too much, though, because he seldom seems to make a sale.

When he finishes a new painting, he takes it off his easel and hangs it beside the others on the fence. Then he sits for a time, usually on the ground, but once with his back to me on the other side of my picnic table, and smokes a cigarette. Two days ago he came over and asked for a smoke from my pack. He had just seen me light up. I gave him one gladly, and I sort of liked the fact that he asked me. In all the time we'd worked here in such close proximity, we'd never spoken. And that was basically the way it should be, I figured. I didn't think either of us was anxious to get real palsy, but it was nice to know that we could share a cigarette when one of our packs was empty. I interpreted Tonto's request as a gesture that he'd found a kindred spirit, a man with whom he held in common a silent bond.

Boy, was I wrong.

Yesterday he came over and asked for another cigarette. Again, I gladly gave it to him. He patted at his pockets as if he were searching for a match, so I handed him my book of matches. He sat down on my side of the picnic table, his back breaking the wind off the ocean, cupped his hand around the Marlboro and succeeded on the third match at getting it lit. He put the match book down on the table and slid it toward me, took a deep drag on his smoke and as he exhaled said, nodding his head back toward the fence and his painting. "Like to buy one?"

I smiled. I might *like* to buy one, but as you might guess, a memo writer doesn't exactly roll in dough. I shook my head. "I'm sure I couldn't afford it," I said.

"I sell it to you cheap," he offered.

However cheap, I was still sure it would be out of my price range, considering that I had a price range. But trying to be polite, I asked anyway, "How much?"

Tonto pointed at the painting on the fence nearest us. "I could get fifty for that one," he said. "You can have it thirty…twenty-five."

I smiled and shook my head. "I'd love to, man, but I just don't have the bread."

"Gimme a check," Tonto said.

"It wouldn't do you any good. It'd just bounce, and I'd hate to rip you off."

"Come on, man," Tonto said.

I smiled once more and raised my palms skyward. He took a last deep drag on the Marlboro, sucking the embers almost to the filter. "Shit, man," he said exhaling. "Rich boy like you. Sit out here all day doin' nuthin'." He stared at me fiercely and ground his cigarette out on the top of my picnic table. "Shit, man," he said again and stood up. He stomped toward the fence and snatched his paintings off, packing them hurriedly into his portfolio. I brushed the crumpled butt of the cigarette off my worktable, but the black smudge where the paint was charred, I'm afraid, is permanent.

Today the painter did not return to my part of the palisades. It just goes to show you how you can think you've sized a person up but really not know him at all.

But the story of my painter friend is a digression from the story I have intended to tell you about an event which occurred in the middle of the spring quarter of 1973, my third term in graduate school. I joined Johnnie Golden late one night in the bar at the LoDaMar bowling alley. He was playing eight-ball with one of the regulars. There was only one other guy in the place, not counting the bartender. I slapped down a quarter to challenge the table. Johnnie acknowledged me only with a nod, so I ordered a beer and leaned against the bar to watch the game. Johnnie ran three balls, called a corner pocket on the eight ball and ran it in, too. The guy he was playing shook his head and hung his stick up on the wall. To me he said, "He's outasight. You better get ready to get your ass kicked."

"That right?" I asked Johnnie and started racking the balls for the next game. He answered with a shrug. Johnnie broke, and we played without our usual banter. He didn't talk to the balls, and he didn't call me the luckiest son-of-a-bitch he'd ever known when I made a difficult shot. Mainly, I suppose, because it was a night when I didn't make many shots at all, difficult or otherwise. Johnnie was so hot that he was running three, four and five balls every turn. In eight-ball, that meant that games didn't last too long. When he sank the winner for the seventh straight time, he asked me without enthusiasm, "One more?"

"Not tonight," I said. "I can't beat you. It's no use. Let's just get a drink."

Johnnie looked around the nearly deserted bar. "Let's go over to my place," he said.

I was surprised at this suggestion, since I'd never been invited before. When I got inside his spartan efficiency apartment, I remarked on how few books Johnnie seemed to own. "Ever heard of libraries?" he said sharply. I was taken aback. Johnnie noticed it and added, "Fucking hick. Ain't New Orleans got any public establishments other than bars?"

"You insinuatin' I'm redneck, asshole, is like Rose callin' Scarlet, Crimson." It wasn't an original line, but I thought he'd enjoy it.

He looked at me seriously, though, and said, "Hey, man, I'm a Jew. And a Southern Jew ain't from the South. He's from Jewland and that's all."

"What's eatin' you?" I asked.

"Shit," he said. He went to a cabinet and got a bottle of tequila and a shaker of salt. He took a small, square cutting board and a knife from a drawer and couple of limes from his tiny refrigerator. He brought all of this to the empty space in the middle of his room. "Sit down," he said, indicating the floor. He began to slice one of the limes. "Know how to do this?"

"I'm sure I can catch on."

Johnnie wiped the back of his hand, right at the base of his thumb, with a lime slice. He sprinkled salt on the wet smear. Then he licked off the salt, took a slug from the tequila bottle and chased it by eating the pulp out of the slice of lime. He passed the bottle and salt to me. "I think I'm gonna hang it up," he said. I followed his example of salt and tequila and lime. It tasted better than I expected. I set the bottle and the shaker between us and waited for him to continue. "My transcript contains nothing but a string of incompletes that I'm never going to finish. I'm wasting my time."

"How long you been thinking about this?"

"Since I got here. Maybe a while before that." He laughed and grabbed the drink ingredients again.

"What you going to do?"

"Go back to newspaper work. That's what I've always really wanted to do. I can't even figure out why I came here in the first place. I hated my job in Minneapolis, and I needed to get away from Diane. But I never wanted to be a historian. So what am I doing here?"

"They gave you a big scholarship," I said.

Johnnie took off his hat and ran a hand through his long dirty hair. He laughed and said, "They gave me a scholarship. An offer I couldn't refuse."

"You gonna stay here?"

"Can't find anything. I've sent out a bunch of resumés. Get this: two offers. One from the *Macon Telegraph and News.*"

"Hey, that doesn't sound bad," I interjected. "It's close to home. How far's Macon from Atlanta?"

Johnnie snorted at me and took another hit of tequila. "Man, it's okay to be *from* the South, but who wants to be *in* the South?"

"Where's the other job?"

"Bismarck, North Dakota. Workin' for the AP again. Ain't that great? Get myself an extra year of education and get demoted from Minneapolis to a fuckin' icebox. Bismarck ain't a town, man; it's an obstacle."

"I'm sure it'll work out okay," I said.

Johnnie snorted again and shook the bottle at me. "Want some of this shit? You're letting me get drunk without you."

I took the bottle, limed and salted my hand and, in the interest of friendship, took a big slug of tequila.

"You think I'm fuckin' up, don't you, Rich?"

"I hate to see you leave. What am I gonna do without you? You're the only pool player I can lick." I smiled at him.

"But you really think I'm fuckin' up, don't you?"

"Shit, Johnnie, how the hell do I know? I think you're probably the brightest guy in this graduate school. You're also the biggest screw off. Maybe I'm the one who's screwin' up by stayin'. Maybe I should never have given up my coaching job. God, I loved that."

"Nah, man, you're not fuckin' up. You're eatin' this place up. You're doin' good." He reached across the cutting board of lime slices and rinds and slapped my knee.

"That's just it, Johnnie. I always do well. I got this big teacher's pet thing, you know. They ask it; I deliver it."

"Bullshit, Janus. That's not the whole of it. That ain't even the half of it. I know you hate this grad school grind. Only an asshole wouldn't. But somewhere down inside you, you must want to be a historian. You couldn't do so well otherwise." I shook my head and started to protest, but he continued quickly. "We're not the same, you and me, Rich. You're doin' well, and I'm doin' nothin'. You'll take your exams next year." He laughed and smiled. "And you'll get your fuckin' Ph.D. and after that a nice job somewhere and maybe you'll have to move once or twice, but pretty soon you'll have tenure and lifetime security. And Faith will bless you with a couple of brats, and your fingernails will smell like baby shit."

"Sounds great," I said. "When do I get midriff bulge and varicose veins?" Johnnie shook his head and took a pull at the tequila bottle.

"And I'll be freezin' my ass off in Bismarck, North Dakota, which I understand is within sledding distance of the North Pole. But I wouldn't want all that life I just gave you if I could have it. I don't want to be Richard Hofstadter, and I certainly don't want a life of failing to be Richard Hofstadter. I want a life of failing to be Edward R. Murrow."

"I don't want to be Richard Hofstadter," I said, but I don't think he really heard me. We had nearly killed the fifth of tequila and were both drunk. It was very late. "I think I gotta be going," I said. I got up unsteadily. "If Faith wakes up when I come in, she's gonna be pissed as it is. If it gets any later, she'll just go right to divorce court."

Johnnie was staring at the floor. "I really love Faith, you know." He looked up at me then. "I really love you, too. I never had such a friend." Johnnie's eyes were filmy behind his thick glasses. I extended my hand to him to help him up. He grabbed it, but in hoisting himself almost succeeded in pulling me down. When he was finally up, he put his arm around my shoulders and walked me toward the door.

I slipped my arm around his waist. "I'm really gonna miss you, Odd Body."

"Ah, LALA," he said and kissed me on the cheek.

I squeezed him, said good night and stumbled into the hall.

Within two weeks, Johnnie was gone. In the first two months after he left, we corresponded frequently. He wasn't enjoying his work. "I have discovered new heights of assholery," he wrote. "New depths of temperature." After a time his replies were longer in coming. Finally they ceased altogether. In the fall I had a letter returned Addressee Unknown.

I anticipated that the summer after Johnnie left would be a lonesome time. It didn't turn out that way. It was a busy summer, but one I remember mostly with fondness. Faith was out of school, of course, and we spent about all our time together. We weren't quite as carefree, somehow, as we had been our first summer in L.A., but all in all we were happy.

I decided to register for a summer school course. You may remember, Dr. Burden. It was your course in the social history of early America. I wrote my second paper on King Philip's War for you. Faith decided to take a course, too. She signed up as a special (non-degree candidate) student for a seminar in abnormal psychology. We rode our bikes up to campus every morning. She'd go to the library while I was in class, and afterwards I'd accompany her to hers. I was doing the reading for her course as well, thoroughly enjoying the quasi-break from history. Usually we'd eat a salad at the union for lunch and then bike to the beach to spend the afternoon reading on the sand. At night we might play tennis (Faith was really getting good) or go to a movie, often with our friend Danielle LeBlanc. Sometimes Faith's colleague, Kate Banford, who had recently separated from her husband, went along as well.

On Saturdays and Sundays, Faith and I worked together in a small amusement park out in the Valley. We were doing all right financially. She took her salary on a twelve-month basis; I had my stipend from the Fortran Foundation; we still even had money in the bank from our days in St. Louis. But the opportunity for these jobs kind of fell into our laps. Kate Banford's father owned a little park that rented itself out on the weekends for company picnics. There were a half-dozen rides, several booths where you could win worthless prizes by knocking things down and lawn games that included three-legged, wheelbarrow and sack races. It was a sexist operation, unfortunately. Faith and I worked the same ten-to-five day, but much to Kate's embarrassment and Faith's frustration, I was paid forty dollars while Faith made only thirty. But the bottom line on the job was that we liked it. The work was easy. It gave us an extra $140 a week. And more important, in those days we were finding it fun just being together.

Over the Fourth of July weekend, Faith and I drove up to northern California to visit with our friends Paul and Grace Taylor. Grace, the former Grace Lamm, was a sorority sister of Faith's and a short-term flame of mine when we'd all been at Lancaster. Paul and Grace were newlyweds, honeymooning in their Berkeley apartment before Paul began a job in Oakland as an officer with the National Association of Government Employees. They drove us across the Bay Bridge for drinks on the top of the Fairmont and dinner at the Basque Hotel. We took the ferry to Sausalito. We wore sweaters and sat for hours on the Berkeley shore at Solomon Grundy's. Through the glass windows of the bar, the city lights reached toward us across the frigid black water. It was the high point of our summer, and it was a grand time.

As Yeats has mentioned, though, things fall apart. I know, I already stole that line once in this note, but is that any reason not to steal it anew? Is it any less true now than it was then? It is certainly more true now than when Yeats first asserted it. But as I'm sure he knew even in the back when, things fall apart gradually, not all at once. Like an automobile. The day-to-day progression from the shiny machine you drove home from the showroom to the faded, rusted, hunk of junk you have to pay to get towed to a junkyard is almost imperceptible.

Our summer didn't end well. Faith had to start teaching again during the last week of summer school. She was in an absolute panic about her term paper, which she had planned, but failed, to finish early. She stayed up all one night, completing the rough draft and going to teach the next day without even an hour's sleep. I stayed up the next night and typed it for her. Her school year had just begun, and she was already exhausted and irritable. Somehow our second year never recovered from that hectic start. Faith seemed busier, more preoccupied. The number of hours her job required never lessened. She continued meeting with her women's group on Wednesdays and tried to recuperate from her weekday pace by sleeping most of the weekend. After our summer together, I felt a little abandoned.

But that second year I was more anxious, of course. Trying to cram three years of work into two, I began preparing for my doctoral exams and in the process experienced a sense of fear rivaled only by my terror of the draft. I mean, there was a lot to learn. And my first year in graduate school had mainly taught me how little I knew.

In my anxiety, I'm sure I wanted more of Faith than she had to give. I wanted her to be, in addition to wife, the friend I had lost when Johnnie left. But she couldn't do that, of course. She hated watching sports on TV, hated viewing them in person even more. We played tennis occasionally, but she wouldn't have known which end of a cue stick to hit the balls with even if I had ever been able to get her into the LoDaMar. And she was long asleep by the time Sherlock Holmes hit the late night tube.

Our second year in L.A., I had to drink my *wein kuhlers* alone.

But I shouldn't give the impression that I became a kind of hermit with a somnolent spouse. I was on friendly terms with a number of other graduate students in my department. And if I tended to think of them as "associates" rather than "friends," it was only because I had not gotten close enough to any of them to bridge the gulf that separates the two. Friendship for me means something very personal, something intimate, something shared. It is sacred, one of life's things worth fighting for. But graduate school isn't an environment terribly conducive to friendship. We may like each other, but we're nonetheless forever in competition with one another: for grades, for the inside track with our professors, for the too few jobs that await us when our degrees are finished. With all that built-in competition, it's hard to make the leap into friendship.

When graduate students get together, we don't talk about spouses or lovers or dreams or fears, topics which might really forge a bond between us. We sometimes talk about our futures, but almost never about our pasts. Rather, we talk about books and articles and papers and professors and jobs.

Academic chess, I call it. One guy drops a name of somebody or something he hopes the other guy doesn't recognize. The second guy counters with another name. When they finally break away from each other, they feel both supremely confident and superior for what they knew and absolutely terrified and stupid for what they didn't know that the other guy did. Academic chess could be played anywhere and anytime that graduate students met. It was the most popular of party games. And my social life that second year consisted mostly of parties.

Parties. Where were the parties of my past? The parties at Earl K. Long High School to which I never got invited? The parties at Lancaster College to which I didn't want to go? Where were the King Cake parties I loved in the sixth grade? Where were the Kincaid parties, the best parties of all, the ones I had only imagined?

Graduate school parties: parties where jovial acquaintances while away the time along the path to never becoming friends, parties where the same topics get discussed to the same conclusions or the same impasses with only the dialogues' partners changing, and sometimes, frighteningly often in fact, not even that. Parties where energy is expended trying to impress. Parties where spouses and partners are excluded. Parties in the end, perhaps, which exist as excuses for drinking to excess in the company of others and hence without guilt.

At the end of the fall quarter in 1973, Professor Crotchet had a party at his home. It was a beneficent gesture, occasioned only by the term's end. Had it not been for my orals upcoming, I might have felt a touch of the party spirit.

Walter Crotchet, of course, was a fortyish Yale Ph.D. who taught U.S. religious and intellectual history. I found him an odd but oddly likable man. Eccentric is perhaps the word. As y'all know, he had the strangest dressing habits, the first reason I both noticed his peculiarity and liked him for it. For as y'all also know, at UCLA the style is casual, particularly in the leftist history department, where jeans are statement as well as style. So perhaps, I thought, Professor Crotchet's sartorial habits also constituted a statement. Though, of what sort, I could never tell. But he was not blind, and in a department as determinedly scruffy as this one, he must have noticed that he was the only faculty member ever to wear an orange turtleneck shirt with a zipper up the back or a double-breasted burgundy blazer or bright green plaid slacks and certainly that he was the only one to wear them all at once.

I hesitate to confide this next thought to my writing tablet, but since there is considerable difference between draft and text, memo finished and memo mailed, I will forge ahead. I have wondered whether Professor Crotchet selected his wardrobe as a visible rebellion against people like those of you on my committee, who may dress like hippie-radicals and may even believe in radical political solutions, but are, in your academic values and actions, as establishmentarian as any faculty anywhere.

But maybe that wasn't it. Professor Crotchet had a certain prissiness that might explain his manner of dress. He was the sort of man who always spoke in class with his nose, slightly but perceptibly, in the air. It was a mannerism rather than indication of snobbishness, I think. He was the sort of man who always had his little finger extended when he held a cup of coffee, even if it was only a paper cup from the vending machine on the first floor of Bunche Hall. Professor Crotchet was the sort of man who entered a toilet stall in a public restroom and locked the door to pee, even when there were ample numbers of urinals available.

Or maybe rather than rebelliousness or prissiness, Crotchet's delightful characteristic perversity accounted for his gaudy attire. His favorite novel was *Lolita,* understandable enough except that one suspected he identified with Humbert. He announced in seminar one day with lip-smacking relish that his favorite film was the Dirk Bogarde-Charlotte Rampling sadomasochistic romp, *The Night Porter.* Now, that's downright weird, folks.

But my fondest memory of Professor Crotchet is of his joyful readings of those lengthy passages from William Bradford's *Of Plymouth Plantation* that deal with the harsh punishments meted out by the early New Englanders to those of their members who engaged in such disreputable practices as miscegenation, bestiality and particularly buggery. Crotchet could pronounce this last word with such precision that his whole face seemed to get involved in its enunciation—bulged eyes, wiggled ears, flared nostrils, strained lips, flicked tongue. I rather assumed that Bradford's publishers had set the word in boldfaced type. They did not, but I have nonetheless done so here. **Buggery,** just for you, Walter.

I'm sure it surprises you, Dr. Burden, that I regard Walter Crotchet with affection. It shouldn't, of course, since I confided my liking for him to you in person once. It was on the day that you and I were discussing prospective members of my committee. I mentioned Crotchet, and you remarked what a tight ass he was. Do you recall this incident? I doubt it.

But you were right, of course, that Crotchet was a tight ass, if by that term you designate someone terribly different from yourself. He was stiff, and you're loose; he was formal, and you're casual; he was a family man, and you're into "alternative lifestyles"; he was an unreconstructed Kennedy liberal, and you've spotted the weaknesses of that approach and have moved on to Marxism.

You were a poor kid who has made it to the top of your profession. With a strong nose for the scent of current trends, you have managed to stay on the cutting edge of your field. Walter, on the other hand, was a middle-class kid who managed to make it only to the middle of his profession. He didn't give a damn about current trends of scholarship, and that hurt him. His work, as you once assessed it, "was competent but utterly out of date."

But he was a purer scholar than you, I think. He did work that interested him, not work on topics or with methodologies just because they were in vogue. And now he has done something unspeakable, quite insane really. He's left UCLA for a job at a small liberal arts college, not even one particularly well-heeled, where his teaching load is doubled and his leave time is halved. But lest I make him a hero, as you pointed out, "He couldn't take the heat here, so he got out."

I knew what to do when we had our conversation, Dr. Burden, and I did it. Like Hubert Humphrey earning the vice presidential nod from LBJ by screwing the black-based Mississippi Freedom Democrats at the 1964 convention, I crossed Walter Crotchet off my committee list.

Walter Crotchet was terribly different from you, Dr. Burden, and he was different from me, too. He did what he wanted, not what others wanted him to do. He was strange, and he was original. While I was just a copy of you.

To the party that Professor Crotchet gave in December of 1973, he invited the members of the seminar he had directed in the fall quarter and their spouses. His invitation seemed to discriminate against those members of the class who shared their lives with people to whom they were not married. But I think Professor Crotchet failed to extend the invitation to unmarried partners out of oversight, not malice. In the end, of course, they were blessed because being uninvited, they did not have to attend. Faith was not so fortunate.

When we arrived at Professor Crotchet's home high in the Hollywood Hills, he greeted us at the door with a drink in one hand and a cigarette smoldering in a long black holder in the other. He was actually wearing a smoking jacket, one of those sashed, robelike garments out of some Noel Coward play, with satin lapels and suede elbow patches.

"This is Faith Cleaver, Professor Crotchet," I said. Faith stepped forward, and shook his hand firmly.

"I'm Rich's wife," she said to assure him that I had not violated the invitation by bringing a mere girlfriend.

"Faith," he smiled. "Cleaver? Is that right? Not Janus?"

"Yes, Cleaver," Faith said.

His smile broadened. "Well, young lady, I know something about you already." Standing behind Professor Crotchet, dressed in a floor-length evening gown and also holding a drink, was a plump woman with bobbed hair. He turned to her as he closed the door behind us. "Richard Janus and Faith Cleaver," he said, "this is my wife, Mrs. Crotchet."

Faith was annoyed because she took Walter's refusal to identify his wife's first name as a slap at her, a woman not only with a first name, but also with a last name different from her husband's. And maybe she was right, though I doubt it. He was making a joke, I think, which no one got but me. And I lacked the courage to laugh. Had I done so, I'm sure Walter would have told us his wife's first name and put us all at ease. Instead, I cast my eyes away and left Walter with egg on his face.

Mrs. Crotchet took us through the kitchen for drinks and then into the living room, where a few other party goers were already gathered. The beginnings of such affairs are always incredibly awkward. You sip your drink and nod at people over the lip of your glass. You struggle for some conversational topic. You wish not to have to talk about your field or your department, but you know that inevitably you will. You wonder how in the world your spouse will be able to survive.

Faith, being gracious, engaged Mrs. Crotchet. Quickly she discovered that the Crotchets had a sixth-grade daughter, and from there Faith was able to ask her hostess countless questions about the young girl's school and other interests.

I fell into conversation with Anne Norton, a bright, attractive classmate who had a particular distaste for Crotchet. "In a moment," Anne giggled mirthlessly, "Wally's going to ask you if you want to traipse across the back yard to see his view." She raised her fine blond eyebrows. "God, you'd think he had an original Paul Klee out there or something. He's already told me *twice* that he wanted to show me but should probably wait until the rest of you arrived." She took a sip of her drink and said, "Wherever *is* everyone?"

I looked around the room as if I might discover them hiding behind pieces of furniture, determined not to join the party unless we spotted them.

"Wally's got his nerve," Anne said. "Really. Throwing this shindig before he's posted final grades. I wouldn't dare not have come, but I'm afraid I might die before I can leave gracefully."

Anne and I did not really know each other well. We had talked around the coffee urn in the history department lounge, but that was the extent of our intercourse. She was friendlier than other graduate students, and I liked that about her, but I did not like the way she assumed that I must share her judgment that Walter Crotchet was a jerk. So I changed the subject by asking Anne if she planned to take her exams in the spring. She said no and confessed her astonishment that I was going to.

I'd been lucky, I explained. I hadn't had to work, not even as a teaching assistant. And I'd gone to summer school for two additional quarters. In other words, I stressed, I wasn't really taking my exams as early as it seemed. When I stopped talking, she asked if I had selected a committee chairman yet.

"Warren Burden," I said.

"Oh, I should have known," she said, a little smile teasing at the corners of her mouth. "You even look like Burden."

"I do?" I said, quite surprised.

"Of course," Anne said. "Your hair's the same color and about the same length. You both have beards. You're even nearly as tall as he is."

I laughed. "I've got a good two inches on him."

"No! Surely that's not right. Burden is huge."

"I've stood right beside him many times," I said. "Maybe he just stands up straighter." I drew myself up and tried to appear convincingly tall, but she tucked her chin against her neck and looked at me sideways, and I knew she was skeptical.

Crotchet walked up at that moment with two more guests he'd just shown in and asked what we were arguing about. Anne laughed and said, "Janus here claims he's taller than Warren Burden."

"Quite right," Crotchet said to my jubilation and Anne's continuing disbelief. "A good two inches, I judge." I wanted to turn to her and say in a very nasty nasal tone, seeeeeeeee. But I try to keep a lid on my childishness. Crotchet looked from my face to Anne's and back. He took a puff from his cigarette holder and said, "Well, I really don't know what's keeping the others, but I do want you to see the view. Why don't we do that now, and if the late ones miss it, then they're just out of luck, aren't they?"

Walter gathered everybody together, but Mrs. Crotchet said she'd stay inside and put out some hors d'oeuvres. As we walked across the back lawn, Crotchet said, "We're right at the top of the Santa Monica Mountains, you know, and when we peer over the fence we can see the entire valley, that forgotten half of Los Angeles where Barry Goldwater, Jr., lives and Scott Fitzgerald died." The lights came into view perhaps three-quarters of the way across the yard. Beyond the waist-high wire fence was a sheer drop. We peered over the edge. The valley below us was shrouded in a diaphanous mist through which a sea of lights twinkled their silent conformity.

I leaned out over the fence in order to look straight down into the blackness of the hillside. When I stood back up, I said, "It's breathtaking."

Without looking at me, Professor Crotchet said, "You've settled for cliché, Richard, my boy. I'd have expected better of you."

"Not at all, Professor," I laughed. "As it happens, I'm a bit of an acrophobe, and the cliché describes precisely the feeling I get when I venture to the precipice." I bent over the fence again and exaggerated my panting.

Crotchet looked over at me now and said, "Touché."

On the way back, Anne sidled up beside me. I rather expected her to hiss something like, "ass sucker," but all she said was, "What a big deal that was. My feet are soaking wet from the dew." But to Crotchet, who held the sliding glass door open for us as we stepped back inside, she said, "Thank you, Professor; that was lovely."

"Well, I'm glad you liked it, Anne. I know it's damp out but our guests often enjoy the view."

I enjoyed the view, thereby confirming my suspicion that I was a guest. It was the same view, basically, that Faith and Johnnie and Danielle and I rode along Mulholland Drive for. I never seemed to tire of it. As I have not yet tired of sitting at my picnic table at the corner of Wilshire and Ocean Boulevard, where, with a single turn of my head, I can see from Palos Verdes to Point Dume, from Santa Monica to Catalina. And on clear days, beyond.

Sadly, the trip to the back yard fence was the highlight of Professor Crotchet's party. Much of its slowness thereafter was his own fault, however. He kept his booze in the kitchen, so that those of us not talking were unable to keep our nervously emptied glasses filled until such time that creeping inebriation would have broken us from a roundtable, seminar-like situation into groups of twos and threes. My experience has proven that even academic conversations can become, with enough alcoholic lubricant, if not fascinating exactly, then at least tolerably interesting. But Professor Crotchet kept us sober and so kept us uncomfortable.

When it came time to leave, I lingered in Crotchet's hallway, fighting an attack of the El Cholo Feeling. It was not so much the affection I felt for this man, so different from me, as it was a selfish desire to wrest something lastingly personal from him and from my classmates, with whom I had spent ten weeks of my life. I didn't want us all to pass through his front door and behave forever after as if those ten weeks had never happened. Finding nothing pertinent to say, I merely lingered as the partiers said their good-byes and departed. I lingered, absent-mindedly examining some photographs the Crotchets had hung on the wall near their door. Anne Norton and two others lingered also. Perhaps they did so for similar reasons. I hope so.

Finally, I said to the professor, "How do you react to your son's playing on a Little League team called 'Indians'? I'd think you'd at least protest, if not refuse to let him play." I pointed to one of the hallway photographs where his son posed with the other members of his team, the name *Indians* diagonally blazoned across their uniform shirts. This tease was my feeble attempt to effect something personal before I left.

"Not at all," Professor Crotchet responded seriously. "I suppose you're referring to the events at Stanford." That fall Stanford had ceased being Indians in favor of becoming Cardinals. "I really think all this business of protesting the use of Indians as a sports nickname is needless breast-beating. Where's the rub? Other ethnic groups are used as nicknames. Notre Dames calls itself the 'Irish' and Boston's professional basketball team is the 'Celtics.'" I was surprised that Professor Crotchet knew this much about sports.

But I had not really intended my remark to spawn a serious discussion. So I said, "Well, I suppose you've heard that the National League has authorized a new Tennessee franchise, the Nashville Negroes." The various lingerers rewarded me with a burst of laughter.

"That's choice, Richard, old boy," Professor Crotchet said. "That's quite good, really. I fear I must concede." In higher spirits, the others said good night. Anne Norton even kissed my cheek lightly, and we promised to have lunch on campus when school resumed after Christmas. Faith stepped through the door and onto the front porch. I turned at the doorway, thanked Mrs. Crotchet again for having us and put my arm out to shake my professor's hand. He was smiling broadly when he took my hand warmly in both of his. "Nashville Negroes," he said. "I like that. A really choice retort, Richard." He patted with his left hand at my elbow. "You're a fine student, Mr. Janus. And I'm going to expect fine things from you." I smiled and thanked him. He unclasped me, and as I stepped through the door into the night, he shook his head and laughed again, "Nashville Negroes. Choice, Janus. You're choice."

And he was right, of course. It was still my choice. But I didn't choose you, Wally. You were tight-assed and formal and out-of-date. I had doctoral exams to take, a doctoral committee to form. And you couldn't be on it, because you didn't fit in. From my picnic table at the corner of Wilshire and Ocean, I ask your forgiveness.

16

1974

Richard Janus was tired. He had been studying since before noon, and it was after nine P.M. He put his palms against the edge of his desk, pushed his chair back on two legs and stared out the window in front of him at the gray Santa Monica night. I need a vacation, he thought, and laughed because it was the Sunday night before winter quarter began. He'd had a vacation, and it was within a night's sleep of being over. But he hadn't really had a vacation at all, not in the sense that he'd always had them in the past. In college, while he was teaching, even his first year in graduate school, Christmas had been a time of relentless idleness, so much so that he normally found himself restless and ready for work by the time school resumed. This Christmas, though, had been nothing but work. His doctoral exams were in five months, and his fear of them had driven him to a pace of study he had never known before.

Janus yawned and lowered his chair back to the desk. He bent over his book again. The words were like insects and ran all over the page. He rubbed his eyes and called out to Faith, who was making lesson plans at the dining room table, "I need a vacation."

She didn't answer. She was punishing him, he guessed. They'd had a squabble earlier in the evening, though he couldn't remember what about. He sat up in his chair and tried to recall. What had they fought about this time? The phone on his desk rang. Janus did not immediately reach to answer it. He was irritated because he expected it was Kate Banford for Faith and that he'd have to move to the living room while they talked. Kate was having some kind of problem and called Faith almost nightly for counsel.

On the third ring, Faith appeared at the doorway to the bedroom and said, "Have you gone deaf?" Janus looked around at her. "Jesus," she said and started across the room toward him.

He picked up the phone before she got there and said, "Hello." His voice was dull and vaguely hostile. He was instantly sorry. It was Paul Taylor calling from Berkeley.

"Tricks, baby, you sound like an old grizzly." Janus laughed, and Paul told him that he and Grace were taking a late vacation and were driving down to Los Angeles on their way to San Deigo and Tijuana. Paul was going to knock off work about two, he said, and they should arrive in L.A. Friday night about eight. They were planning to stay only the one night, but Janus prevailed on them to agree to stay Saturday night as well.

When they rang off, Janus scooted out of his chair to tell his wife the good news. Faith was standing in the doorway, leaning against the jamb. Janus wondered if she'd been standing there since he picked up the phone.

"Who was that?" she said.

"Didn't you hear?" He was sure she must have heard the conversation.

"Paul Taylor," Faith said.

"You did hear, then." Janus felt a rush of dread that forced away the momentary elation he had felt about Paul's visit. "He and Grace are stopping through here next Friday on their way to San Diego." He looked at his wife, who seemed to be chewing at her bottom lip. "They can only stay a couple of nights. Only a day and a half, really," he added.

"They can't come," Faith said.

"Why? I already told them we'd be looking for them."

"This is my first week back in school. I have too much to do."

"They're not coming until the weekend."

"I have too much to do this week to get ready for them."

"What's to get ready?"

"Look at this place," Faith said, gesturing at the room with a sweep of her arm.

Janus looked around the room. The bed was unmade. The closet door was standing open. His tennis shoes were flung in a corner, one lying upside down. Next to them were four balled-up white socks. A jock hung on one door knob, a pair of gym shorts on the other. He laughed at the disarray. "I promise to pick up my jock before they get here." Faith cocked her jaw the way she did when she was girding for battle. "Hey, come on," Janus said, hoping to soothe her. "Paul and Grace are old friends. They don't expect us to pretend we live in the pages of *Good Housekeeping.*"

"They can't come," Faith said.

"Are you crazy? Of course they can come."

"They can't come!" Faith screeched.

"Goddamnit, why not?" Janus's voice was now loud, too.

"Who's gonna buy the groceries and clean the house? I won't have the time, I tell you."

"I *always* do the grocery shopping," he said incredulously.

"Yeah, ground beef and Hamburger Helper. We can't feed that to them. When we were in Berkeley, Grace fed us as if we were gourmets."

"Well damnit, Faith, Grace cooks like that all the time, whether we're there or not. They know we don't like to cook much. We talked about that when we were raving over Grace's meals." Faith began to pace alongside the bed. "They're coming to see us, not eat." She turned on her heel and glared at him. "Look, if you're concerned about meals, why don't we go out to eat? They'd love El Cholo. We could go there on Saturday. Friday night we could just run up to Piece of Pizza."

"They can't come," Faith said.

"Faith," Janus implored, "I already told them they could come. Do you want me to call them back now and tell them that they can't?"

"Yes."

Janus looked at her a long hard moment before licking his lips and telling her in a low growl. "Well, I'm not going to do it."

"Then I'll do it," Faith said calmly. "You make like this is such a big deal. I'll just explain that this weekend is inconvenient for us."

"Us?" Janus said. *"Us* my ass. You explain that *I* want them to come but that this weekend is inconvenient for *you."*

"Well, it ought to be inconvenient for *you,* too. You've got exams to study for, you know."

Janus continued to stare at his wife. She was absolutely flabbergasting, he thought. "What the hell do you think I've been doing in here all day for the last month, jacking off?"

"You're repulsive."

"You're insane."

"Just call Paul Taylor and tell him he can't come here!" Faith screamed.

"I'll be damned if I will," Janus said through gritted teeth.

Faith glared at him. She squeezed her fists together until her arms shook, then spun around, walked into the bathroom and slammed the door.

Janus tried to follow her, but she had locked the door. He rattled it. He felt a surge of fury and started to smash at the door with a forearm. But controlling himself, he stepped back from the door, breathed deeply and said, "Faith, will you open the door? We've got to settle this?"

"They can't come," she said.

"Come out here and sit down and explain to me why you're so uptight about this."

"They can't come. Get it? THEY CAN'T COME."

Janus was on top of the door then, his lips practically against it when he said, "Goddamn you, Faith. You better get your ass out of that bathroom, or I'm gonna kick this fucking door into splinters."

Janus felt a sharp blow delivered to the bottom of the door; Faith had presumably kicked it. "Come on, Janus. Why don't you kick it down, you son of a bitch. Then when you get inside, you can knock me out again the way you did in St. Louis." Faith kicked the door again, but her words had succeeded in puncturing his anger. He felt the violence pour out of him like air out of a balloon. He walked away from the door and sat on the edge of the bed. "Bully!" Faith screamed. "Lousy bully. When you can't have your way, threaten me, why don't you. You big baby."

"Who's a baby about not having her way? Who locked herself up in the bathroom to pout? Poor little put upon Faithy." Though his anger had ebbed, Janus felt a loathing for his wife that was foreign to him since they had moved to L.A.

"Shut up!" Faith screamed.

"Christ, you're sick," Janus said, as much to himself as to her. He doubted that she could have heard him through the door.

But she yelled, "Shut up," again anyway.

Janus got up from the bed, picked up his tennis shoes, dropped them in the bottom of the closet, closed the closet door and gathered up his athletic gear. He stood in front of the bathroom door, holding dirty clothes in his hands. "Faith," he said quietly. "Could I please get you to come out and talk about this?"

"Will you call them back and tell them that they can't come? They're your friends."

Janus started to argue again, but he took a deep breath and let it out in a loud sigh. "If you explain to me why you think it's necessary, I might. But I won't do it if you don't come out of there and talk."

He heard no stirring of motion from inside the bathroom. He looked at the soiled gym gear and wondered what to do with it. The hamper was in the bathroom. He wadded the clothes into a pile and dropped them in front of the door, off to the side so that Faith wouldn't trip on them if she ever emerged. He went to the bed and began making it. Halfway through, he stopped and laughed. It was nearly ten o'clock. He pulled the sheet and spread taut up to the pillows and lay down, arms clasped behind his head.

While he was staring at the ceiling, Faith came out of the bathroom and stood over him. "The house is a mess," she said, "and I won't have time next week to clean it up. Grace keeps her house clean enough to eat off the floor."

Janus kept his eyes on the ceiling. "I thought it was clear that I'd clean it up. I don't mind. If you're busy, it's only fair that I do it. Besides, half of the cleaning chores are mine anyway. So I'll only be half doing something, not wholly doing it."

"That's just the problem," Faith said.

"Meaning?"

"Meaning that whenever you clean, you only do it halfway."

Somewhere deep inside him, Janus felt the rumblings of anger again. But he was becoming skilled at controlling himself. When he spoke, his voice was very flat. "I'm sure that under your supervision I can manage to get things acceptably clean."

"You don't even know how to clean things right. Sure, you help out, but everything you do is inadequate."

"It seems clean to me."

"I'm sure it *is* clean to you. We just have different notions of what constitutes a clean house."

"How's this?" Janus offered, still looking at the ceiling. "I'll clean the house Wednesday. By the time you get home from school, I'll have it my version of clean. Then you can inspect." He looked over at Faith and suddenly a bubble of rage, like a hiccup, burst to the surface. "Like in the fucking army," he said. But the rage passed as quickly as a hiccup, too. "Forget that," he added hurriedly. "Anything you don't like after the inspection, I'll do over until it meets your approval. I'll have two whole days to get it right before Paul and Grace get here."

"It won't work," Faith pronounced.

Janus sat up. "I can't believe you. How about if I kiss your ass, too? Will that suffice?"

"Go to hell."

"I accomplished that feat when I married you."

"God, I hate you," Faith said through clenched teeth.

"Unfortunately, I know that."

"I hate you so much."

Janus lay back down, an arm thrown across his face to shade his eyes from the light. "Why does it always come to this, babe?"

"Because you always get your way."

Janus pulled the arm away so that he could look at her again, still standing beside the bed. "Faith, these are friends of ours. Old friends. Dear friends. How can we let the condition of the house impede our desire to see them?"

"I don't have any desire to see them. They're your friends, not mine."

Janus snatched a pillow from under his head and covered his face. From underneath it he said, "Jesus, that's such bullshit. Didn't we have a great time visiting with them last summer? Or were you just faking?"

"Grace keeps her house just perfect, and she wouldn't understand my not doing the same thing."

Janus sat up again and scooted backwards so that he could lean against the headboard. "I don't get this at all. You don't even believe that the condition of the house is *your* responsibility. It's *our* responsibility." He stared at her, but she refused to make eye contact. "Look. I'll clean the house. When they get here, I'll tell them that you've had a very busy week and that I've had to do all the cleaning and if anything is amiss that it's my fault. I'll make a joke out of it, but it'll be clear how we do things."

"That'd just give you an excuse to do your usual half-ass job. You wouldn't give a shit if your friends visited you in a pig sty."

"Christ." Janus shook his head and rubbed his arms back and forth across the pillow that he had pulled into his lap. "You know, you want to be a feminist, but you don't want to accept the fact that involved in the process which requires me to do half the work is the compromise that things can't always be to your standards. And besides, this place is hardly a pig sty."

"No thanks to you."

"What can I say? I told you I'd clean the place to your specifications this time and tell them that this week the responsibility was all mine, in case there was a slip-up of some sort."

"That would just embarrass me. It would make me look disorganized and selfish. And Paul and Grace would just think it was weird. They both think housework is the woman's responsibility. Anything wrong they'd blame me for no matter what you told them. In fact, anything you said would just make you the long-suffering martyr in their eyes."

"If that's their attitude, then fuck 'em."

"I don't want your crummy friends to judge me."

"What in the world is the matter with you? Why are you so down on them? I know that you think Paul is too much sometimes, but you and Grace have been friends for ages, longer even than Paul and I have."

"But we continue to be friends only because you and Paul are. She would never come to see me. And I would never go see her. We don't have anything much in common."

"Jesus, Faith, that's just nuts. You both teach school. You went to the same college. You were in the same sorority." Janus thought about adding, "You've slept with the same man," but he knew better.

"We have nothing in common. Grace thinks that picking up after a man is her duty. Making her man comfortable is her destiny. That and having a baby."

"You want to have a baby," Janus pointed out.

"Yeah, but Grace thinks it would be *nice* if Paul would do ten percent of the parenting. That's what she told me." Faith moved away from the bed. She went to the dresser and wiped away dust from the top with her hand. "What bullshit," she said.

"Baby shit is more germane."

"Oh, go to hell, Janus," Faith said with her back to him. But her voice lacked much edge.

She moved things from place to place on the dresser top and continued to wipe at the dust with her hand. Janus didn't say anything. He could never understand why she got so angry when he made jokes in the heat of battle. He always did it to try to cut the tension, but usually he succeeded in making things worse.

"I wish I were dead," Faith said. She came back to the bed and sat down facing away from her husband. She put her face in her hands and began to cry.

Janus moved close to her and put his arm around her. "Babe, why does stuff always upset you so much?"

"Leave me alone," she sobbed.

"Is it that repulsive for you to be around Grace? I know she's no feminist like you, but I always thought you two got along. She's awfully nice."

Janus reached in his back pocket for his handkerchief and handed it to Faith. She blotted her face and blew her nose. "You wouldn't understand, Rich."

"That's the old bottom line, babe. But think back. Sometimes I do manage to understand." Faith offered him his handkerchief back but he refused it, shaking his head, screwing up his face and saying, "Yuck."

She laughed at that a little. "I'm not sure you *can* understand, Rich. I'm not sure any *man* can. Grace *is* nice. She's very nice. But women like Grace are a threat to me and everything I believe in. It's not Paul's fault that Grace waits on him. She wants to. And it's not your fault that you think she's nice. She is. But, you see, women like Grace make women like me look like bitches. We're feminists, not bitches. Those are two very different things."

"You're not a bitch, babe," Janus said softly. "You're a witch. Remember? Where's your witch hat? Maybe you should get it out and wear it while Paul and Grace are here so they'll know the difference."

"If you really understood, Rich, you wouldn't let them come this weekend. I'm just not up to it."

To prove his understanding, Janus got up right then, stepped to the phone and dialed Berkeley. He told Paul that he was sorry but he had committed himself without speaking to Faith and that next weekend was an especially bad time for her. Paul said he understood.

When he came back to the bed to find Faith crying again, Janus was pleased with himself. He felt he'd demonstrated that his loyalty to Faith took preeminence in his life, was greater even than his love for someone as special to him as Paul Taylor. And he did somewhat grasp what Faith felt about Grace, or at least about women like Grace. He saw how, in the movement Faith was ever more caught up in, that women like Grace were the Uncle Toms.

But as time went along, Janus's first rush of satisfaction ebbed. Of course, Faith had cause to resent the Aunt Graces of the world. But Faith's politics, he came to feel, did not have the right to trample on something more important than politics. To Richard Janus, friendship was the most important thing in the world. Faith had made him hurt a friend. She had reason, but as time passed the reason seemed hardly great enough, seemed ultimately selfish and small. Janus's satisfaction atrophied into resentment that Faith had made him do something shameful. At first he was only vaguely aware of this resentment, but it was like a cancer which ate silently and steadily at his insides.

For the most part, as the time before his exams dwindled, Janus managed to stave off panic. He was often irritable, of course, but he was aware of it, admitted it readily and asked Faith's forgiveness when she was victimized by it. Remarkably, he was able to save weekend nights for Faith right up until the end. Usually at midweek, he would announce with great fanfare that this weekend she would have to entertain herself, that he had finally reached the critical stage of his preparations and would, hereafter, have to work night and day until the exams began. But by the weekend he was so sick of studying that a night alone while Faith went to a movie with Danielle or for a drink with Kate loomed as unbearable. So at the last minute he would join in whatever plans Faith had made. With Danielle this eleventh-hour intrusion caused no problems. The three of them still went to El Cholo sometimes, and the experience never lost its specialness.

Evenings with Kate were another matter. Kate and Janus had never warmed to one another. They'd gotten off to an awfully bad start back when Kate was married and she and her husband had come for dinner. Janus had mixed up a wine punch, a sort of embellished wine cooler with slices of lemon and orange, and served it in a decanter he and Faith had gotten as a wedding present from Grace Lamm. Kate remarked on the decanter's handsomeness. "It has such an interesting shape," she said.

"Almost as interesting as that of the lady who gave it to us," Janus joked, rolling his eyes and looking over his shoulder toward Faith, who was busy at the stove. It was one of those things he shouldn't have said, one meant for Faith's ears and actually meaningless to Kate or her husband, who guffawed loudly nonetheless. Janus really *hadn't* been intimate with Grace the night of Winter Festival all those years ago, but he knew that Faith had never quite believed him, and he enjoyed teasing her sometimes about Grace, greatly magnifying any attraction he'd ever felt for her.

Janus wasn't sure whether it was the rudeness of his remark or the exaggeration of her husband's reaction which most aggravated her, but Kate was offended. "That was a sexist thing to say, Rich," she reprimanded him. "I'm surprised at you."

Janus wondered why she was surprised. They barely knew each other. He guessed she was referring to some body of praise Faith must have thrown his way. If so, then her correction was likely aimed more at Faith than at him. "Was it?" he said pleasantly and smiled. "I'm sorry." He was sorry, too. He guessed he could understand how the remark *seemed* sexist, though he was certain that, however ill-advised it was, it *wasn't* sexist. He saw no denigration of women by recognizing that Grace Lamm had a nice body. He was guilty of being thoughtless for making an in-joke in front of guests, but damn it, he was not guilty of sexism. He hoped that his apology and smile would encourage Kate to let the matter drop.

But she didn't. "Of course it was. You've just compared a woman, a friend of yours evidently, to an object. Like most men, you've indicated an attitude, subconscious I hope, of contemptuous ridicule for the female form."

"All that with just one little line?" Janus said. He smiled again, but this time only with his mouth. His acid eyes said, "Gee I think you're a galloping asshole." Kate started to say something else but decided against it. The entire evening after that became enormously strained.

As Faith's relationship with Kate developed, Janus regretted he hadn't done a better job of wooing her that first night. He could never escape the feeling that she disapproved of him. Worse, he felt that Kate made Faith ashamed of being associated with such a large, bearded, deep-voiced, latently sexist MAN. Janus joked that he must smell like a chauvinist because Kate's nose always seemed to wrinkle when he was around, but he didn't hesitate to accompany Faith on her outings with Kate. It was one of his faults to believe that he was innocent of the charge of sexism, to believe that he was basically decent enough to win Kate's approval if she only saw enough of him.

Then somewhere along in the spring of 1974, Kate announced that she was a lesbian. After that Janus accompanied Faith and Kate because he wasn't keen on the idea of their being alone together. Faith held that such an attitude was ridiculous.

"But look," he argued. "If Kate is gay, that makes you a sexual object for her. You wouldn't like it if I took to having drinks with Anne Norton or some other attractive woman I go to school with, would you?"

"Nonsense," Faith said.

"Then it's okay if Anne and I go out together?"

"Is that what you want?"

"Of course that isn't what I want. I want you to see why it bothers me if you go out with Kate."

"Kate isn't interested in *me,*" Faith maintained. "She's interested in *gay* women."

Janus wondered if that was right. He could imagine being attracted to a gay woman. In fact, he was sometimes attracted to Kate herself. She was not terribly good looking; that is, her face was rather plain. But she was a dedicated jogger, slender and firm, and much as she disbelieved it, Janus liked the passion of her feminism. And when she relaxed and laughed and flirted, Janus liked *her.* These things didn't change because she declared herself a lesbian. So, he reasoned, if he could be attracted to a gay woman, why couldn't a gay woman be attracted to one who was straight?

Janus hated this lesbian development, though. He had trouble enough with Kate as a straight person. As a lesbian, it seemed, her ability to reject him was total. But he couldn't expect Faith to abandon her friend. He didn't believe their friendship *ought* to be affected by Kate's sexual preference. On the other hand, he couldn't conquer the feeling that when Faith went out with Kate, it was the rough equivalent of her going out with a man.

In addition to weekend nights out, Janus also refused to sacrifice his lifelong habit of exercise while he prepared for his doctoral exams. But for him, exercise had to be associated with a ball. Jogging may have been a more efficient way of staying in shape, but the very idea of it made him sleepy. Running was rife in Santa Monica, but Janus avoided it, maintaining that *jogger* and *masochist* were synonyms. So whenever he was on campus, he normally allowed a couple of hours for gimpy-ankled basketball at UCLA's Pauley Pavillion. On the days he worked at home, he normally knocked off around four to join a group of dedicated basketballers on the outdoor courts at Lincoln Junior High. On Sunday afternoons, he continued to play in a recreation department league at Santa Monica High. And on Saturday afternoons and sometimes on Thursday nights, Janus played tennis with his wife.

In the two years she had been playing, Faith had become quite good. She could slice a forehand down the line with deadly accuracy or hit it with crisp topspin cross court. Her backhand lacked much pace but was steady and improving. Her serve was soft, but she could move the ball from side to side, and she never double faulted. Her volley and overhead were weak, but she never used these shots. Staying at the baseline, she climbed to the top of Santa Monica's B challenge board in only one year. She had more trouble the second year playing in the A division, but she won as many matches as she lost.

The only problem with Faith's tennis game was that she couldn't beat her husband, a fact that frustrated her enormously. She rightly considered herself a fundamentally better player than he was. After playing under Janus's instruction for a while, she'd taken lessons from a professional, who had helped her game become remarkably sound. Self-taught and fonder of basketball, Janus retained the tennis strokes of the novice he really was. His forehand was passable. He could knock hell out of a first serve but had to dink his second to avoid double faulting. His backhand was embarrassing, always, it seemed, either sailing long or fluttering helplessly into the net, a problem Janus solved by refusing to hit it. Still, weak as his game was, Faith couldn't beat him. He was fast enough to run around his backhand, smart enough to hit the ball constantly to Faith's weaker backhand side and quick enough to get to the net. Faith often succeeded in passing him but not often enough. He was rangy and agile and could always get to enough volleys to beat her.

She absolutely hated it. Once she'd had lessons and realized the potential of her game, she figured it was only a matter of time until she could beat Janus regularly. But that time never came.

After one particularly frustrating loss, when sharp passing shots had given her a 4-1 lead only to have Janus rally to claim the set, Faith threw her racquet against the back screen and screamed so loudly that people on adjoining courts stopped to stare. "Damn you, God. The problem in this world is that you're the original male chauvinist pig."

Janus laughed, but Faith wasn't joking. She refused to speak to him on the way home and refused to play with him for a while. Finally they agreed just to rally, each standing at the baseline hitting balls back and forth without playing points or keeping score. Probably they should have kept that system up, but Faith was tempted to play. Her ground strokes were better than his, and it always appeared to her that she was ready to win.

She agreed to start playing sets again, but a new round of losses produced threats by Faith to stop playing altogether. "It's not fair," she complained. "You win at everything else. Why do you have to win at tennis, too?" That seemed a legitimate gripe to Janus. Faith never understood it, but he didn't take great pleasure in beating her. He agreed that her game was more fundamentally sound. And he agreed that if there were justice, she would win. Further, he knew she was right when she asserted that he won *because* he was male, because he was born bigger and stronger and quicker.

And she never understood how proud he was of her tennis ability. He told her, but he knew she always felt patronized. Janus enjoyed playing tennis with his wife, even if the workout was not strenuous enough to suit him. He took pleasure in watching her play and in participating with her at something in which she excelled. It saddened him that his winning ruined the fun for her.

So he began throwing points, throwing them often enough to make their sets very close. He was adept enough that sometimes he could make a set go sixteen, even twenty games, long enough to fill their hour without producing a victor. At first he cheated stupidly, deliberately hitting balls that were headed out, or calling balls good that had clearly landed wide or long. But Faith protested, called him condescending and demanded the right at least to lose with dignity. Janus admired this stance, but he was still faced with her frustration about defeat. Then he discovered a method for helping her that worked rather well and led to their tight matches. Once he got to net, he would continually hit volleys back to her rather than putting them away. She was a steady enough player that sooner or later she would hit a winner to earn the point. Janus was pleased with this system. Faith couldn't accuse him of cheating for her, and he still spared her having to suffer defeat.

One night after they'd played a 9-9 tie, Faith beefed about her failure actually to win. She had served first, and Janus let her hold service all night. The pressure he put on himself to win his own service games had increased his enjoyment of the night's tennis, so he was additionally disappointed that tying had not proved enjoyable to Faith.

"You're so macho, you'd die before you'd let me win," she said. "I had a chance to beat you from 5-4 on, but you just couldn't let me do it. You should have seen yourself digging for points. You'd have thought you were in a tournament."

Janus found these remarks annoying. Of course he had hustled for points to keep from losing the match. Wasn't that the way one was supposed to play? Wasn't that the challenge that made sport fun? "Isn't it enough that I let you tie?" he snapped.

"Is that what you did? You let me tie?"

"No," Janus said. He was already sorry that he'd lipped off. To admit what he'd done was to ruin having done it.

"You didn't?"

"No."

"Then why did you say that you did?"

"I was being an asshole," Janus said. "I'm sorry. I *did* have to hustle to stay with you tonight. You're really getting so much better."

Faith didn't reply instantly but finally said, "If you have been deliberately letting me have points and games, then you're even more macho than I realized. Because you've obviously never had the guts to let me win."

In Janus's relationship with his wife, he couldn't win by tying.

Faith's observation got to him. He had congratulated himself on being big enough to throw points to her, but she was right; he was still protecting himself, shielding his male ego from the humiliation of being beaten by a woman. Willing to forgo victory, he had not been willing to embrace defeat. If he was really capable of sacrifice, then he would actually let her win.

In Janus's relationship with Faith, however, he couldn't win by losing, either. To put it in the words of Mrs. Brisket, words that Janus should have lived by, cheaters never gain.

The next time he played Faith, he lost. He didn't even try to make it close, afraid that she might choke and start making unforced errors. She won the first four games and then held serve for a 6-2 win. It was the first set she'd ever taken from him. After the winning point, he called out, "You were sensational, babe."

He went to the net to congratulate her but she stayed at the baseline. She'd dropped her racquet and was dancing in a circle with her hands clasped above her head. He laughed and said, "Now that you've finally broken through, you'll probably win a lot of the time."

"I hope I win all the time," she said. "All the sets all the time. I want you to feel what it's like always to lose."

"Well, that's not very gracious," Janus said and found himself thinking that Faith could use some lessons in sportsmanship.

"Ha," she said. "Let's play again before we have to give the court up."

They started a new set. Faith won the first three games with Janus hitting all his volleys right at her.

When they changed sides, she said, "How does it feel?"

That was a mistake. One for which both of them were to be penalized. Janus got mad, and as often happened when he was mad, he behaved badly. He began angling all his volleys away from her and easily took the next five games. Not a word was exchanged as they changed sides. They didn't even call out the score to one another.

Faith served to try to save the set. In order to set up a sure forehand return, Janus positioned himself far to the left of the service box, defying her to hit a serve hard enough to put it past him. The strategy worked. Trying to hit a service winner, she faulted on every first serve. Three times in a row, he charged her second serve, driving it deep to her backhand. The first two times, he blocked volleys away from her for easy winners. The third time, when she tried to lob, he hit an overhead so hard that it bounced over the back screen after being pounded inside her service box.

At set point, Faith again tried to lob his deep service return. She began back pedaling when she saw him set up for the overhead. But instead of smashing the ball, he just tapped it softly into her forecourt. Faith never had a chance to get it, but the ball hung up long enough to entice her forward. "You son of a bitch!" she screamed as she dashed in, bent low, trying to scoop the ball up before it bounced a second time. When her racquet came through without touching the ball, she just loosened her grip on the handle and it went flying right for Janus, who was standing at the net.

Had the racquet not hit the top of the net, he probably could have dodged it. But when the racquet ricocheted off the net cord, it jumped in the same direction he did and drove into his groin. He bent double and sagged to the ground. The pain was great enough that not even he realized immediately that the racquet handle had missed hitting him in the balls.

Among Faith's many astonishing qualities was her capacity for remorse. She was powerfully penitent that she had hurt her husband by throwing her tennis racquet. She would cry sometimes during the subsequent couple of weeks just looking at the grapefruit-sized bruise she had caused on the inside of his upper thigh. The night it happened, she clung to him in bed, her face bathing his chest in tears. When he would stir from sleeping, he would hear her whisper, "Oh, Bubba, I'm so sorry."

Oddly, it was after the tennis incident that she first spoke again of thoughts about leaving him. The manner of her broaching the subject, the first time she had done so since they reached L.A., was different from any of her threats in St. Louis.

Janus had come in from playing basketball, showered and pulled on a clean pair of gym shorts before he walked into the living room and plopped down in a director's chair. The short pants showed the yellow-green bruise on his thigh. Faith was sitting in his wing-back chair. When she saw him, her eyes filled with water, but he told her to please stop feeling guilty. "It never did hurt nearly as bad as it looks," he said.

Then Faith made one of her remarks that never failed to shock him. There was a logical progression to her question, but it was delivered without introduction. Her voice was small and timid. "Do I make enough money to live on all by myself, Bubba?" she asked.

Janus laughed, not grasping the gravity of her question. "You live on it, don't you?"

"Well, we live on it," she said. "But we have two incomes and only this small apartment. If I had to, could I live by myself on what I make? In my own apartment?"

"Why?" Janus asked.

She shrugged her small shoulders in a way that struck her husband like a stab. He felt himself begin to tear, too. Faith made eight thousand dollars a year from her teaching job. Of course she could live on it. How incredibly sad, he realized, that she didn't know it. They maintained joint checking and saving accounts, and Faith had her own checkbook, but she never paid a bill like rent or utilities or phone. Since Janus did the grocery shopping, she didn't pay the food bills either. Most of the check writing she did was for her own clothes or for other personal items. She didn't go to the bank, didn't compute a monthly balance, didn't even keep a running balance in her own checkbook. She brought home her paychecks, endorsed them and gave them to Janus, who took care of depositing them during hours while she was teaching. When she wanted to purchase something, she always had to ask him whether there was money enough in the account to cover the amount of her purchase. It was a system Faith had never complained about, one in many ways that was a convenience to her. But all at once Janus grasped why it was that she wouldn't know the value of her own salary. She was a full-grown, working adult, and she'd never managed any money. She had no sense of what their monthly expenses were compared with their joint income.

"Of course you can live on what you make, babe," he told her. "I never realized you didn't know that. Maybe we ought to let you handle the bill-paying chore for a while so you can get a sense of things."

"I thought maybe I'd have to get a roommate."

"Is this a theoretical discussion?" Janus asked with a nervous laugh. "Or are you planning on moving out in the near future?"

Faith's head was down, her teeth clamped over her lower lip. Her eyes darted a glance at him. "Sometimes I do think I should move out," she said. "Don't you ever think so?"

Janus was torn between two competing responses. The first one, the one he rejected, was to give her a lecture about the selfishness of raising this kind of issue while he was studying for exams, to accuse her of treachery for jeopardizing his concentration at this critical time with this kind of talk. The second, the one he chose, seemed called for by the sad rather than angry way that Faith had raised the topic. "No, I don't, babe. In fact, I thought you were happy, that you'd been happy since we moved to L.A. I know that this year hasn't been as good as last year, of course. But I...." He didn't try to finish his thought.

Faith was still looking at him only in fleeting glaces, immediately casting her eyes back down. "I *have* been happier, Whaley, but I hate it that I get so mad at you sometimes. That's not right. You deserve someone better than that."

Janus moved across the room and sat at Faith's feet. He put his arms around her legs and his head on her knee. "I'll just have to work harder at not making you mad," he said.

Janus and Faith went to the Piece of Pizza restaurant that night. When Janus saw the company slogan, "Had a piece lately?" on the sign outside, he teased Faith that he hadn't. But she cried rather than laughed.

When they got home and had gone to bed, Janus began to caress her.

"Not tonight, Bubba," she said. "Okay?"

"Okay," he said and pulled her against him and held her until they slept.

In June, the week of Janus's written exams finally came. He was astonished by how easy he found them, convinced that he'd been preposterously lucky. Questions were provided on the very material he knew best. The gaps in his knowledge, which he was sure were numerous and vast, were not exposed.

His oral was scheduled at noon on Friday of the next week. Janus worked all day the last Thursday. He and Faith ate a leisurely supper, and he reviewed outlines for a couple of hours afterwards. Around nine, he stopped. He opened a bottle of red wine, and he and Faith talked about their plans for the coming summer. She was going to take another psychology course at UCLA. She'd done quite well in the one last summer and had begun to think about doing an M.A. at some point after Janus finished his degree. He promised to do nothing other than lie on the sand and get brown. She suggested that he ought to get started on his dissertation, and he said that he would, of course, but that he didn't plan to work so hard that he couldn't attend her course with her.

When they went to bed, Faith cuddled against him, threw a leg over him and purred in a way that indicated she was interested in having sex. But Janus did not try to find out. Their sex life recently had been lacking. Often she had refused him when he approached her. They had not fought about it, but Janus didn't like the feeling of rejection. So he kissed her, loud and perfunctorily like a parent kissing a child, or like a brother kissing a sister, and made settling noises and motions as if in a hurry to sleep.

Faith rose first the next morning. She fixed Orange Jewels, something she seldom did, and woke Janus with his. He was touched by her thoughtfulness.

When he'd finished half of his drink, she asked if he planned to study this morning before the exam.

"I guess I'll read over my outlines one more time." He smiled. "Not that it could conceivably make any difference."

"Would you go to the pancake house with me?"

Janus set his drink glass down on the night stand and pulled her down to kiss. "Sure, Sleeping Greasy, why not?"

"I'm not Sleeping Greasy. I'm wide awake."

"Sure, Waking Greasy, why not?"

"I'm not Waking Greasy. I already washed my face."

"Sure, Nolonger Greasy, why not? I'll have a nice protein breakfast to stimulate my brain. And you can tell me that you'll love me even if I fail?"

"You're not going to fail."

"You can never tell. Cardinal Newman failed and studied a lot more than

I have."

"Who is Cardinal Newman?"

"I never can remember. And that always worries me."

"Oh, my God, maybe you *are* going to fail. How depressing. And you'll probably expect me to love you anyway."

"You mean you don't want me to fail?"

Faith looked at him very seriously and shook her head slowly side to side. "No," she said.

Janus kissed her on her nose and said, "Then I promise to try not to."

At the pancake house, when they had finished breakfast and were talking amid a jumble of dirty dishes, Janus betrayed his nervousness by musing about how he was going to structure his dissertation, how he was going to start off with a review of the pertinent literature and then end the first chapter with an analysis of how and why other scholars went wrong. Faith listened patiently for a while before she began to fidget. "Do you need to go to the bathroom?" Janus asked her.

"I just need you to shut up," she laughed.

"Oh, you aren't just entranced by the actions of men long dead, events ardently disagreed upon by other men more recently dead or all too soon to die?"

She reached across the table and cupped her hand over his mouth. When she moved it, he instantly started talking again. She pinched his lips shut. "If you don't hush a minute, I'm going to stuff a napkin so far down your throat you'll have to take your oral today in sign language." She fumbled in her purse and brought out a jewelry box that she set on the table in front of him. "It's for luck today, Bubba," she said.

Janus opened the box. Inside was a chain and a silver medallion. On the front side was the picture of an old man with a walking stick carrying a haloed child on his back across a body of water. Around the edge were the words *St. Christopher Protect Us*. On the back was inscribed: *The Patron Saint of Whales*. Janus took the medallion and hung it around his neck. There were tears in his eyes.

"You don't have to wear it if you don't like it," Faith said.

"I won't ever take it off," he answered. "As long as it's around my neck, you'll know I still love you. And that will be forever."

In the car riding eastward from Santa Monica to UCLA, Faith said to her husband, "Do you really love me, Whaley?"

"Of course I do," he said. "I'm no dummy, you know."

"You're not going to think I'm dumb when you have a Ph.D., are you?"

Janus looked over at her and shook his head. "No."

"Are you going to fall in love with some smart woman then? Someone who's on your own level?"

"I'm already very much in love with a smart woman who's at least on my level."

"If I said let's go home and fuck now, would you do it?" She opened the top buttons on her blouse and nudged her right breast into his view. "This still turn you on, big fella?"

Janus laughed. "You're a wonderful wild woman, Faith. But no, for once in my life I wouldn't go home and fuck right now." Faith stuck out her lower lip and buttoned herself back up. "On the other hand," Janus said, "we probably have time to fool around in the parking garage for a while before I go up to the exam."

Faith reached over and tugged at his pants zipper. "In honor of this special occasion," she said, "I think we should engage in *oral* sex."

17

The El Cholo Feeling. The year after I passed my exams, it was with me like sand on a desert. I was teaching again. As y'all know, UCLA had awarded me a very lucrative teaching fellowship that I loved so much it almost proved my undoing. I had to teach only two classes a week, but I found I could devote almost the whole week to preparing those sessions. My dissertation work inched along painfully.

I committed to a trip back east to work with primary sources over the long Christmas break, and before I left I wanted to exhaust the resources in UCLA's research library. Fat chance. There were a couple of million pages I still needed to turn when the fall quarter ended. The trip to Boston and New Haven was cold and gray and fraught with the feeling of being premature.

I was in the library at Harvard when I finally admitted to myself how absolutely loathsome I found this whole business. I should leave this kind of work to someone who enjoys it, I thought. King Philip's War was pretty exciting when I first started working on it, but I'd probably been working on it too long.

I discovered the project in my second quarter at UCLA when I managed to convince you, Dr. Burden, that all published accounts of the war were in error and that I and only I understood the origins of the war for what they were. You told me there was a first-rate dissertation in that idea, once I'd convinced you I was right. I loved those words: first rate. And I'd been working on the project ever since.

But I didn't care any more. Worse, I knew that no one else cared much either. Most people in America had never heard of King Philip's War and weren't going to listen when I tried to tell them about it. A handful of my fellow historians would be interested for a while, and that should have been enough incentive for any historian worth his salt. But I never really wanted to be an historian. I wanted to please teachers. And I'd pleased you, Dr. Burden, just by demonstrating the validity of my analysis. After that, I was talking to myself. And I already knew what I was going to say.

I forced myself to keep working, but I was in agony. The more I did, the more I hated it. I tried to confide my feelings to Faith, from whom I was separated for the first extended time in our marriage. She mouthed the proper mix of sympathy and encouragement, but I couldn't escape the feeling that she found my condition contemptible.

I returned to L.A. for the start of winter quarter with the gnawing feeling that I hadn't accomplished enough on my trip, that if the dissertation were to be any good I'd have to go back East again. I'd gotten a decent amount of material digested, but I'd also spent a decent amount of time watching football games on my rooming house television set.

I was experiencing, I think, what psychologists call a crisis.

In other words, I was fragile and tentative. I was irritable. In still other words, I was an asshole. I wanted Faith to love me more than ever and kept accusing her of loving me less. By the end of the winter quarter, we were in the midst of our domestic version of World War II.

I had finally finished my research at UCLA and had only the sources at the Huntington Library to investigate before I began writing. I was sure unforeseen monsters lay awaiting me once the drafting began, but at least I was making progress. It began to seem that I might actually finish and survive this ordeal. The back of my brain burned with the terror that finishing meant committing myself to a lifetime of something I hated. But how often have I paid the least attention to the back of my brain?

"I'm really getting there," I bragged one day to Faith, who was forever pestering me for progress reports. "I have to work at the Huntington for a few weeks when I get back from the Fortran conference, but after that I think I can roll paper into the typewriter."

"It's about time," she suggested.

I am twenty-eight years old. I am a graduate student. A successful one. God has blessed me with intelligence and the capacity for hard work if, unfortunately, with little courage. And I have gone far. "Success," you have told me, Dr. Burden, "in teaching, in writing, in *thinking,* comes from the same source: the ability to ask the right questions. Rich," you've said to me, "you have that ability. You should go far." And I have. One doctoral dissertation more and I'd be a Ph.D. One last requirement met and I'd be a certified, sanctified, emulsified historian. But this success would obviously *not* arise from asking the right questions. Like, why am I doing this? For an historian is something others told me I *should* be, not something I decided I *wanted* to be.

I finally admitted that to myself at last year's spring Fortran conference. You all know of the Fortran Foundation and the fellowships they award for graduate study. Second to the Rhodes, I suppose, they're the most prestigious scholarships a graduate student can land. My senior year in college, I was Lancaster's only nominee in a nationwide competition that included top students from every academic major. I was outrageously lucky to win, of course. But I was proud, too. I'm always proud of my awards. And this one has had the added advantage of putting books in my library and groceries on my table. Of course, it was supposed to put a diploma on my wall.

The spring conference last year was held at Asilomar on California's Monterey Peninsula. Asilomar is serene and beautiful, a rambling resort with sandy bedrooms and shared baths. It stands on the dunes that guard Spanish Bay, in which swimming is not recommended.

The conference was an unqualified success. Everyone said so; therefore, it must have been. The participants were bright and articulate, the cream of the nation's graduate schools, as each of the meeting's leaders remarked. We were reminded that we were different from the rest of the nation's academics. Different, mind you, not necessarily superior. Fortran Fellows are awesomely aware of the pitfalls of elitism.

The general sessions, led by notables like Erik Erikson, who brilliantly and affectionately explained to us Ingmar Bergman's *Wild Strawberries,* were supplemented with small group workshops where important issues like sex discrimination in the hiring practices of colleges and universities were discussed, where mock seminars were videotaped and teaching styles were analyzed.

It was a congenial group. We seldom disagreed. We were all sympathetic to the problems of women and minorities, all liberal Democrats who hated Richard Nixon and admitted sadistic satisfaction at his national embarrassment. I once admitted sadistic glee, but that was going too far. I didn't do it again.

Everyone at the conference had spotted the preview which *Newsweek* ran on its "Periscope" page of Watergate reporters Bob Woodward and Carl Bernstein's new book, *The Final Days,* chronicling the events leading to Nixon's resignation. Everyone has since surely read the lengthy piece *Newsweek* did on the book when it finally appeared a year later. And if they didn't actually read the book, they did read Nicholas Von Hoffman's review in *The New York Review of Books,* the current copies of which we had all brought to the conference in our briefcases.

At Fortran Conferences, the El Cholo Feeling is rampant.

The first day of the conference that March, after the cheese and sherry party and after an informal meal, I met my roommate, a chubby historian from Stanford. When I entered the corner room that we were to share, I found him sitting on the bed by the windows, grinning out at a stand of redwoods before the dunes. He had just a trace of yellowed mayonnaise in his mustache. He was dressed in a kelly green print shirt with the tail hanging out over lime-colored Bermuda shorts, and white low-cut tennis shoes with lime socks.

My roommate was a large man, flabby and balding. He kept the thick hair on the sides of his head slicked back like the gill fins on a fish. He looked a lot like a fish—one of those rare species that puffs itself up to avoid being swallowed by its predators. His thick glasses for acute myopia made his eyes appear to bulge. A sinus condition (I gathered since he rasped and snorted in his sleep) made his mouth hang open in a vertical oval. I was not surprised to learn later that his name was Leonard Bass.

"This is certainly a beautiful place, isn't it?" Leonard Bass said as I came into the room.

"Yes, it is," I agreed. It was the first of many agreements we were to have. I slumped onto the bed where I had dumped my belongings, making room for myself between the plaid gym bag stuffed with clean underwear and a change of jeans, and my briefcase, which contained, among other things, the note cards to the doctoral dissertation I've decided not to write.

Grinning broadly, the man came across the sandy floor to greet me. "I'm Leonard Bass," he said, extending a moist and flaccid hand.

"Rich Janus," I said, shaking his hand.

"I'm in U.S. history at Stanford. Nineteenth-century intellectual," he said.

"I'm in Indian history at UCLA. American Indian."

"What period?"

"My dissertation is in seventeenth-century."

"Ah, a colonialist," he said.

And so soon it started. Academic chess. How many times I'd played before.

"Have you read Herring's book on Springfield artisans?" Leonard Bass asked. (KP to K4)

Woodsmen and Woodworkers? Yeah, I read it when I was studying for orals. Traced the movement of second-generation pioneers into the carpentry trade." (KP to K4)

"Well, what do you think of it in light of Nitworth Quibbler's analysis in the *Journal of American History?*" (KB to QB4)

"I'm afraid I'm not acquainted with the piece," I admitted. (QP to Q3)

"It's in the most recent issue," Leonard Bass said in a tone somewhere between surprised and reproachful. "You really must have a look at it."

(Q to KR5)

"I'll have to remember to do that. You know, I thought Herring did a good job at capturing the tension of frontier society at the onset of industrialization." (KN to KB3)

"Ah, but that's just Quibbler's point. Herring's methodology was diametrically wrong. He worked from lists of carpenters rather than from the census records and probates that could have gotten him at the whole of frontier society. Quibbler has no data, of course, but his approach throws Herring's entire thesis into doubt." (Q to KB7, check)

"Well, I can see that I really need to read Quibbler," I concluded. (Resign)

What I really thought at the end of this exchange was: well, now at least I won't need to read Quibbler.

I found it difficult to like Leonard Bass, but I did not give up immediately. A short time later, when he came out of the shower with a towel wrapped around his waist and his glasses pushed far down near the end of his nose, his freshly washed hair was standing out, tousled and wild, from the sides of his head.

"Hey," I said smiling, "did anyone ever tell you that you sort of resemble Woody Allen?"

He quickly shoved his glasses up to his eyes and said suspiciously, "No."

"Woody Allen's one of my heroes," I said, wanting him to understand that I had mentioned the resemblance as a compliment.

"Oh. I've always regarded him as rather frivolous." I took that to be Leonard Bass's conclusion about anything humorous.

Not that Leonard was an unhappy sort, for he was utterly happy, I think. A humorless, blindly cheerful sort of happy. He grinned incessantly through his unwieldy mustache, cheerfully agreeing with everyone at the conference. Except when his face momentarily contorted while he fashioned thoughtful, articulate sentences with which everyone else agreed. Even me, usually.

When Leonard Bass had dressed, he checked his watch and said, "It's almost time for the evening session. Shall we head downstairs?"

"You go ahead," I said. "I need to settle in a bit." All I had was my battered gym bag and a briefcase. It was not the best excuse, but it sufficed. I wanted him to go so that I could climb upon his bed, which unlike mine was near the windows, and stare out of them at the parched scrub brush and the greenish-black ice plant that dotted the dunes between me and the fog on Spanish Bay. I wanted to throw the window open to feel the breeze spread from my face to my shoulders to the backs of my arms and up into the back of my neck. I wanted to feel the chill and let it build until it passed in the spasm of a shiver.

I arrived at the teaching workshop just in time to see Leonard Bass raise his hand and say, "Query." The videotape machine was switched off, and Leonard continued. "Why were you so nervous at the outset of your presentation? It put me off." He looked around the room to find a semicircle of faces nodding in agreement. "Frankly, I think your nervousness made all the rest of us nervous."

My corpulent roomie was making *me* nervous.

"I'm sorry," the Fellow whose teaching style was being analyzed said. His name was Rod, and he was in English at Harvard.

"Yes, of course," Leonard Bass persisted. "But why *were* you so nervous?"

"I was just afraid that no one would be interested in the topic I'd chosen, that my questions would go unanswered. That no real seminar-type situation would develop and I'd be forced to lecture," Rod explained.

"Hmph," Leonard Bass announced. "I would think a Fortran Fellow would be comfortable on the other side of the pedagogical chasm." Indignation flashed across Rod's handsome face.

"Before I start the tape again," counselled the female workshop leader, an expert on teaching from Berkeley, "let us keep in mind that the purpose of these workshops is to help one another to learn, and there is no reason for any of us to feel embarrassed." She paused and then added, "We're all among friends here." This wasn't really true, but we believed her because she spoke with the exaggerated softness and patience of a first grade teacher. I was seized by the impulse to stand up and proclaim something outrageous. SUCK EGGS. But I didn't do it. She switched the tape back on, and we watched in silence for a minute or so.

"Caveat," Leonard Bass said. "Rod's just asked two questions at once."

"Good point," the leader commended. She stopped the tape once again. "How do we know which question to answer when the teacher asks two questions at once? Don't you think this promotes confusion and is akin to a related problem called 'insufficient wait time'? What do I mean by insufficient wait time? When you fall victim to insufficient wait time, you nervously ask a second question before getting a response to the first, or you simply supply the first answer and go on to a new question. Try to avoid this. Have faith in your students. They'll get involved. Wait for the answer to the first question before asking a new one."

When the workshop on teaching was over, I confided to Rod that I also sometimes asked two questions at once. He laughed. "I admire your courage for volunteering to go first," I said.

"Shit," Rod replied. "I wished I hadn't, once that asshole from Stanford began dumping on me."

"Well," I said, "I don't think he meant to be so officious. He's just mastered the graduate seminar manner." Rod laughed, and I added, "That's where we're trained by assholes in the fine art of assholery." He didn't laugh again, and I feared that he was sizing me up as an asshole of a different color. "But I'm probably just an asshole of a different color," I said. This time he laughed, and that gave me hope.

But of course I had been full of hope for Tommy, one of the guards on my J.V. basketball squad. "Squatsky," the kids called him, because when he tried to shoot a jump shot, he dropped his behind too low and pushed the ball from his chest rather than raising it above his head and flicking it from his wrists when he reached the peak of his jump. Every day after practice, I spent a few extra minutes trying to teach Tommy to shoot, but he just couldn't get the hang of it.

The varsity coach used to tease me about working with him so much. "Rich," he said. "Old Squatsky ain't ever gonna learn to shoot that jumper. Kid looks like he's gonna crap every time he puts the ball up."

"You're probably right, coach," I said. "But don't you think Tommy's got some promise? He really works hard on defense. He's selfless, and he'll do anything you ask him. If he can just learn to shoot, he can help you when he moves up to the varsity."

"Naw," the coach said. "It's too late. Kid should've learned how to shoot in junior high. If he ain't learned yet, he ain't gonna. I couldn't afford to use him. We see too many zones. Against zones you gotta have guards who can stick that ball in the hole from downtown."

Still, Tommy and I worked. Fifteen minutes after every practice. But the coach was right, of course. Tommy never did learn to shoot the jump shot.

Leaving the dining room the next morning after breakfast, I quickened my pace to fall in stride with Rod. "Morning," I said when I caught him.

"Hi," Rod said. We walked several steps in awkward silence.

"How would you like to get up a game of volleyball before the morning session?" I said. "Or maybe this place has a basketball hoop somewhere."

"You sound like an old jock," Rod said.

"I used to play basketball," I said. "Actually, I *still* play basketball, only not nearly so well."

"I'd like to get some exercise, but I've got a stack of compositions I need to get graded before I get back to Boston. My wife'll kill me if I come home without finishing them."

"She keeps you on your toes, does she?" I laughed.

"Yeah." He joined my laughter, but then added seriously, "She's pretty anxious for me to wrap my thesis up and get a job. We'd like to start a family."

"Does your wife work?"

"She's a social worker for the city schools."

We had reached my dormitory. For a while we stood outside, shifting our weights from one leg to the other, and continued to talk.

"How's it worked out?" I asked. "I mean, with you being in school and your wife working full time?"

"Fine," he shrugged. "Not all modern marriages encounter problems."

I laughed nervously. "Yeah," I said. "My wife teaches grade school, but she gets pretty resentful sometimes because she feels that whereas she works, what I do is something like fun." Rod brushed with his fingers at his short blond hair. "I've tried to disabuse her of this fun theory of graduate education, but I doubt that I've ever convinced her of anything other than that she's married to a fast-talking bullshitter."

Rod, I think, was made uncomfortable by these revelations about my personal life. And who can blame him, really? We'd just met, and here I was bending his ear. "Well," he said, "if I'm going to accomplish anything this morning, I better get going."

"Right," I said.

"Maybe tomorrow we'll look for a hoop," he added.

He headed off, and I went upstairs to my room. I sat on Leonard's bed for a while and stared again out the windows. There was no breeze. Soon I found myself lying on my back gazing emptily at the ceiling. "I couldn't stand it. I went to my briefcase and took out a notebook in which I had logged the bibliography for my dissertation. I tore out the pages I had filled with the titles of old books, folded them once and tucked them carefully away. I lay down on my own bed and wrote JOURNAL at the top of the fresh, blank, first page. I began to write down the thoughts and memories that ultimately spawned this note.

At lunch I met Rita, an anthropology student at Michigan. She was an attractive woman, nearly six feet tall, with a trim, athletic body. Long dark hair framed an oval face. Tinted aviator glasses only partially obscured irreverent eyes.

"I'm dropping out of school," she told me confidentially. "I'm choking on the bullshit." She extended her right hand toward me in a kind of stiff Shirley Temple manner. "My name is Rita Gates, by the way. I'm twenty-eight years old and single. People say I'm confused."

"Maybe they meant confusing," I said with a laugh and shook her hand.

"Could be," she said, raising her eyebrows. She watched me as I chewed a bite of tuna sandwich and took a sip of coffee. "You can ask me any questions you like."

"Okay," I said. "What are you going to do when you drop out of school?"

"Who cares? Rent a beach house. Lie in the sand. Write science fiction."

"Sounds good," I said. "How are you going to eat?"

"I don't know. But I'm a Fortran Fellow, am I not? And as I understand it, we're just about the smartest people in the whole world. Right behind Nobel prize winners, I think it is. Surely I'm capable of doing something besides writing up case studies for the perusal of some wizened old farts at Big Deal U. Or teaching intro anthropology to a bunch of bug-eyed freshmen who want to look at pictures of sagging black tits." Rita picked up my sandwich and took a bite. "Mind?" she said with a full mouth.

"Be my guest," I said and pointedly moved the rest of my dishes to a corner of the table away from her.

"My twin brothers are med school dropouts. They operate a shop now where they build and refinish furniture. How does carpentry sound? I could go to work for them." Before I could comment, she grabbed my shirt front and twisted it toward her so she could read my name tag. "Are you *the* Richard Janus?" she asked.

For just an instant I had the strange sensation that I had somehow become a famous person but had forgotten for what accomplishment. But then I realized that she was only teasing me for failing to introduce myself. So I said, "The most important one I know."

"That's just fabulous," she said, "because I've always wanted to go for a post-lunch walk on the beach with the most important Richard Janus you know. We'll have to do that just as soon as you're finished." She picked up the last bite of my sandwich and put it in her mouth. "Ready?" she said.

After our walk, Rita and I sat together at the afternoon session, a presentation by an administrator from the University of Chicago on the strides being taken to increase the number of faculty appointments for women. He admitted there was a long way to go before something approximating parity was achieved, but he stressed the gains that had been made since 1970.

When he finished his talk, Rita was the first to respond. "Frankly," she said, "I think we can dismiss the figures you've presented as inherently sexist. You'd have us take hope from a recent trend. What you have failed to point out is that the percentage of tenured women faculty members was substantially higher in 1900 than it is in 1975. At the turn of the century, this country was dotted coast to coast with small women's colleges staffed predominantly by female instructors. Today those institutions are rapidly disappearing, often being devoured by nearby co-ed schools staffed overwhelmingly by men. The effect is to inflate artificially the sex ratio at the larger school, while terminating the existence of positions that were formerly a nigh-exclusive female province."

When the session was over, Rita said to me, "I really nailed that slippery bastard, didn't I?"

"That you did," I agreed.

"I loved it," she said.

Before dinner the two of us tried to organize a game of volleyball. "Everyone out for volleyball," we alternately called to anyone who neared the net over which we batted the ball to one another. No one stopped for more than a puzzled glance.

"Goddamn, these Fortran Fellows are *creeps,*" Rita declared, underscoring her final word by smacking the ball toward my side of the net.

"Weeps," I concurred, batting it back at her.

"Eggheads."

"Bookworms."

"Drones."

"Drudges," I yelled, hitting the ball deep to her side of the court.

Gracefully and quickly, Rita ran back for the shot. "They're a bunch of *chicken* shits," she grunted, lofting the ball short to my side.

"And candy asses," I proclaimed, smashing the ball to the sand.

Giving up on volleyball after that exchange, we improvised a game of one-on-one soccer, using two cedar trees for a goal. And when we tired, sweating and panting, we walked back toward our dormitory together.

"Rich," she said, "why are all these people so afraid of having fun?"

"Give them a chance," I counselled. "Maybe they'll play tomorrow."

"Tomorrow. Tomorrow never comes."

"Now, now, we mustn't wax bromidic. After all, perhaps there's only been an insufficient wait time."

I hurried through my shower to join Rita for dinner, but when I got to the dining room, she was sitting next to Rod at a full table. Through dinner I watched them. She was as animated with him as she had been with me a short time earlier. And after dinner, as they were leaving the dining hall, Rita slipped her hand inside the crook of Rod's arm.

I put a dime in the pay phone and dialed O. "I'd like to make a collect call to Faith Cleaver," I told the operator. Surprisingly, someone else answered, and Faith had to be called to the phone. "Who was that, kid?" I said. "I'd say here's looking at you, kid, but, well, I'm not lookin' at you, kid." Kate had come over for a glass of wine, she said. "Well, what ya been doing when you're not gettin' schnockered with our old friend Kate, kid?" She knew I wouldn't like it that Kate was there, but I didn't want to fuss about it long distance.

"Well, since all of us aren't lucky enough to get wined and dined by the

Fortran Foundation, I've been working."

"A real change of pace, huh? Well, at least you'll be glad to know that I haven't been having any fun."

"What did you call for?"

"No reason. I was just sort of feeling kind of lonely. Wanted to hear a friendly voice."

"How can you feel lonely surrounded by all of your intellectual soulmates?"

"Faith, you know I never enjoy these conferences."

"Then why do you go?"

"I don't know," I said. I wished I hadn't called her. "I go because I'm supposed to."

"It's not like you don't have anything better to do. There's a dissertation to write, for instance."

"I seldom forget that, Faith."

"It seems to me you seldom remember it."

"Right, I know you feel that way. Well, we shouldn't run up a bill, I guess."

"You're mad now," Faith said.

"No. No, I'm not mad."

"Well, you shouldn't be. I'm just trying to help you."

"I said I'm not mad. Just lonely."

"Well, I'm sorry you're lonely, Rich. I wish you weren't."

"Thanks, babe. I miss you. See you soon."

I lay in bed that night unable to sleep. I stared at a ceiling that was too dark to see.

It was years ago, and Faith lay beside me. Unlike now, I switched on the light. Moving to get the pad from beside the phone, I accidentally woke Faith, who asked what I was doing. "I wanted to make a note of something that happened in tonight's game," I said. "We won. Tommy hit two free throws at the end that did it."

Faith said, "He's the one they call Squatter, isn't he?"

"Squatsky," I said.

"I thought you said he couldn't shoot."

"He can't. But at the foul line there's no one to block that awkward shot of his. All the pressure in the world on him; he stood right up there and knocked home both shots. It was wonderful."

"You're a good coach, honey."

"Not so good that I've been able to teach the kid to shoot from the field. That's what I wanted to jot down. His release isn't bad. Maybe I can get him to *feel* his release and then transfer it up over his head. Then it's just a matter, maybe…."

Faith yawned noisily.

"I forgot you're not interested," I said.

"Well, it's just that I don't know what you're talking about."

"If you came to the games, I'd be glad to…."

"We've been over this before, Rich."

"I know."

"If I'd been born male, I'd understand something about basketball. But I wasn't. And I'm not going to waste my time supporting something that has systematically excluded me."

"I understand," I sighed.

"Then why do you bug me about it?"

"I shouldn't. It's just that I enjoy it so much. And it's hard to share that with you."

"Well, you ought not to worry about it so much. You won't be coaching again after this year."

"I know."

"Really, Rich, you take it altogether too seriously. If you can't sleep, instead of taking notes about basketball, you ought to do something about getting a head start on next year."

"What in the world could I do?" I said. "I don't even start school for six months."

"Well, I don't know," Faith said. "You could brush up on your German or something. You're going to have language exams to pass."

From my bed at Asilomar, I told her, "And I passed them, Faith. I passed them." I flicked on the light by my bed, tilted the shade so as not to wake Leonard, took out my new journal and once again began to write. Wrote until finally I could sleep.

I slept late the next morning. When Leonard Bass returned from breakfast, he found me still in bed, writing in my notebook.

"Morning," he beamed. "What did you think of the evening session last night?"

"Fine," I said. I couldn't remember a thing about it. "It was enjoyable." I strove to put a lilt in my voice. Not wanting to answer in a single word. Wanting to seem jovial. Trying not to notice the egg on Leonard Bass's face. "How did you like it?"

"Just superb. Litwack is a brilliant scholar. The Foundation certainly affords us a marvelous opportunity to rub shoulders with first-rate minds."

I tried to picture the several conference speakers walking around stooped over so that the Fortran Fellows could use their shoulders to massage the speakers' heads. "Indeed, it does," I agreed.

Leonard Bass leaned against the dresser into which he had placed his clothing, thoughtfully reserving a drawer for me that I had not bothered to use. He noticed that I was writing. "Fashioning an epistle, I see," he said, surreptitiously attempting to glimpse the scrawl on my notebook.

"This is my journal."

Leonard sidled over the by the door. "You keep a journal?"

"Yep," I replied.

Leonard nodded his head several times quickly and adjusted his glasses. "Why do you do that?" he asked.

I shrugged and sat up on the bed, propping the notebook on my knees. "Some people take photographs. I don't own a camera, so I thought I'd try a journal." I scribbled a furious sentence. I did not *want* to be rude, but even less did I want intellectual discourse with Leonard Bass about the craft of journal keeping.

"Do you do this for therapy?" he asked, moving to sit on his bed. "We historians are supposed to analyze other people's journals, not keep them ourselves." He laughed. Very thin. Ha ha ha. He ran his fingers through his thinning hair. Why didn't he ever run them through his mustache.

"In a way," I answered reluctantly. "A journal is a place to save one's thoughts. In the hope that they're worth saving. A friend when you're lonely, a key to the prison of your mind—that sort of thing." It was all so bullshitty. I hoped it would turn him off. On the other hand, it occurred to me that I believed it.

"What constitutes the substance of a normal entry?"

"Pardon me?" I said after reading from my notebook a moment.

"What sort of stuff do you write in your journal?"

"Personal stuff," I said quietly.

"Of course," he said. His mouth hung open but he was silent. He twitched, then lay back on the bed with his hands clasped behind his head. He sat right back up and said, "Mind if I glance through your *Newsweek?* I noticed it in your briefcase."

"Not at all." I tossed it over to him.

He flipped through the pages. "Did you see that Woodward and Bernstein are working on a new book they're calling *The Final Days?*" As he tried to find the article, I said pleasantly that I'd seen it.

He rapidly turned several more pages before handing the magazine back to me. "It's about time for the morning session. You'd better get going if you're going to make it."

"You're right," I said, and we both smiled.

"See you later," he said and went out the door.

But he was wrong, of course.

The last session of the conference was over. I was alone in a lounge. Sitting. Smoking cigarettes. Rita stuck her head in the doorway. Her glasses were pushed on top of her head, pulling her hair back off her face, "I found you," she announced. "You've been avoiding me."

"I have?"

She came and sat in a chair facing me. She surveyed the room as if trying to get her bearings in a foreign environment. "What are you doing in here?"

"Nothing," I said.

"Nothing?"

"Thinking. Brooding. I don't know."

"Are you from the South, Richard Janus?"

I laughed. "You're the master of the non sequitur."

"Not at all," she said. "I just leave out a lot of the in-between parts."

"I see," I said.

She moved her chair closer, bent forward at the waist, rested her hands on her knees and stared at me intently. "So, are you from the South?"

"Why?"

"You sound sort of Southern. I always wanted to go out with a Southern boy."

"Whyever?"

Rita smacked me on the side of my knee. "See, you are from the South. Who but a Southern boy would say, 'Whyever?'"

"I used to be a Southerner. A long time ago."

"But no more?"

"No more, forever."

"My word," Rita said, affecting a British accent. She sat up in her chair. "You sound as if your liberal conscience has turned your nose up at your homeland."

"Shouldn't it?" I lit another Marlboro.

"I hadn't taken you for a fool," she said. I puffed my cheeks and let out a long slow breath. She leaned back away from me. "Seriously, Rich, are you really into this enlightened expatriate business?"

"I guess so," I said. "I don't give it much thought, actually. The South mainly seems long ago to me. Something pristine, something gone. And when I think of places to live, I never think about anywhere east of California that's south of Chicago."

"Do you go back to visit?"

"Not in years," I said.

"You should. A person can only know who he is in terms of where he came from."

I smiled. "You think so, huh?"

"I know so."

"Maybe you're right. I certainly wonder who I am often enough."

"Do it," Rita urged. "Because that would make you a Southern boy for sure, and I'd want to go out with you again." She sat forward in her chair again and put her hand on my knee. "Do you know Rod the Bod?" she asked.

"Who is Rod the Bod?"

"He's Rod the Bod, of course."

"Of course," I said.

Rita scooted her chair still closer to me. "What would you think if I reached over and grabbed you by the crotch?" she whispered.

I tried to mask my astonishment. "Whyever would you do that?"

"Because Rod the Bod just grabbed me by the crotch."

"So?" I threw my hands out and dropped my cigarette in the process. Casually, as if I had done it on purpose, I crushed it out under my foot.

"I believe in do unto others," Rita said.

"Well," I said, speaking slowly. "I suppose the question is whether or not it was fun." I did not look at her. My remark surprised and frightened me.

"What?" Rita said with a smile.

"Who?" I said.

"Where?"

"When?"

"Why?"

"How?"

"Uh, uh," she said, and we both laughed.

"Well?" I said.

"Well, what?"

"Was it fun?"

"Why not?" she said. "We're all among friends." Rita squeezed my leg. "We're friends, aren't we, Rich?"

"Sure," I said and patted at her hand, which was still on my leg. "You know, Rita, you're a very unusual person." I smiled toward her but still did not look in her eyes.

Rita inched forward again. "You know why you like me?" She was almost on top of me now. Our chairs were nearly touching. She had put one of her legs between the V of mine, and now she knocked the inside of my thigh with her knee. She moved in her chair and my knee grazed the material in the crotch of her jeans. She leaned over and reached behind my head, pulling me forward until our foreheads were touching.

"I give up. Why do I like you?" I said. Her breath was sweet. I thought she was going to kiss me. I was afraid she was going to kiss me. I was glad that our foreheads were touching and not our cheeks.

"Because I grab at that part of you that wonders what you're doing here."

"You're right," I said, and I was very frightened.

"Let's go skinny-dipping," Rita said.

I laughed. "You're crazy."

"You're not afraid of the Fortran people, are you? Surely you don't think any of them will be on the beach at this time of night."

"You're thinking of going swimming in the bay?"

"There won't be anyone around if you're modest. Except me."

"Swimming in the bay isn't recommended," I pointed out. "The undertow is really powerful. It would be especially dangerous at night."

"Christ," she said with an exasperated shake of her head. She took my hands in her hers. "Hey. Let me show you what else Rod the Bod did. Stand up." We stood. She put her arms around me and slipped her hands in the back pockets of my jeans and pulled us snugly together. She turned her head sideways and laid it against my face. I could smell the scent of her shampoo. My arms inadvertently circled her waist. "I'm locked out of my room," she whispered. "I wonder where I can sleep."

"I'm married, you know," I said.

"So?" she said and looked into my face. We stood a moment together. "Does it matter?"

"It matters to me."

"Then you're happy with her."

I took a deep breath and let it out noisily. "I'm not happy with her tonight," I said.

"Then?"

"Then it matters all the more to me," I said.

Rita brought her arms up around my chest and hugged me, her chin hooked over my shoulder. I realized that I had never embraced a woman so tall. She pulled her head back and looked steadily into my eyes. She smiled a little and said, "You could have helped me find a janitor or someone to let me into my room." She raised her head and kissed me quickly on the bridge of my nose. Something moved past the door. "Hey, Rod the Bod," Rita called. She broke away from me and left the room. Through the window I could see them talking in the dark.

Later that night, I lay in bed awake. The conference was over. Tomorrow was the return to L.A. There, history and Faith awaited me. During a brief and fitful sleep, I dreamed that Rita was trying to get into my room. A noise in the hall awoke me and sleep would not return. Across the room Leonard Bass snored peacefully.

I got up and pulled on my jeans without underwear. It was after three A.M.

I zipped my jacket up over the St. Christopher medal on my bare chest, walked downstairs and stopped outside the door to Rita's room. She had evidently found her lost key. The hall was quiet; the other Fortran Fellows were asleep. But from Rita's room came muffled laughter, her voice and Rod's, and the unmistakable, tantalizing green fragrance of marijuana smoke. I smiled and allowed myself one, short, soundless burst of laughter.

Outside, walking along the dunes, I found a gnarled tree to climb. The sky was heavy and dark. No moon or stars, but from my weathered perch I could see a few pinpoints of light from Asilomar. Beneath and behind me was Spanish Bay, in which swimming is not recommended. The wind cut through my jacket. Shivering, I held tightly to the tree and turned to stare at the black water.

When my fingers began to numb, I dropped to the sand and walked slowly to the water's edge. Still shivering, I let the water run up over my sandals. Then quickly, defying hesitation, I kicked the sandals off, unzipped my jacket and pulled off my jeans. I dived into a breaking wave and swam.

I could feel the undertow pulling me out and down. The water was so cold it hurt. I fought my way to the surface, gasping for air. The indiscriminate sea swelled under me, lifting me high above the shore, but I was inside the swell. I started sliding down and the sea continued to rise. The white water swallowed me like the jaws of a leviathan. I was somersaulted once, twice, and dashed against the sandy bottom.

Again I made the surface, and this time I attacked before the surf could strike. Swimming out, swimming hard. My shoulders ached. My legs felt like lead. But I reached the point where the sea lies calm, where the waves only rock as they gather force. There, treading water, I rested.

Swimming in, I rode the ocean's back. The whale hurled me toward the shore, but I was a passenger on his nose, atop, not within his foamy teeth.

On the beach, I shook the water from my skin and tasted the salt on my lips. I felt clean, finally ready. The running tide had carried me far down the coast. But looking back I could see Asilomar—and beyond it the first gray light of dawn.

18

1975

Richard Janus returned to L.A. from Asilomar feeling as if he lived in a jar of molasses. Every action seemed to be executed in slow motion but with a tremendous expenditure of energy.

Spring quarter should have been a breeze; his course assignments were the same he'd taught in the fall. Yet they seemed to take all his time. He needed to put in several weeks, perhaps a month, of hard work at the Huntington Library but could never seem to find the time to get there even once. Halfway through the term, he abandoned any intention of embarking upon the last stage of his research before summer.

His stomach began bothering him for the first time since St. Louis. He was sleeping very poorly, sometimes unable to fall asleep after lying in bed for as long as four hours. He awoke in the morning feeling as if he hadn't slept at all. Though he seemed helpless to effect a solution, Janus was fully aware of what was happening to him. He wrote in his journal, "I am suffering from anxiety. I am experiencing what the psychologists call a crisis." The only cure he knew was to make some tangible progress on his dissertation, to get moving again. But he couldn't.

He hadn't looked at the dissertation materials since returning from northern California. The thesis was constantly on his mind, but he was unable really to think about it at all. All he thought about was how much he hated the very idea of his dissertation, of how impotent he felt about ever finishing it. More seriously, he knew that a part of him wanted not to finish it, wanted not to have to face the implications of finishing it and having then to be, for the rest of his life, an historian—"something," he wrote in his journal, "I never much wanted to be."

Janus began to worry that he was going crazy. When this thought crossed his mind, he would laugh the dry, cynical laugh he had taught himself to hide behind when he was in high school. Then he would think of theatrical renderings of lunacy. The insane always laughed maniacally. "Perhaps I've just always been crazy," he wrote. "But even if I lose my mind, I must remember not to lose my sense of humor."

Janus's condition was aggravated by his inability to confess his problem to Faith. She would, he was sure, see herself as a victim. He'd brought her to L.A., largely against her will, so that he could earn a Ph.D. in history. Now, three years later, he found he couldn't do it. How could she possibly forgive him? His graduate career had delayed her having a baby. Faith would not have delayed the bearing of a child, but Janus had passionately argued that graduate school imposed enough tensions on a marriage without adding the problem of children as well.

The baby issue had arisen at various points in their five years of marriage. Faith had tried to get her husband to consider parenting shortly after they arrived in St. Louis. He had the draft as an excuse then. "You want to raise the child of a fugitive?" he asked. "Or the child of a dead man? Maybe the child of a convict?" When the draft disappeared from his life, it was replaced by the graduate school excuse. "What kind of life is it for a child to have a father who's a student?" Faith basically agreed that financial security was a plus for child rearing, but even after they arrived in L.A., she occasionally used her desire for a baby to goad Janus along faster in his work.

The issue came up again when Janus got home from the Fortran conference. Faith picked him up at the airport, obviously in a bad mood. Janus was feeling down himself, but he rallied to try to save their reunion. He told her about the conference, making it sound funnier in its idiosyncrasies than it really was.

He even told her about Rita Gates, making Rita sound hornier than she may have been and a lot less attractive. "I'm confident now that dogs respond to me," he said. "If I could only work the same magic with foxes."

"Don't be sexist," Faith said.

"Sound advice," Janus agreed, still trying to be cheery.

"Do you have to go to these conferences to keep your scholarship?" Faith wondered. She was driving home from the airport, and the conversation had an air of the perfunctory.

"I don't know," Janus said. And he didn't know, either. But he suspected that he was better off with Faith either not knowing this or his pretending that participation in the conferences was mandatory. "Why?" he asked, affecting nonchalance.

"Well, they just take so much time. A long weekend in the spring, another in the fall every year."

"That's two long weekends a year," Janus observed.

Faith glanced over at him disdainfully from behind the wheel. "My point is," she said, "that even Fortran Fellows have work to do, like *dissertations.*" She looked at him pointedly. "And these conferences just take you away from your work. Some of the rest of us, like me, whose lives are hung up waiting for our spouses to finish school, might just as soon see you working as chasing each other naked through the halls of some resort."

"I couldn't get anybody to chase me naked," Janus said. His voice had gone flat now. Faith drove on without further comment until Janus suddenly snapped, "So what big delay are you suffering by my going to Fortran conferences?"

"The sooner you finish, the sooner I can have a baby." She kept her eyes fastened to the road.

"Yep. You're a whole twenty-seven years old," Janus snorted. "I guess menopause'll probably take you out of the running just any day now."

"I want to have a kid before I'm thirty. Haven't I made that clear? The earliest you say you'll finish your thesis is a year from now, and I might not be able to get pregnant right away. So we're already pushing it, as far as I'm concerned."

Janus rammed his hands into the waist pockets of his denim jacket and slumped down in his seat with his head against the Toyota's high-back seat. He looked out at the ubiquitous L.A. traffic, heavy even late on a Sunday night. As they drove north on the San Diego Freeway, cool air gushing through their lowered windows, he felt the call of an irresponsible freedom, one in which he would suggest to Faith that they just keep driving north beyond their turnoff to Santa Monica, across the mountains, through the valley out to Oxnard, and on up the coast on Highway 1, up to Carmel and maybe farther; that they run away, in other words, to escape from a life that seemed to be pressing in all around them. He wanted to suggest this to Faith, but he didn't. Even though she wouldn't have taken him seriously, he knew she hated his occasional flights of romantic fancy, feared them as a sign that lurking within him was some vast reservoir of weakness.

Faith jerked him back to their conversation by saying, "See what I mean?"

Janus wanted to argue that her deadline of thirty for bearing a child was evidence of determined paranoia, that no study showed a significant increase in complications before age thirty-five, but he let it go. They'd fought to no decision over this territory before. "What's got you back on the baby kick again?" he asked.

"It's no kick," Faith said. "I've wanted a baby all along. You know that."

"Why are you thinking about it tonight, I mean?"

"Kate and I were talking," Faith said. Her voice shifted, lost its hint of annoyance and took on a quality almost dreamy. "We think a lot of feminists are making a mistake by renouncing motherhood. In seeking equality, women shouldn't seek to imitate maleness, shouldn't reject qualities which may be uniquely female."

That seemed to make sense to Janus. He wasn't sure, though. A fervent feminist arguing that the very idea of gender qualities was the result of, and for the benefit of, male domination could probably convince him of that notion as well.

"Kate's going to have a baby," Faith added.

Janus sat up straighter in his seat, wondering if he'd heard correctly. "Kate Banford is going to have baby?" he said, failing to mask his astonishment.

"Uh huh. Isn't it wonderful?"

Janus was puzzled. Kate Banford was an avowed lesbian. Now she was pregnant. "California," Janus wrote in his journal, "is a place where people call wonderful those things which make no sense."

"Uh, who's the father?" Janus asked tentatively.

"Oh, she's not pregnant yet. What I mean is that she believes just because she decided to embrace her lesbianism shouldn't mean that she has to forsake her basic maternal instincts. In fact, her lesbianism reinforces those instincts, makes her more attuned to her womanhood."

"She going to arrange for artificial insemination?" Janus asked.

Faith slowly turned her head in his direction and glared at him for as long as she dared keep her eyes off the road. "Why are you such an asshole?"

"What have I done now?" Janus didn't know, though he assumed that his artificial insemination comment indicated some colossal insensitivity. But at least the insensitivity arose from seriousness. This was one time he hadn't been acting flip. If Kate was a lesbian, wasn't the idea of heterosexual intercourse repulsive to her? Wouldn't she prefer to achieve her impregnation without having to involve a man?

Faith suddenly smashed both palms of her hands against the steering wheel. "Why are you *such* an ASSHOLE?"

Janus raised his hands, palms opened outwards to shoulder height in his characteristic gesture of innocence. "What'd I do, babe?" He was genuinely confused.

"You think it's ridiculous for a lesbian to want to have a baby."

"No, I don't," Janus protested. This was the smart reply, and he knew it. And he wished it was altogether true. He certainly hated those cases he'd read about where the courts took children away from lesbian mothers. On the other hand, he worried that being a child was routinely hard enough without having to explain that your dad was named Sue.

"You even think it's ridiculous for *us* to have a baby," Faith said.

Glad to have escaped from the other, shakier ground, Janus said, "That's not true at all, babe. I just want things to be stable and secure for our child."

They'd finally arrived home. Inside, the conversation continued for a while as Janus unpacked the few things he'd taken on his trip. Faith suggested that perhaps children were a lot more adaptive than he thought and perhaps security and stability were so relative and so elusive that there was always an excuse for delay.

Janus had to admit that she had a point. He was always impressed by how passionate she was on the baby issue. He had idle ideas about the joys of a little boy or little girl to cuddle and teach, but he felt no greater urge toward parenthood than toward barrenness, which to his mind had significant attractions of its own. But he recognized in Faith's desire for a child a desperation that he didn't want to aggravate. So how, as his dissertation remained dormant for weeks, could he face her with the news that all she had sacrificed was for naught?

He couldn't, so he led her to believe that he was still chipping away. He had to admit to her that he hadn't started writing yet. He couldn't risk lying and having her ask to see pages. But he couldn't admit that he'd stopped all other work. "I need to read and organize my note cards," he told her. "There's another book I've discovered I have to look at. Joe Makeupsomename has just done an article that's quite relevant to chapter three. I'm working on some provisional outlines."

The subterfuges he undertook to deceive her would have been comic had they not been so sad. He had piles of note cards spread about his desk surrounding a yellow legal pad with a scrawled outline on the top sheet. Janus rearranged these items into different positions on a daily basis, adding a tattered book held open by a paperweight today, a xeroxed journal article tomorrow, to give the impression of the desk's having been labored at.

Faith was not familiar enough with the process of his work to know that he wasn't really doing anything. If he was home when she came in from school, he made sure that he was sitting at his desk. The subterfuges worked in that Faith never complained that he didn't seem to be working. Any suspicion she may have had arose from aspects of Janus's behavior other than the doctored appearance of his desk.

And there were several occasions for suspicion. Once after a night of sleeplessness, Janus had decided to try an afternoon nap. He fell into a slumber so deep that he was still sleeping when Faith got home from school. He tried to camouflage his real situation by claiming to be ill.

On another, more serious occasion, Faith discovered a copy of Dreiser's *An American Tragedy* beside his chair in the living room. Under the pretense of going to the library to check the accuracy of his bibliographical notations,

Janus had been attending, twice a week since the start of spring quarter, classes in a course on modern American fiction, for which Dreiser's novel was one of the readings. Janus escaped with minimum damage from that episode when he claimed he'd gotten momentarily saturated in his thesis work and had started reading the novel as a way of clearing his brain.

Noting that the volume was open to page 360, Faith said, "This is an awfully long book just for the purpose of clearing your brain." But after that she let the matter drop.

Faith finally found him out, though, when a woman in the English class called him at home about midway in the quarter. He had to talk to her, and he couldn't keep Faith, who had answered the phone, from overhearing.

"Who was that?" she asked when he hung up. "She told me she was in a class of yours. What class are you taking?"

Janus opted not to risk lying. "I've been sitting in a class on American fiction," he admitted. "I've just gotten sick of reading nothing but history. I feel so compartmentalized. I thought maybe a course in something completely different might be good for my spirits." This tactic, writ small, had worked once before. Would it satisfy Faith once again?

"You haven't been working on your dissertation?"

Now was the time for the lie. "Oh, of course. I work on it every day. This novel course is just a sideline."

"Well, I guess," Faith said. "Maybe you should have done your work in English."

"Maybe so," Janus laughed, knowing that his problems arose from the expectations of academic scholarship, not from the particular field of history. "But it's too late now."

"It certainly is. Anyway, what did this chickie want?" Faith would have been incensed to hear a man use the term chickie, but she often used it to refer to women with whom Janus had relationships. A female professor he admired was, "Your teacher chickie." Anne Norton was his "fellow student chickie." Female Fortran Fellows were "hot shot chickies."

"I wouldn't call her a chickie," Janus said. "First of all, she's hardly attractive. Second of all, she's blind. The whole thing is very sad. Her name's Sally Dawson."

"She's blind?"

Janus nodded. "She sits right in front of the teacher's desk with her head turned so that she can hear him better. Whenever he writes something on the board, she asks the girl sitting next to her to repeat it."

"What's this got to do with you?" Janus was surprised at the harshness of Faith's tone. She must be annoyed with the whole idea of his attending a fiction class, he decided. It was not at all like her to be callous to the world's unfortunate.

"Just as the period ended today, she raised her hand and asked if she could address the entire class. She said she needed someone to read to her several hours a week, that the person who had been doing it had to quit. No one spoke up to volunteer right away, and the teacher dismissed the class, asking Sally to wait in case anyone wanted to speak with her about her request. 'I can pay you,' she called out as the class members filed into the hall. She continued sitting at her desk with her milky eyes rolled back in her head, wearing a smile somewhere between expectant and resigned. She kept tilting her head back and forth, like blind people do, listening, I guess, for the class to be empty before she got up. After a while she took her cane out of her purse and started unfurling it. I never realized they were collapsible. I couldn't stand the fact that no one was going to help her."

"That's horrible," Faith said quietly. "So you told her that you'd read to her."

Janus nodded. "I kept thinking of the passages from Camus's *The Fall* where the narrator is tormented by his failure to answer the cry of the lonely girl on the bridge who jumped into the water after he walked by: 'that cry which had sounded over the Seine behind me years before,' he says, 'never ceased.' It goes something like that. Later he cries out himself, 'O young woman, throw yourself into the water again so that I may a second time have the chance of saving us both.'"

Janus took a breath and looked over his wife's head and up at the ceiling. "I don't think much of anything I've done or ever will do is likely to result in saving anyone, even myself. But I kept thinking that I didn't want the memory of leaving a blind girl in that empty classroom following me around for the rest of my life. She had finished fashioning her cane and was starting to get up when I went up to her. She had a funny, all-knowing sort of smile on her face. I kept looking away from her wasted eyes, the way you do when you don't want to get caught staring, and thinking all the time how stupid that was since she couldn't see me. I talked to her for a while and gave her my telephone number and told her to call me if she couldn't find anyone to help her. I didn't like her very much, actually. Isn't that awful? She kept calling me Mr. History Doctoral Candidate. I guess she thought I had tried to impress her. I told her I was doing a dissertation and really didn't have much time. Who knows? It doesn't matter. I told her I'd read to her for two hours on Tuesday and Thursday afternoons."

Faith came over to his desk where Janus had sat while he spoke with Sally and where he was still sitting after having described the experience. She put her arm around his neck and kissed him on the top of his head. "I think you're doing a wonderful thing for this girl, Bubba."

Janus stared straight ahead out the window beyond his desk. A scraggly palm tree brushed against the screen. "That's just it though, babe," he said. "I'm not doing it for her at all, you see. I'm doing it for me."

The remaining weeks of the spring quarter saw Janus's anxiety ease somewhat. The development was irrational and short-term, both of which he knew. Basically it came about because his reading to Sally Dawson gave his life a focus on Tuesdays and Thursdays. Mondays and Wednesdays he taught. So only on Fridays did he have to fight the knowledge daylong that he was drifting. The other days just lacked enough time before other duties beckoned him to get up enough steam to making working worthwhile. This was nonsense, of course, and he knew it, but somehow, nonetheless, the vice that had been tightening around his guts loosened a bit.

In the last week of the quarter, though, Faith confronted him with startling news. "When she first started to tell me," he wrote in his journal, "I thought she must be pregnant." But she wasn't. She had decided to resign her job and to enter the UCLA graduate program in psychology full time.

The hesitance and then the belligerence with which she announced her decision seemed to indicate that she expected Janus to try to dissuade her. Both her attitude and her expectation, Janus believed, arose from her own doubts about the wisdom of the decision. But she was right that he was not thrilled at the idea. Not at first, anyway. They had grown quite comfortable on their two incomes, and living only on what he could provide from his Fortran stipend and his teaching fellowship would prove a struggle, he felt certain.

But it was the timing of the decision, not the principle of it, that surprised Janus. Faith had voiced a desire to do graduate work as soon as she saw she could compete at UCLA when she took her first course two summers ago. She had always labored under a poor self-image, and the A she received in that course had been a significant boost to her confidence. Janus had been nearly as happy as she was. And in the long term he believed that doing graduate work was precisely what Faith needed.

Still, had his circumstances been different, he might have argued with her, might have tried to convince her to wait until he had a full-time job. But he felt so stymied in his own work that he no longer believed he was ever going to get a full-time job. So despite his misgivings about finances, Janus gave her his blessing from the first. And the more he thought about it, the more he began to see her starting back to school as a personal relief. When angry with him, Faith often asserted that her whole life was structured around his plans, that *his* career needs were met first and then her career was shaped to mesh with his.

Janus wrote in his journal, "I always resented it when she jabbed me with this point." He resented it because he recognized it was true. However benevolent he may have been or aspired to be, however much he conformed to a role that was handed to him and not wholly of his own design, however much he wanted what was best for Faith as well as for himself, it was true. With Faith's embarking upon a graduate program of her own, though, the point ceased to be true, and Janus was relieved of a measure of his burden of guilt.

Janus hoped that with Faith involved right away in summer school, he might be able to get himself back on track. After all, not so much time had been lost, really. But when the routine of the spring ended and even his flimsy excuses for procrastination ended, too, his anxiety returned like a thunderclap. He still couldn't work. It was madness. He could barely get himself to his desk, and he couldn't sit there more than five minutes without feeling as if he was going to hyperventilate.

Discipline. His life had always been full of discipline. He had to exert it anew. He decided to revamp himself completely. He would make himself go out to the Huntington, a good hour from Santa Monica. Once there, he wouldn't let himself leave until he accomplished something. Discipline was the key. Discipline in every facet of his life. He would quit smoking. He would lose twenty pounds. His weight had gradually climbed from the 180 he weighed in college to 195. The 175 he had weighed in high school sounded like the proper figure. He would keep all these resolutions simultaneously, he decided. Discipline breeds discipline.

He made a fair start. He got himself to the library and undertook the last stage of research he had to do before starting to write. To replace the oral gratification of his Marlboros, he bought packages of sunflower seeds, which were salty and caloric enough that he could eat little else and shed the pounds he wanted to lose. Sadly, however, all this provided no relief from his anxiety, save during the moments he was actually working. He remained afraid that the next morning light would bring the day he stopped working on his thesis forever; he remained afraid that finishing his research would provide no impetus to start the harder work of writing. His insomnia returned, and he found that he could escape a terrifying sense of desperation in the wee hours of the morning only by writing in the journal he'd begun at Asilomar, a journal of haphazard musings that already spilled from the pages of its first notebook into a second.

Sadly, too, Janus's new routine not only failed to give him much comfort but proved aggravating to his wife as well.

"I have begun to infuriate my wife," he wrote in his journal, "by the merest act of breathing."

What infuriated her more than his breathing was his infernal habit of eating sunflower seeds. Janus had discovered that he could pop a handful of seeds into his mouth and could extract the tasty nugget from each seed assembly-line fashion with dexterous teeth, tongue and lip work. Unfortunately, the process resulted in a loud pop each time a shell was broken. Or Faith claimed the pops were loud, anyway. Janus doubted that he would have noticed had he been the listener rather than the eater, but Faith was so annoyed by the sunflower seeds that she wouldn't let him eat them when she was in the same room.

This meant that while Faith studied at the dining table, a starving, smokeless Janus had to sit every evening in his living room chair without touching the inviting bowl of seeds which sat nearby on the floor. Without sunflower seeds to munch, Janus resurrected a habit he thought he had conquered: nail biting and cuticle chewing. Unfortunately, he discovered that this habit drove Faith nuts, too. At least, Janus would have sworn, the habit must be noiseless, however visually offensive. But Faith maintained violently that she could *hear* him chew on a cuticle.

"You make wet, nasty sounds," she said. And it must have been true, because she would demand that he stop doing it even when she was working at her table with her back to him. Her demands always surprised him. When he bit on a finger, he was utterly unaware of it. But in his particular state that summer, anxious, hungry and deprived of cigarettes, he evidently gnawed at himself all the time: Faith was forever yelling at him to stop.

"Quit biting," she would snap.

"Okay," Janus would agree.

"Quit biting," she would demand again within minutes.

"You could hear that?"

"YES. Now stop it."

He would agree, but it was never terribly long before she would catch him again. His finger munching drove her crazy, he knew, but he never did it on purpose. Her constant correcting drove him crazy, and she *did* do it on purpose.

The impasse on this issue produced one of the more ridiculous scenes in their stormy marriage. Janus absent-mindedly slipped a finger in his mouth one night while reading in his living room chair. From her post at the dining table, Faith warned him to desist. He did but then backslid. After several corrections, promises and betrayals, Faith suddenly loomed up in front of his chair like a ghost in a fun house. She grabbed his hand away from his face and stuck her own finger in her mouth, producing a series of exaggerated, slurping noises. She screwed up her face into a gruesome mask. She pretended to jerk at the skin on her fingers with her teeth. "You make me SICK!" she screamed. She threw his hand back at him and went back to her table, managing several slamming sounds as she reseated herself.

Janus was stunned. He didn't stir in his chair for a long moment. Then he rose and walked deliberately to a spot just behind Faith's chair. She knew he was there. He could sense with some animal instinct that she knew he was standing right behind her. But she did not turn her head even slightly so that she might see him, did not acknowledge this presence in any way.

He spread his arms wide, his hands slightly curled inward like Tarzan, perhaps, in the last moment before he beats on his chest. Janus held this pose for just an instant, as a ballet dancer hangs for just an instant at the top of his *grande jeté* before beginning to fall back toward the floor.

Suddenly, with a burst of sound, Janus began to move from behind Faith, circling around the table to the other side where he could face her. He moved his feet sideways, never crossing over, like a basketball player on defense. Arms still outstretched, he sang to a tune he created as he went along: "Cuticle Surgeon. Dada dada dada dada. Cuticle Surgeon. Dada dada dada dada." He dropped his arms and in the resonant voice of a TV announcer said, "In tonight's gripping episode, Doctors Mountebank, Charlatan and Quack are confronted with a case of emergency hangnail."

"You've lost your mind," Faith said. "But you're not funny. Now, please leave me alone so I can study."

"Cuticle Surgeon," Janus sang while dancing, arms outstretched again, sideways across the room and back. "Dada dada dada dada. Cuticle Surgeon."

"Shut UP!" Faith screamed.

"Oh, doctors, doctors," Janus said in a high-pitched, squeaky voice. "Doctors, come quickly. Poor Mr. Janus has just been brought in with an awful case of hangnail. The medics don't know if he'll pull through." Faith closed the book she was reading and began to gather notebooks and pens. "Thank you, nurse." "Thank you, nurse." "Thank you, nurse," Janus said in three different voices: one bass, one baritone and one like Donald Duck.

"Are you going to leave me alone?" Faith asked.

Janus held his hand up in front of his face. "What do you think, Dr. Charlatan, Dr. Quack?" Dr. Mountebank said.

"Amputate," Dr. Charlatan said.

"Amputate," Dr. Quack clucked.

Faith stood up, her study materials in her arms, and began to move toward the bedroom. Janus moved right along with her.

"Amputate?"

"His entire nail!"

"His entire finger!"

Faith bent over Janus's chair and picked up his bowl of sunflower seeds.

"Doctors," Mountebank said in a tone of reprimand, "a simple hangnailectomy will surely suffice."

"I think we should play it safe and take the whole finger," Charlatan recommended.

"Vee must do a radical armectomy," said the third doctor, who suddenly began quacking with a German accent.

At the door to the bedroom, Faith stopped and said, "I'm going to work at your desk. If you know what's good for you, you'll leave me alone." Very deliberately she closed the door in his face.

He waited long enough for her to get set at the desk, then eased the door back open.

"Sorry, gentlemen," Mountebank said. "I'm senior cuticle surgeon here, and I think your measures are too extreme. We're going to do the hangnailectomy, and we're going to do it now. Let's get cracking before the condition spreads."

Faith turned around in the chair and stared at him.

"Knife," Mountebank demanded.

Janus reached in his pocket for his knife. He slapped it from hand to hand.

"Knife," Charlatan said.

"Get OUT of here!" Faith screamed.

Janus sawed with his knife at the flesh he'd been gnawing on his index finger.

"Clippers," Mountebank ordered.

Janus closed the knife, slipped it back into his pocket and brought out his clippers.

"Goddamn you, leave me ALONE," Faith warned.

"Clippers," Quack quacked.

Janus took the clippers, squinted and brought them at arm's length down on the jagged flesh of his finger as if he were lighting a fuse.

As he pinched off the sliver of skin, Faith came toward him carrying the pottery bowl of sunflower seeds.

Janus held the little piece of skin toward her. "Look, Mom," he said. "No teeth. A perfect operation. Should we perhaps preserve the extraction in formaldehyde?"

"SHUT UP!" Faith screamed. She slung her arm toward him and launched the contents of the bowl, a thousand sunflower seeds, right in her husband's face. The seeds nestled in his hair, went down his shirt front and lodged in the tops of his shoes.

He picked a seed out of his shirt pocket as if nothing had happened, put it quickly between his teeth and snapped it open with a loud pop. "Sticks and stones can break my bones," Janus said, smiling lewdly, "but seeds can only pelt me."

Faith slammed the door. "LEAVE ME ALONE."

"A pity about zee operation," Quack said.

"Quite so," Charlatan agreed. "If only we'd considered a wifectomy."

In the ebbing days of summer, Janus finished his work at the Huntington and set immediately about some serious procrastinating. It was unquestionably time now to write. What more research was needed would be dictated by the drafting of his thesis when he discovered the questions he'd failed yet even to ask. But he didn't start writing. He puttered around the house fixing things. Faith probably sensed that he was troubled, but she had her own work and jealously guarded her emotional reserves. There was a tension between them, but for the most part they remained at truce. Janus's insomnia worsened, and he still found he could dampen the embers of panic only by writing in his journal.

To fill his daylight hours once everything in the house was put in working order, Janus went on a building kick. Out of a telephone cable spool, he made a coffee table. While picking up sandpaper, brushes and varnish with which to finish it, he spotted at the lumberyard an old, ornate door to some renovated apartment A. The door had a wrought-iron peephole from which the outside grate was missing. Janus decided immediately to buy it and build Faith a desk. When he finished with the coffee table, he sanded down the outside of the door and attached legs to the inside. He left the metal A in place as a symbol of all the grades Faith would earn while working at her desk. The peephole he turned into a built-in pencil holder.

Faith was touched when she discovered what he was doing. "I'm slow to figure things out, sometimes," he told her, "but sometimes, too, I finally get there. How's it fair that I've got a desk and you have to work at the dining table? When this is finished, we'll set it up for you in the living room." Faith hugged him while he talked to her. "Until we get a little richer, babe, this'll have to do as a room of your own."

"You love me, don't you, Bubba," she said. It was not a question.

Summer gave way to fall, though the change was registered primarily on the calendar. Santa Monica retained its year-round yellow-green color, and the air remained balmy enough in the day to make shorts and sandals comfortable. Only the brisker temperature of the water in Santa Monica Bay provided a clue that summer had passed.

Faith began her fall quarter work. Janus resumed his teaching but otherwise continued doing nothing and feeling rotten about it. He received his notice that the fall Fortran conference would be held near Chicago and cringed at the realization of how much time had passed since he'd last made real progress on his thesis.

One day while Faith was at school, he took his journal to his desk and began thumbing through it. Reading it made him short of breath. He felt like a cinch was being tightened around his intestines. As a joke, he began to write a memo to Warren Burden and the other members of his doctoral committee, telling them that he'd decided to withdraw from graduate school. He wrote things that made him laugh. Laughter spurred him on to write more.

His typewriter buzzed and clattered at a pace it hadn't known in months. The noise of its clack, it must have been, kept him from hearing Faith come in. Before he realized it, she was standing behind him.

"My God, is that your dissertation, Janus?" She hooked her chin over his shoulder, but he spun around in his chair toward her before she had a chance to see the words he had written. "I can't believe you've finally gotten the drafting underway."

He made a crucial error. He lied by implication and set himself up to be discovered and embarrassed. "It's been long enough in coming, hasn't it?" he said.

"Let's see what you've got."

He tried to dissuade her. Had this situation arisen at some prior time in their marriage, he might have been able to bluff his way out of it, might have been able to intimidate her by telling her that what he had written was too technical for her to grasp. But such a time was gone. It was good that such a time was gone, of course, but it made his present situation very difficult. "It's just a rough draft. Very rough really," Janus said. "I doubt that you would…."

But it was too late. "Nonsense," she said. "Of course I want to see." She gathered the several pages he had typed and read them with widening eyes. "What's this?" she asked, shaking the pages in front of her face like a fan. "This is your dissertation?"

Janus couldn't look at her. "No, of course not," he said.

"What's the matter, Janus?" Her voice rained on him from above and ate at him like a corrosive. "Don't you like Indians anymore?"

By reflex, he tried to joke his way free. "Sure, I still like Indians," he replied. "Some of my best friends are Indians. It's just that I don't want my daughter's father to spend the rest of his life writing about one."

Faith looked at him without smiling. "You haven't got a daughter, Janus," she said. "And if you don't do your dissertation, you're not *gonna* have a daughter. Or any other kind of child. If you don't get your Ph.D., you won't get a job. If you don't get a job, we're too poor to have a kid."

Janus wrote in his journal, "Faith was always literal when it suited her purposes." Still trying to survive via humor, he told her then, "I know we don't have a daughter." He looked at her scowling face and explained, "I was just trying to make a joke."

"A joke? You're making a joke out of your life is what you're doing."

With his best Groucho Marx impression, he responded, "I'd rather be making my life out of a joke." But Faith was genuinely upset and not to be teased out of it. The truth was that he could hardly blame her.

She put the sheets of paper back on his desk and brushed her fingers across them. She shook her head and said in a gravelly whisper, "What a waste, Janus, what a waste." She looked hard at him. "Are you seriously entertaining the notion of not finishing your dissertation?"

"Of course not," Janus said. "I told you. This stuff is just a joke."

"As with most of your jokes, I fail to see what's funny."

Suddenly Janus said something that ultimately changed his life. He was basically such a careful man, it is ironic that this statement slipped out of him without his planning it. But all of a sudden there it was out in the open between them—ugly, wrinkled and in need of total care, like a newborn baby from an unknown pregnancy. "Maybe it isn't a joke then," he said. "Maybe it's the truth, the whole truth and nothing but the truth."

"You're crazy," Faith said.

"Undoubtedly. But perhaps I've just turned onto the road to recovery."

"Don't do this," Faith said.

"As Martin Luther said, *'Ich kann nicht ander.'* Perhaps I can do no other."

Faith shook her head. Her eyes blinked rapidly. Her lower jaw moved slowly from side to side. "I can't believe this. I worked for three years to put you through graduate school. Now you get this close, and you're going to throw it all away. That makes my sacrifice seem pretty worthless, doesn't it?"

"Sacrifice?" Janus laughed. "What big deal sacrifice did you make?" He deeply hoped their conversation was not about to assume the direction he sensed and feared it was about to take.

"You know goddamn well what sacrifice. I worked teaching shitty grade school so you could go to graduate school."

"You didn't put me through school," Janus said. His anger had come all at once, like a bomb hitting an oil tank. One moment there is quiet, the very next an inferno.

"The hell I didn't," Faith said. "What do you think I was doing for three years? You think I wanted to be a sixth-grade teacher?"

Janus's voice assumed a false calm. "You were working, and I was in graduate school. And there's no denying those events were coincident. But *I* put myself through school, Faithy, and I'm sick of your trying to have it otherwise. There's been some putting through school in this marriage, okay. *I* put you through school in St. Louis. Then *I* put me through school here. You held a job. Tough life that people have to work, isn't it? You took care of yourself. Period."

"That's not true. I earned more than you did."

Janus was ready for this argument. The debate was one they'd had several times before, one that in the absence of figures had never been settled. So one day, instead of doing his dissertation, Janus had gathered all their income records for the years of their marriage and computed who had earned what and who had spent how much on schooling. He had even bothered to make a liberal estimate of the tips Faith had collected during her period as a barmaid. Now he yanked open a file drawer and took out a manila folder into which he had placed his computations. "Here you go, Faith, girl," he hissed. "Here you go, right here. I've heard your woe-is-me-gotta-support-hubby routine too many times, so I got it for ya right here, all in black and white. And in your case, red. Take a look at it, kiddo, or as the poker players say, 'Read 'em and weep.'"

Janus tried to hand the folder to Faith, but she refused to take it. She slapped against it with the back of her hand. "I don't believe that *shit*," she said. But Janus could detect in her voice a tone that belied her assertion. He knew he had her, and in his anger he relished his advantage.

"Oh, I don't expect that you'll trust *my* figures," he said. "Why should you do that?" He snapped open the file drawer again and extracted the records from which he had worked. "You go through these yourself, shit-for-brains. I want you to. Because the truth will set *me* free."

"Don't you call *me* shit-for-brains, you son of a bitch. You're the one who's got shit for brains. You're the one who's who's quitting on himself and on me."

"You're right," Janus said in mock acquiescence. "I shouldn't call you shit for brains when you've got no brains at all. How could you possibly have any brains if you ever thought you were supporting me when you weren't doing shit but supporting yourself? I don't owe you a goddamn penny. It's you who owes me, you who owes me money for putting *you* through graduate school, in St. Louis and now."

"Shut up. SHUT UP!" she screamed.

Janus waved the folder at her again. "Read 'em and weep, Faith baby."

She hit him then. First one hard slap across his face, and when he grinned and thrust his chin at her, a series of quick slaps back and forth that gradually weakened in force until she burst into tears and ran from the room.

Janus later recognized that he'd been cruel, intentionally cruel to his wife for the first time in their marriage. He had been wrong many times. He had failed to understand her many times. But he had never before been cruel.

At the moment Faith fled, though, he saw not cruelty in his proclamations but only truth. He had facts and figures to back up his statements. Only as time passed would he come to understand what he did not that day as he sat at his desk and carefully returned the income records and his folder of computations to their places in the file drawer. At the moment, he was fixated on his proof that Faith had not made the larger financial contribution to their marriage. His tax-free fellowships were too lucrative for that to have been possible.

But at that ugly moment Janus was blinding himself to the enormous investment Faith had made in his graduate career. She had put her own ambitions on hold while earning an income that made possible their avoidance of the common poverty endemic among graduate students. She had made *his* success her first priority.

Only as time passed would Janus come to understand the severity of the blow he delivered that day, the cruelty he practiced in the name of truth. By announcing his decision not to finish his dissertation, he had negated the dividend on Faith's investment. By attacking her with his manila folder of figures, he had denied that the investment had ever been made. But no matter the verdict of Janus's figures, her investment had been made, of course, if not neatly in dollar and cents, then pervasively in psychic capital. Hard as Janus's first blow was for her to absorb, the second was far more devastating.

After he closed his drawer on its vindictive treasure of records, he sat for a time at his desk, staring blankly out the window. He stacked the pages of his memo and rolled the half-finished sheet from his typewriter. As he opened his journal notebook, intending to tuck the pages of his joke memo inside, his eyes fell on a passage he'd written describing a fight he'd had with Faith in St. Louis when she had demanded a car of her own. He remembered anew how he'd ridiculed her and how he'd felt like a blind man suddenly allowed to see when he finally understood. All at once Janus felt a rush of love. Faith was so vulnerable, it seemed to him. He had bruised her too often not meaning to. His love and his residual anger mixed together. He felt unsteady, volatile. But he rose from his desk and went in search of his wife. He felt very low; it was his intent to apologize.

Faith was sitting on the stoop outside the apartment's front door. She had stopped crying and had drawn her legs up against her chest and laid her face against her knees.

"Hey, Faith," Janus said to her in his softest voice.

She didn't attempt to look at him but said as if she were commenting on the weather, "I'm leaving you."

"Come on, babe, let's quit it now."

She sat up and looked straight at him. Pronouncing her words slowly and carefully, she said, "I'm leaving you, Janus."

"Come on, Faith, that's such an old tune."

"This time it's true, Janus. You've never been horrible like this before. I don't know you. I can't stand this. I've got too much work to do. I have to make a success of myself now because you've quit on me." She shuddered. "I want you to get this. We're through."

Janus's anger flared anew. "When are you leaving? Oh, and by the way, where are you going? How are you going to live? Need I remind you that you've got no job, no income? Need I remind you that you're in school? I may have quit on you, but I seem to be supporting you."

Faith looked away from him. "I can move in with Kate," she said. "Kate told me that I could move in with her any time I wanted to." She looked back at Janus in steely accusation. "Kate is my friend. I can count on her to help me."

Just the mention of Kate Banford as a source of refuge fanned Janus's anger to a new intensity, and his responding laugh was nasty. "Maybe you can help her too, huh? Maybe you can lick her cunt for her."

"You shut up, you," Faith said without separating her teeth.

"You shut up, you," Janus mimicked her.

Faith's crying, which began again, now lacked its usual effect on her. Tears streamed down her face but did not wash her anger into the helpless eddy of sobs. "I hate you," she said. She laughed without a pause in her crying. "I hate you so much I'm going to tell you something that will make you hate me back. And then we can both finally be done with each other."

"I hate you so much, I'm gonna finally whatever, whatever," Janus mocked.

"I slept with Johnnie Golden," Faith said.

Janus was shot right through the heart, and the fight went out of him as if he were dead. "Don't," he said.

"I slept with him more than once." Janus shook his head, trying to signal her to quit. "Sometimes I'd deliberately tell you we needed something from the grocery, and I'd fuck him while you were gone. I'd fuck him standing up in the kitchen or sitting in your chair in the living room, knowing that you'd be back any second. Knowing you might catch us made it that much better."

"Stop it, Faith," Janus said. His voice was breaking. Tears were already on his cheeks. "It's not true," he said.

"Why do you think he had to leave town so suddenly, you fool? He couldn't take it anymore." She snorted. "But I was the fool, wasn't I? He wanted me to go with him, and I chose to stay with you."

"This isn't true," Janus said.

"Ha! You dope. I used to give him blow jobs in the car when we'd drop you off to get our names on the waiting list at El Cholo."

Janus kept shaking his head. "No," he said.

Faith looked at her husband straight in the face. Her eyes were bright behind their wetness. Her face relaxed from its contemptuous grimace.

"I'll never let you, but I let him fuck me in the ass."

19

If I may engage in a little self-analysis, my problem, I think, has always been the tendency to define myself in terms of my accomplishments. In high school I was a basketball player who made good grades. In college I was a war protester who played basketball. In my first (and only) full-time job, I was a coach with long hair and better things waiting who wouldn't be staying at the school long. In graduate school I was a Fortran Fellow with a hot-shot dissertation topic on King Philip's War.

In my marriage I was an asshole. But that's another story.

The problem was, you see, that after my basketball days ended I could never kick the addiction to being special. I don't mean special to some other person, like a mom or a wife or a friend, but special as in, well, hot-shot. That's how I ended up in this big predicament. People told me I had a special talent for history and should pursue it. I loved the words *special talent,* so I pursued it. But I never liked *doing* history. I didn't especially like reading it, and I hated doing research. But I craved to fill that need of mine to excel, so I hustled along and more or less excelled as an apprentice historian.

By the fall of 1975, I had come to grips with the awful truth: I had made a gigantic mistake. I was nearing thirty years old and was trained to do something I loathed. So I took a terrifying step. I quit. I started writing this note to y'all as a joke, stating that I'd quit before I'd really decided to. But then Faith caught me, and the jig was up. (Gosh, I hope that isn't a racist expression deriving from the lynching of a black person.) Since the note couldn't be a joke anymore, I either had to stop writing it and start working on my dissertation or admit the note wasn't a joke. I couldn't possibly write my dissertation, so I was forced to follow the second option.

The problem was, as you can imagine, that note writing isn't much of an occupation. Oh, I still had income from my Fortran and teaching fellowships, but they would both run out in June. In other words, I knew what I didn't want to do with my life but not yet what I *did* want to do with it.

These were not happy times.

Faith was laboring away in her own graduate career and was at once irritable and content. She was content with being in graduate school. She really liked psychology, really wanted to be a scholar. She was irritated that I was an asshole.

We had a colossal fight when she discovered this note. She threatened to leave me, and, it hurts even now to mention this, she told me about sleeping with our friend Johnnie Golden. Isn't that a funny euphemism? What she did was commit acts of sex upon Johnnie Golden's body. They never had the time or opportunity to sleep together because I was always around.

You won't be surprised when I tell you that all this gave me a significant case of the El Cholo Feeling.

Oddly, Faith didn't move out. After the revelation about Johnnie, I expected her to be packed and gone within a few days. But she was in the middle of the quarter, she pointed out, and hardly had the time to arrange a move before Christmas break. I made my usual bold proclamations, of course. I told her she could damn well get her ass out immediately. I told her the next time she came home from class to be prepared to find her possessions boxed and waiting for her on the front step. She said I didn't have the guts.

She had me pegged, as usual.

It was a strange time. Always in the past, Faith quickly retracted her threats of separation. This time she refused to. And yet she didn't leave. She came home from school. We made our meals together. We still talked. Not every moment was one of anguish. Things were tense, of course, but we got along better than we had in St. Louis. We even laughed occasionally.

I could go periods of time forgetting that, according to Faith, our marriage was in its deathwatch. But she would not take back her promise that come the quarter's end she was leaving, probably to move in with Kate Banford. I couldn't understand this behavior. I couldn't grasp how she could feel driven to do something as important as end a marriage and not feel compelled to do it instantly. Had it been me, I thought, I'd have been gone inside a week.

I shared this sentiment with her and she turned it on me, making me feel doubly guilty: first because I was such a jerk that she wanted to leave me, second because I was so selfish as to want her to leave now rather than at some later, more convenient time. Looking back, I am forever amazed at Faith's ability to rope me into ridiculous attitudes.

The end result of her staying, in the midst of promises to leave, was that I doubted from day to day that she really intended to leave at all. These doubts were a source of comfort, but at the same time they made me hate her for being so cruel. If only I could have stopped loving her, things would have been so much easier.

Or perhaps if I could have started working on my dissertation again. I don't want to give the impression that Faith gave me any ultimatums. She didn't. As a matter of fact, after that one night she had little to say to me about my career plans. "Your career is altogether your own affair now," she told me once when I raised the issue with her. But in the back of my mind, I couldn't help believing that I could perhaps melt her glacier of indifference by making some significant headway on my thesis.

But I couldn't. I couldn't because once I started writing this fucking note, I couldn't quit. When I sat at a typewriter, my fingers began tapping out additional pages of this memo. When my pen scratched at a legal pad, sentences turned into passages to be included here. I was obsessed.

I was feeling monumentally crummy, and the obsession of this note provided my only relief.

Working on this note carried me from the night of the Johnnie Golden revelation to the middle of November, when I had to go to Chicago to attend my last Fortran conference. Actually, I *didn't* have to go. I could have waited until the following fall. The final conference was a big wingding at the Illinois State Beach Lodge in Zion, and the Fortran people let you attend it either your fourth year in graduate school or your first year in teaching. They supposed, I suppose, that for some, the fourth fall would be a time too busy with thesis writing for an all-expense-paid intellectual vacation.

I figured I'd better go that November, since a year later was unlikely to find me with a teaching job. Also, I'll admit, I was anxious to get away from Faith about then. It's pretty lonely living with a person who's going to leave you.

But the El Cholo Feeling, I remembered too late, is rampant at Fortran conferences. And by the time I arrived at Chicago's O'Hare Field, I had it, as my childhood chum B.F. Johnson used to say, like goosebumps on a virgin.

To accompany the El Cholo Feeling, I also had the goosebumps. California boy that I'd become, I arrived in the Midwest with only a sweatshirt and a denim jacket to protect me from the cold. I'd forgotten that in the world outside L.A., winter means something other than the time of year when it might rain.

The good news was that I found the old army-green lodge bus as soon as I emerged from the airline terminal. The bad news was that the bus wasn't heated. It was nearly empty when I climbed aboard. A gregarious sort, the sort I always wanted to be, would have struck up a conversation with one of the other Fellows waiting for the bus to fill. I opted to freeze to death in silence.

It was late afternoon. I sat on the left side of the bus with my hands tucked up in my armpits trying to head off frostbite. I wanted to put the hood of my sweatshirt up around my head but feared that doing so would make me look foolish. If I was going to freeze to death, I didn't want it to appear I'd been cold. Outside my window, the airport's architecture and the waning day blended into uniform grayness.

Gradually the bus filled. I kept hoping someone would sit next to me. I needed the warmth both physically and spiritually. I wondered if Rita Gates would be at the conference. I doubted it, but I wondered how I would react if she were. This would be my sixth Fortran conference, one the first year, two each of the next two years. I suddenly realized how few of the Fellows I'd gotten to know. I wondered if Rod the Bod would be there. I wondered if I was once again to room with Leonard Bass. Behind me some smokers lit their cigarettes. I had started up again myself, but I didn't join them. A woman whom the smoke annoyed pulled down her window. The gray smoke drifted out; the gray cold afternoon drifted in.

A last couple of Fellows came aboard, one a tall man in a furry parka with the hood around his face, the other a tall slender woman with curly hair hanging out from underneath a wool cap. The woman found a place up front; the man brushed past me to sit in the rear. They were followed quickly onto the bus by the driver and an official from the Fortran Foundation, who counted noses before we pulled away from the curb at the dreary arrivals area. Inexplicably, we did not merge with the expressway traffic but hugged the inside lane, made a complete circle and returned to the tomblike position we'd occupied before in front of United Airlines. Presumably the Fortran representative thought we'd left someone, but no one else came aboard. We froze while waiting anew before the order to depart was finally given. We edged away again, this time for good.

The bus found its way to Interstate 94 and headed north. It was dark inside. A few wisps of conversation drifted into my hearing, but largely we rode in silence. Several miles to the east of us, I knew, lay the grimy green water of Lake Michigan. I looked out of my side of the bus, toward the west. We were passing an expanse of open land covered with a thin layer of snow. Soon, I was sure, it would be covered with shopping centers and fast-food franchises, but at the moment it stretched an incredible distance to a coral sunset low on the horizon.

The woman whom the smoke had annoyed decided that the icy air was a worse menace, but she couldn't get her window back up. The wind through her window blasted over me, deadening feeling in my toes and ear lobes. My fingers were so cold they felt hollow and detached from my hands. I finally pulled the cloth hood of my sweatshirt up around my head, leaned back against the seat and studied that western horizon where all the clouds in the sky appeared concentrated. The sunset seemed to light them from below. I had the strange thought that I was confined to a tiny universe bound by the thin metal sides of this decrepit old bus, a universe that was at right angles to another one far to the west, which began in a perpendicular plane just below those amber clouds.

Between the bus's world and that other flew a flock of birds heading south for the winter. I could see them strung out for several miles, fluttering, seemingly struggling. Occasionally there were gaps in the spacing of the flock. But until darkness hid them from me, they kept coming. I wondered why.

Thirty-four miles north of O'Hare, we turned east toward Zion. It was totally dark now. I could barely make out the figures of the Fellows sitting around me, but a burst of chattering conversation registered the excitement that we were nearing our destination. Behind me I heard a familiar voice, although I didn't instantly place it. The red tip of a cigarette with an Eastern accent said, "Monterey...Asilomar...spring conference." Most of the lit cigarettes I knew were from L.A.

We filed from the bus at the three-story lodge. The red cigarette tip came off just after me and followed me into the light inside the lobby. It was Rod the Bod. We shook hands and made small talk while waiting to register. He was given a first-floor room; I was on the second. As we separated, we promised to get together and chat. I gathered my briefcase and small suitcase and walked slowly toward the elevator at the lobby's far end. I could hear the buzz of others getting their room assignments. I felt the stupid, self-pitying loneliness with which Fortran conferences always began for me.

The elevator came, and I blocked its doors open with one foot and used the other to nudge my bags inside. As the doors were closing, I heard a female voice call out, "Hey, hold that for me." I jammed my foot back between the doors. When they opened, I stuck my head out and saw the person who turned out to be Cally. She was the tall curly-haired woman who had come onto the bus just before we left. She was still wearing her knit cap and was struggling toward the elevator all leaned over her right side, clutching a large suitcase.

Holding the elevator doors back with my left hand, reaching out with my right hand toward her bag, I said, "I really am a gentleman, but if I come help you with that, we're going to lose this elevator, and it might never come back." The person who turned out to be Cally smiled and shoved her suitcase along toward me.

"That's okay," she said, setting the suitcase on the floor and dragging it along. "You know modern women. We travel light but manage heavy thoughts." When she got close enough to me, I took the suitcase from her and slid it inside next to mine. "Thanks," she said and smiled at me again.

The person who turned out to be Cally was among the most attractive women I had ever seen. She was like a movie star, I thought. Her face was absolutely flawless. Her long green skirt, blue turtleneck sweater and high-peaked cap exaggerated her slenderness and made her look slinky like Lauren Bacall in *To Have and Have Not*. But there was something besides the perfection in her face that attracted me. I am cold to many beautiful women because so often their beauty is accompanied by a face that communicates haughtiness. The person who turned out to be Cally had a face that was somehow soft and sweet, somehow hinting at a compassionate nature.

"What floor are you on?" I asked to stop myself from staring.

"Three," she said. I pushed the three button, and we started up. She peeled off a beige mitten and stuck her hand out to me. "I'm Calliope Martin. Cally, actually."

She had a nice firm handshake. "Rich Janus," I responded.

"Your hand is freezing!" she said and put her other hand around mine and rubbed it between them.

"My hand is freezing," I agreed. She laughed.

Suddenly she dropped my hand. "Are you *Richard* Janus?"

"Yes," I nodded.

"The Richard Janus?"

I had exactly the same feeling I had had six months earlier when Rita Gates had asked me the same question, the disarming feeling that I had somehow become a famous person but could not remember when or for what accomplishment. "I'm the main Richard Janus I know," I said.

Cally knitted her eyebrows. "Did you run for Congress in Maine last year? If so, my husband and I sent money for your campaign."

I shook my head and laughed. "That must have been the other Richard Janus. But I wish it had been me. I might have liked being a Congressman."

Cally smiled. "I'm afraid you didn't win," she said.

The doors clattered open as we arrived at the third floor. Cally and I both reached for her bag at the same time, her hand grabbing mine just after I'd clasped the suitcase handle. Both laughing, we shoved her large valise into the hall. I stepped back into the elevator, and she made a slight turn in my direction, indicating that she expected me to bring my own bags off. I was embarrassed when it dawned on me that I had failed to push the button for my own floor.

"Aren't you getting off?" she asked. "I'm afraid you can't go any higher." Again that warm smile.

"I'm afraid you've taken me higher than I'd intended to go." I cleared my throat. "I forgot to push the button for two."

"Oh," she said.

"See you later," I said. The elevator door closed, and I dropped back down.

My room was large and warm, and unlike at Asilomar, I had it all to myself. The Foundation liked to give the final conference a touch of luxury. I had two double beds and my own bath. The only thing missing, I thought, was a desk to write my memo on, or else I could have just moved in to stay. I dumped my briefcase and suitcase on the bed farthest from the windows against the southern wall. Opening the briefcase, I found the conference schedule and discovered that I was due downstairs shortly for wine and cheese.

To fill up the minutes before our first gathering, I changed out of my sweatshirt and into a green ski sweater. I hoped I looked like a proper conference goer.

The meeting room was packed when I got downstairs. Fellows were munching and sipping everywhere. I didn't see a single face I knew. I looked for Rita. I even looked for Rod the Bod. Finally, I spotted Leonard Bass, who was in an animated conversation about something or other. As I moved stealthily in his direction, I noticed that a piece of cracker clung to the right side of his mustache. I moved around him without his catching sight of me and made it to the bar, where I poured myself a glass of chablis.

With the wine in my fist, I edged through the jam of bodies to the cheese table, which was littered with emptied glasses, wadded-up napkins and dirty ashtrays. There were bowls of soft cheese and blocks of cheddar and Swiss and Brie. At the end of the table, next to the napkins, was a stack of paper plates. Have you ever noticed how few people ever use plates at affairs such as these? Probably not. Well, I wish I hadn't noticed, too, but I get so supremely uncomfortable at these mixers sometimes that I start analyzing such things. Was it any wonder my wife thought I was a jerk? I cut myself a couple of hunks of cheese and opted to forgo a plate. I didn't want to be identified so early on as a plate man.

Beyond the cheese and cracker table was the room's eastern wall, made of plate glass and looking out across a narrow, snow-covered beach to Lake Michigan. I went to the windows and stared out at the night. The daylong cloud cover persisted and was lit now from below by the gray light of Chicago. But the waters of the lake did not glimmer in this reflected illumination, and I could not tell exactly where the dark shore ended and the black water began.

As I squinted out, trying to see through the mirror of the party behind me, I wondered how long I could stand in front of these windows before stamping myself as antisocial, with latent plate-man tendencies. Fortunately, I didn't have to ponder this question too long. A voice behind me said, "Hey." It was Cally.

And that quickly the party was fun. She and I shared the essential information. Cally was a Harvard Ph.D. in classics and was in her first year of teaching in an honors program at the University of New Orleans. Her husband was a physicist with a doctorate from MIT. He was teaching at Rice in Houston, and they were finding their new weekend relationship a strain. Cally revealed this personal data with a matter-of-factness which utterly lacked the hint of neuroticism that often accompanies such divulgences to a stranger.

I told her that I was not writing a dissertation on King Philip's War for a degree I wouldn't finish in U.S. History at UCLA.

"Your writing isn't going well?" she said and smiled.

"My writing isn't going at all," I told her.

"Well, I'm sure you'll get back on track. Everybody has problems at some stage or other."

I started to tell her that I was pretty sure I wouldn't get back on track but decided against it. I told her instead that I'd grown up in New Orleans. That led us to a pleasant discussion about places and sights in New Orleans, which she had only recently encountered, and I could barely remember.

While we were talking, Rod the Bod joined us, throwing his arm around Cally's waist as he walked up behind her. "Rod!" she said. "I'm so glad you came this year." She kissed him quickly on the cheek and put her arm around his waist, too. "Do you know...?" she said to him, starting to introduce me.

"Rich and I met last spring at Asilomar," Rod said.

"Rod and I are old friends," Cally said to me. "We always felt rooked because we were in different classes and never got to go to the same conferences."

"I always figured if I could get her alone at one of these meetings, I could steal her away from the scientific genius she married," Rod the Bod said.

"Rod's opinion of his attractiveness is matched only by his attractiveness," Cally said, deftly complimenting and teasing him in the same sentence.

Rod and Cally talked about Boston, and she asked about his wife. She was very considerate of me, explaining things that I was obviously ignorant of, including me in the conversation whenever possible. She had just switched the conversation from Boston to New Orleans by telling Rod that I was going to clue her in to all the best things to do in her new home town when she was approached by another old friend, a woman who turned out to be Virginia Brown, art history Ph.D. from the University of Chicago.

While Cally and Virginia talked, one of the Fortran officials tinkled with a spoon on a wine glass until the room grew quiet, then announced that dinner was served. Like steers at the beginning of a cattle drive, we moved slowly to the stairwell at the north end of the room and up the stairs to the dining room. Rod the Bod and I continued to talk, but we became separated from Cally and Virginia, who straggled somewhere in the crowd behind us. As we seated ourselves at an empty table, I hoped that the two women would be able to join us, but the remaining places had filled by the time I saw them enter the dining hall.

Rod asked if Rita Gates was at the conference. I was tempted to tell him that he'd have better reason to know than I did, but I simply said that I hadn't seen her.

"What a crazy broad," he said.

"Yeah," I said, not agreeing but wanting to seem so. "I really liked her."

He misunderstood me, I think. "Rita Gates could really give good convention." He laughed and shook his head, remembering. Then he looked at me. "But I wouldn't go so far as liking her." He laughed again.

"Did she drop out of school?"

"Who the hell knows?" he said. "Just because I fucked the chick doesn't mean I want to write her biography."

"Isn't it interesting," I wanted to say, "how people with a string of advanced degrees, with years of humane education, can manage to remain such complete assholes?" But I didn't, of course. Instead I just smiled, acknowledging his witticism, and then deliberately changed the subject. "How well do you know Cally Martin?" I asked.

"Not nearly as well as I'd like to," Rod replied.

"Cally Martin?" the Fellow to my left asked. I turned to him, and he added, "Excuse me for butting into your conversation, but since I was eavesdropping anyway, I thought I might as well participate."

"You know Cally, too?" I asked.

"Red's the name, and math's the game," the new Fellow said, extending a hand for me to shake. I introduced myself and then Rod, and they nodded at each other. "I went to school with Cally's husband, Robert Dodge, at MIT," he said.

I smiled at Red. "Cally seems awfully nice." I'm such a penetrating conversationalist.

"What Janus here means is that Cally seems awfully gorgeous," Rod the Bod said to Red. Then he turned to me and said, "Watch out now, boy, that's married stuff you're sniffing after."

I have to admit I was shocked. Not because I hadn't heard far cruder language, but because the circumstances for such crudity seemed so unlikely. I managed an awkward shift of topic by asking Red about his work at MIT. He was another Fellow who had finished his degree and was in his first year of teaching.

I made some comment of approbation, and Red held up his hands as if trying to quiet an audience's applause. "I know what you're thinking," he said. "You're thinking what a lucky guy. Young. Good looking." He paused, staring first at me and then at Rod until each of us shifted our eyes away from his. "You're not thinking good looking? I'll have you know that underneath this squat, freckled, baldish exterior lurks the body and charm of Warren Beatty. Brilliant. Well-heeled. Well-educated. MIT, Ph.D, M-O-U-S-E." I laughed, and Red hurried on. "Well, I've got my problems too, you know. I broke up with my girl. I suffer from heat rash. My application to be Woody Allen last year was turned down for inadequate Jewishness."

"How did you do in neuroses?" I asked.

"Straight A's in neuroses from sixth grade on, when I discovered that short round people are seldom tall and thin."

"Are you finding professional achievements to offset your lingering physical, shall I say, shortcomings?" I asked.

"None whatsoever, tall doctor," Red said.

"My tallness may be only a conjecture," I said. "And please try to remember that I'm not the doctor; you are."

"I keep forgetting, tall doctor."

I suddenly realized that Rod had been silent through this silly exchange. I wondered if I should try to get him involved in the conversation again but didn't know exactly how. People, I've learned, either possess a capacity for silliness or they don't.

"My students hate me," Red continued, flashing his eyes from side to side as if one might be nearby.

"Perhaps they only strongly dislike you," I said consolingly.

"They don't take me seriously. They see me as part of some conspiracy to bore them to death while simultaneously lowering their GPA's so they can't be accepted to the Wharton School of Instant Affluence. I'm thinking of wearing my Richard Nixon mask to class." Red paused to take a sip from his water glass. "I hate Richard Nixon," he added.

"Who doesn't?" Rod the Bod said.

"Mrs. Nixon," Red said quickly. "And David and Julia and Tricia."

"I don't think Eddie *really* likes him, though," I said. "I think he just pretends to."

"Ron Ziegler likes him," Red said. "He's a masochist."

"And don't forget Bebe Rebozo," I added. "And for inscrutable reasons, the citizens of the People's Republic of China."

"You know, Rich," Red said confidentially, "I am deeply afraid we don't really have Richard Nixon to kick around any more." I nodded sympathetically. "I have another fear too. I'm afraid I'm going to quit my job."

"Why?" I asked.

"Because I hate it."

"Too bad you don't have a good reason," I said.

"I know," Red said, looking forlorn. "You see, I really want to do something else, only I'm already too old, I guess. I'm nearly twenty-eight. I used to be a whiz kid. Do you think it's too late for me to be a late bloomer, tall doctor?"

"My tallness is largely a matter of reputation," I pointed out. "At home I'm as short as any other man. And please try to remember that it is you, not I, who is the doctor."

"How true," Red observed. "How bitterly true."

To make a long story short, Red and I hit if off. After dinner we headed for the general session together. Rod the Bod managed to give us the slip and turned up later sitting with Cally and Virginia. I was beginning to feel unkindly toward him.

When the session was over, Red and I adjourned to the reception room for a beer. We had just seated ourselves at one of the plastic-tablecloth-covered tables when we were joined by Cally and Virginia. Cally introduced us to her friend. "Red McAuliffe," she said, "is a friend of my husband. Bob calls him the smartest fuck-off he knows."

"I don't accomplish much, but I'm very bright about it," Red said.

"Richard Janus," Cally went on, "is a man who did not run for Congress in Maine last year."

"I also didn't run in California," I pointed out. "It's rumored that I didn't run in several other states as well."

"While not running for Congress, coast to coast," Cally said, "Mr. Janus explains that he's found ample time not to write his dissertation."

"I've been not writing it for six solid months now," I bragged. "And the funniest thing, you know—since I began not writing, I've discovered that millions of people, all over this country, fail to write dissertations every year. And yet they seem otherwise perfectly normal. They don't gain weight, and they aren't grouchy with family and friends."

"You've been holding out on me, tall guy," Red said. "Here I was crowing about quitting my job, and you're probably not even going to get one."

"Probably not," I agreed.

"Are these guys for real?" Virginia asked Cally. She had long, straight, brown hair and a pronounced Southern accent.

"Who knows?" Cally said. "Why don't you ask them?"

"Are you really quitting your job?" she asked Red.

"Well, I'm not really *quitting* my job," Red said. "But I'm really *thinking* about really quitting my job. That has always seemed rather brave to me."

"I see," Virginia said. She shifted her attention to me. "And what does a person who hasn't been writing his dissertation do for six solid months?"

"That's an easy one," I said. "There's lots to do. There are ulcers to grow and sleepless nights to be awake in."

Red announced that he was going to the bar for another beer and asked if anyone else was ready. I told him I was. Each of the women held up bottles that were more than half full.

"Where are you from, Rich?" Virginia asked.

"UCLA."

"But you're not a native Californian," she judged.

"Rich is from New Orleans," Cally said.

"Ah ha," Virginia laughed. "I thought I heard a little grit in your voice."

Red returned with the beer, and I was glad for the respite. Frankly, I was always surprised and a little embarrassed when people spotted my accent. I couldn't hear the Southern tinge that I guess I never managed to lose. I suspected it was aggravated by the dinner wine and the bottle of Budweiser in my belly and the influence of listening to Virginia.

As I twisted off the cap and tilted the fresh beer to my lips, Virginia turned to Cally and said, "You know, I think our friend Mr. Janus here has probably been using all his time not writing his dissertation to write the great American novel. Scratch a Southerner, and you'll find a writer. All Southern men are either writers or scoundrels."

"Some are probably lucky enough to be both," Red said.

"I was planning on writing the great American novel up until two years ago when it came out by Philip Roth," I said.

"That's true," Virginia admitted. She turned to Cally again. "Oh, well, he must be a poet then. Scratch a Southerner, and you'll find a poet."

"All Southern men are either scoundrels or poets," Red said.

"I *am* writing a memo," I told them.

"He's probably a memo writer," Virginia told Red.

"Scratch a Southerner, and you'll find a memo writer," Red replied.

Cally laughed. "What's your memo about, Rich?"

"It's a letter to my doctoral committee telling them I've decided to quit graduate school."

"It must be some memo if it's six months long," Virginia said.

"It's kind of turned into the story of my life," I explained. "I'm already up to long pants, though, so I should finish this century."

"To the last of the great memo writers," Red said, raising his bottle in a toast. He swallowed down the rest of his beer and headed to the bar for more, returning with a whole new round. We drank and bantered and became friends. At one o'clock, the barman said he was leaving but that we were welcome to stay. He set out a tub of ice with a dozen more bottles of beer in it and told us to pay for whatever we drank the next day. He blew out the candles on the other tables in the room and went home. We drank another round before Virginia said she was going to bed.

"I think I'll join you," Red said. There was a moment of silence and then the three of us burst into laughter. Red had gotten his best laugh of the night, albeit inadvertently, and the skin on his face began to flush as orange as the sparse hair on his head.

"That's the most offhanded proposition I've ever received," Virginia said.

Red stammered out that he hadn't meant, of course, that…. Virginia stood up a little unsteadily and pulled Red to his feet. She was at least four inches taller. "Come on, short stuff," she said. "Blow in my ear and I'll follow you anywhere."

"But I can't reach your ear," Red said, leaning toward her on tiptoes.

"Now you're catching on," she said. She put her arm through his, and they trudged out of the darkened room toward the stairwell.

Cally and I were alone. I felt very nervous about being with her by myself. I was powerfully attracted to her. Remotely similar feelings toward other women had possessed me since my marriage, but never before had I been of a mind to act on those feelings. Even now I felt something strongly akin to sinfulness in being alone with her. "Shall we call it a night, too?" I said.

"Let's split another beer."

"Sure," I said, ecstatic but hopeful that I had managed to sound casual, or in California lingo, laid back. I went to the ice bucket and brought back another bottle, twisted off the cap and handed it to Cally. She drank from it and handed it to me. I felt an erotic rush as I touched my lips to the cold, wet rim where hers had so recently been. Isn't that just ridiculous? It was true, though.

"Are you really writing this long letter you were telling us about, or is that tale just part of your social chitchat?" Cally's voice lacked the flipness that we had all been using to entertain each other earlier.

"Yes," I said.

Wouldn't it have been nice to have tried a little sincerity?

She laughed. "Yes, what?"

"Yes, I think it's very nice being all alone here with you. You're a very nice person." Now, that was sincere, but it was also potentially disastrous. It was too dark in the room to see if I had made Cally blush, but I'm sure I did.

She laughed, this time nervously, then sort of cleared her throat and laughed again and thanked me for the compliment. I was dying a thousand deaths, sure that the next words out of her mouth would announce her intention to retire immediately. She reached for the beer bottle which stood on the table between us and took a drink.

As she did so, I said, "Yes, I am writing this long letter I was telling y'all about. My flip manner helps conceal the fact that I normally tell the truth."

"Tell me about the letter," she said, sliding the beer back towards me.

I laughed. "How can I tell you about it. It's a crazy obsession. It started as a joke. One I was telling to myself. Now I just keep writing on it. Did you ever start out to do something very small, I don't know, like washing out a coffee cup, and when you got to the kitchen decided to do all the dishes and then, of course, you ought to wipe the counter and the stove and maybe use a little cleanser on the top of the icebox, which was really filthy? And pretty soon you've just cleaned the entire house? Well, this is sort of like that." I had avoided Cally's eyes as I made my little speech, but I looked into them now. They seemed incredibly large. I could see the candlelight flicker in them as she looked back at me.

"Do you ever let people read this memo of yours? I would think it would provide a shortcut at getting to know you."

"Nah," I said. "It's just a place I can tell all the lies I'm too afraid to tell in real life." Cally smiled at me. "And vice versa," I added.

We finished our share of the beer and walked up the staircase to the first floor, where we boarded the elevator in the main lobby. Cally pushed the button for three. When the doors opened on her floor, she held them ajar with one hand as she turned to me and said, "That's twice today I think I've taken you higher than you wanted to go." I smiled and patted her back as she stepped back into the hall. Facing me, she smiled warmly as the doors began to ease shut. Bending from the waist, I bowed to her.

Why did I bow?

The next morning the Fortran Fellows were asked to meet in small workshops according to field. "To initiate dialogue we hope will last the whole conference," the program schedule said.

"Perhaps the best way for us to begin," the convener of the history meeting said, "is for each of us to introduce ourselves and state briefly the contours of our interests." The contours of my interest at the moment took a sinfully female form. On the note pad I had rested on my knee, I wrote of the foregoing thought, "I seem to suffer from congenital assholery."

The first to introduce himself was in French social history at Berkeley. "My dissertation is a quantitative assessment of the decision-making influence of the Orleans proletariat during the French Revolution," he said.

A Princeton student in English history reported, "My thesis examines avenues of upward mobility among Cornwall peasants in the second third of the nineteenth century."

A woman named Charlene Taney said, "I finished my work last spring at Michigan and am now teaching at Southern Illinois. My thesis was a study of the economic functions of housewives in Cheyenne, Wyoming, during the first decade of this century. Essentially, I tried to arrive at dollar value assessments of female work by comparing it to wages paid hired male laborers."

A Harvard student named MacDonald Ford said, "My dissertation is a study of the Philadelphia police force as a vehicle for social mobility from 1880 to 1890. Included are profiles of the various ethnic groups which sought police employment. I have been fortunate enough to get the first two chapters published in the *Journal of American History.* Those of you who are Americanists may be acquainted with the two pieces which appeared last fall."

When my turn came, I announced, "For several years I have been a graduate student in U.S. history at UCLA. For the last six months I've not been working on a dissertation on King Philip's War, which for those of you who may not know was not an obscure engagement fought on behalf of a sixteenth-century monarch."

I looked around the room. No one laughed. I know it wasn't the wittiest line ever uttered, but people will normally reward attempts at witticism with at least a polite titter. But I realized no one had heard. Those yet to speak were mentally preparing what they would say; those who had already spoken were trying to gauge what impression they had made. But I was no different, was I? I made a grandstand play for a laugh and was thwarted because my associates were just as self-obsessed as I was.

I felt a rush of the El Cholo Feeling. It had taken a summon of nerves, I thought, for me to admit that I wasn't working on my thesis. I expected at least a response. A cluck of condolence. A glance of disparagement. But my expectations were unfair. Why should any of these people who had worked so hard at sustaining their difficult academic careers have taken notice of someone who had lost the will to sustain his?

Virginia, Red and Cally were already seated for lunch when I got to the dining room. Fortunately, there was an empty chair at their table, and I joined them. Cally asked me what I planned to do during the afternoon.

"I think I'll attend the session on alternative careers," I said to chuckles from my companions. "I sort of suspect that the session was placed on the conference schedule for my particular benefit. What are y'all doing?"

Red said he was going to the session on faculty relations. "I have a lot to learn about relating to my faculties," he admitted.

"I'm taking a nap," Virginia said.

"I'm taking the nature walk," Cally said.

"The nature walk?" I asked. "There's snow on the ground."

She laughed. "What a California softy. Snow is part of nature, you know. Why don't you come with me?"

"It's cold out there," I observed.

"I think Rich might make a good weatherman," Red told Virginia. "I don't know; I just sense he has the instincts for it."

"Weatherperson," Virginia corrected.

"So, it's cold," Cally said.

"So, it's cold," I repeated. "Isn't the fact that it's cold a negative reason?"

"No," she said.

"Oh. Then I guess I'll have to go with you."

The nature walk was a meandering trail which wound its way along the lake shore and through a forest preserve that bordered the lodge on the south. But the little tour brochure with which the lodge provided us was obviously designed for spring, summer and fall use. It told us how to identify trees by the shapes of their leaves, only there were no leaves. It told us to watch for flowers which obviously weren't there. It told us about birds, which I had probably seen heading south for the winter. It told us how to spot marine creatures by the kinds of tracks found on the wet sand of the beach, sand which now was trackless, covered with snow or frozen to a thin crust. Our walk provided us, though, with the opportunity to contract very red noses, cheeks and in my gloveless case, hands. In other words, the nature walk was wonderful. We nearly froze to death and had immense fun doing it.

Cally kept trying to convince me to wear her mittens for a while. I kept thinking how I'd so much rather warm my hands by tucking them into the crevices of her body. And I kept feeling ashamed for having such thoughts about a person who was clearly so decent, so friendly, so worthy of my respect, so married to someone else.

But on the walk I realized that something so dangerous was happening to me that it was silly: I was falling in love with this woman. Or I was falling infatuated with her. I was certainly utterly in lust with her. And I knew it was stupid. We *had* spent a lot of time together, I pointed out to myself. We had known each other about twenty-four hours.

At the general session after dinner, I sat next to Cally. The bulky sleeve of her sweater brushed against my arm every time she moved, and every time it touched me I thought I was going to get an erection. I was like a teen-ager again, heartsick with wanting something forbidden. She had used some kind of light scent after her shower, and I was drunk with the smell of her.

When the session was over, we drank beer again in the makeshift bar until after the barman had gone home and Red and Virginia had ambled off to bed. I drank too much. And I had to keep reminding myself, as we talked in shifting red shadows of the candlelight, that I couldn't reach out and take her hand. Suddenly, drunkenly, I said, "You know, I think Red and Virginia are making whoopee."

Can you believe I said "making whoopee"? I was hopelessly attracted to this woman. I wanted to make her feel the same way toward me. I wanted to turn the talk to sex to give things a whiff of the risque. So I said, "Red and Virginia are making whoopee."

I wanted to be run over by a bus.

Cally merely smiled at me. She had had a lot to drink, too, but she didn't show it. "Are they?" she said. There wasn't a hint of the facetious in her voice, not a pinch of coy, false innocence. It was as if she had said: perhaps it appears so, but perhaps they aren't, and anyway, whose business is it? But saying it that way might have called for a tone of reprimand, and that was absent, too. It was as if, in other words, she weren't sitting at a table with an asshole.

"People do that at these conferences, you know."

I have an instinct for my own jugular, remember.

"I'm sure they do," Cally said. She continued to smile. If she perceived that I was coming on to her, however ineptly, she refused to let on, refused to humiliate me even by the gentlest deflection.

"Perhaps we should call it a night," I said. "I feel like I've drunk Lake Michigan." I was trying to get out of it now, trying to save face by running away.

Cally knew better how to save my face, though. "And here I thought you could drink Lake Superior," she said. She got up and brought us back another beer to share. When we'd finished, she blew out the candle and said, "Tomorrow night I'm going to see if you can drink an ocean."

As we walked toward the stairwell, she slipped her arm around my waist. Though I hoped otherwise, I was sure she meant nothing sexual. When we started up the stairs, she squeezed me a little and said, "I like you, Richard Janus. This is a better conference because you're here."

Jesus. "If that old husband of yours ever breaks your heart," I said, "I want you to call me so I can break his face." She laughed a little, and then we were silent as we walked to the elevator. Waiting for it to come, I added, "He doesn't lift weights or anything?"

In the elevator, I pushed the button for three. At the third floor, she stepped out and grabbed the doors to keep them from closing. With perhaps just a little thickness of tongue, she asked, "Why do you always ride with me all the way up?"

"It's the only ritual we have," I said.

The air in my room was so hot it seemed like a soft obstacle trying to bar my entrance. It was the dry, suffocating heat that reigns in closed Midwestern buildings once winter descends. I undressed and lay on the bed uncovered, but even naked I was too warm. I opened the sliding glass doors and stepped out on the balcony, which overlooked the forest preserve where we had taken our walk. Somewhere above me was Cally's room. I imagined that she was standing naked on her balcony, too. Thinking of me.

Cally came by my room early the next morning to make sure that I sat with her at breakfast. While we were eating, she asked me what I planned to attend during the morning session.

"I think I'm going to the forum on women's studies," I said. She looked mildly surprised. "I like women," I explained. "Some of my best friends are women."

"I think you really do like women, Rich. Like them as people, I mean."

"I like them a lot as women, too." I said.

She laughed politely and sipped her coffee. "Not all men like women as people, though, not even those who think they like them a whole lot as women."

"I like you," I said, wishing instantly I hadn't, not because it wasn't terribly true, of course, but because there's a stark difference between such confessions made bleary-eyed in the wee hours of the morning and those made in the full light of day.

Cally looked at me evenly and said in a voice a shade more quiet than usual. "I know."

There was a short silence in which each of us filled our mouths with food. When she had taken another sip of coffee and had dabbed at her mouth with her napkin, she said, "Why don't you ever talk about your wife?"

If one can feel a blush, I blushed. All the hairs on the back of my neck and sides of my head felt like they were standing out straight. I was like a fish on a stringer: able to squirm but unable to wriggle away. "How did you know I was married?"

She laughed, reached across the table and picked up my left hand. "You're wearing a wedding ring."

I looked at the silver band on my finger as if it belonged to someone else. "Ring around the finger," I said weakly.

"You must have had that on a long time to forget it was there."

I nodded that she was right. "My wife's name is Faith Cleaver. She's a first-year psychology graduate student at UCLA. We've been married since the dawn of time." I finished my coffee in a large, scalding, swallow. My burning mouth made my eyes water. "We don't get along so well, I'm sorry to say. In fact, she's planning to move out in about a month when our fall term ends." I took a drink from my water glass. "Which perhaps explains why I don't talk much about my wife."

"I'm sorry," Cally said.

I laughed. "Please don't be sorry. Let me be sorry. I'm very good at it." Cally laid her hand on my wrist and rubbed a moment at the back of my arm.

"Our profession is especially hard on marriages," she said, "especially when both people are academics. There's the competition, and, of course, the great difficulty of both finding jobs in the same area."

"Like you and Bob," I said.

"Like me and Bob." Cally looked at me hard in the face and then with the splayed fingers of both hands raked her curly hair back from her face. It was a gesture I had seen her make before. Her eyes shifted away from mine, and she blew out a stream of air. "Bob and I have had our difficulties, too. We met our first year in college, two bright kids away from home for the first time. We were both virgins." She paused and laughed, remembering. "It was the sweetest time of my life. We loved each other very earnestly. We married our sophomore year. Now we're very adult. We live in separate cities, and we see each other twice a month. We have different careers and friends and, more important now, different interests." She shifted her gaze back to meet mine. "I've cheated on him," she said. "I've...."

"Don't tell me, Cally, please...."

"But I want to tell you, Rich." She picked up my pack of cigarettes and shook one out. "Do you mind?" she asked. She put it to her lips, and I lit it for her. She took a puff, then crushed the cigarette out. "Isn't this ridiculous? I don't smoke." She looked at me again, hard, unblinking. It was as if she were a ball rolled toward the crest of a hill in that moment of suspended movement before it picks up momentum and rolls on or begins to fall backward in the direction from which it came. "I cheated on him when we were still in Boston. He was so busy he never suspected. It was just a fling. And when it was over, I felt so cheap and small. And I pledged to myself never to do it again. It's inexcusable behavior. But now that we're separated, I've been thinking about divorce. For Bob's sake, I tell myself, as much as mine. He's so loyal, such a straight shooter that he'd never ask me to sacrifice my career so we could be together...."

"Do you want that?"

Her answer was a dry, breathy laugh. "No. Not now. I might have once, though. Poor Bob, he would deny himself all the pleasures of regular companionship out of loyalty to a woman who's been unfaithful to him."

"It sounds to me like maybe you're being a little hard on yourself."

Cally shook her head. "We live in a world in which people are constantly untrue to their own principles. I deplore that. And yet I let myself become one of those people."

"Christians," I said, "believe in a very strange idea which I find ever more attractive as I grow older. Forgiveness." It was my turn to reach for the cigarettes, for I am always uncomfortable telling people about my religious notions. I lit up and took a drag. "The hardest thing for some of us, though, is that if forgiveness exists, it's there for us, too, not just for others." Cally looked at me strangely, and I was sure I sounded like a jerk. I took another drag on my Marlboro. "But it's too early in the morning for my half-baked theology." The dining room was mostly empty now, and I told Cally we'd better hurry if we were going to a meeting. She was silent as we walked to the workshop on women's studies.

Which is where I got in trouble, because I was the only male who showed up. And my presence was not uniformly appreciated. Just after the meeting was convened by a tweed-suited senior professor who taught political science at Bryn Mawr, one of the women Fellows stood up and asked the moderator if the meeting was open or closed.

The moderator was thoroughly flustered. She didn't know the answer; she may not have understood the question. Which would have been understandable, I think, because I didn't understand the question, at first, either. The questioner stood up to explain herself. She had short blond hair and wire-rimmed glasses, which she adjusted on her face before speaking. "I don't see how we can conduct an effective meeting," she said, "with a man in the room."

The cards were on the table. I was the cards.

"Ahem, yes, well, no," the moderator said. She adjusted her suit jacket, smoothing it around her hips. "This isn't a political meeting, dear."

"Dear," the blonde said, "all meetings are political. *Everything* is political." She turned around and pointed at me, making things personal for the first time. "I want him *out."*

A Fellow I knew from UCLA, Diane Bonds, stood up and said, "I know Richard Janus, and I don't see how his presence harms us."

Another called out from her seat, "His presence is disrupting us, isn't it?"

Diane said to me, "Rich, will you consent to a vote on whether or not you should stay?"

Before I could answer, Cally said, "Any such vote is outrageous. Where does it say that any of the sessions at this conference are segregated by sex?"

"Get rid of the pig," someone else muttered loud enough for all in the room to hear.

"Rich?" Diane pleaded. "Before this gets out of hand, is a vote okay with you?"

"If you vote him out," Cally said, "I'll walk out with him. And any fair-minded woman in this room will walk with me."

I stood up. What I wanted to say was, "Those of you opposed to my innocent presence here are cordially invited to suck my undershorts." But what I far more wisely did say was, "I am deeply embarrassed by the commotion I've inadvertently caused here. I'm interested in women's issues and women's studies programs and that alone explains my presence."

I spoke directly to Diane and said, "Thank you for supporting me. I would certainly leave if I were voted out, but such a vote would inevitably leave some people feeling unhappy no matter how it turned out. So I think the best course is for me to just withdraw and ask that all the rest of you remain and have a productive session. I'm sure that someone can fill me in on the highlights at a later time." I made a slight bow and edged my way toward the door. What I wanted to say to the blonde was, "Fuck you."

What I wanted to say to the audible mutterer was, "Fuck you with a Buick."

Outside I did say, "And furthermore, my undershorts are too good for you." But there was no one to hear, of course.

That afternoon Cally, Red, Virginia and I played a ragged game of volleyball on a snow-slicked court in the lodge's courtyard. There were few Fellows out and about, but every few minutes we managed to harass someone into batting the ball with us for a while before the cold drove him or her away. Red kept us passably warm with the flask of brandy he had in his jacket. He was a marvelously inept player who cheated with admirable honesty. "I get to add two points to our score because I thought to bring the brandy," he declared several times a game. Or, "I'm afraid that one's going to have to go against you, Rich. It was in, but I thought it was going to be out and so didn't play it."

Lanky Virginia was quite a good player: agile and strong. But Cally was the real volleyballer of the group. She knew words like "dig" and "set" and "spike" and moved for each ball with grace and precision. "I've played before," she explained when I complimented her skill. I spent most of my time freezing to death. When I finally lost all feeling in my little finger, I insisted that we quit.

"Fine. But that's an extra one thousand points for my side," Red contended.

Sitting on the sofas in the lobby, we entertained ourselves with nonsense chatter. I told Cally she was so good at volleyball that she ought to have her number retired.

"You can hand your shirt to me any time you want," Red offered. "And speaking of retirement, I should announce my retirement as a math professor and my debut as a comic. I'm sure you all will want to be in attendance at the talent show tonight when I launch my new and spectacular career."

The talent show was evidently a tradition at the final year conference. Fortran officials had been talking it up since we first arrived. Anyone who could sing or dance, read a poem or a short story was encouraged to participate. Those requirements left me out. My nonacademic talents were restricted to games involving balls. Red, I thought, was remarkably courageous. Nothing seemed to me more daring than standing before a crowd with the announced intention to make them laugh.

The show began shortly after the evening session. We all helped to set up the room like a nightclub. A portable bar was placed against the wall. Virginia and Cally and I were seated at a front row table when Red came in dressed like Bozo the Clown. I laughed just looking at him. Red seated himself with us to watch the opening acts. There was an extra beer on the table, and he reached for it, but I snatched it away from him. "No drinking before the show, Clarabelle," I told him. "I don't want you stepping on all your own lines." I wasn't really serious, but Red must have been nervous because he agreed that I was probably right.

The first number was by a Fellow from North Carolina. He sang an original song he called "The Still Talking Fortran Blues," which was a send-up of the Fortran Foundation. It was received with stomping, cheering and finally a standing ovation. Next came a modern dance by a female Fellow from Michigan. She was followed on stage by one of the Foundation's leaders, a hairy-legged, round-chested man wearing a long blond wig, a silver, sequined evening gown stuffed in the chest with what appeared to be basketballs and a long feather boa which dangled to the floor from either side of his thick neck. He lip-synced to a record of "Let Me Entertain You," swaying and swirling in a pouty-mouthed imitation of Marilyn Monroe. We were slack-jawed with laughter at this performance by a man we had all seen for the years of our association with the Foundation in the guise of a quiet, self-effacing administrator. As the song ended, off came the slippers, the gloves and the dress, leaving the performer in the wig, a stuffed undershirt and striped boxer shorts. People were on the floor.

And our friend Red had the great misfortune to be the next act. His plight was perhaps analogous to mine in having to follow you, Dr. Burden.

"There's an old rule of show business," he said in opening. "Never try to follow children or dogs or Fortran officials doing striptease." That got him a warm response, but afterwards he struggled. His material really wasn't so bad, but the acoustics were poor and after the broad humor of the striptease, Red didn't have a chance.

He was understandably dejected when he came back to our table. The three of us each assured him he'd been a knockout, but he knew better. Cally was so effective, though, that she took the sting out of his wound. She laughed when he arrived at the table and kissed him, smearing herself with his makeup. She told him which jokes to do away with and which ones to be sure to keep. She gave him firm evidence that she took the whole business of being funny quite seriously. She was solicitous without being condescending; she consoled without being consoling.

In a word she was marvelous.

It was the last night of my Fortran Conference, easily the best I'd ever attended, though that fact probably had more to do with me than with the conference. I felt a surge of affection for my companions, those at my table and all the others in the hall. By midnight we were all pleasantly enough drunk that we seemed to one another like the best and brightest people in the world. Only in the backs of our minds did it register that tomorrow we would leave, likely never to cross paths again.

"I want to dance on the table top," Cally declared. "I always dance on the table top when I'm drunk."

"If you'll dance naked, I'll dance with you," Virginia drawled.

"I don't want to dance on the table top," Cally decided.

"I'll dance naked with you," Red offered.

"I don't want to dance naked on the table top," Virginia decided.

"I want to go for a walk by the lake," Cally declared.

"A perfectly insane idea," I said. "Shall we get our coats?"

"I'd rather dance on the table top," Red said.

"I'd rather Red dance on the table top," Virginia said.

"I really want to walk by the lake," Cally said.

"A perfectly insane idea," I said. "Shall we get our coats?"

Cally kissed Red and Virginia and ran upstairs for her warm clothes. I started to leave for mine but Red grabbed my arm. "Hey, tall fellow, we may not be here when you get back." He put a joint in my hand. "In as often as you smoke this, do so in remembrance of me."

"Good old Red," I said. I slapped him on the back.

"Easy, tall person," he said.

I kissed Virginia and went upstairs for my sweatshirt and jacket.

A Lake Michigan beach on a November night is not exactly ideal for strolling. The wind screamed off the lake so loudly that talking was fruitless. After a short distance, I began to lose feeling in the skin over my cheekbones. But the roar and bite of the night were in odd contrast with the calm, clear sky overhead, which seemed as still and hopeful as a night in June. I huddled my head down inside my jacket and lit Red's joint. Wordlessly, I handed it to Cally. Like two Powhatans before the coming of the white man, we passed the little stick of smoke back and forth between us. Under the twinkling umbrella of sky, we bore on against the swirling wind until each of us knew, without even a touch of communication, that it was time to return.

When we got back to the lodge, we went into an orgy of stomping and rubbing ourselves. It was as if outside we had been in a dream, but now awake we were a burst of activity. "I like the cold," Cally said. "I like to feel the numbness attach itself to my finger and toes. And I like knowing that there's a warm place waiting where I can rub myself and feel the sensation return."

I put my arm around her and pulled her toward me. She laid her head against my shoulder. "You know, you said exactly the same thing to me when we went on the nature hike. When was that? Yesterday or the year before?" Cally shrugged against me as if I'd asked her a question she couldn't answer. "I know when it was," I said. "It was when I first knew how much I liked you."

"Then I'll say it again," she said. And she did. She slipped her arm around my waist, and we walked from the lodge entrance to the banquet room, which was now dark.

"I can't even offer you a last beer, my friend," I said.

"It's just as well. If I had anymore to drink, I would dance naked on the table for you."

I laughed. "Excuse me while I run into Zion to find an open liquor store." Cally rubbed her hand up and down my side.

In the elevator, I pushed the button for three. When the doors opened, she stepped off ahead of me and turned. I blocked the doors with my foot. Her face was flushed, her eyes teary from the wind. I smiled and brushed with the back of my hand at the smear of Red's makeup that still clung to her cheek.

"I'm afraid," she said, "that tonight you've taken me higher than I intended go."

"Only because," I said, "it's the only ritual we have." I bowed slightly, slid my foot from in front of the door and let myself be closed off alone.

In my hot room, I peeled off my coat and sweatshirt, opened the glass door to the balcony and stepped outside. I was beyond now merely imagining that Cally was on her balcony above me. I was beyond merely imagining that she was somehow thinking of me. As I stood there in the wind, I was praying for it.

Inside, I stripped to my shorts and went into the bathroom. I brushed my teeth. I studied my ruddy face in the mirror. I was twenty-eight years old. I wasn't in the movies or a professional baseball player. I wasn't a lawyer who could cancel tennis games because he had to be in court. I wasn't an historian and probably wasn't going to become one. I was nearly thirty years old and had a crush like a teen-ager. And the woman was married. I shook my head, wondering who it was that I stood watching in the mirror. I laughed my tiny dry laugh and flicked off the light.

Then I heard the hesitant knock on my door. My breath caught in my throat. I knew who it was, and I knew exactly what I was going to say, had been planning the words for the next moment, I think all my life. I opened the door. Cally stood in the hall, barefoot on the red carpet. She was wearing an ankle-length, white flannel nightgown, checked with small pink squares out of which grew light green plants sprouting tiny yellow flowers. Her curly hair was wet and left spreading damp spots on her shoulders. Her cheeks were extraordinarily pink from having been rubbed, I guess, to remove the clown's makeup. She stepped into the room shivering.

"I came down here, Rich," she said.

"What took you so long?" I said. There, I'd said it. I planned it for years and got my chance and said it.

It's a miracle she didn't flee from the room screaming.

"You knew I was coming?"

"I only hoped you were coming with all my heart, hoped it so much that I planned exactly what to say if you did."

"I couldn't sleep."

"I didn't try." I stepped closer to her. She looked up at me and smiled. When I put my arms around her waist, I could feel her naked body tense, if only slightly, under her gown. "Cally…."

"Don't say anything, Rich." She put her arms around my neck and laid her damp head against my chest. I kissed the top of her head. We stood there like that a long time, not moving, neither of us speaking. Finally, she turned her face up to me, and I kissed her. I gathered her nightgown up around her waist and ran my hands over the curve of her buttocks.

"I like you, Cally Martin," I said. Her laugh was perfect. Like the rustle of backyard trees on an evening in early spring. Her face—I was so close now—had little flaws: a mole, a small blemish at the point of her chin, a scar, perhaps from the chicken pox. Her face was perfect. She reached behind her and gathered her nightgown and pulled it up over her head.

I squeezed her as if she were a lifeline and I a drowning man. She rubbed her face in a circle slowly against my chest.

And I began to cry.

I took a deep breath, because what I had to say next was so very difficult. "I'm not going to make love to you, Cally. I want you. I want you. Jesus, I want you."

"Because I'm married," she said, stating a fact, not asking a question.

"Because you're married and because you've had too much to drink. And mostly because I want you so much. If I make love to you now, I run the risk of ruining it, of becoming just a fling. But if I don't do it, then maybe you won't be able to forget." I stepped back to look at her. Skin like fine china. Large eyes. Small breasts on an agonizingly thin upper body. Surprisingly wide hips and thick thighs. "Jesus, I want you," I said.

I took the nightgown she had dropped to the floor and tied the arms around her neck and let the rest fall down between us, a curtain separating her nakedness from me.

"I can't go out like this," she said.

"I wouldn't let you go out," I led her to the bed and pulled back the covers. She slid between the crisp sheets. I turned off the lamp and drew back the curtains to allow the night's remaining starlight inside. I showered quickly and crawled into bed beside her.

"You're going to sleep with me, Rich?"

"Yes," I said.

"But you're not going to make love to me?"

"No."

"Because you're afraid you'd make me violate my principles."

"Yes."

"Are you the only man in the world who would do that?"

"How many others do you know so crazy?" She laughed and snuggled against me. I adjusted my arm under her head. We lay still for a long time and gradually Cally's breathing became deep and steady. Finally, I said, "You know, I'm abstaining for me too, though. I don't want you to think I'm so noble as to be able to resist you for just your principles. But mine, too. I can go home now and remember forever that you came to my room. If I made love to you, I'd have that memory sullied by the fact that I broke a promise I made to myself a long time ago."

Cally did not respond.

And I lay there in the ebbing night fashioning the smart-ass line to summarize this night in my journal: "The principled life is often unrelievedly hard."

A splash of sunlight awoke me the next morning. Cally was still sleeping against me. I stroked her hair to wake her.

"It's the day we leave," she said. "What time is it?" I took my watch from the lamp table next to the bed. It was ten o'clock. "I'm in trouble," she laughed suddenly. "I'm down in your room in only my nightgown." We lay in bed for a while. The stretch of her warmth alongside me seemed the privilege of a god. I offered to go up to her room and bring back her suitcase so she could dress.

She was in the bathroom when I returned. I opened her suitcase for her on the unused bed. She was wearing her nightgown when she came out. I watched her sift through her valise for a bra and clean underpants. She held them in her left hand and smoothed her green wool skirt on the bed with her right. She seemed hesitant. I could catch her glancing, occasionally, in my direction. Finally, she turned full to face me. "Haven't you ever seen a woman get dressed before?"

"I've never seen you get dressed before." She shook her head at me but smiled. She laid her blue turtleneck sweater on top of her skirt. It was the ensemble she'd worn the first day of the conference, the outfit I put on her whenever I think about her. She looked at me again, and I said, "Would you do me a favor, Cally? Would you get dressed in the bathroom?"

"Okay," she said. She laughed and regarded me quizzically. "Care to expound on that request?"

"If I see you take that nightgown off again, I might not let you put anything back on."

Dressed and packed, we carried our clothes bags downstairs, left them in the lobby and went to the dining room for a late breakfast. A final session was taking place elsewhere. I doubt that it occurred to either of us to attend. I remember Cally ordered a sweet roll and juice and that I settled for a cup of coffee which I didn't finish. And I remember that we talked quietly together.

But for the life of me I can't remember a single thing we said.

In a while we could hear the stirrings in the lobby that meant the first bus was loading to leave for the airport. It was the bus I had to take. Cally was staying the night with Virginia in her Hyde Park apartment. We stood together in the lobby facing each other, holding hands. I saw Rod the Bod walk by and leer at us as he headed for the bus. He tried to catch my eye, but I wouldn't acknowledge him. Red came over and patted my back. He told us some joke, and I let go of Cally long enough to clasp his hand. The bus driver called out that he would be leaving for O'Hare in three minutes. I pulled Cally against me. She was taller and thicker than Faith, and embracing her seemed an altogether new experience.

"Oh, Rich," she said.

I squeezed her hard enough perhaps to hurt. I could feel her chest heaving to breathe, but I didn't let her go. I had to squeeze her hard enough to last me a long time.

20

1975

J anus came to what he thought were his senses on the flight from Chicago
back to Los Angeles. The ache he felt for Cally Martin, he decided, was
the irresponsible longing of an unhappy and even cowardly man. Love
was not something which could spring to life in a long weekend. His feelings
for Cally, he told himself, were a demon which had to be exorcised. He must
not fool himself. By avoiding sex with Cally, he had not avoided sinning
against his marriage, for he had wanted her with a dangerous desperation.
And if she had suggested that he abandon Faith at that moment and forever,
he felt certain he would have done so. In fact, he thought, his appearance of
restraint was all facade. If Cally had questioned his grand gesture, even for a
moment, he felt sure he never would have followed through with it.

It was odd, he realized, his thinking of his feelings for Cally as sin. Sin was
not a term he ever used, not a concept whose existence he even exactly
acknowledged. But sin, he knew, best described the treachery of his wanting
another woman the way he wanted Cally Martin. He had promised his
fidelity to Faith long ago. It was a pledge made not so much to her as to
himself. Until now he had been true, but he had never before been really
tested. When tested, only his body showed strength; his spirit had proven very
weak, indeed. On his long flight home, he resolved a greater fidelity. He
could still make his marriage work. In his journal he wrote, "I must go and
sin no more."

Faith was determined to make that resolve difficult for him, however. She
seemed committed to shut him out of her life altogether. Well into her first
regular quarter of graduate work, she had become obsessed with the notion
that she was destined to do poorly. To flee this fear, she began to spend most

of her waking moments working. It was not enough for her merely to read the books for her courses; she insisted that she had to read them twice, had to sample additional literature about each topic before she attended her seminars. She developed a new threat against her husband, a new method to finger his ragged propensity for guilt.

"You *don't* want me to do well in school," she would storm. "You'll be secretly pleased if I fail. You've decided to fail yourself and could only be embarrassed if I managed to succeed." This attack Faith brandished whenever she felt that Janus was trying to thieve her of study time. Increasingly she resisted his trying to engage her in practically any kind of intercourse. She even used this threat to negotiate a new alignment of house duties which, lawyerlike, she required each of them to sign before she taped the agreement on the icebox door. And she used the threat to demand that they exchange work spaces.

"You don't need the privacy of the bedroom anymore. You've gotten to where you do most of your writing on that insane note down in the park anyway." Janus had to agree to the fairness of her being given the bedroom study space, since she was the one now in school. He thought it extreme, however, when she began to insist that he knock on the bedroom door before he entered any time she was studying. But she had taunted him, saying, "You promised me a room of my own. When are you going to be able to give it to me? Well, during the time I'm studying now, this *is* my room. And I want you to knock."

Janus didn't take all this goading calmly, of course. It wasn't part of his nature to do so. He stormed back. He yelled and cursed occasionally. But more often he tried to stay out of her way, sought to see that she was undisturbed and comfortable and without reason for irritation. He took to going to movies at the Nuart and the Fox Venice, where the double features of old and foreign films changed daily. In the month after he returned to Los Angeles from Zion, he saw forty-one films, an average of more than one a day.

He employed other strategies toward her as well. He read some of her textbooks and talked with her about them at mealtime or before bed. He offered to type papers for her. He donated his mornings for a routine of tutoring her in German. His own German, of course, was no great shakes, but he knew enough to coach her toward passing the ELS exam. The German study met with mixed success, though. It became the largest block of time they spent together anymore, but the teacher/student relationship which necessarily arose provided a fertile ground for resentment. Faith had become so unrestrained in her irritability toward him that these sessions regularly became unpleasant. Janus began to feel battered by the ceaselessness of her ill will. The

German lessons were a gift from him but were hardly received gratefully. He began to wonder if there was perhaps something masochistic about him, something sordid and sick that craved her hostility and thought it deserved.

About two weeks after his return from Zion, Janus tried to get Faith to sacrifice a Sunday morning's study for a hike into the Santa Monica Mountains. A friend had told him about a trail from Temescal and Sunset that led to an eroded boulder that hikers had dubbed Skull Rock. From Skull Rock one supposedly had a view of Santa Monica and the entire bay, on a good day, clear to Catalina and San Thomas.

But Faith wouldn't go. "You promised me that you wouldn't interfere with my studying," she complained.

It was only for a few hours, he pleaded. "And remember, when I was in graduate school, I had plenty of time to spend with you."

"Perhaps if you'd studied night and day like I do, you'd have finished instead of quit."

Janus felt the well of his anger begin to heat, and rather than allow it to boil over into still another ugly scene, he let the matter drop. But as his anger cooled away, it was replaced by despair. He and Faith had drifted so far apart that hopes for hanging on to each other seemed painfully thin.

A week later, the festering boil of their marriage came to a head.

Janus and Faith were both up early. Faith had washed her face and gone directly to her desk. Janus had dressed quickly in a sweatshirt and cutoffs and collected the Sunday *Times* from his doorstep, made a cup of instant coffee and settled into his chair to read and breakfast on sunflower seeds. It was Faith's new duty to make the concoction of juice and milk and honey they called Orange Jewels, but Janus harbored no great hopes she'd actually do it. She hadn't made it for the last four days. Twice he'd made it himself; twice he'd simply gone without. He resented the fact that she had made such a big deal of renegotiating and restructuring their house duties and then failed to perform hers.

He wasn't seething exactly when she came into the room, still wearing her nightgown, her unwashed red hair tied back in a blue bandana. But he was agitated. She opened the refrigerator and grabbed a Seven-Up. So she wasn't going to make the Orange Jewels.

Janus cracked down on a sunflower seed.

"Quit eating those while I'm in here," she said. Her voice was quiet but nonetheless biting. Janus snapped another seed, and she spun around on him. "Goddamnit, I said quit eating those while I'm in here."

"I'm hungry," he said.

"Fix yourself something to eat."

"I was hoping you might fix the Orange Jewels." Janus rustled his paper, loudly turning the pages. He hadn't looked at her yet.

"I don't want Orange Jewels," Faith said.

"I do," he said.

Faith took a swallow of her Seven-Up and belched. "Why should I fix them just for you?"

Janus was on his feet as if he'd been hoisted out of his chair by a catapult. He was livid. "Why should you goddamn make them? Because it's your goddamned house duty to make them. That's why, asshole."

"Eat shit, maniac," Faith said. She picked up her soda bottle and walked back into the bedroom, but Janus was all over her like a baseball manager in a dispute with an umpire.

"I want you to make the goddamn Orange Jewels, Faith. I got a piece of paper taped on the refrigerator out there that says that it's your house duty. Now get your ass out there."

"Sue me," Faith said as she sat at her desk with her back to Janus. He gritted his teeth and felt for the first time that he understood why husbands and wives sometimes kill each other. "Close the door on your way out," Faith said.

In a deliberately calm voice, achieved at the expenditure of perhaps more control than he knew he had, Janus said, "This is my bedroom, and I think I can stay here if I please."

Faith turned in her chair to look at him. "We agreed that this was my workroom now and that you'd leave me alone to study."

He plopped down on the bed, lay back and interlaced his fingers behind his head. "Yep," he said to the ceiling. "And we also agreed that we would alternate the cooking, that I'd do the vacuuming and the wash, clean the bathroom, make the bed, change the linens, pay the bills, empty the trash, and that you'd do the dishes, dust and make the goddamned Orange Jewels. So I do my chores, which by the way constitute one fucking lot more than fifty percent of the domestic duties. But you'd think that when the dust bowl blew out of Oklahoma in the 1930's, it blew directly to Santa Monica and settled in our apartment. Every dish in this house is dirty, and now you won't even make the Orange...."

"GET THE FUCK OUT OF MY ROOM!" Faith screamed.

"What have you been studying in here, anyway?" Janus said. "What vocal cords you've got. Here you've been taking voice lessons, and all the while I thought you were doing psychology."

"Get out of here, you derelict asshole."

Janus turned on his side and looked at his wife. "Fuck you," he said. He rolled back on his back and stared at the ceiling again.

But Faith was out of her chair and looming over him. "You'd like to fuck me, wouldn't you? How long's it been since you had a piece of ass, Janus?"

He refused to look at her. "Don't compliment yourself, Faith. I lost my desire for you shortly after the Great Flood."

"I'll bet you did. You haven't been laid in so long you'd fuck a dog if you could manage to turn it on."

"A dog might be an improvement," Janus laughed. He was so mad he thought he was going to cry. His eyes watered even as the sound of laughter came from his mouth.

"GET OUT OF MY ROOM, YOU SON OF A BITCH."

Janus sat up and stared at her. In anger, she was bent over from the waist, leaning slightly toward him. Speaking very precisely, he said, "Fuck you, Faith. Who are you to tell me to get out of my own bedroom? Just fuck you."

"I'm sick of your telling me that," she said.

"So do something about it."

"I will, asshole. You want to fuck me? Come on, fuck me." She yanked her nightgown up around her waist and pulled the front of her underpants down to reveal her pubic hair. "This what you want, asshole? This what you want?" She pulled her underwear off and thrust herself at him lewdly. She took the nightgown off and then with both hands at once rubbed her nipples erect. "Look, Janus, look how you've turned me on. Here I am now, the perfect woman for you: a big piece of meat. Why don't you fuck me now?"

"Jesus, you're sick," Janus said. "You can't even think up any new routines."

"What's the matter, big man? Is your prick limp?" When Janus didn't respond, Faith climbed on the bed beside him. She was still wearing the yellowed wool socks she wore instead of slippers. "Can't get it up any more, Janus?" She put a hand between her legs and rubbed herself. She put a finger inside and then rubbed it on his face and under his nose. "Hey, Janus, I'm ready now, FUCK ME."

He moved as if in slow motion. Rolling over on her, he pinned her arms and held her legs apart with his knees. He expected that she would struggle, even wanted her to struggle perhaps, but she didn't. Without speaking, she mouthed the words, "Fuck me." He let go of one of her arms carefully, guarding against an attempt to slap or scratch him, but she didn't resist. He unzipped himself, and when he entered her she was wet. He touched her clitoris, but she knocked his hand away and replaced it with her own. She rocked her hips against him as he thrust repeatedly into her, her swirling fingers at work steadily on herself. All the while each stared venomously into the face of the other. And even when they came, they both refused to close their eyes.

Janus did not collapse his weight on top of her as he usually did when they made love. He rolled away from her immediately onto his back and flung an arm across his face in profound dismay.

After long minutes, Faith said, "I wish I had syphilis and had just given it to you." When he did not respond, she said, "I find you repulsive." Janus shifted a pillow from under him to cover his head. He lay very still beside her. "You can't even make me come anymore. I have to do it myself."

Slowly he got up from the bed. At the dresser he gathered a jock, two pairs of socks, shorts and his green basketball jersey. From the closet he picked up his tennis shoes. He went back into the living room and dumped his athletic gear beside his chair. In the kitchen he put water on to boil and watched it simmer. The vapors rising from the pot seemed to drug him. When the first bubbles formed in the bottom, he poured the water over instant coffee and carried the cup to the living room chair, where he sat and turned through the rest of the pages in the paper.

After a while, Janus walked past the bedroom on the way to the bathroom. Faith still lay naked on the bed. The morning sun cut into the room at an angle that obscenely illuminated the lower half of her body and made the yellow socks on her feet seem to glow while leaving her upper body in shadow. Her rigid body, legs still splayed wide, was motionless. It was as if she had died.

But she saw him pass, evidently, and called out to him, "I've got something you ought to know, Janus. I've been sleeping with Kate."

As if he hadn't heard, he continued on into the bathroom, used it, and when he passed by her door again, didn't so much as glance in his wife's direction. "I've been sleeping with Kate, Janus. And I'm in love with her," Faith said. In the living room he changed into his basketball uniform. He put his sweatshirt back on over his jersey; his other clothes he abandoned in a pile near his chair. He searched the room absently a moment as if he might be forgetting something. Whatever it was never came to him before he left the house.

Richard Janus played in his basketball league that afternoon as if he were still in college. He was quick and graceful. Every pass he threw found its man. His shooting touch had its special soft magic. Gentle, feathery, all day long his shots touched nothing but net, dropping through the basket almost soundlessly without the thong of vibrating rim or even the rip of stretched nylon. On defense he was like a snake: poised, cocked, never seeming to move at all until his long arms suddenly flicked out to bat away a pass or snatch away a dribble.

After the game, which his team won easily, Janus stopped with his teammates in a bar near the Long Beach gym where they'd played. They drank pitchers of beer for a couple of hours, sharing yarns, teasing each other, slapping one another on the back or arm. Janus was fond of these men and wondered suddenly why his association with them was limited to basketball. Faith didn't like them much, of course, but that wasn't all of it. In his years in L.A., he just never considered socializing with them beyond their Sunday afternoon post-game beers. He'd have to change that in the coming days, he thought.

Driving home on the San Diego Freeway, he felt mildly chilled by the wind through the window, which whipped his stiff number thirty-four against his nipples, already chafed raw during the game. The salt in his shirt made them sting. The beer in his otherwise empty stomach made him giddily, strangely optimistic. He sang with the radio as he drove along, beating time to the music with his fingers on the steering wheel.

He was still whistling after he'd parked the car in front of their apartment complex and made his way through the perpetually blooming courtyard. When he stuck his key in the lock on his front door, it swung open from that slight pressure. The living room was a clutter of boxes.

Janus walked through the house. Many books had been shifted from the shelves he'd installed to the boxes which were stacked and scattered in each room. Faith's dresser drawers had been emptied, and many of the clothes from her closet were gone. Most of the kitchen utensils were still in place. On the dining table he found a note:

Dear Rich,

I've taken mostly just my clothes for now. I'll be back in the next few days to get books and other things. You can keep the furniture for now, though I'm going to get my desk as soon as I can arrange some help moving it. Can I count on you? I guess I'd understand if you'd prefer not to be home. I'd like to have the dining table, too, but we can decide all that later.

I'm afraid this isn't going to be too coherent.

I really wanted to wait to do this until after the quarter ended, but things have just gotten too much. You won't believe this, but I appreciate that you were letting me stay until then. I hoped that when I had some time at break we might have been able to talk, and I could have perhaps explained things a little.

I was really ugly this morning. I have been ugly to you on many occasions, I know. I don't even know if this was the worst. But please don't think this morning really had anything to do with my leaving. It didn't. It has made me leave today, perhaps, but I had to go some time. I'd already decided that, as you know.

I know you won't believe this either. And I can hardly blame you. But I don't really blame you for all this. In fact, what I remember and what I will remember are all the ways in which you were more than any woman could hope for in a man. I remember your gentleness. I remember your sense of humor. God, you and Johnnie used to make us laugh when we went to El Cholo. I remember your getting me the car and grading my papers for me and teaching me German. I remember all the trying you've done. I do remember all that. I remember you were willing to give up your job in St. Louis so I could take the one in Chicago. Most of all I remember how you loved me, you know. Jesus, that meant a lot. You were my best friend, Richie. You still are my best friend.

I really remember only two bad things. There were other things, but not so important. I guess I should tell them to you. You always say "explain things so I can learn from them." I don't really think you've been sympathetic to me as a graduate student. Though I do think you've tried. But you just never seemed to understand that working night and day is the only way I can do things. If I don't work, I start to panic. You could do things differently. You were always so calm and confident. But you should have let me do things my own way. You should have let me be me, in other words. I think you always thought that my manner of doing things was just a stubborn protest on my part against the right way of doing things, the way you did them.

The other bad thing, of course, is your quitting your career. I counted on you. And then suddenly you weren't a safety net anymore. But more, I resented your denying that I had supported you in school. Maybe all the facts and figures don't show that I supported you. But in my mind that's what I was doing, and that's what counts. I really think you wanted to hurt me that day. You were never mean like that before.

I've got everything I'm taking with me in the car now. I'll be at Kate's, but I don't think we should talk just yet. I think we'd probably just fight. It's true what I said to you this morning before you left. I have been sleeping with Kate. And I do love her. She's made me understand that for some women only a woman's love is right. That's true of me. That's why things couldn't ever work with you; that's why I know you're not to blame, why neither of us is to blame.

I've got to go now.

But there's one other thing I need to tell. Two things really. The first is that I never slept with Johnnie Golden. I was mean enough to tell you that I did and even to let you go on thinking I had. I hoped that would hurt you enough that you'd leave or throw me out. But he was your good friend, Rich. He'd never have slept with me even had I encouraged him, which I never did. The second thing I want to tell you, you won't believe most of all. It's that I still love you and that I'll always love you.

Faith

Janus put the letter back on the dining table. He walked around the house studying the boxes Faith had filled or half-filled. He opened the linen closet in the bathroom and then the medicine cabinet. He didn't know in particular what he was looking for.

He walked outside and sat on the front step. Two bees worked busily over a flower in the courtyard flower bed. On the sidewalk a long string of ants labored to and from a snail shell.

Back inside, Janus searched for the clothes he'd left by the chair earlier in the day. Faith had moved them to the laundry hamper in the bathroom. He left them there and piled his basketball uniform in on top. He showered quickly and dressed in clean cut-offs, sandals and a knit shirt.

He read Faith's letter again. He had imagined her leaving for years and had always wondered how he'd feel when she finally did. Heartbroken and crippled? He didn't feel that way now. Relieved? Yes, he guessed. Empty. Lousy to be sure. But mostly, he felt pensive. He wanted to figure out what the lesson was, for there was always a lesson, he believed. Surprisingly, he didn't feel angry. She loved him, she said. He'd doubted that. She loved him. He was glad. Wasn't it odd that something he'd feared for so long, something that was so wholly sad could provide him, in however qualified a way, with an occasion for a measure of joy? She loved him. If she said so at a time like this, then it must be true.

Janus put his sweatshirt on and walked to the picnic table at the corner of

Wilshire and Ocean. There, he wrote in his journal for a long time.

Janus didn't hear from Faith for two weeks, but after the quarter ended, she called and wanted to talk about arranging to get the rest of her belongings. "Just come and get them," he told her. "You've got a key."

"Well, it's not that easy," Faith protested. "I mean, there are things we have to discuss. What I take, what you keep."

"Take what you want," Janus said.

"Come on, Rich, I know this can't be fun, but we don't have to make it unnecessarily unpleasant."

It may not have been time yet, but Janus told her to come over. In the course of a long conversation, she tried to explain her decision to live with Kate. She'd talked to Kate a lot, about her doubts and fears, and Kate had helped her see how difficult it was for certain kinds of women to thrive in relationships with men. "We aren't strong enough; we lack the self-assurance to resist a man's natural tendency to dominate." Living with a woman, Faith maintained, was a much more naturally equal situation. Few women were instinctive dominators; most women were instinctively understanding. "You always insisted that I explain things, that I make myself clear in logical, rational terms. But Kate has helped me to understand why I was always so frustrated with you—because I felt deeply I was right about certain things, but I was unable to defend my positions when you attacked them. The thing about two women living together is that that kind of adversary relationship doesn't exist."

Janus might have argued with her, but he knew she'd just use the fact of his arguing as evidence that what she said was true. So mostly he listened, saddened, perplexed, amazed. And sometimes, he grudgingly admitted, enlightened. But Faith seemed to say things as if she'd been brainwashed. At the same time he recognized that she seemed more relaxed, articulate and self-assured than he'd ever seen her. She seemed happier, too.

Tentatively, he asked her about the sex. She was remarkably tolerant in her response, though in a condescending sort of way. "Men always want to know that," she laughed. Sex, she said, was, as with all people, a part of her new life. But it wasn't the central part, not even an important part. She laughed again, gently, and said, "That's hard for a man to understand, I think. What's important between me and Kate isn't the sex but the companionship, the calm and natural understanding of two people who don't question one another's equality."

"But, well…." Janus felt very uncertain of himself. "I thought a person sort of was or wasn't gay. Like…it's something you prefer, not something you just decide."

Faith smiled and let her face slip into composed somberness. She told him in college she'd had an affair with Cassie Sears.

Janus felt totally embarrassed by this revelation, monumentally foolish that he'd not even suspected. His embarrassment, he decided later, explained the nature of his response. He was angered but determined not to let Faith see it. Furthermore, if she'd had an affair with Cassie Sears and then lived with him, for a time happily, he knew, too, that she could have an affair with Kate Banford and return to life happily with him in the future. He had been numb for the two weeks she'd been gone; now he was on fire with a desire to have her back. He became obsessed with the notion that she was meant for him and that he'd be forever sorry if he didn't do his utmost to win her again.

The nature of the game had changed vastly, though, he knew, since he'd won her originally. He had to camouflage whatever disapproval he had of her present lifestyle or associates. He had to woo her with his acceptance, his patience, his vulnerability.

Quickly and to a remarkable extent, this new strategy worked. He and Faith became friends of a kind. They met for lunch; they went on a picnic in Palisades Park once; they went to movies occasionally; they talked on the phone. Faith continued to live with Kate, of course, but Kate was never a party to their outings, and they talked about her very little. That Faith would spend time with him, and that she confided her special liking for him, encouraged Janus to believe that his campaign was succeeding.

Buoyed, he took an even more radical step: he began to think about his dissertation. He'd been away from it so long that he couldn't just start in writing, but he really began working on it, reading his note cards and outlines. He could make some substantial progress, he decided, finish a chapter or two and then surprise Faith with his progress. Playing this trump card, he hoped, might get her all the way back.

In accordance with his renewed scholarly endeavors, he accepted an invitation to serve as the History Department's graduate representative on its Appointments Committee. This position was arranged by Warren Burden, Janus's doctoral advisor. Burden remained unaware that his protegé wasn't at work on his thesis, wasn't about to make an important scholarly contribution to his field. Earlier Janus had resented the fact that Burden had kept their relationship professional, that somehow they'd never managed to bridge the gap between professor and student to become genuine friends, but now he realized what a stroke of luck this distance was for him. A friend, Janus would have told about quitting. Burden, he'd never bothered to tell. That allowed him now to pick things up and appear at worst just slow.

To be sure, Janus battled misgivings about his decision to resurrect his academic pursuits. He felt no greater urge now to be an historian than he'd ever felt. He desperately hoped that two magical occurrences would take place in his life: first, that his dissertation would succeed in winning Faith back; second, that as soon as his thesis was finished, he'd be offered a job at a small liberal arts college where he'd never be expected to do anything but teach well. Janus still liked teaching a great deal.

It was a season of nervous energy for him. He tried to rekindle his enthusiasm for a piece of work he thought he'd put out of his life forever. He began his Appointments Committee work. He spent as much time as possible with Faith, and other nights, as a hedge against loneliness, with Danielle LeBlanc and Anne Norton. He bought them all lavish Christmas presents in a fit of generosity one night when he went shopping because all of the women had other plans.

Work on the crazy note of resignation ceased, but late at night Janus still wrote in his journal. "My wife sleeps with women," he wrote. "My wife leaves and says that she loves me, and I believe her. My wife has gotten me to do the unthinkable and resume my career. My wife is unbelievable. My wife is the wizard of odds."

21

A t the end of the fall quarter last year, I was asked to serve on the History Department's Appointments Committee. The "search committee," it is generally called. The search committee's mission, as y'all know, is to select nominees for vacant positions in the department, of which there are always frightfully too few. The nation may or may not be heading for depression, but the university teaching profession is already there. I am one of the depressed.

I was selected as the graduate representative on the search committee because of all the students considered, I was judged the brightest and best. "The most mature of our young scholars."

After an extended period of stagnation, I felt honored and eager to serve. I spent all my Christmas vacation reading the doctoral dissertations of the year's hopefuls, documents which in every case were intended as the bases for future books. My service on the search committee did require a bit of sacrifice. It curtailed my efforts to get my own dissertation, the basis for my future book, back underway; or, to put it a different way, it gave me a new excuse not to work on my dissertation. But the work I was not able to undertake was not undertaken with far more ease and considerably less guilt than the work I had not undertaken in the previous six months. Which gave me the breather that I'm sure I needed.

Working with the search committee gave me the opportunity to gauge the quality of theses which had actually been completed. It provided me with a standard by which to judge my own work. It offered me the chance to sit as nearly equal with men (not women) who had really become university professors, the chance to measure myself against them, the chance further to demonstrate to them my depth and breadth and strength of mind. It allowed me to impress them with my incisiveness and my wit and with my dedication to our mutual craft, which at times, of course, I have failed to possess.

I was feeling somewhat better about myself as the result of this work. I felt that I was getting in a good warm-up, rounding myself into top condition, and that when the search committee work was completed, I would burst forth in a frenzy of production on my thesis that would save my life (not to mention my wife). I was bolstered by every implication that I was in the process of becoming, that I was almost, that one day soon I surely would be, "one of us."

After guiltlessly reading away my Christmas vacation, immersed in the scholarship of bright, mature young men and women who made subtle distinctions on issues I cared not one whit about, I joined the professors for a crucial meeting of our committee. The field of candidates for the year's three vacancies was to be winnowed, and nominees were to be chosen. It was the first week of the bicentennial year.

I was prepared to make my contribution, for I had been able to identify the strongest candidate for each position. For our regular tenure-ladder appointments, these were bright, mature young men (not women) who used the language with greater precision than their competitors, who made the subtlest distinctions on issues I cared not one whit about, whose scholarship was the most rigorous. These were men, I assured myself, much like me.

The meeting got underway, and we quickly got down to the business of rejection. The candidates we rejected were dismissed most often as "pedestrian." For God's sake, run, don't walk. For some, however, was reserved the sop "interesting but small; we need a man of scope, of vision." On the other hand, a few were rejected as "too broad; the candidate has not demonstrated his abilities to do in-depth scholarship." And for a very few, the committee offered the commendation "shows potential, but not presently of our caliber." This last was awarded to several candidates who might be hired somewhere else, candidates who might ultimately emerge as "one of us" whether we liked it or not.

Finally, having selected the best and brightest candidate for each of our regular positions, we set a date for each to come to campus for an interview. We then turned our attention to the task of selecting a nominee for a one-year replacement position in nineteenth-century intellectual history. Richard Boeotian, as y'all know, was tenured in the position but had won a Guggenheim Fellowship to finance stimulating new research in Boston, which had developed naturally from leads uncovered in his book, *Bulls in a China Shop: Fabian Socialism Among the Boston Brahmins*. Professor Boeotian hoped that the Guggenheim would pave the way for a new book, tentatively titled *Bulls in a Closed Shop: Unionism Among the Boston Brahmins*.

The candidates to replace Professor Boeotian came down to two. The first was Frank Jobe, a fifty-four-year-old Vanderbilt Ph.D. who had resigned a tenured position at Alabama two years earlier due to emotional difficulties he suffered over the sudden death of his wife. The second was Anne Saxton, a twenty-seven-year-old Yale Ph.D. who was looking for her first job. To make a long story short, the committee voted to hire the woman, because, as Professor Boeotian, who acted as chairman, pointed out, "She's female. And we're under rather heavy pressure to hire some more of that persuasion."

You may remember, Dr. Burden, that I tried to make an argument that because our position was for one year only, and especially because Ms. Saxton had a postdoctoral fellowship available if she chose, that perhaps we should hire Professor Jobe and thereby provide him a lifeline for getting back into the profession he'd abandoned in a time of personal distress. I'm sure you remember how you sought to dissuade me from that view: "I share your concern for Mr. Jobe's situation, Rich, but in matters of hiring, just as in matters of promotion, we simply cannot take human considerations into account."

That's why history is classified as one of the humanities, I might have remarked with appropriate sarcasm. But, of course, I didn't.

The committee did not meet again until after the first candidate for one of our regular positions had come to campus for an interview. MacDonald Ford was our choice for the position in late nineteenth-century social history. A Fortran Fellow, MacDonald and I had met briefly at the final year conference at Zion. He was from Harvard and had just turned twenty-nine. His long, straight hair was not parted and was brushed straight back from his face. There was a studied carelessness about MacDonald Ford, a manner that indicated, I think, a preference for ponderous reflection over such details as clean fingernails.

The day of the interview he wore a plaid sports coat and gray trousers. His narrow striped tie had a crooked knot which he hadn't bothered to pull snug against his neck. I'm sure he chose his attire as a compromise between formal and casual, but he was still the only person in the room with a tie of any kind on. Even Boeotian, who normally wore suits, was dressed that day in slacks and a pullover sweater.

Ford was a chain smoker; he lit up even during the meal that preceded the interview. And yet, he struck us as completely calm. He had that marvelous Boston accent in which he bantered with wit, thrusted with rapierlike sharpness, parried with chivalry. His voice dripped with tradition and money.

MacDonald Ford impressed us all with his depth and breadth and strength of mind. He answered questions with confidence and occasionally with respectful, winsome levity. Questions which neither he nor anyone, including the asker, understood. Questions designed to display the intelligence of the asker rather than to elicit information from the respondent. And MacDonald Ford had plans for future research projects which developed naturally from leads uncovered in his dissertation, which he'd titled *The Blue Movement: An Examination of the Philadelphia Police Force as a Vehicle for Social Mobility, 1880-1890.* MacDonald Ford was unquestionably "one of us."

Wasn't he, Dr. Burden? "He's one of us," you proclaimed to the members of the committee when we convened to assess Ford's interview. "I am thoroughly impressed with this candidate's depth and breadth and strength of mind. Unquestionably, he's one of us." You didn't realize, of course, that your statement of enthusiasm made me uncomfortable, for I was not a professor. And I had not yet finished not writing my dissertation.

But you went on, "His research is brilliant. I think we're all agreed on that. He's already published two of his thesis chapters in the *Journal of American History.* And Oxford has contracted to take the entire book." You smiled at each member of the committee, including me, before continuing. "And leads uncovered in this project have suggested to him the stimulating new research needed on Philadelphia firemen. This man is a rare find. Is there any question that he's one of us?" Your gaze shifted from face to face, carefully making eye contact with each. I wasn't sure you'd seek your unspoken consensus in my face as well, so I lowered my eyes to my notes.

You were always an enigma to me, Dr. Burden. Did you know that? I suspected you at times of being intentionally inscrutable. People often say we look alike, I suppose, because we both have beards. You're thinner, though. And I'm taller. In class, you never hesitate to voice your aggressive sympathy for the plights of minorities, poor people and women. It was this concern which first attracted me to you. You display it in your undergraduate lectures, which I attended purely for their eloquence. And you display it in your scholarly work, which you term the history of the inarticulate. And in your politics, which are Marxist. And in your lifestyle, which is nonmonogamous. And in your dress, which is the garb of a counterculture that has all but ceased to exist, preserved primarily in the formaldeyhydic halls of academe.

Surely you know of your reputation for being deliberately distant. With most students, you maintain a rigorous formality, always addressing them as *Mr.* Smith or *Ms.* Jones. I know no tales that depict you as having ever been outwardly rude to a student. But you do create a certain atmosphere during your office hours that makes students very efficient at conducting their business and taking their leave in as short a time as possible. I think it's your habit of fidgeting. You tap a foot or gnaw your nails or drum your fingers. Time and again you reach inside a faded jean pocket and pull out your gold watch, which you open with an upward flick of your thumb and close immediately with a snap. Thus students are convinced that they must be detaining you from some pressing task, which is far more important than whatever question or piece of advice they wanted to ask.

But you were always friendlier to me than to most students, for reasons that I never fully understood. Somewhere along the way, I did something that impressed you, and evidently you never forgot it. You became my mentor and in many ways my guardian angel, helping me to procure teaching fellowships, travel grants and appointments to the departmental search committee. I appreciated your support, you know, and for a time I wanted to be just like you. But our relationship stalled out short of the haven of friendship where failings can be forgiven. And unfortunately you let me see you close up enough so that you could not remain my hero.

I greatly appreciated it when you paid me $100 to review manuscripts you'd been hired to judge for publication. And I tried to believe it justified when I discovered that the publishing houses paid you $150 for the services I rendered. I couldn't count it justified, however, when you agreed to write a letter of recommendation for a friend of mine and then wrote one so tepid and qualified that it did him more harm than good. And I simply hated it when you failed to support Max Blanton for tenure because Max's book, though published by the University of California Press, "was finally rather disappointing." Max was your friend, goddamnit. And you screwed him. I know you think you stood up for principle, but you screwed him. And somewhere, deep inside you, you know it.

So that's why I couldn't join you, Dr. Burden, in your rush of enthusiasm for MacDonald Ford, even though I shared your judgment that he was very, very good. But I admit now with consummate shame that I averted my eyes from yours that day, as you sought acknowledgment that MacDonald Ford was "one of us," not because I feared your gaze would next flicker, beamingly, to mine, but because I feared it wouldn't.

I can imagine the outraged astonishment that will spread across your face when you read this. Now, if only I can harness my outrage one day so as to put it in the mail.

The second scholar to come for an interview was Bryan Jennings. You remember—he was the candidate for our position in American Indian history. The committee was lukewarm about Jennings's application, because Bryan Jennings had gotten his Ph.D. at the University of Nebraska at Omaha. And his dissertation, *James Logan and the Delaware Walking Purchase: An Ethnohistorical Perspective,* was sought for publication not by Harcourt or Norton or Oxford but only by the University of Oklahoma Press, and they were requiring substantial revisions.

I took a special interest in Bryan Jennings's candidacy. He was in my field and thought about issues I cared at least one whit about. He, too, was about my age. He had thick, curly black hair which hid his ears and the temples of his wire-rimmed glasses, which he seemed to have difficulty keeping properly in place.

The day of his interview, Bryan Jennings wore a brown corduroy sports coat and plaid pants and had his broad striped tie pulled snug at the neck. Unlike MacDonald Ford, he did not smoke. Unlike MacDonald Ford, his hands shook when he talked, and his voice, which contained the slightest hint of a lisp, cracked occasionally when with neither confidence nor wit he sought to answer questions that neither he nor anyone, including the asker, understood. Sadly, he had not developed a single new research project from leads uncovered in his dissertation. Bryan Jennings failed to impress the committee with his breadth and depth and strength of mind, despite the fact that he was the best and brightest of the applicants for our job.

Hence, in the interval between the morning interview and the afternoon committee session, I was asked to accompany Bryan Jennings to lunch. You took MacDonald Ford to lunch, you'll recall, Dr. Burden.

"This is really an exciting place," Bryan Jennings enthused to me over his poorboy sandwich. "Such a stimulating intellectual community. Such a challenging group of scholars to work with. You know, I read that piece Warren Burden did for the *William and Mary Quarterly* on the Boston working class. It was such a fine piece. Quite useful for my own work, interestingly. Who better qualifies for inclusion among the inarticulate than the American Indian?" Bryan smiled and took a large bite of his sandwich. "You must really love it here," he said politely, covering his full mouth with his napkin.

"Well," I said. This was difficult. I was practically positive the committee was going to reject his candidacy. How did I go about preparing him for it? "There are a lot of bright people here, but I'm not so sure I'd term the place a community. The department is riddled with political divisions and personal jealousies. As David Halberstam might say, the brightest people aren't always the best."

Faith has always maintained that when pushed I can be as pompous as the next asshole.

"Of course," Bryan Jennings said. "But that's true wherever you are. I can't imagine many places I'd rather work than here. This school is at the cutting edge of the important work in social history." Bryan Jennings's glasses slid down to the end of his nose. He took them off and ran a hand over his face and up through his curly hair. Then looking skyward in an unabashedly prayerful way, he said, "This is really the place for me. Among men who are genuinely committed to studying the forgotten man, women, the poor man, Indians, the common man."

Neither of us spoke for a moment after that. Finally I asked him how he'd gotten into history, if he'd grown up planning on becoming an historian.

Bryan Jennings laughed. "I'm your classic late starter. When I started college, I had no idea what I wanted to do. I just took classes at random. I wasn't a very good student. I just sort of drifted along forever on the verge of dropping out. If I hadn't been so afraid of the draft, I'm sure I would have. I took a lot of science courses for a while and thought about becoming a nurse. I would have thought about medicine, but I figured out early on that I could never get into medical school."

"How did you finally make the move into history?" I asked. "Did you finally have a good professor who told you that you were cut out for scholarship?"

Bryan Jennings laughed again as if I had just told him a joke. "Gosh, no," he said. "I was always such a poor student there was never a professor who'd have had reason to encourage me. My undergraduate professors would be absolutely shocked that I'm even being considered for a job at UCLA." He punched his glasses back up on his nose again. "My senior year in college, I read *Black Elk Speaks*. I was fascinated by the world of Indian thought. I had to understand it. I've been trying to ever since."

"Why did you choose to do your graduate work at Omaha?"

To this question, Bryan Jennings laughed especially hard. "Hell, it was the only school I could get into. They don't even have an Indian historian there. I had to learn the field by myself."

I assured him that he'd done a pretty good job of that and confided that he was the only candidate we had decided to interview. But then suddenly I remembered again that I needed to find a way to prepare him for bad news. "I'm sure if they fund the position that you'll get it," I said. I had found the lie I was looking for.

Bryan looked startled. "The position might not be funded?"

I worried that I might get caught out in this deception, but it was too late to backtrack. "Yes, sadly, as I understand it, funding has recently become an issue. I don't want to alarm you; I was just trying to say that I think finances are the only thing standing in your way."

He raised his eyes skyward again. "Please let there be funding."

"I hope there will be," I said. "I think you deserve this job." And that was the truth. But, of course, you disagreed, Dr. Burden.

"He just isn't one of us," you said that afternoon when the search committee convened. You reached in your jeans to find your pocket watch, promptly opened it with an upward flick of your thumb and just as promptly closed it with a snap.

"Well, his thesis shows potential," Richard Boeotian said. "But I was awfully disappointed with his answers to our queries. Sadly, he hasn't developed a single stimulating new research project from leads unearthed in his dissertation. That's really disturbing, when one thinks about it."

"Really, Dick," Samuel Haddock, our diplomatic historian said. "I find his work irredeemably pedestrian. And he's gotten his training at Omaha of all places. Is it possible he could have learned anything there?" Haddock laughed and said, "Can anyone remember why we decided to interview him in the first place?"

You certainly couldn't remember, Dr. Burden. "He just isn't one of us," you concluded, drumming your fingers on the table. "And I cannot vote to recommend his appointment. The American Indian field is an important one, but it's a young one, too. If Bryan Jennings is the best and brightest Ph.D. the field has to offer at the present time, then I think we should wait until the field produces a better one."

You raised your eyebrows and shifted about in your chair before going on. I remember well, because what you said next was so shocking. "And I think this very room may contain the man we're looking for." That's when you reached over and drummed your fingers on my knee. "This young gentleman," you said, meaning me, "is one of us. And he's at work on a dissertation of absolutely first-rate promise. Rich has been serving us as a teaching fellow, as you know. I think we can trust him to handle himself in the classroom. I move we seek permission from the dean to hold the regular position in abeyance and that we offer Mr. Janus a Visiting Assistant Professorship for next fall. I think I can speak for Rich when I say that he'll be eager to accept."

You had to speak for me at that moment, Dr. Burden, because I couldn't have uttered a sound had my life depended on it. I felt like B.F. Johnson the day in junior high he stood mute and seemingly dazed before a furious vice-principal, who had caught him peeking into the faculty women's restroom where he saw Sally Brisket, her scoop-necked blouse down around her waist, standing at the lavatory soaping under her arms, her large, pendulous breasts just grazing the top of the cool porcelain.

"I knew I was doin' wrong," B.F. later explained. "But it was so beautiful, it was like it wasn't wrong at all."

Professor Boeotian asked me to wait in the hall while the committee considered your proposal. I could see the darkness outside the windows. I gathered my blasphemous notes and walked into the abandoned corridor outside the meeting room. In less than a minute, you swept out beside me. "Done, old man," you said, slithering out a hand for me to shake. And then you added, "If I were you, I'd give that thesis a big run in the next nine months. You're going to be a busy young man come next fall." With that, you were off at a brisk place toward the elevator at the center of the building. I walked in the opposite direction, toward the exit sign at the head of the stairway. I opened the door and started down.

I had been at UCLA for nearly four years. In all that time of passing through the Sculpture Garden behind Bunche Hall, I had never paused to look at the statues. It was time. I came out of the history building and into the late winter moonlight. For a long time I looked at Francisco Zuniga's *Desmudo Reclinada.* And then at Henry Laurens's *Esquisse D'Automne.* I liked Jacques Lipshitz's *The Song of Vowels.* My favorites were Gaston Laschaise's *Standing Woman* and Auguste Rodin's *The Walking Man.*

Leaving the Sculpture Garden, I boarded the bus to return to my empty apartment in Santa Monica. I had no one to tell my news, no one to help me decide how to judge it. Around me in the bus, other solitary figures clutched their briefcases and hunched with long faces in the stiff plastic seats. We made our way through downtown Westwood and then out to Wilshire. The night was still clear enough in West Los Angeles. But as soon as the sun goes down in winter, the fog begins to creep off the ocean until by late evening it covers all Santa Monica. We were headed directly toward the bay. Past the Brentwood Twins at 26th street. *The Sailor Who Fell From Grace with the Sea* was in Cinema One. In Cinema Two was *Bound for Glory.* Past the porno house, where *Beyond Fulfillment* was playing. Past Yale Street. Past Harvard Street and Princeton and Berkeley.

At 24th, the driver stopped for a drunk who was reeling against the bus stop pole, carrying a bottle of wine in a brown paper bag. He was wearing a khaki shirt and pants that once had matched, the trousers badly patched at the knees. His faded, tattered plaid sports coat was flecked with pieces of dried grass as was his long, filthy, matted hair. He staggered up a step or two of the bus but then lost his balance and rushed back out to keep from falling over. The driver waited patiently for him to make another attempt to board, but he took a long drink from his bottle and waved the bus on. "Aw, fuck it," he said. As we pulled away, he turned his face up toward the window where I sat staring at him. I could see him clearly in the pale blue white of the street light. Under a scraggly, matted beard was a face I knew. Johnnie Golden's face. It wasn't Johnnie, of course. I knew it wasn't Johnnie. It couldn't have been Johnnie.

We rode on and were swallowed by the fog.

22

1976

When Richard Janus got home from the search committee meeting at which he was offered a full-time position at UCLA, he called Faith and asked her to come over. She couldn't, she said, not even when Janus said he had something important to tell her. She was sorry, but she and Kate had plans, she said. She'd be glad to meet for lunch tomorrow.

Janus was tempted to just blurt his news out over the phone, to just tell her and then demand that she come back to him immediately because he'd so miraculously solved the major problem that stood between them. But he didn't. Because he knew, on one hand, that their problems went much deeper than his career disarray. And because, on the other hand, he felt a strange lack of euphoria over what had been offered him. Had this stroke of good fortune befallen him back in December when he resumed work on his dissertation, he would have thought that he was the luckiest man in the world. But now in the first week of March, his attitude was uncertain. He wanted to *talk* to Faith as much as he wanted to exult to her.

Since the winter quarter had begun, Janus had finished the introduction and conclusion of his thesis and had written about half of the first chapter. The work was torturously slow, and Janus had still failed to ignite within himself the spark of enthusiasm he would need to keep his work from becoming drudgery. He had planned on showing Faith the progress he had made when the first full chapter was complete. With the news today, he figured it was no longer necessary to wait. He was going to make it as an academic after all. But he couldn't shake the gnawing feeling that he was being trapped. What he'd admitted to himself nearly a year before was still true: he didn't want to be an historian.

He couldn't tell Faith all this over the phone, so he agreed to meet for lunch the next day.

After an initial upswing in his hopefulness about getting Faith back, Janus had begun to doubt that he would finally be successful. At times he wanted her back with an intensity that was overwhelming.

"I must want her back worse than anything," he wrote in his journal. "I'm doing my fucking dissertation for her, am I not?"

But at other times, occasions such as the moment he wrote these lines, he wondered if he really wanted her back at all. He was very lonely living by himself. He missed the presence of someone else just to share the comings and goings of the day with. "I think even boredom is more tolerable," he wrote in his journal, "if you have someone to be bored with." But he wondered if it was so much *Faith* he missed as it was that he didn't like living alone. He sometimes felt that his life was actually better than it had been because it was free now of the storms of acrimony that had lashed so much of his marriage. "On the whole," he wrote to himself, "boredom is probably preferable to war."

In the end, Janus didn't know. He didn't know how he felt or why he seemed to feel so different from one moment to the next. This hour he desperately missed his wife; the next hour he wondered if her leaving him weren't a very special blessing. "I think I'm all fucked up," he wrote in his journal.

He felt particularly confused the night he received his offer of a Visiting Assistant Professorship. He really *needed* to talk to someone, to share with someone the turmoil of his emotions. He was vaguely angry that Faith had not sensed his need and responded to it. "I possess the ability," he later wrote, "to blame Faith for practically anything."

After talking to her, Janus wandered around his apartment like a caged animal. Whatever room he found himself in seemed unsuitable for whatever he was doing. "There's just no proper place," he wrote in his journal, "for doing nothing."

It was just after seven o'clock. He considered going to bed. He had spent a massive amount of time sleeping since December, but he found that whereas he could sleep late in the morning or take naps in the afternoon, he could not go to bed early in the evening—not even on occasions like this one, when falling asleep would provide him with an escape from his aimless restlessness.

He thought of calling Paul Taylor. One thing he could always count on from Paul was a sympathetic ear. After Faith had moved out, he'd called, and Paul had flown down to see him the following weekend. In January Paul had mailed him a PSA ticket to the Oakland Airport and had insisted that Janus fly up for a visit. But Janus knew essentially what Paul would say: "Tricks, man," he could hear Paul telling him, "why don't you just shuck this academic shit like you should have a long time ago and get about doing something important?" And Janus would tell him that this was serious and that Paul's little imperatives failed to take account of the complexity of the situation. And Paul would say, "Tricks, if the job's what you want to do, then you should take it and be glad you got it. But if the job isn't what you want to do, then you should pass and thank God for the good sense to do that."

"The problem with Paul Taylor," Janus wrote in his journal, "is that he makes things so goddamn clear he's no help to you at all."

Janus considered calling Anne Norton and asking her out for a drink. They'd been out several times since he and Faith had separated. Janus often found Anne attractive, and when things were working between them, they had fun together. Oddly, they almost always concurred on matters of historical interpretation, but they talked about history too much. Not academic chess, as Janus liked to term a certain intellectual gamesmanship, but still they spent long evenings talking about books or articles that were important in their field, or about personalities and politics in their department.

Underlying their relationship, Janus knew, was a competitiveness that he hated. It would flare sometimes when they talked, rising suddenly to a sharp edge of determined disagreement over very minor matters. There were never "scenes," nothing at all like that. Everything was entirely pleasant. But there was a stubbornness present sometimes that boded ill for a serious relationship, a stubbornness that he tended to blame on Anne but recognized that he was probably equally responsible for. "The problem with seeing things from my perspective," he wrote in his journal, "is that it inhibits me from seeing things so clearly from the perspective of others."

There was a quality about Anne, in other words, that reminded Janus of Faith. She was attractive and quite sexy, and he'd been repeatedly tempted to take her to bed, a temptation he'd intimated to Faith that he had succumbed to. But he hadn't. He hadn't, because in the final analysis, he wasn't even sure he liked her. And though he knew he could manage to sleep with her, he wasn't so sure he could handle waking up with her.

So finally Janus decided to call Danielle LeBlanc, his actress friend. He'd spent a lot of time with her, too, since his separation, and the affection he'd always felt for her had grown into closeness.

"Guess who's got the El Cholo Feeling," he said when Danielle answered the phone.

"Johnnie Golden, you old scoundrel," Danielle said, "and here I'd thought you'd dried up and blown away."

"Guess again, sugar tits," Janus said.

"I just love it when you talk dirty. Do you know any words that start with F?"

"Frantic," Janus said. "Fulmination. Foolish. Fist. False."

"Oh, please don't stop," Danielle whispered.

"Farther. Farm. Fast. Famous. Fable."

"Oh, I just can't stand it."

"Famished," Janus said.

"You'd better pick me up quick then," Danielle advised.

The El Cholo they entered forty-five minutes later was vastly different from the tiny restaurant Johnnie Golden had first taken them to. The remodeled waiting room was huge, and there were plenty of seats so that few customers had to stand anymore. The wait had been reduced to only half an hour or so. The food was slightly more expensive, but it was just as good, and the margaritas remained the best in the world. Janus and Danielle ordered a pitcher as they talked.

They talked about Danielle's ever-stumbling career and about the fact that Janus had started working on his dissertation again. Inevitably, they talked about Faith.

"She still loves you, you know," Danielle assured him.

Janus laughed. "Like a brother," he said. "That's what she tells me. 'I do love you, Bubba. You're the brother I never had, and you always will be.'" He snorted and refilled his margarita glass.

Danielle reached over and took his hand, a gesture she often made when they talked. "Oh, Rich. Please don't be so unhappy. I used to love the good times we had when we came here."

"It's just that she drives me crazy. All the time we're together. Sometimes she loves me, sometimes she never loved me. Which is true?"

"Both," Danielle said.

"You're a big help."

"I have this theory about Faith. I'm the sort of person who is very consistent to my convictions. It's just that they don't last too long. They change depending on the opinions of the last person I talked to. Faith isn't like that, though some people may think so. Her convictions are strong and enduring. It's just that she has a lot of them, and she's never been able to deal with the fact that they're contradictory."

Janus smiled. He patted Danielle's hand and said, "Ah, Daniella, my good old pal. You're a reservoir of untapped wisdom and insight." He took a cigarette from her pack, lit it and blew out a cloud of smoke. "You know, maybe the problem between men and women is sex. Maybe if we could all just be friends and eliminate sex, everything would be so much better."

"You really believe that?" she said.

Janus nodded gravely, exhaling another puff of smoke. "Sometimes."

"I thought the problem was too little sex, not too much."

"That too," Janus said, and they both laughed.

Their table was ready, and they followed the hostess into one of the dining rooms. Janus ordered another pitcher of margaritas, ensuring that he and Danielle would go home drunk.

When their food came, Janus suddenly blurted out, "What I don't understand, though, is how she can be a...," he hesitated, "lesbian." He felt uncomfortable uttering that word about Faith or any other lesbian. He guessed it was because until his move to California and the recent developments in his life, lesbians, like homosexuals, had been creatures alien to his experience, creatures strange, exotic, unfathomable. Not evil ever, but foreign, different in some way that was supposed to be forever a subject of mere speculation for him. In other words, lesbians were supposed to be people for whom he could feel a kind of condescending compassion. Lesbians were not supposed to be his wife.

"What's a lesbian?" Danielle asked. Janus looked at her slack-jawed. She laughed. "I'm just trying to get a definition in terms, Rich. We *are* on the far side of the Sexual Revolution, you know."

Janus felt cross. Indeed, they were on the far side of the Sexual Revolution. They were in California, the land of anything goes. Seemingly rational people would undertake consideration of practically any manner of behavior. "I'll try anything once," was the unofficial state motto. But Janus was not in the mood for subtle distinctions. "You know damned well what I mean by lesbian," he snapped. "A cunt lapper."

"Don't be foul," Danielle said. Janus could see that he had irked her and was instantly sorry.

"I'm sorry, kiddo," he said. "As I told my dear departed wife sometime before she joined me in the bonds of matrimony, I'm most adept at giving misimpressions of myself. I'm an asshole, but maybe not as large a one as I seem."

Danielle smiled her forgiveness, drank from her margarita glass and dabbed at her lips with a napkin. "I hope you're a cunt lapper, Richard Janus, and I have strong doubts that you're a lizard."

"A lizard," Janus said. "I love it. The term lizard seems to describe my wife so perfectly." He raised his margarita glass and said, "To the lizards of my life. And the lizard who's my wife."

Danielle didn't join him in the toast. She shook her head, and the smile she offered him was sad. "I wish this hadn't happened to you, Rich. You like women so. I hope this doesn't turn you against us all."

"The problem is," Janus said somberly, "that I don't know how to deal with this finally. It's so frustrating. I feel like if Faith had left me for a man that I'd know how to respond. I could beat him up. Or I could be too big to beat him up. I could threaten him and have him beat me up." He smiled. "I could study him to figure out what he had that I didn't. I could tell myself that he didn't have anything I didn't and that Faith was obviously a fool for leaving me for him. But this…. This doesn't seem to allow me much response at all. I feel more than personally rejected. I feel that I've been put in a position where response is impossible. There's nothing I can do. There's nothing I could ever have done."

"That's probably not true," Danielle said.

"I could cut it off, I guess."

She shook her head and there followed a silence in which Janus's most recent ripe remark seemed to envelop them in a noxious cloud. Finally, Danielle said, "The problem with you, Rich, and it's a problem with almost all men, is that you don't realize what it's like being a woman. You don't understand how frustrating it is for us having to deal with men who are naturally so much more assertive and demanding. I'm not even married anymore, but I sometimes feel so pushed about I want to scream."

"But you haven't decided to become a lizard," Janus said. He found he could use the word lizard much more easily than lesbian. In his journal he judged, "Just further evidence that I'm a hopeless asshole."

"No, but I can understand it," Danielle said.

"But understanding it and doing it are different things."

"Not as much as you think. I've had fantasies about sex with women."

"You have?" Janus said. Again he was astonished.

She nodded. "It's an odd sexual fantasy. Its basis isn't even erotic, exactly, but something else. I imagine being loved by a woman, and the sensation I get is one of luxurious comfort."

Janus took a deep breath. Daily, it seemed, he discovered something incredible. "You can imagine doing it? The whole thing?" He hesitated because he wasn't being flip. "Tongues against…organs? Breasts?"

Danielle looked at him open-faced and said, "Yes, but it's not so much imagining a specifically sexual act. I think of that, I guess. A woman kissing me instead of a man, a woman's lips on me instead of a man's."

"And you think of doing it to a woman?"

"I think of suckling, yes. And the rest, too, I guess." Danielle pushed her plate of food, half-eaten, toward the center of the table and poured more margarita into her glass. "But the point is," she continued, "that what I think most about is being held by a person who is gentle and implicitly knows me."

Janus ate his last forkful of relleno. He pushed his plate aside, took another cigarette from Danielle's pack and lit it. "Are we all supposed to become bisexual now? Have we reached Brave New World?" Janus took a deep drag on the Salem. "I can't even specifically imagine myself in a homosexual situation. Even the thought is repellent." Janus would have gone on to say that he didn't mean that statement to be macho or smug or superior or anti-gay. He didn't even mean it to be ignorant of such situations, like prisons, where otherwise heterosexual men sought out homosexual contact. But before he could add those qualifications, Danielle interrupted.

"I think I can understand that," she said. "I suspect the ease with which a woman can imagine herself in a lesbian situation has to do with the amount of contact a little girl naturally has with her mother. Little boys also have that contact with their mothers, but neither has it with their fathers."

"Danielle Freud," Janus said. "Is what you just told me true, or are you just able to make it up so that it sounds that way?" She laughed, and Janus poured the last of the margaritas back and forth between their glasses. "You aren't going to become a lizard, too, are you, Daniella?" he asked.

She sipped some of the foamy liquid from her glass. "Want some empirical evidence, big boy?"

The truth was that Janus didn't want empirical evidence that Danielle was heterosexual. He liked Danielle enormously. She was a wonderfully good sport. She rewarded all his jokes with peals of laughter. She had been very good to him. But as he wrote in his journal about her, "Daniella does not turn me on." Why, he couldn't say. It had something to do with her physical type, he guessed. He was sexually attracted to lean women. And though Danielle was not really fat, as she imagined, she was thick waisted, heavy legged, and large breasted.

She made it clear that night, though, that she wanted to sleep with him, felt even that sleeping with him was something that he needed.

When they got back to her Santa Monica apartment, she invited him in. She showed him to the kitchen and told him to fix drinks. He assumed she had gone to the bathroom, but when she returned, she had taken off her shirt and jeans and was wearing a baggy, sleeveless, slipover smock. She had brushed her hair and sprayed herself with perfume.

They carried their drinks to the living room, and Danielle sat beside him on the couch with her feet up under her. She gathered her thick brown hair in her hand at the base of her neck and then shook her head, letting it fall back in place. When she did so, her smock swelled like a sail across her chest and a plump breast flashed into Janus's view. They drank and smoked cigarettes. Janus made his stark, ironic remarks, and Danielle rewarded him with giggles of appreciation.

When they finished their second drinks, Danielle kissed him. She cupped her hand along his face and kissed him. He pulled her against his chest. "Oh, Daniella," he said. She looked up and kissed him again.

He knew he shouldn't, but he let himself be led by the hand into her bedroom. She seated him on the bed and slipped the smock over her head. Naked, she knelt before him, untied his shoes, peeled off his socks. She pulled him to his feet and unbuckled his pants.

When he too was naked, Danielle crawled between her sheets and beckoned to him with outstretched arms. The room was dark, but light from the street spilled across the bed from the window over Danielle's head. Janus rose on his knees at the head of the bed and drew the curtains. In total darkness, he surrendered to her embrace, glad she couldn't see that he was not aroused.

He kissed her eyes and neck. He let her tongue probe inside his mouth. He rolled her large nipples between lip-covered teeth. He laid his head on her thick, soft stomach and stroked his hands between her legs. He buried his face in her vast wetness.

When she had come, Danielle pulled Janus on top of her, squeezing out the aftershocks of her orgasm with her arms locked tightly around him. As she relaxed, she nestled her hands in the long hair on the back of his neck and ran them down the length of his spine. Aroused by her pleasure, he was hard when she reached to place him inside her.

Janus was shocked by the sensation of making love to Danielle. His sexual experience was really rather limited. There had been women before Faith, girls before Faith, that is, girls when he was still a boy, hot moments with Janice Martin in the front seat of his parents' car, or seemingly more sophisticated nights in his apartment at Lancaster, but those times were very long ago and lit forever by an aura of youthful ignorance. Since his first night with Faith, there had never been anyone else. He had lain his night at Zion beside Cally with an erection so desperate that he awoke with testicles as sore as those Janice Martin used to give him when she would restrict their encounters to heavy petting. But until this moment of thrusting himself into Danielle LeBlanc, for more than seven years Janus had made love only to Faith. Danielle felt so different to him. She was much softer, fuller-breasted, wider-hipped. He gripped his hand about her shoulders and thrashed inside her. She was so much looser and wetter than Faith. He wasn't supposed to like the looseness, he remembered. "There's no pussy like tight pussy," B.F. Johnson always maintained. But Janus had always doubted the wisdom of that attitude. Faith was so tight that Janus always feared he was going to hurt her. And she was often sore after they made love. Danielle, it seemed, could never be made sore. He wondered if that was true. He liked her looseness, he decided, and suspected that she was lucky to be built that way.

Janus thought all this as he plunged himself into his friend. Then suddenly he realized he wasn't going to come, a condition having everything to do with himself and nothing to do with Danielle. He was aroused, he felt close to

Danielle, and he was glad that he had gone to bed with her, but he wasn't going to come. He had never experienced such a thing before. He didn't even know that such a thing ever happened to males. He speeded up the timing of this thrusts, and Danielle began to coo. But his orgasm was no closer. "Come, my baby," Danielle whispered. "I want you to come inside me. I like that. That makes me feel so good." Janus thrust still harder. He began to moan. He tightened his legs and shuddered and his body collapsed on top of her. "Oh, baby." Danielle said. "Oh, baby."

Janus had done what he hadn't known men ever did: he had faked an orgasm. He was afraid that Danielle would feel she was an inadequate lover, that she lacked some crucial attractiveness if he failed to come, so he had faked it and collapsed on top of her. After a while he kissed her gently about the face and then on the mouth. He rolled beside her. She snuggled in the crook of his arm, and they slept.

Danielle still slept when Janus awoke the next morning. He lay in bed, wide awake but uncertain what to do. He didn't want to be rude by rising and leaving while she was still asleep. On the other hand, he feared that if he remained in bed she would wake and try to stimulate him to another bout of sex. He had always thought himself fond of morning coupling, but he was not attracted to a repeat of last night's affair. The course of action he adopted was to dress and begin to prepare breakfast. That way he would appear fond of her, which he really was, but would remove the temptation of their lying warm and naked together.

Janus recognized his depression as he cooked, a depression that he knew did not start with the previous night's events. He reflected on what had happened. How odd to make love and not come. How odd to enjoy making love and not be able to come. He wondered if he should be embarrassed. He didn't feel embarrassed. No one had been harmed. If someone was shortchanged, it was he. But he didn't feel that way at all.

His depression, he recognized, sprang from something much deeper than an unusual sexual experience. It concerned not one night but his whole life, the direction of which had brought him to that one night. He was still carrying around inside of him the news of his job offer. He had intended to tell Danielle but never had. He now decided not to. He was supposed to meet Faith for lunch to tell her. He decided not to do that either.

All at once he felt closed in, boxed by America's most open city. He wanted to get away. He wanted to do something different. He had bacon draining on paper towels, toast in the toaster and eggs in the skillet when he decided that he would use his two-week term break, which would begin in ten days, to take a bus trip. But a bus trip to where? A bus trip to New Orleans, of course.

He was in a much brighter mood when he woke Danielle with her breakfast tray and the news of his impending vacation. She was concerned that his decision to leave town had something to do with their relations. "I hope you're not feeling bad, that you're not sorry about last night."

He assured her otherwise. "How can you be sorry," he said, "when you've spent the night with someone special to you?"

Faith's reaction to the news was caustic at first. He hadn't told her about the progress he had made on his thesis, and she saw the purposelessness of his trip as just more evidence of his drifting. And she was right, of course, though Janus felt a strange prescience that this journey was to be the beginning of something new for him. He was going home, or at least going to the place that was the home of his boyhood. He felt driven to make this journey, though he had no idea what it was about. It was as if he believed in magic and that in New Orleans some revelation would show him the true way.

He revealed little of this to Faith, however, and she suddenly guessed that he was going to New Orleans to see Cally Martin. He had told her of meeting an attractive woman at Zion who taught in New Orleans.

"That hot-shot Fortran chickie lives in New Orleans, doesn't she?" Faith remembered. "You're going to see her."

Faith was partially right, of course. Janus did indeed plan on seeing Cally. Maybe, even, he *was* making the trip in order to see her, but he didn't think so. He felt his need to walk the streets of New Orleans again was greater than just the need to see Cally Martin. But given their circumstances, Janus was content for Faith to think him interested in another woman. That's why he'd hinted at a relationship with Anne Norton that he'd never allowed to develop. He could have told her about Danielle, of course, but Danielle was Faith's friend, and he didn't want to damage their friendship. "I hope she's gotten the divorce she was talking about," Faith said of Cally. "I'd hate to see you ride the bus across country only to get shot."

Janus laughed. He knew for a fact that Cally had gotten her divorce or at least that she'd started the proceedings. She had written and told him so several weeks after Zion. What he didn't know was whether Cally would even consent to see him now since he'd not answered the three letters she wrote him. But he didn't laugh about the knowledge of Cally that Faith didn't know he possessed; he laughed at what seemed a jealous reaction on Faith's part. "Why would I need to go to New Orleans for a woman," he said, goading her, "even a very special woman like Cally Martin?" Janus raised his eyebrow in a leer. "Isn't L.A. the Mecca of good nooky?"

"You're disgusting," Faith said. But she wasn't mad. Since she'd left him, Janus had discovered, he could get away with almost all the provocative remarks that used to infuriate her. As he wrote in his journal, "Faith never ceases to amaze and mystify me."

The night before he left on his trip, Janus went with Faith to the movies to see Lina Wertmuller's *Swept Away*. Afterwards, Faith suggested that they go to the Piece of Pizza for a carafe of wine. There they discussed the film. Faith was disturbed about its sexual politics, feeling that it seemed to suggest that what a woman needed to make her loving was to be brutalized for a while. Janus had to agree, but he was struck by the film's beauty and moved by its romanticism. Somehow they managed to share their different reactions without lapsing into the struggles that had marked such conversations in the past.

As they were leaving, Faith glanced at the establishment's slogan and asked, "What about you, Janus, had a piece lately?"

He didn't know how to respond. Lately Faith had taken to asking questions about his sex life. The habit irked him a little since he felt she was hardly open to discussing her relations with Kate, but they'd had a pleasant evening, and he didn't want it to end with a display of irritation. So he smiled as he let her into his van and said, "Who wants to know?"

Faith grinned at him as he slipped behind the wheel and then asked bluntly, "Are you really fucking that snotty slut Anne Norton?"

"Fucking her brains out," Janus said. He started the car and pulled it into traffic ocean bound on Wilshire. "Her. I.Q. has dropped ten points in the last month."

"You really fucking her, Janus?"

"Sometimes I fuck her on top of my desk at school."

"Really?"

"Once we did it on the observation deck on the top of Bunche Hall. Boy, was that a high." Janus laughed.

"Come on, are you really fucking her?"

Janus's grip on his emotions slipped a notch. "Why should I tell you, Faith? How's it fair that you even ask me?"

"It's not. I'm sorry. I guess I shouldn't even want to know."

Janus looked over at her. She had positioned herself back against the door so that she could stare at him while he drove. The street lights flickered on and off her face like a slow strobe light as he passed them. He laughed. "Oh, Faith of my soul. You can be reasonable when you want to."

As they neared the turn Janus would have to make to take Faith to Kate's Venice apartment, she said, "If you want I'll go back to our apartment with you."

"Why?" he said.

"I'd like to sleep with you tonight."

Janus was flabbergasted. He almost said something ugly like, "Don't I have the wrong equipment for you?" But he didn't. And against his better judgment, he took her home with him.

It seemed to Janus that Faith acted much like she had long ago, the first time they'd made love. She talked to him in that silly, little girl's voice that had always charmed him. She insisted that he undress her. Janus felt weak, a little bit used, but he wanted her very much. When she came, Faith screamed in a high-pitched tone. It was a sound she had never made before in their lovemaking.

Afterwards, they lay in bed, side-by-side in the dark, close to one another but not touching. Faith was so still that Janus thought perhaps she'd fallen asleep. When he said, "Where's Kate tonight?" his voice was barely a whisper.

"She's not home," Faith said. Janus didn't ask why. He wondered, of course. He knew next to nothing about the manner of Faith and Kate's relationship, but he was afraid that anything she might tell him now would make him feel worse than he already did. He did not want to learn that Faith was using him as some pawn in a struggle with Kate.

He let another period of time pass and finally asked, "You'll be going back there tomorrow?"

Rather absently, it seemed to Janus since her voice wasn't directed right to him, Faith laid a hand on his arm and said, "I'm sorry, honey. Yes, I am. I thought you understood." She rolled on her side to face him and stroked his hair back off his forehead. "Was it good for you, baby?"

Janus snorted his studied, cynical laugh and quoted an old Woody Allen joke: "The worst one I ever had was…right there." Faith didn't comment and ran her hand over his face another time or two before finally shifting onto her back again. After a time, Janus asked, "Was it good for you, Faith?"

"I guess I'd forgotten it could be like that with a man," she said.

23

S pring had not yet come to L.A. Not that spring, as it is known in other parts of the country, ever comes to L.A. But the fog, which by summer would daily retreat offshore, now in March seldom cleared beyond the city's western border. And Santa Monica lay shrouded throughout the day; the sun was but a tiny amber disk visible intermittently through the swirling mist.

It was time for me to get away.

Los Angeles had become an omnipresent, gray, sugar-coated tar baby that stuck to me everywhere I touched it, that was pleasant because it was sweet-tasting but was empty and expelled the intoxicating breath of decadence. With visions of Faith again in my life, with the smell of Faith again on my body, I bought a bus ticket to New Orleans. For fifty dollars, I could ride that bus from L.A. until it stopped somewhere on the East Coast. But New Orleans was far enough for me.

I was going home. From the station on Sixth Street to a terminal at El Monte, to another in Claremont, through Riverside and out into the desert, which I would not wholly leave until Houston, then across the bayous and the swamps to New Orleans, after so many years, I was going home.

I had planned to sit up front so I could watch the country as it came rushing toward me, but I discovered that the leg room there was even less than elsewhere, so I picked a place on the right side about halfway back and hoped that no one would take the seat on the aisle next to me. Behind me a man jammed his legs against the back of my seat and refused to yield to any pressure I attempted to exert by tilting my chair back. I was uncomfortable from the beginning. Going home, I decided, was no easy business. By the time we reached El Centro, my legs ached from not being able to extend them fully.

Since the bus left at six in the evening, I also had planned to read to tire myself and then sleep the night away. That way, the trip would be nearly one-third gone by the time I awoke. I had a lot to learn about bus travel.

Across the aisle to my left, an old man in a rumpled suit and a new hat of the old-fashioned, feather-in-the brim style had contracted severely clogged nasal passages. He began wheezing before we left L.A. By the time we reached the desert, he sounded like an old steam engine unable to generate enough power. The wheezer, I called him. If I could have gotten to a drugstore, I'd have bought him a bottle of nasal spray just for the peace and quiet.

In front of the wheezer was the cougher, more grizzled even than the man riding behind him. Whereas the wheezer had a look of lost respectability in his old gray suit, faded tie and decaying, wing-tip shoes, the cougher's look was of respectability neither lost nor even missed. He had soiled tennis shoes on his feet; old gray work trousers, rolled up at the bottom, bagged about his veiny, hairless legs and failed to reach the tops of his thin, black socks. A bright green cardigan sweater was buttoned neatly over his white T-shirt, though, and a new red St. Louis Cardinals baseball cap was pulled snugly down to his eyebrows. His cough was shallow but unceasing. There seemed something lodged inside the man that was choking him.

After a time, the cougher's calls elicited antiphonal responses elsewhere in the bus, first from the wheezer who decided to move into coughing, too, a regular germ-spreading conglomerate, then from places behind me. These human voices, communicating on the most elemental level, called and answered one another throughout the night, a hacking chorus that hailed the miles as we passed.

I thought I was going to throw up.

As the long night dragged toward dawn, I ached for the haven of sleep, but I seemed doomed to a weary wakefulness. Then, stung by the first yellow rays of morning, I lapsed into the sleepless reverie that I had been on that bus my entire lifetime and that I was condemned to be there always. In my daydream, the bus was the "real" world, and all that I remembered from before having boarded was merely fantasy. The scenery scarcely changed and repeated itself with a regularity that led me to believe that even the bus's motion was illusion. We were trapped on a platform in some Hollywood studio on a hydraulic machine that swayed the vehicle to and fro, creating the sensation of movement, while outside the windows a series of pictures was slowly pulled past us on a large revolving drum. And every hour the initial pictures reappeared to start the sequence again. The notion was supported by the identical nature of the isolated stations where we stopped to refuel every second hour or so. Studio employees, I came to believe, masters of illusion, merely changed the station signs each time we stopped to convince us that some progress had been made.

I squirmed and sweated and stank through an endless desert day. For a while I had to share my cramped space with a damp young woman who confided that she was fleeing her husband of seven months and had gotten the money for her bus ticket by stealing it from a church collection plate. She made me promise to do the same if I was ever in her situation. At some nameless, dusty town, she departed, and I was left again with the indifferent companionship of the rushing wasteland. The sun slowly settled into a fiery ball behind us and disappeared at the exit sign for Alamogordo. In the spreading darkness to the south, I could see a lone cactus raise its angry middle finger in defiance.

And finally I slept.

I awoke when the cougher loomed up next to my chair. His face was shaven. He was holding his red ball cap in his hand. We were in a darkened station stall, and he obviously had just come from inside. His thin white hair was freshly combed and lay wet and slick against his shiny scalp.

"Excuse me, mister," he said in his high-pitched, deceptively youthful voice. "Do you mind if I ride next to you?" There was a touching tentativeness in his voice, but the fact was that I did mind. I minded powerfully. I had heard his cough for too long already, and I'd been lucky, blessed with two seats to myself the whole trip, except for the brief time with the runaway wife. So I could almost hear myself saying nastily, "You've already got a seat." Or something truly horrid: "Buzz off, you old geezer." Or something merely cold: "It's a free world, isn't it?"

Thank God, I said none of these ugly things, for the charming man who was to ride the next leg of my homeward trip with me was to remind me of an important lesson about living. What I fortunately said to his request was, "No, of course not." But I didn't smile, and I wasn't warm, and I remember those failings now with shame.

I straightened myself in the seat against the window. The cougher slid a plastic gym bag, so shiny it appeared to have been rubbed with oil and buffed, under his seat, placed some other article in the aisle next to his chair and sat down.

I instantly began to suffer from claustrophobia.

The cougher fidgeted. I had not yet noticed that he was no longer coughing, but as he tried to pull that shiny gym bag back out from under his seat, I did notice how long his legs were. He was probably about my height. When he had finally extracted the bag, he unzipped it and pulled out a small box wrapped in cellophane, Vicks Wild Cherry Mentholated Cough Drops. He took out one of the triangular lozenges and placed it in his mouth. He tucked the tongue of the lid back inside and started to shove the box into the bag. Then he stopped. His upper body made a kind of quiver, the jerk you make when you remember something almost wrongly forgotten, something you had determined not to forget.

"Would you like a cough drop, mister?" He pulled the box open again and offered it to me. "They got medicine in them. And they taste good, too. Take as many as you like."

I told him that I didn't care for any. His face seemed to register disappointment as he put the box away again, and I wished I had accepted his gift. "Where are you headed?" I asked to make up for my apparent unfriendliness.

"Houston."

"Well," I said. "Only a few more hours." My abilities as a scintillating conversationalist never fail me.

"I'm going to visit my sister," the cougher said. I nodded. "I've got my present for her right here." He held his left arm toward me with his hand bent backward to the wrist. Tucked under the watchband was a stick of chewing gum. "This isn't really her present," he explained. "I got her one of those large packs they sell at the Drug King. I just put this piece there so I don't forget to give it to her. She really likes gum. I remember."

I nodded and the cougher settled back in his seat. He folded his hands in his lap, occasionally turning his head to glance around the bus. His cheeks swelled in and out as he sucked on his cough drop.

"How long has it been since you've seen your sister?" I asked.

"Well," he said, "it's been a long time. She couldn't come for Mom's funeral. But she wanted to. She sent the money so I could make this trip."

The man brushed his hand across his head to make sure his hair was dry and pulled his ball cap back down to his eyebrows. "Do you mind if I talk to you, mister? I don't want to bother you or anything. My sister, Katherine, told me to be sure not to bother anyone on the bus."

"I don't mind," I said.

"This is the first bus trip I've been on. Out of town like this, I mean. I ride the bus to work every day."

"What kind of work do you do?"

"I'm a messenger," he said. "I work at the offices downtown."

"In L.A.?" I said.

"Uh huh. I know just where all the buildings are and what floors all the businesses are on. It's a real good job. I get ninety-six dollars a week plus bus fare and a uniform. I have to pay to clean the uniform, though. But I don't mind. I brush it every day with a brush Katherine gave me for Christmas."

"How long have you had this job?"

"Forty-two years." He took the piece of gum out from under his watchband, carefully laid it on his leg and then slipped the watch off over his hand. He turned the band inside out and showed me an engraving on the back of the watch: *To Derek Adams For 35 Years of Loyal Service.* "My boss gave me this. He's a real nice man. I have to retire next year, but he told me I could keep my uniform. I'm not supposed to wear it when I'm not at work, but I brought it with me, and Katherine said I could wear it in Houston. I don't think my boss would mind because Houston is a long ways from Los Angeles."

As we rode along, I learned a lot about Derek Adams. He was sixty-four years old, had been born in L.A. and had lived all his life with his mother until she died ten years earlier. When he was older than those boys who went to high school, his mother married Katherine's father. At the time Katherine was born, she was the prettiest baby in the world. He called her Katie then, but he was supposed to call her Katherine now.

When our conversation lagged after a while, I took out my book to read again. When I did so, Derek said that he thought he'd read, too. He reached beside his chair and grasped a plastic briefcase, rippled to make it appear like leather. He opened it and showed me that inside he had placed two copies of Classics Illustrated: *Oliver Twist* and *Kidnapped.* "Lots of people don't think I can read," he confided. "Because I never went to school and all. But my mom taught me at home." He began to read to me the first balloon from *Kidnapped,* carefully placing his index finger under each word as he pronounced it. "I'm not going to read any more to you," he explained after that, "because you have your own book to read."

I had read perhaps a page when Derek said, "Excuse me, mister." I asked him to call me Rich. "Well, Rich, I hope you don't think I ever read the messages at work just because I could. I wouldn't ever do that."

I assured him that such a thought had never occurred to me. "I can tell just by talking to you, Derek, that you're a man of integrity." His wrinkled brow indicated that he hadn't understood me. "I can tell you're an honest man."

"Thank you, Rich," he said. "I appreciate that."

A while later Derek asked me where I was headed, and I told him New Orleans. "Are you going there for business? Are you a businessman, Rich?"

Inside I laughed at the notion of my booted, blue-jeaned, long-haired self as a businessman. "No, Derek, I'm not a businessman." I said. "I'm a...." My mind choked on the end of that sentence. "I'm a...."

What is it that I am? I know what I'm not, I thought. I'm not an historian or a baseball player or a doctor or a movie star or a lawyer who has to be in court or a jeweler like my grandfather or a messenger like Derek. I'm not an

Indian. I *am* a basketball player, I thought. I was a coach. I've been a memo writer and an unsuccessful husband. I'm a bus rider.

"I'm a teacher," I said to Derek, and it sounded right.

"A teacher," Derek said with excitement. "I should have guessed you were a teacher."

I laughed, thinking how little I probably looked like a teacher, too. "Why should you have guessed?" I asked Derek.

"I don't know," Derek said, looking at me sideways as if he were sizing me up. "You just seem like a teacher; I can tell."

That was as nice a compliment as I've ever received.

By the time we reached Houston, Derek was in a state of agitation. He pulled both pieces of his luggage onto his lap before we reached the terminal. He was at the door before the driver opened it and had bounded into the station before I was able to get out of my seat. I was just getting inside when I saw him greet his sister. She gave him a hug. The man with her allowed Derek to pump his hand. I started to make my way past them, but Derek spotted me and waved me over. Very formally, he introduced me to his sister and brother-in-law. "Rich is my friend," he explained to them.

And as he did so, I felt for the first time that I understood what was meant by the term *grace*.

The world of the bus was transformed when I boarded it for my journey's final leg. Immediately I noticed the difference in my fellow travelers. They seemed unquestionably more prosperous. For the riders from Houston to New Orleans, the bus was a cheaper, perhaps more convenient means of travel, not a means lacking an alternative. A neatly groomed white-haired couple, probably in their seventies, sat holding hands across the aisle. In front of me a young mother talked lovingly to her son about whales and their visit to his grandmother's. When he grew tired and fell asleep against her breast, she snuggled him close and kissed him gently on top of his head. Behind me an attractive blond woman in a smart green suit was reading *Fear of Flying*.

The new brightness inside the bus, however, was not reflected outside, where the day was overcast. But the cool, green-shaded day was a refreshing contrast to the stark yellow brilliance of the departed desert.

The swampy gray terrain between Houston and New Orleans was meant to be traversed only by the wily, the alligator and the moccasin, the muskrat and the Cajun in his pirogue. It is such a soft and dense area that it swallows highways whole. The dual ribbons of concrete that span it rise on pilings twenty feet above the marsh; I-10 represents the wiliness of technology, and it allowed us to fly across the swamp at the level of the treetops.

But if I-10 makes it possible to defy the swamp, it has by no means subdued it; the swamp remains forbidding, untamed. It is thick with death and decay. And the soft soil rules. It will not support life which becomes too great. Countless trees lie lifeless in the swamp, dead from having grown too large, unable to support their own weight. But the soft soil rules with an even hand, and the swamp swallows its death in a thickness of living things.

From the tidal basin of Lake Pontchartrain through Jefferson Parish we sped. At the Orleans Parish line, the bus turned south toward the river. I found that Greyhound had taken over the old Union train station terminal. Knapsack on my back, a gentle, evening breeze in my hair, buoyed by the spirit of Derek Adams, I walked from the bus station toward Lee Circle. The red azaleas were in bloom, and the air was redolent with the smell of sweet olives.

I had been gone a long time. But finally I was home.

24

1976

At Lee Circle, Janus caught the outbound St. Charles Avenue streetcar. The clacking old trolley was like a transfusion of youth for him, and he felt an incautious sense of elation. At Napoleon he transferred to a bus and rode twenty blocks or so to a neighborhood just beyond Claiborne, to the home of old family friends with whom he'd arranged to stay.

Jerry Schwartz was a Baptist preacher. Like Janus's father, he'd grown up in central Louisiana. The two men had met each other in the seminary and, united both by their rural roots and their liberal attitudes in matters of race, religion, and politics, had become fast friends. After the seminary, Jerry had gone into the parish ministry back in north Louisiana while Janus's dad had done doctoral work and ended up teaching at the local Baptist college. But even though separated in terms of locale, the two men remained close and were frequent visitors in one another's homes. Jerry and Anne Schwartz had been like second parents to Janus when he was growing up. In the sixties, the two men had suffered similar misfortunes when each espoused the outrageous notion that white churches ought to accept Negroes into their memberships. Janus's father's firing had led to their family's relocation to Chicago. Jerry Schwartz had moved in the opposite direction. Dismissed from a church in Shreveport and given one week to remove his family and belongings from the parsonage, Jerry had moved to New Orleans. He was pushing fifty at the time and was a pariah in his profession, but he found work as a laborer in a shipyard and survived. Sometime later, as attitudes softened, he was able to reenter the ministry. By the time of Janus's visit, he was a chaplain at Baptist Hospital—happy and full of vinegar.

Janus admired Jerry Schwartz enormously, saw him as a man of courage and principle and perseverance. He had not seen the Schwartzes in ten years, since he was eighteen, but Jerry and Anne had called him at least twice a year during that time. When he arrived at their house with a backpack over one shoulder and his beat-up gym bag in the opposite fist, they greeted him as if they'd seen him only yesterday.

"It's about time you got here, boy," Anne told him at the door. She was a moon-faced woman who wore no other makeup but always painted her lips a bright, cheery red. She was shaped like a figure eight—large breasts and hips and a cinched-in waist. She was drying her hands on an apron as she came to the door. Her pugnacious manner was belied by her twinkling eyes. "You're so late we'd almost decided you were gonna wait another ten years before coming to see us. I hope you brought your work clothes. No one stays at this house without earning his keep. Now, bend over so I can kiss you hello, and then go out in the kitchen and help Jerry pull heads off those shrimp, or else you don't get any for dinner."

Janus laughed and shook his head and followed her into the kitchen. Jerry Schwartz didn't even get up from the ice chest where he was working. "You just a California beach boy now," Jerry asked him, "or do you still remember the head end from the eatin' end of a shrimp?" Anne hadn't mentioned what she wanted him to do with his bags, so he placed them in a corner, more or less out of the way, rolled up his sleeves and pitched in. As they worked, they gradually caught each other up on their respective families.

After dinner Janus volunteered to wash dishes. "Don't think you're butterin' me up, Richie Janus," Annie said. "The dishes are Jerry Schwartz's job, and if you do them for him, fine, but you still owe me."

"I think the boy's got good sense after all," Jerry observed. "I think he's figured out who's the boss, who to please and how to get invited back."

When the kitchen was clean, Janus sat with Anne and Jerry in their living room while Jerry told stories of the shenanigans he and Janus's dad used to pull when they were in school together. White-haired and overweight but still handsome at sixty, Jerry was a man of imposing charm. He was mischievous and irreverent, and for all his denials, he had a love for his fellow beings that was clear in everything he said.

All through the evening he would amble back and forth to the kitchen, spinning a yarn all the while, always returning with a dollop of ice cream that he had spooned into a coffee cup. "Have some more, blimpo," Anne would chide and then add to Janus something like, "I hope he eats himself to death sooner rather than later, while I'm young and have still got my looks." After midnight, Anne finally showed Janus to the guest room and made him promise to sleep late the next morning. "You look tired, buddy," she said. "We better keep you down here and give you some conditionin' in shootin' the bull."

Before she left for work the next day, Anne stuck her head in Janus's room and told him that there was breakfast in the refrigerator if he knew how to fix it. He went back to sleep until after eleven. When he finally rose, he called Cally Martin's office at the university but was told she wasn't in. When he asked for her home number, the secretary told him she wasn't permitted to release that number. He checked the New Orleans phone book but no Cally Martin was listed, only a C. Martin and a C. L. Martin. Janus dialed both numbers but got an answer at neither.

"Why are things never easy?" he wrote in his journal.

Janus made himself a sandwich for brunch and decided to travel across town to revisit his old neighborhood. He walked up to the end of Napoleon and caught the Broad Street bus, which ran out to the Gentilly section of town where he'd grown up. He marvelled at the experience of being at large in New Orleans again. The street names that he passed reverberated in his brain and unlocked with their sounds the sealed chambers of his memory. Earhart. Poydras. Toulouse. Barracks.

At Elysian Fields, he transferred buses and rode out toward the Lakefront. He stood in front of his parents' dream house and imagined himself mowing the lawn, shirtless and brown on a warm Saturday morning. The basketball goal he and his dad had installed over the garage was still there. He wondered who shot baskets at it now.

He went back to the bus line and made his way to the neighborhood where he'd lived until high school. He almost failed to recognize the house he'd lived in until he was fifteen. The hackberry tree was gone from the front yard, and the brick flower bed had been replaced by a row of ligustrum. The front walk was hedged, and the two mimosa trees that he had helped his mother plant were full grown, ageless, as if they'd been there always.

He walked to the playground where he'd gone to shoot baskets with Billy Buck. Five black teen-agers were tossing a scruffed leather ball at the metal backboards. Janus watched them shoot and jostle one another for the rebounds. Things had changed dramatically, he realized. When he had been a resident of this neighborhood, there was never a black face to be seen. A black kid would have been beaten up before he would have been allowed to shoot at these baskets. Now the only white face belonged to Janus.

The ball took a crazy carom and rolled toward him. He scooped it up and started to roll it back to its owners, but then he stepped onto the asphalt surface of the court, took one dribble and went up for his jumper. The chain net sang as the ball dropped through.

Janus grinned as one of the kids called out, "Nice shot, dude." He watched them play a while longer and was about to leave when they asked him to play.

He agreed, glad that he'd worn tennis shoes for the day's walking about. He worried that his ankles weren't taped, but promised himself he'd take it easy and be extra careful.

In the early going, Janus contented himself to dominate the rebounding and pass off to his teammates. But his opponents, finally wise to that strategy, began to leave him all alone. One of his teammates demanded, "Put it up, man." Janus was at the top of the key. He went up, still hoping for a passing lane, but finding none, rammed the shot home. Eight times in a row they insisted that he shoot, and each time he made good. "He caint do that forever," an opponent maintained, and on certain days that would have been true. But that day he had the range and everything he put up fell in. When the game ended at dusk, one of the boys said, "Man, you shoot like Pistol Pete. Where'dya learn to shoot like dat?" Janus laughed. "Naw, come on, man. How you shoot dat way?"

"Practice," Janus said. The kid asked if Janus could teach him to shoot that way. "I don't know," he said, "but I can make you a *better* shooter." He showed the boy that he needed to position his hand farther underneath the ball for better leverage and more control, that he needed to center his point of release and make his whole shooting motion from front to back in a straight line, not in a half-circular motion as he had been doing.

"Feels funny," the kid said.

"Sure it does," Janus said. "But do it often enough and it won't."

"I'm gonna practice this," the kid promised.

"Do that, and it'll make you better," Janus said as he walked away to catch a bus back to the Schwartzes'.

"Pistol Pete," the kid called out after him.

Before dinner, Janus called C. Martin and still gòt no answer. C.L. Martin told him that no one named Cally lived there. While they ate, Janus got Jerry to talk about the days of his Civil Rights activity. It was an exciting tale for Janus. Finally, he asked how it was that a small-town Louisiana boy came to have such benign attitudes about race at a time when it was more than unpopular to hold them, at a time when it was dangerous not only to your career but even to your health.

"You keep callin' me a liberal, Richie," he said. "Now, you quit that. I'm no liberal. I'm a conservative now and always have been. I'm so conservative that I wear both a belt and suspenders. Would have done it when I was a youngster, too, 'cept that I was so poor I couldn't afford anything but some twine out of the Sears and Roebuck catalog to hold up my dungarees."

"Howwww poor were you?" Janus said, doing Ed McMahon.

"We were so poor when I was growing up that we had tumbleweeds for pets. We were so poor out there on that plot of ground near Winnfield that my parents couldn't even afford toys for the kids."

"Try not to be vulgar," Anne counselled.

"Nope, never had a toy as a kid. My mother made corncob dolls for the girls. But for me and my brother there wasn't anything. All Momma could do was just cut holes in our pockets."

"Tellin' him not be vulgar is like tellin' a cow pie not to draw flies," Anne said.

"There's a point to this, Annie," Jerry told her, but she just harrumphed at him. "See, Richie, I was as poor as the blacks I grew up all around, poorer than some. So my attitudes didn't have anything at all to do with being conservative or liberal. It had to do with what seemed fair, and fair as far as I ever could tell ain't got no color. I never could find anywhere in the Bible that said that heaven was for white folks only. So I couldn't much see that those of us on earth had any business making distinctions that God himself didn't make."

Janus told Jerry, for the first time probably, how much he admired him, but Jerry tried to deflect the compliment. "You put it on the line," Janus said, "and there weren't many who stood with you."

"Naw," Jerry maintained. "You make it sound all brave when that wasn't it at all. When you believe something, you ain't got any choice, and doing what you ought to do makes you free. That's the kick of it. How can they hurt you? They can kill you, but you can defy 'em while they do it and they know that. But not so many of 'em want to hurt you as you think. I've had people who stayed my friends for a long time even when I told 'em they were wrong. They'll take that from you if they know all along that you love 'em. They'll get mad, but usually they won't hurt you too much if they know you love 'em."

"Is that why you didn't leave?" Janus asked, thinking that his dad had left and that he had never recovered from his flight.

"Where the hell was I gonna go?" Jerry said. "This is my home. What do I know about anywhere else? You gotta do your work where you know somethin' and you know somethin' about the people you're workin' with. Now, ain't I tellin' the boy the truth?" Jerry asked Anne.

"Yeah," Anne conceded. "But even a blind pig sometimes finds an acorn."

Janus dialed C. Martin again after dinner and again got no answer. He was beginning to feel anxious about reaching her.

He told the Schwartzes that he thought he'd like to go down to the French Quarter, and they insisted that he take one of their cars. But his return to the Quarter was ill-timed. With a companion, he would have had fun, but he was not very skilled at carousing alone. He found a place he liked, the Napoleon House, and had a Dixie Beer sitting along one of the open sides so that he could watch strollers as they passed. It felt pleasant enough there in the cool spring air, but Janus decided against a second beer.

He thought of his friend Johnnie Golden, who was comfortable in bars, who would always strike up conversations with those near him. Johnnie never seemed to feel the isolation Janus experienced when he went into bars alone.

Leaving the Napoleon House, Janus walked the length of Bourbon Street, which was as honky-tonk as ever. The only additions that Janus recognized, besides the ubiquitous T-shirt shops, were a couple of places which featured nude dancing by female impersonators. He thought for just a moment about seeking out The Dairy, where he'd drunk his fill of Tom Collinses with his high school chums a decade ago, but he wasn't really interested. He went to Pat O'Brien's and ordered a hurricane. The first sip of the rum punch seemed too sweet, but he decided before he finished it that he liked it well enough to perhaps order it again sometime.

He ended his evening at Café du Monde, with a café au lait and an order of doughnuts. The breeze there by the river was gusty, and Janus enjoyed the experience, savoring the memories evoked by the strong, sweet coffee, the tepid water and the grit of sugary residue which coated the table. But he admitted to himself, too, that he was lonely, that home had to do with people as well as place.

"The El Cholo Feeling," he wrote in his journal that night in the Schwartzes' bedroom, "is not confined to L.A."

The next morning Janus sat with the New Orleans phone book in his lap and looked up the names of kids he had known growing up. Some were there; surprisingly many were not. B.F. Johnson's name was there. So was Carter Percy's.

On impulse, without analyzing why, he dialed Carter's number. A woman answered, and Janus asked for Carter. "Why, he's at work." Then she laughed and added, "At least, he'd better be." She offered to take a message. Janus told her he was an old friend and thought he might see Carter while he was in town. She gave him Carter's work number and made him promise to call there.

"Orleans Parish School Board," a secretary said when Janus rang the work number. He asked for Carter Percy, and another secretary said, "Department of Athletics," when the call was transferred. Carter was Supervisor of Athletics for New Orleans Public Schools. The first thing he wanted to know after he answered the phone and identified himself was whether Janus now lived in New Orleans again. When Janus told him no, Carter asked how soon he was planning to move back. Janus laughed and told him he was just in town on vacation, that he was still in graduate school at UCLA.

"Well, you sound bright enough then to exercise the sense to move home," Carter said.

Janus laughed again and asked how long Carter had been a big-cheese administrator. It was only his second year, he said, and maybe his last, too. He liked the money, but he didn't much like the responsibility. Mostly he missed the contact with the kids. And there was nothing like the weekly anticipation of the weekend's games. Janus told him he certainly knew that and related briefly his own coaching background. Carter had to ring off shortly; he had another blasted meeting, he complained, but he insisted that Janus meet him for lunch at Liuzza's, a neighborhood restaurant near Warren Easton High School, where Carter had another meeting that afternoon.

"Good old Carter," Janus wrote in his journal when he got off the phone. Janus hadn't seen the man in eleven years, had not seen him since he'd become a man, but he greeted Janus as if their friendship had never been interrupted.

Carter didn't look at all as Janus had imagined in his dream. His hair was thinning, but there was no sag to his powerful physique. He looked in good enough shape to resume his old tackle position that very afternoon and go both ways the entire game, the way he did when in high school.

Over fried oysters and large, stemmed bowls of Dixie Beer, they caught each other up on the last decade. Carter had won a football scholarship to Louisiana Tech and had been one of the offensive linemen who protected Terry Bradshaw in his collegiate days before the Steelers made him a number one draft pick. Carter had even landed a tryout with the New Orleans Saints but hadn't been quite good enough for the NFL. He'd earned a teaching certificate at Tech and taken a job as a biology teacher and junior varsity football coach right out of school. New Orleans was in the last stages of achieving full racial integration at the time, and white teachers were leaving the school system in droves. Carter became head varsity coach at Jefferson in his second year. Three years later he was promoted to his present position and was the youngest supervisor in the system. He had married a girl from Tech, who was now a senior at LSU Dental School. They didn't have children, weren't sure they were going to.

The two men also talked about old acquaintances, naturally. Janice Martin, Janus's old flame, was married to a CPA, seemingly happy, mother of three. Pamela DeVane was an actress; she lived in New York but had appeared at the local Beverly Dinner Theater about a year ago. Carter didn't know what had happened to Adrienne Bandeau. Billy Buck, whom Carter had never known well, was a prominent local physician. B.F. Johnson was a Parish Councilman from Kenner. And Ronald Demart was dead.

Before the lunch ended, Janus asked Carter if he was really serious about giving up his administrative position. "You're damn straight," he said. "I didn't go into this business to be a paper pusher and a meeting attender."

"And the money?" Janus asked.

"Once Ruthie's into her practice, I can coach 'em for free," he said.

Janus questioned Carter about what it was like teaching in an inner-city school.

"You mean, what's it like teaching mostly black kids," Carter said and grinned. "Inner-city is just a euphemism for schools with mostly minority students."

Janus laughed and admitted that Carter was right.

"It's a whole lot like teaching school in this town when you and I were kids," Carter said. "There's a bunch of tough kids, and they are a lot more interested in what girl they're gonna make next or how they're gonna get a hold of their next quart of beer than they are in learning anything. And there's a bunch more kids who will learn something if you know how to teach it to them, and some even who are determined to learn no matter how inept you are."

Carter's voice had that evangelistic quality common among Southerners who had to speak frequently in public. "We've got a long way to go in this business," he continued. "We don't even know how to teach a lot of these kids yet. And we don't have their full cooperation yet. But I think we may be right on the verge. And the fact of the matter is that if you want to make positive change in this society, there's no better place to be than a teacher in inner-city schools."

"That's some rap," Janus said. "It's not exactly the speech you hear from public school teachers anymore."

"Well, it's either believe you can make a difference or slit your throat," Carter laughed. He looked at his watch and quickly wiped a napkin across his face. "And even suicide is preferable to life as an administrator."

They paid the bill, each insisting on the right to buy the other's lunch, and walked outside. Janus agreed to call him again before he left town.

"And more than once," Carter said.

"And more than once," Janus promised.

As Carter walked away, he called out, "If you ever want to get away from the college hayride and do some teaching where it counts, let me know. I can get you a classroom where you can help 'em learn to think right and a basketball court where you can teach 'em how to go to their left."

"I may just do that," Janus called back. Carter waved and climbed into his car. Janus had made this last remark in a perfunctory, bantering way, but as he walked toward Broad to wait for the bus, he began to think about the idea as if it might be serious.

That afternoon Janus finally reached Cally at her office. She was obviously shocked to hear from him. "I'd like to see you yesterday," he said. "But if I have to wait until today, I guess that will be okay." He volunteered to come out to the Lakefront campus immediately, but she told him she was so busy that that would be inconvenient.

Janus was enormously disappointed. He had hoped she would greet him with a burst of joy. In his journal he had written, "If she says 'this time I insist that you fuck me,' then I'll know she missed me pretty much." The reception he was getting was somewhat less enthusiastic. She seemed distracted. He worried that perhaps she was even cool.

And so, as was his lifelong way, he was about to retreat, to hang up without plans to see her, when he said, almost whispered, "I came down here, Cally."

"What took you so long?" she said.

That night Cally picked Janus up at the Schwartzes' in her battered VW bug. They had agreed to go out for dinner, but Cally took him to her apartment instead. "We'll have a drink here where we can talk," she explained, "and then go out to eat later."

They never went out. Things were awkward at first, but finally Cally admitted her hurt when Janus didn't answer her letters. He explained the situation as best he could. He asked for her forgiveness, and she gave it.

They drank Scotch and water and talked about things that had been left unsaid in the hazy rapture of Zion. Janus told her the whole long story of his relationship with Faith, and Cally explained in detail the deterioration of her marriage to Bob. Their situations were starkly opposite, Janus's marriage expiring in the fire of hot words and violent actions, Cally's in the ice of different goals and unfused commitments.

"I can't image anyone being lukewarm about a life with you," Janus said late that night.

"Maybe you just haven't known me long enough," Cally said.

"I'd like to get to know you better," he admitted.

"You mean, you're not going to give me brave speeches about my principles tonight?"

Janus laughed. "You mean, you're gonna give me another chance to find out?"

The next day, Janus said his goodbyes to the Schwartzes and moved his belongings to Cally's. Though it was very short-term, of course, they fell into a routine during his stay with her. Janus got out the long letter of resignation he'd worked on for a year and began to add to it. He adopted the habit of writing on it while Cally was at work. At night they went to films or out to eat. After several days, she came home and found him adding the details of his bus trip to New Orleans.

"So, this is your famous memo," she said.

"Yes," Janus admitted uncomfortably. No one else but Faith had ever seen the baroque note, and Faith's response had not been exactly enthusiastic.

"So, it isn't finished yet," Cally said.

"No. It can't be finished until I decide what to do with my life."

"You've got to decide that, you know."

Janus frowned. "You sound like Faith."

His response made Cally mad. "If I sound like Faith, then Faith was right. Or at least right that you have to stop resigning and get about acting." She went into her bedroom and put her books away and changed clothes. When she returned to the dining table where Janus was sitting, she said, "And don't ever tell me I sound like Faith. Or look like Faith or act like Faith or anything like Faith."

Janus looked straight at her with a deadpan expression. "When I used to irritate Faith," he said, "she sounded an awful lot like you."

"Asshole." Cally laughed. She stood behind him and rested her hands on his shoulders. "What am I going to do with you, Richard Janus? You've charmed the pants off me. But I won't sit idly by and let you waste yourself." She walked around the table and sat down facing him.

"I'd like to hear some more about that part where you don't have your pants on," he said.

"Sex fiend."

"I didn't bring up this business of your being bare-assed."

Cally shook her head and laughed again. "What am I going to do when you're gone?" She had insisted on paying his plane fare to L.A. so that he could stay two extra days, but even that time would soon end, and he'd have to go back for the spring term. "You're kind of a son of a bitch, you know, for coming here like this only to leave."

"What would you say if I told you I was going to live here permanently?" Janus said.

"I'd say you'd better learn to cook." Janus smiled, and Cally added, "Are you serious?"

"I'm having a beer tomorrow afternoon with Carter Percy. I'm gonna talk to him seriously about a coaching job at one of the high schools here. I'd probably have to go out to UNO to finish a teaching credential."

"Are you really gonna do this?" Cally said. Her eyes were bright but disbelieving.

"I don't know," he said, and for the first time he told her about his offer at UCLA.

"Jesus," Cally said.

"What should I do?" Janus asked her.

She got up and went to the kitchen, where she began mixing drinks. "You want Scotch?" she called out. Janus said yes, and she brought the two glasses back to the table with her.

"What should I do?" he repeated.

Cally took a sip of her drink and stared at him carefully. "UCLA's a very big job, but, of course, you know that. If you want to be an academic, you'd be a fool to turn it down."

"Do you want me to move here?"

"Yes," she said.

"Then just tell me to take Carter's job offer."

"No," she said, sipping her drink again.

"Why not? Would it embarrass you to have a boyfriend who was just a high school teacher?"

"You're not serious?"

Unfortunately, he really was, and she saw it in his face.

"Jesus Christ," she said. "I wouldn't have thought you were such a macho asshole."

"Some women wouldn't feel…."

"I'm not some women, Rich. And besides, we're not really talking about how I might feel. Are we? Aren't we really talking about *your* feelings? About whether or not *you* could stand living with a woman who holds a supposedly more prestigious position?"

"I guess you're right," he conceded.

She shook her head and looked at the ceiling. "Jesus, Rich…."

"You know," he said. "Women are awfully big these days on getting other women over the hump of defining themselves only in traditional ways. Maybe men sometimes have a similar problem."

Cally looked at him searchingly then. She sipped her drink and seemed to try to order something in her mind. Finally she said, "Do you want to coach, Rich?"

Janus curled his lower lip and blew a breath upward over his face. "The problem with coaching," he said, "is that some of the time you get beat." He smiled. "And some of the time, you get beat all of the time." He raised his eyebrows and rubbed his fingertips across the bridge of his nose. "But yeah, I think I want to do it. I sure enjoyed it a lot when I did it before. And I know that coaches can sometimes affect a kid's life in a way a college teacher probably never could."

"Then you should take it," she said.

"If I were a high school coach," Janus sang, "and she a professor, would she live with me anyway? Would she let me possess her?"

"You should definitely take the job," Cally said.

"Why?"

"Because you're just not going to make it as the new Christy Minstrel."

The next afternoon Janus asked Carter for a job. Carter couldn't believe the request at first, but as he came to realize that Janus was serious, he became elated and began to brainstorm with his friend about getting both of them in the same school. "We can make a difference, Richie," he enthused. "Maybe not so big a difference, I suppose, but a goddamned important one."

In the time remaining to them before Janus's return to L.A., he and Cally made their plans about his move in the early summer. They decided that it was probably best if Janus didn't move in with her right away but rented an apartment of his own to give them time and space to adjust to one another. Janus boasted in his journal, "Haven't I always been mature?"

On the night before he left, after they'd made love, Cally lay with her head on Janus's chest and fingered the St. Christopher medallion he wore around his neck. "Why do you wear this?" she asked. She turned the medal over and read the inscription, "The Patron Saint of Whales."

"Faith gave it to me on the day of my orals," he explained. "One of her silly names for me was Bubba the Magic Whale. Detailing the term's etymology would take us into next month."

Cally studied the medallion, turning it over and reading the inscription again. "You still wear it?"

"Yes," Janus said.

"You don't wear your ring."

"I don't feel married anymore."

"Then why do you wear this? She gave it to you."

"When she gave it to me," Janus said as he slid his fingers into Cally's long curly hair, "I told her I would wear it as long as I loved her."

Janus could feel Cally's head move on his chest. "Then you still love her?"

"I told her I would love her forever," Janus said.

Cally ran her hand over the medallion as if she were trying to smooth it into the texture of his skin. "Bubba the Magic Whale," she said. "It's a good name for you. I wish I'd given it to you, not her."

Janus squeezed her and caressed her back from one shoulder to the other with the flat of his hand. "I don't want to ever hurt you," he said.

"How?"

"By loving her. If I could quit, I would. Maybe I will someday."

"No, you won't," Cally said. "And I wouldn't want you to. If you could quit loving her someday, then you could quit loving me."

But Cally admitted she was worried about Faith. Janus had told her that

Faith had slept at his house on the night before he left for New Orleans. Cally wasn't sure that Faith wouldn't try to get him back now.

"Faith's a lizard," Janus reminded her. "She lives with her fellow lizard in Lizardland."

"Don't be ugly about her," Cally said. "It's not becoming." After a moment she added, "Much as I wish otherwise, it bothers me that your feelings for her run so deep."

"I'm sorry," Janus said. "She drives me crazy. I love her, but when I think about her sometimes, I hate her, too."

"Don't hate her," Cally urged. "As much unhappiness as she's caused you, I think she's had a positive impact, too. As a result of your living with her, for instance, you're probably a better person for me."

"Yeah," Janus said in mock irritability. "If she made me so special, how come she left me?"

Cally snuggled against him. "She never knew what she had."

Janus lay quietly with her then as the rhythm of their breathing drove them toward sleep. But just before dropping off, he asked aloud, "Could I maybe get that last statement notarized?"

25

The first thing I saw when I entered my apartment upon arriving in Santa Monica from New Orleans was a huge banner, stretching the length of the living room, that read: "Welcome Home Bubba."

Then I saw Faith.

She was sitting in my chair with her feet folded up under her, wearing a shorty jump suit which zipped from crotch to neck. She had the zipper undone to about mid-stomach. There was a glass of white wine poised on the chair arm. Faith had been reading, but she put the book aside when I came in. "Welcome home, Bubba," she said.

I was not terribly friendly. "What are you doing here?" I carried my bags into the bedroom and tossed them on the bed.

"Maybe I ought to ask you the same thing," she called from the living room.

"I live here," I reminded her.

"I used to live here," she giggled.

"I vaguely remember."

"I've been waiting here for three straight nights. I'd about decided that hot-shot New Orleans chickie of yours had trapped you down there." I came back into the living room and sat across from Faith in one of the canvas director's chairs. She uncrossed her legs and splayed them wide. "She teach you any tricks I ought to know about?"

"You want me to give you a blow by blow description?"

"Your hot-shot chickie's into oral sex, huh?"

I laughed in spite of myself and shook my head. "What do you want, Faith? What's all this about?"

"I missed my Bubba Whale," she said. "And I wanted him to know."

"Well, that's just great, Faith, really sweet, I mean, but doesn't your life have, uh, other priorities?"

"Not tonight," she said. "I've got a present for you."

"What's that?" I asked.

She came and stood in front of me. "See how tan I am?"

"You're very tan, Faith."

"But I'm really tan, you know what I mean?" She turned around so that I could see the half moons of ass that peeked from under the back of her jump suit. "See anything you like? In the tan department, I mean?"

"What's your present, Faith?"

She turned back to face me, put her thumbs through the large ring attached to her zipper and tugged it an inch or so lower. "Me," she said.

I stood up and walked away from her. I went into the kitchen and searched for something to eat. I finally put a glass on the table and poured myself some of the white wine Faith had brought. When I turned around to put the bottle back in the icebox, she was right behind me. "Is that Southern nooky so good that you don't want some of this good California stuff?"

"Cut it out, Faith."

"Cut what out, Bubba? I'm just trying to give you a warm welcome."

I brushed past her, went back to the living room and sat in my chair. Faith followed and sat in my lap.

"Faith," I said.

"Are hot-shot chickie's tits as good as mine, Bubba?" Faith lifted her clothes away from her chest so that I could see her breasts. She had evidently been sunbathing topless.

"Get off me, Faith."

"Uh uh," she said. "I like it here. I like where that knee of yours is." She wiggled herself around on my lap until she was straddling one of my legs. "I don't have on any panties," she said. "I hope you didn't notice."

I laughed, but my voice cracked, and I thought I was going to cry. "Goddamnit, Faith, what's this all about? Where's Kate? Why are you here?"

She bent over and kissed me. When she pulled away, I started to ask her questions again, but she said, "Ssssh," and kissed me again. She whispered in my ear, "Wanna fuck, Bubba?"

"No," I said.

She traced a tickly hand down my chest to my groin. "Part of you wants to," she said.

Goddamn, but I'm a weak person.

When I was in New Orleans, I was sure that I was absolutely through with Faith. I would have bet everything I owned (which, granted, wasn't much) that she would never be able to cast her spell on me again. In Cally I'd found a person with whom I was sure I could be forever happy. Cally was so absolutely mature that it was inconceivable to me that things could go awry. And I was madly in love with her. But there I was, not back in L.A. a whole hour, and I was in bed with Faith.

And Faith's newest guise was as sexual athlete. She wanted to do all sorts of things now that I think she'd have tried to have me arrested for if I'd suggested only a year earlier. And I *would* have suggested most of them if I hadn't been afraid of prison for the sexually demented.

But there was something brutally sad about all this. Though I was too weak to resist her sexually that night, I remained steadfast in my determination to leave Los Angeles and take a coaching job in New Orleans. I told her so, too, and I continued to tell her so in the days that followed.

"I know you're leaving, Bubba. You don't have to keep telling me," Faith took to replying. But I know she didn't believe it, or at least didn't altogether believe it. I'd been in her position or one like it before, and I knew how dread and wish can mix to screen our vision of what we know is certain. It's like our attitude toward death. We know it's going to happen, but it always surprises us when it does anyway.

For the nth time in her life, Faith became a completely new person. I was back teaching my two courses at UCLA. And she was still in graduate school. But she had molted the grinding life of the paranoid student as thoroughly as she had earlier shed her fascination with glossolalia. She continued to live with Kate at first, but she called me every day practically with plans to go to movies or the theater or to eat at some neat, out-of-the-way restaurant she'd heard about.

Why I did those things with her I don't exactly know.

Or maybe I do. I still loved her, and at her best, when she showed that bouncy, energetic side of her personality, I still liked her. Now, for the first time in years, we were really having fun together again.

I told myself that I was spending time with her to help convince her that I was really leaving soon. And I was assiduous about asserting that intention frequently.

But, of course, I'm sure I saw her for me, too, to help myself adjust to the notion that our days left together were numbered. So I'm sure that my repeated declarations of my intent to leave were made to remind myself as much as her.

I tried to learn how it was that her relationship with Kate worked. "If we were still married…," I started to say.

"We are still married, Bubba," Faith interrupted and flashed her finger at me. She'd taken to wearing her wedding ring again.

"If we were still married," I began again, "in any sense other than the eyes of the law, I would hardly be pleased if you were fooling around with Kate three days a week."

"Kate and I aren't married."

"Well, what exactly are you? That's what I'm getting at."

"If you won't tell me about Cally hot Southern pussy, then I won't tell you about Kate," Faith insisted, so I remained in the dark about how their relationship worked.

About two weeks after I got back, though, Faith asked me if I was interested in living with her and Kate together. Faith never ceased to amaze me. She didn't surprise me anymore, but she amazed me. That she looked at things from a different perspective, I had come to understand, but I could never learn her logic. She assured me that I'd like Kate a lot better once I got to know her. She was probably right about that, too, but I was still hostile to her suggestion.

"Do we all sleep together in the same bed?" I asked.

"No!" she said. "That's...that's revolting."

I might have argued with her that trying *ménage à trois* was not so long a leap from what had already been tried, but I wasn't interested in a meaningless argument. I told her that, number one, I was not interested in living with my wife's lesbian lover, and number two, that I was moving to New Orleans in two months.

Faith didn't propose that we cohabit with Kate again, but three weeks later she moved back into my apartment. I found her replacing things on shelves and refilling drawers when I came home from teaching one day. "Have you and Kate broken up?" I asked.

"Kate and I are very good friends," she maintained. "Nothing has changed."

I loved it when she did stuff like that.

"Does it ever occur to you to ask a person's permission before you just barge into his life?"

"I know you talk to Magnolia Blossom several hours long distance every day," she said. "I get a busy signal ninety percent of the time when I call here after six. But don't worry; I don't plan to interfere. I'll go sit on the steps so you two can coo in private, if that's what you want."

I was really annoyed. I had tremendous guilt feelings just about spending time with Faith. I couldn't even deal with the fact that I had slept with her again. My bogus rationale that all my dealings with Faith were a benign strategy to help her adjust to my leaving wasn't elastic enough to cover living with her again. I told her so.

But as was usual with Faith, she had not only a ready but a disarming answer. "I know you're leaving, Bubba. How can I forget it? You tell me every day, so I can't forget it even if I wanted to. And that's why it makes perfect sense for me to move back in here. We're friends." She looked at me pitifully, as if she were about to burst into tears. "Kate and I decided we should live apart now, so I need a place to live. And I can just keep this apartment after you're gone."

So I let her stay. And soon it was like we were married again. We consulted one another about our daily plans, shared expenses and duties. There were only two differences: we got along much better than we had when we were married, and I remained steadfast in my determination to leave when my teaching responsibilities were over. I gave Faith the bed and insisted on making myself a pallet in the living room. I didn't resist her one night, though, when she slipped under the blanket beside me and whispered tearfully, "I thought you'd always be there for me to come back to, Bubba."

For the most part, in that period, Faith and I talked about current rather than past things in our lives. But one night, a couple of weeks after she moved back in, I went into the darkened bedroom after she'd retired and asked her to explain it all to me.

"All?" she said.

"All," I said and sat down on the bed. "How we made such a mess of ourselves. How it ended up that you're a lesbian and that I never knew it."

She didn't say anything, so I prodded her. "Faith?"

"I don't like that word *lesbian*, Rich."

I snorted.

She turned toward me in the dark. I could feel the bed move as she shifted her position though I couldn't see her face. "A lot of Kate's friends used that word about themselves comfortably, but I never did."

"Well, Faith," I said, "whatever you call it, it amounts to the same thing. You had a lesbian affair in college and now another one.

"I didn't exactly have an *affair* with Cassie at Lancaster," she said.

"That's not what you told me before."

"I kissed her. I let her fondle me, but it never went farther than that."

"That's pretty far."

"Yeah," Faith admitted, "I guess it is. And I was turned on, too. The whole thing just felt, well, sinful."

"But it didn't feel sinful with Kate?"

"It felt different."

"Meaning?"

"Meaning I don't know. It felt good, but it never felt right, either. It always seemed like something I was only doing for right now but wouldn't be doing forever. Do you understand?"

"In part," I said. And in part, maybe I did. "Does that mean you aren't going to be a lizard anymore?"

"I don't know, Bubba. If you stayed with me, maybe I wouldn't."

"But if I stayed with you, maybe you would too, huh?"

"Maybe," she said. "I don't feel that way now, I guess, but I've learned enough about myself to know that things never seem to stay the same with me."

"Oh, Faith."

"I love you, you know," she said. "You're going to leave me soon, but I still love you."

I hugged her and stroked her hair. And she wet the shoulder of my shirt with her tears.

When she pulled away from me to dab at her face with the hem of her flannel nightgown, she sniffled and said, "I'd make it, if you stayed, you know."

"Come on, Faith," I said.

"You don't know what you mean to me, Rich." She smiled a little and expelled a sad snort of a laugh. "Look at me. I'm a graduate student. Whoever would have thought that?"

"You're a graduate student with a straight A average," I told her.

"It's because of you," she said.

"Well that's crazy. I don't know the first thing about psychology."

"No. But you always encouraged me to believe I could go to graduate school if I wanted to." She looked away from me and brushed wet strands of red hair back away from her cheeks, and her eyes brightened. "I might actually get a Ph.D. Wouldn't that be a kick? You and I could teach at the same school."

"I don't think you'll want to teach at Thomas Jefferson High School with a Ph.D., babe."

Faith looked at me as if she hadn't heard what I'd said, and her hazel eyes suddenly lost their momentary luster. "When I was in high school, my old man made me take typing and shorthand. 'So you can support yourself,' he said. I was in the fucking National Honor Society, and he couldn't imagine I'd be anything other than a secretary." Tears streamed down her face again, but she seemed oblivious to them, only absent-mindedly brushing at her cheeks with the backs of her fingers. "By the time I started college, he'd decided I might make it as a grammar school teacher, 'if you work really hard.' Spring of my freshman year at Lancaster, I came home all excited to tell him I'd decided to major in psychology. He wouldn't even turn off some lousy TV program he was watching. He just sipped at his goddamned Southern Comfort and said, 'Don't do it kid. Your degree wouldn't be worth the paper it was printed on.'"

"Well, he was wrong," I said. "And if you keep on the way you're going, you'll be a bigger deal in the field than he is."

"Maybe," she said. "Maybe then he'll be proud of me."

"Old Sleeping Greasy," I said and laid my hand against her face.

"It's all because of you, Rich. It is. You gave me the courage."

"Naw, babe," I said. "You've done it all on your own. I'm the bastard who used to call you stupid. Remember?"

Faith pressed her lips against her teeth with a trembling thumb. "But you never meant it, Richie. I knew that. I knew you never meant it."

I held Faith a long time that night. I held her against me, and she cried into my chest, and I loved her anew. And the ache of tenderness I felt for her was like a stab wound in my soul.

In late May, I was called into Richard Boeotian's office to sign the search committee's letter to Bryan Jennings telling him that his application had been rejected. Boeotian greeted me conspiratorially. "Well, there's dirty work to do here, Rich," he said. "We don't enjoy it, but it's part of our job." Nothing in Boeotian's manner gave evidence of much regret.

He showed me the letter that you, Dr. Burden, had drafted for us all to sign. The letter stated that we had looked upon Jennings's application materials favorably—a technical truth since it was the interview that did him in—but regretted we'd be unable to offer him a position because the spot for which he had applied had not been funded—another technical truth, since he'd applied for a regular position and the title of the one they'd offered me carried the word *Visiting* in front of it.

Academics are masters of fine distinctions.

I signed the letter.

"Great letter, isn't it?" Boeotian said when I handed it back to him.

"Yeah," I agreed. To what, who knows?

"Burden really has the knack of killing them painlessly, you know, with the stiletto. My style runs more to the sledge hammer. Ha ha. Dear Schmuck, we found you wanting. Ha ha ha."

We shook hands before I turned to leave. "You're finishing that good work of yours I keep hearing about, I hope," he said.

"I'm just about finished, sir," I said. He didn't get the irony, of course.

I felt sick

I felt sicker a couple of weeks later when I received a letter from Bryan Jennings thanking me for the kind attention I'd shown him when he was at UCLA for his interview. He hoped we might keep in touch. He would be hearing great things from me, he was sure.

As the quarter drew to a close, I began gradually to pack my belongings. I was letting Faith keep most of the furniture. I was mailing my books. What things I couldn't pack into my bus, I had arranged to ship.

It took me longer after the end of the quarter in late June than I had anticipated to put my affairs in order to leave. There were checking accounts to close, savings to divide with Faith.

Two nights before I planned to leave, Faith kept me awake for hours arguing that I shouldn't go. She'd gone through my files, she said, to winnow out those things there which were hers or were pertinent to her. But she'd found the materials I'd completed on my dissertation before my trip to New Orleans. "If you can do this much, Rich, you can do it all. You don't want to be a high school teacher if you can do work like this. This is good stuff, Janus, important stuff. I can tell."

I explained again what I'd been trying to tell her for more than a year: I didn't want to be an historian. Just because I had the abilities to be a successful one was not reason enough to do something I detested. I wanted to coach, I told her. I was really excited about it. I might be able to make a difference in some kid's life off the court as well as on.

I can wax as idealistic as the next guy.

"That's just shit," Faith said. "You want to run to the honeysucking arms of hot-shot magnolia pussy."

"I'm not even moving in with her," I pointed out.

"Big deal," she said. "You don't have to live with her to fuck her brains out."

"Don't talk about her," I said.

"Big deal. I bet her hick ears are burning. Why are you so dead set on rehickifying yourself when you'd almost escaped it?"

In earlier moments, I would have given Faith a bitter lecture about her regional prejudice. I would have cursed her. But now I didn't. I was silent, and Faith's attacks waned and finally ceased.

She apologized the next morning, and she was so obviously remorseful that I forgave her. And I felt, as was often the case in my life with her, that I had done something wrong by letting her be nasty.

I made my final arrangements, taking boxes to the post office and others to the air express depot. I loaded most of my van, leaving out only those boxes I planned to put next to me in the front seat. I helped Faith rearrange the apartment to cover for those items that I had moved out. Late in the afternoon, Faith spotted the ball gloves, the new one I bought in L.A. for a softball team I'd played on, and the old, smaller, cracked one I'd carried around since my days in Little League. They were lying on the top of one of the boxes still to be loaded in the car.

"Let's play catch, Janus," she said.

"Okay," I said. "You can show me that curve ball of yours again." I offered her the large, new glove, but she insisted on using the old one.

"It's more my size," she said.

We went into the courtyard. The day was overcast and cool for early July. We tossed the tattered hardball I'd had, it seemed, all my life. Once again I was struck by Faith's coordination. There were a few girlish mannerisms in her delivery, but for the most part she had the motions associated with those of a boy. We played for a long time, until my hand was sore from the sting of the ball she seemed unable to throw softly, until her arm ached from the throwing, until the evening fog had crept off the bay and swept through the courtyard on its pervasive course inward.

"Bubba," Faith said when we had finally retreated from the damp and the dark back inside, "when you go tomorrow, can I keep this glove?" She held it with her arms folded across it, trapped against her chest. When she started to cry then, so did I, and it was as if floodgates had been opened.

That night we went to El Cholo. We ordered a pitcher of margaritas and our usual large portions of food. But neither of us was hungry or even interested in drinking. We pushed the food around on our plates, eating some of it but letting most of it get cold. It was hard to talk because the most obvious topic was so painful for us.

At one point, Faith swirled her finger in a large drop of water on the table. "This is the way we were," she said, calling my attention to what she was doing. She managed to separate the drop into two smaller, shimmering pools, divided but close together, seeming as if at any moment they would run back together. "Then we were like this," she said. Then she picked up her napkin and blotted the drops away. "Tomorrow," she said, tears brimming and running down her cheeks, "we'll be gone."

She looked at me and tried to smile. "This salt shaker likes you, Bubba. And so does this fork. They love you, and you're breaking their hearts." She got up from the table and walked toward the staircase at the rear of the restaurant which led upstairs to the restrooms.

As I waited for her, I poured another glass of margarita, but when I sipped it, it burned my stomach. Even though I had eaten little, I had that bursting sensation Johnnie Golden had called the El Cholo Feeling. I sipped at the drink slowly as I waited, no longer enjoying it at all. When Faith finally returned, she said, "I'd like to go home now, Bubba." As I stood to slide from the booth, I accidently knocked the margarita over. The glass broke into two jagged pieces; the greenish white liquid sloshed over the table and dripped slowly to the floor.

Driving home was hazardous. The fog was especially bad, and the pile of boxes in the back of the bus kept me from being able to see out the rear.

Somewhere after we'd turned off the freeway and driven up into the eerie, amber-lighted streets of Santa Monica, Faith took an envelope from her purse. "This came for you today while you were out, Rich. I hope you don't mind that I opened it."

"What is it?" I said.

"It's a letter from the dean offering you the Indian history position. You must have known about this."

"I didn't know when the paper work would go through," I said.

"But you knew that an offer was coming."

"Yes," I said.

"You could have it all then, huh, Rich?"

"I could have what others seem to think is all."

"If you took it, you would have me, too, Bubba," Faith said.

"I know, babe."

"I'd be good," she whispered.

I cautiously pulled to a stop in front of our apartment. The street light was out and our end of the block was very dark. As I held the door for Faith, a car rushed past just behind us, its headlights bouncing so crazily off the mist that I couldn't tell if it were ocean- or inward-bound.

On the sidewalk, Faith threw both arms around me and cried into my chest, "I'd be good, Bubba. I promise. I'd be good."

I tried to steer us toward the apartment, but the fog was so thick around me I feared I would lose my way.

But it's morning now, and the fog has lifted. I have found my way to the western end of Wilshire where I sit at my picnic table finishing this note. The fog will return I'm sure, for New Orleans, too, can be a foggy place. But for this one moment, with a single turn of my head, I can see from Palos Verdes to Point Dume, from Ocean Boulevard to Catalina and beyond.

And so in conclusion, no sir. No sir, no thank you. Your job in Indian history should go to Bryan Jennings. He deserves it, not I. He has written a fine dissertation, and I never will.

No sir, no thank you.

The early morning sun is throwing a swatch of gold on the green water of the Pacific that extends as far as I can see. Above it sea gulls float, effortlessly, endlessly.

From the fence at the end of the bluff, I can look down on the almost abandoned beach. To the north begins a row of houses for the rich, blocking access to the sea. Just this side is a bike path, ending in a loop, beginning its southward course. At a border of red, white and blue trash cans starts the vast expanse of sand covered with the footprints of yesterday's bathers. Walking aimlessly is a lone black dog. Beyond the row of empty lifeguard stations, where the sand is wet and firm, two figures jog toward one another, become for a moment one and move forever away. At the water's edge two lovers wade arm-in-arm. Near them a young man is about to go for a swim.

On the fence there is a faded green sign that reads, "Notice: Bluff Subject to Slides. Use at Your Own Risk." With that counsel I sit for a moment on a bluff-side bench. On its back a loving wife has inscribed:

In the
Evening
Of his life
John P. Kite
Used to
Come every day
To sit in this spot
And
Watch the sun set
Over the
Ocean

In his way, Mr. Kite has challenged the world. And in his honor, no sir, no thank you.

The El Cholo Feeling passes.

The Real Acknowledgements

Richard Janus has his acknowledgments in Chapter One of this book, and I thought I'd add mine here at the end. *The El Cholo Feeling Passes* was originally published without acknowledgments, so I would like to take this opportunity to express my gratitude to the people who helped bring this book into being: to my great friend Will Campbell, who read the book in manuscript and recommended it for publication, to Wayne Elliott, whose family owned Peachtree Publishers in those days and who agreed to publish it, and to Executive Editor Chuck Perry, who first acquired this book and subsequently edited it with great sensitivity.

Most immediately, I hasten to express my profound appreciation to those involved in the 2003 edition. These include the people at UNO Press: Elizabeth Williams, who founded the press in her role as President of the UNO Foundation, Pat Gibbs, who embraced the press and its projects when he succeeded Liz as UNO Foundation President, and Eileen Byrne, whose calm assistance rescued us at crucial moments.

I am indebted to Ron Salisbury, whose family has owned El Cholo since the 1920s. My characters and my friends and I have always treasured the food and entire dining experience at Mr. Salisbury's restaurant, for us a ritual almost spiritual in nature. I am delighted that in this edition he has provided for our cover a picture of the Western Avenue establishment with Richard Janus's V.W. bus parked outside.

My thanks to Libby Arceneaux for her crack manuscript preparation and to ace proofreaders Kerri Barton and Jennifer Spence. Y'all came through for me over and over, and I won't forget it.

I am especially indebted to Mark Bacon, who is astonishingly fast, and more important, who is as good a designer as exists anywhere in the country.

And to Gabi Gautreaux, who edited this edition, all I can say is that I can't thank you enough.

Rick Barton
New Orleans
March, 2003

About the Author

In addition to *The El Cholo Feeling Passes,* Fredrick Barton is the author of the novels *Courting Pandemonium, Black and White on the Rocks* (originally published as *With Extreme Prejudice*), and *A House Divided,* which was awarded the William Faulkner Prize in fiction. Mr. Barton is also author (with composer Jay Weigel) of the jazz opera *Ash Wednesday.* He has written on film since 1980 for the New Orleans weekly *Gambit* and since 1989 for *The Cresset,* a national review of literature, the arts and public affairs. Mr. Barton's many writing awards include a Louisiana Division of the Arts Prize in Literature; the Alex Waller Memorial Award, the New Orleans Press Club's highest honor for print journalism; the Stephen T. Victory Award, the Louisiana Bar Association's prize for feature writing; and the New Orleans Press Club's annual first prize in criticism on 11 occasions. Mr. Barton was educated at Valparaiso University, UCLA and the University of Iowa. He has taught creative writing at the University of New Orleans since 1979 and now serves as Dean of the College of Liberal Arts. Mr. Barton lives in Uptown New Orleans with his longtime attorney, Joyce Markrid Dombourian.

Discussion Questions

1. *What does the El Cholo Feeling mean?*
   A. Does it have more than one meaning?
   B. What does it mean in terms of the experience of dining at the El Cholo restaurant?
   C. What does it mean in terms of the way the book defines the term *cholo*?

2. *How are we to understand the author's choices of his characters' names?*
   A. Richard Janus?
   B. Faith Cleaver?
   C. Warren Burden?
   D. Bryan Jennings?
   E. Johnnie Golden?

3. *How do the novel's epigraphs, the T-shirt slogan, "It takes a secure man to love a liberated woman," and Tennessee Williams's "Security is a kind of death," articulate the novel's themes?*

4. *Why has the author chosen to alternate chapters between Richard Janus's first-person memo and third-person chapters that largely detail his relationship with Faith Cleaver?*

5. *Late in the novel, Richard Janus and Danielle LeBlanc go to El Cholo Restaurant and find that it has been renovated. It is larger and newer; the waiting time is shorter. What is the significance of this change?*

6. *Do you think 1985 audiences would have responded differently from today's audiences to Faith's character? How so? Why?*

7. *Richard Janus's memo is the dissertation he didn't write. In what other ways is the book about not doing rather than doing? In what ways does not doing shape the man Janus becomes?*

8. *This novel is set during the Vietnam War. Richard Janus is a fervent opponent of the war, and much of his story relates to his draft resistance endeavors. How does this aspect of Janus's character relate to other of the novel's themes?*

9. *How does this novel explore issues of friendship?*
   A. Friendship among men?
   B. Friendship among women?
   C. Friendship between men and women?

10. *How does the novel satirize academic institutions?*
    A. How do Richard Janus's attitudes toward the academic calling evolve over the course of his story?
    B. What does he affirm about the academic life, and what does he reject?
    C. How do these judgments reveal his character?

11. *Richard Janus is sitting on a bluff at the novel's end.*
    A. What is the significance of the things he tells us he sees?
    B. What is the significance of the inscription a "loving wife" has placed on the bench where Janus sits?

12. *How does the author employ weather to enhance his themes?*
    A. Fog?
    B. Drought?

13. *What is the author's attitude toward women in general and the women's movement in particular?*

14. *After the UCLA History Department Search Committee offers Richard Janus a teaching position, he walks for a while in a sculpture garden. What significance might be assigned to what he sees there?*

15. *What is the significance of the date Janus writes on his memo to his dissertation committee?*